# THREE ACTION-PACKED WESTERNS
## BY D.B. NEWTON
## IN ONE LOW-PRICED VOLUME!

## *AMBUSH RECKONING*

The bay swung its head; Holden spoke to it and tightened the reins. A bare instant later, he realized his mistake when another horse snorted, somewhere to his immediate left.

His head whipped about sharply, even as he felt the bay's barrel swell to an answering whicker. Against the shadow of the big rock he glimpsed a dark shadow that could only be a horse with a rider motionless on its back. His hand pulled the rein involuntarily just as a gun spoke, in a smash of sound and a spear of muzzle flame.

The bay gave a squeal and lunged straight ahead, down that alley of moonlight descending through the trees. As it did so, either the same gun or another spoke again—behind them now, its roar battering against the face of the big rock. The blow struck solidly. It lifted Holden, slammed him forward onto the neck of his horse.

After that he knew he must be falling, but it felt rather as though he went spinning away into some black and engulfing nowhere....

# AND IN THE SAME ACTION-PACKED VOLUME...
## *HELLBENT FOR A HANGROPE*

Craddock chose this saloon for his next stop. He left the shadow of the arcade and went at an angle across the muddy, hoof-churned street.

It was not entirely dark yet. With the fading of sunset the sky had tempered to a sheet of steel. It would hang like that above the land for some moments of deceptive half-light; then the last of the glow would drain out of the sky, the stars would pinpoint it, and night would rush down to smother the earth. In this moment poised between night and day, the crunch of Craddock's boots seemed alarmingly sharp and clear. Every sound was magnified, every shape and outline keen-edged, yet a little distorted, a little unreal.

But there was nothing unreal in the gunshot that all at once slapped along this street, or in the bullet that split the air a foot from Craddock's body.

## And...
## *THE LURKING GUN*

Gary tried to speak, tried to stir. He could do neither.

Then another voice—the old-timer, Pete Dunn—breaking in on a sudden tone of alarm. "Ain't that blood there on his shirt?"

"Hey! Pete's right, the guy's bleeding!"

Hands worked at his shirt buttons, ripping it open. Somebody swore. "Why, that's a bullet wound!"

"And only about half closed," Pete Dunn said. "That fighting tore it open. No wonder you licked him, Ed! Standing up to you with a thing like that in him—Well, he's a game one, that's all I can say!"

Ed Saxon cried, in a tone of horror, "But how was I to know? He never said—"

"You never asked!" Pete Dunn retorted sharply. "Well, are you gonna just leave him lay there? To bleed to death?"

Hands were under him then, lifting him. And as they raised Jim Gary off the ground, the last gray of twilight seemed to fade. Consciousness ebbed and then darkness swept cleanly over him.

# D.B. NEWTON

## AMBUSH RECKONING/ HELLBENT FOR A HANGROPE/ THE LURKING GUN

**LEISURE BOOKS**　　**NEW YORK CITY**

# A LEISURE BOOK®

November 1993

Published by special arrangement with Golden West Literary Agency.

Dorchester Publishing Co., Inc.
276 Fifth Avenue
New York, NY 10001

# AMBUSH RECKONING

## I

A HARVEST MOON, the size of a bushel basket, had broken above the timbered crests by the time the lamps of Reserve showed ahead. In this golden spill of light Troy Holden tried to make out the expression on the man in the other saddle. A continuing silence, throughout the length of their ride, had held the weight of stern disapproval; Holden felt the pressure more than he cared to admit. At last he was stung to speech.

"I know what you're thinking. So, you might as well put it into words!"

Sam Riggs stared straight ahead, past his horse's ears, at the swimming lights of the nearing cattle town. His voice was stiff with reproach. "Would it do any good?"

"If you mean, will it change my decision any—I'm afraid not." Holden spoke as bluntly as his foreman. "I know how you feel. But, you could try at least to understand my problem. I've told you, I wouldn't be doing this if there was any other way."

"Yeah—you told me." The older man gave a shrug. "Hell —I guess I know! Crown means nothing to you. It never really did."

"That isn't so!"

"Near enough! I don't figure you've lost any sleep over what you're doing. I know damn well it's nothing Vern Holden could ever have done." He added bitterly: "But, you ain't Vern."

Troy Holden nodded. "That's right," he said curtly, "I'm not my father. And I'm afraid there's nothing you can do about it."

Sam Riggs said, in the same harsh tone, "That's why I been keeping my mouth shut!"

That effectively killed the talk between them. Also, by now, the wagon ruts made a turn, picked up a first fringe of houses, and became the main street of the village. They rode in without hurry. Tang of dust, and the smoke of evening fires, mingled with the smells of sun-cured grass and pine left over from the short fall day. Lamplight in windows seemed pale against the golden glow of the round moon that hung above the street, laying shadows as black and straight as if they had been first drawn with a ruler and then generously inked in.

It was early enough that most of the stores were still open, while Reserve's two saloons were brightly lighted but not yet doing the usual Friday night's business. In front of the station, a stage was making up for its run to meet the railroad. The coach lamps were lit and the four-horse team stood restless in harness, while the station agent busied himself storing luggage into the rear boot.

Troy Holden reined in and, from the saddle, spoke to the agent. "Have I got time to mail a letter?"

Melcher, postmaster as well as the stage line's agent in Reserve, peered up at him—a harried-looking man, wearing a green eyeshade and black alpaca sleeve protectors. "You're just under the wire, Mr. Holden. I was all ready to lock the pouch and toss it aboard."

"I'd appreciate getting this into it." Holden handed down an envelope he'd taken from his pocket. One eyebrow quirked as the man hefted the bulkiness of several sheets of letter paper. Holden saw him glance at the inscription—to a Miss Beatrice Applegate, of New York City.

Holden said, "I was wondering if you happen to have any mail for Crown in the office?"

"Why, no, Mr. Holden. Not since your rider picked up the last batch on Tuesday."

"You're very sure? No chance it could have been overlooked?"

Melcher was positive. "No chance at all. Why? Are you missing something? It might be in tomorrow," he suggested helpfully. "When this coach finishes its run to the railroad and back. . . ."

"Thanks," Holden said. "I'll check later." From Melcher's knowing look Holden understood the agent had guessed it was an overdue letter from a girl that had him so concerned. Not greatly caring, he rode on with Sam Riggs, still silent and hostile, flanking him.

At the end of the block, beyond an intersection, stood the hotel—Reserve's largest structure, a graceless, two-story box of a building; catty-cornered from it a lantern burned at the entrance to the public livery. Here, a hunch-shouldered old man who served as night hostler came down the ramp as the two riders stepped off, into dust that had been beaten to flour by countless hooves, and took the reins and the silver dollar Holden tossed him.

Occupied with his own thoughts, Holden turned away without even hearing the old man's respectful greeting; but Riggs paused to exchange a word or two, before hurrying to overtake his employer as he took the wide street crossing toward the hotel. An observer would have found almost nothing in common between these two. The foreman was a rawboned, sunburned man whose rugged features matched his range clothes and sweat-rimmed hat, and the boots whose leather had long since shaped into iron-hard and comfortable creases. By contrast, the owner of Crown ranch —some twenty years his junior—had the mark of a different world on him.

It showed in the careful cut of whipcord jacket and riding pants, in the benchmade boots with the highlight that ran across the polished surface as he mounted the veranda steps and walked inside the hotel. Troy Holden looked out of place against the faded rawness of a cowtown hotel lobby; he was aware of it, and he would have said it made no slightest difference to him—this was not his world and he had no intention of remaining long enough for it to touch him in any way.

Across the dingy room, with its worn carpeting and sagging furniture and its single dusty rubber tree in a pot, the proprietor and his wife were discussing some matter of business. Holden went over and laid a hand on the edge of the desk. "George Lunceford," he said.

They looked at him, and each other. Sid Bravender was short and going to paunch and baldness; his wife, built on a more heroic scale, held an armload of sheets and blankets folded beneath the full shelf of her heavy bosom. The hotel keeper cleared his throat. "I believe he's checked out, Mr. Holden."

The latter frowned, aware of Sam Riggs moving up beside him. "Checked out? That hardly seems possible."

"I was on the desk," the woman said. "Not half an hour ago. He said something about taking the night stage. I don't know if he's actually left his room yet."

8

Holden, too astonished to answer, heard Sam Riggs' grunt and felt the man's touch on his arm. He swung away from the desk, toward the stairs leading from the second floor.

They creaked faintly as a man descended—first only his legs visible, and a hand carrying a carpetbag; then the faint gleam of a gold watchchain stretched across the waistcoat of his business suit. The rest of the man came in view. He was pink-faced, clean shaven, except for thick muttonchops that were frosted with gray. When he saw Holden, below him in the lobby, he halted abruptly as though he half considered turning back.

"Ah—Holden," he said, in a tone of transparent discomfort. "Good evening to you."

"I *thought* it was a good evening," Troy Holden answered shortly, unable to keep the anger from his voice. He nodded toward the hotel keeper and his wife. "These people tell me you're leaving. If I hadn't come early, appears I almost might even have missed you."

George Lunceford came the rest of the way down the steps, still clutching his carpetbag. His eyes slid uneasily from Holden to Sam Riggs and back again. He tried a smile. "I'm sorry. It's something that came up suddenly. Unavoidable. A telegram . . ." He was sidestepping as he spoke, edging toward the open street door.

"You couldn't at least have got word to me?"

"There really wasn't time. You know how it is in business." Sweat was shining on the smooth cheeks; the smile became a painful grimace. "I'm afraid you'll have to excuse me now—really. The stage—"

"Just a minute!" Holden was having trouble keeping his voice under control. He flung an irritated look at the unwelcome witnesses to his private business, but the Bravenders stood rooted, listening with unconcealed curiosity. With

9

a lift of the shoulders, Troy Holden turned back to the businessman.

"I don't have to like this! I've spent three days of a tight schedule, showing you my ranch. I've answered every question you could raise. We agreed I was to meet you tonight and settle on terms. Just what becomes of all that?"

Lunceford swallowed. A tic had begun to pluck at a nerve in his cheek. "I've told you I'm sorry. But in business one can never be certain. Things change in an hour. . . ."

"Then you are *not* buying? If that's what you mean, why can't you come out and say it?"

A voice spoke from the street door, carrying a freight of harsh amusement. "That stage is ready to roll. Friend Lunceford don't want to miss it. . . ."

Holden saw panic break across the face of the man before him. Slowly, he turned.

The one who leaned in the doorway had both thumbs hooked in a heavy shellbelt that dragged at his middle. Untrimmed, rusty-looking hair showed beneath a shapeless hat. The eyes, above slanting cheekbones, were a pale and piercing blue; the full lips held a perpetual sneer. Everything about him hinted of a wild and feral danger.

He spoke again, into the silence. "They won't hold that stage, you know—even if you have bought your ticket. You better run along, little man. . . ."

A sound broke from George Lunceford. Suddenly, without another look at Troy Holden, he was heading toward the door. The redhead made no slightest effort to give room and Lunceford was forced to sidle past, sucking in his middle as though terrified at the idea of their touching. By the time he crossed the veranda and hit the dry plankings of the boardwalk below he was already breaking into a run. The hurried sounds quickly faded.

Holden drew a breath to settle the anger that left him

10

trembling. His stare met the pale eyes of the man in the doorway. "I take it this was your doing," he said into the heavy stillness. "I don't think I know you."

The thick lips quirked; the sneer became more pronounced. "Don't you?"

Sam Riggs spoke hastily. "His name's Seab Glazer. He rides with Bartell's crowd. . . ."

Glazer suggested, with bland amusement, "You've heard of *him*, maybe?"

"Luke Bartell? The cattle rustler? The man that runs a traffic in stolen beef and horses, back and forth across the Canadian border?"

"Is that what Sam told you?" The pale eyes narrowed a trifle, as they cut to the foreman's scowling face. "Why, now, you shouldn't listen to talk, Holden. Some people don't care what they say."

"It's common knowledge!" the foreman retorted.

"It's never been proved. Not in a court of law."

"Law courts are pretty far between, out here." But having said that, Riggs appeared to lose some of his aggressiveness. Looking at him, Troy Holden guessed that the Crown foreman was beginning to feel the full weight of threat from the man in the doorway. Meanwhile both Bravenders, yonder by the desk, were watching with the shocked expressions of people afraid to move or almost to breathe. He didn't need any stronger hints that he faced a real danger.

But Holden was too furious at the moment to weigh precautions. He told Seab Glazer, coldly, "I'm not concerned with who Bartell is, or how he spends his time. I want to know if it was his orders that you should go to work and run George Lunceford out of town—just when we were about to close a deal."

Glazer countered with an amused question. "And, supposing it was?"

"Do you think I'm going to stand tamely by and let him interfere in my business—whatever his reasons?"

The pale eyes studied him, insolently noting the lack of gun or holster, the well-tailored Eastern clothing, the smooth features that showed no mark of sun or elements. Seab Glazer let him have that mocking half-smile.

"You talk real good," he said with a sneer. "I'd like to hear how well you say some of that to Luke, himself. So happens he's gonna be in town, later tonight—over at the Montana House. I think he'd get quite a kick out of it!"

The sound of a four-horse team breaking into a gallop, of creaking leather and slamming timbers and rolling iron, suddenly was born in the street outside and went sweeping past the hotel. Through the door Troy Holden had a quick glimpse of the stagecoach, its lamps gleaming; then it was gone and a fog of dust was settling. Seab Glazer had turned his head to watch the stage go past. When he swung back again he was grinning wickedly, showing a glint of strong white teeth.

"Well, your friend Lunceford made the stage," he remarked pleasantly enough. "That's good. I wouldn't have wanted to worry about him." He straightened then, lazily, pushing away from the doorframe with an easy movement. As he did his arm dropped, the fingers of his right hand carelessly brushing the handle of the holstered gun. Holden sensed the way Sam Riggs, at his side, stiffened and caught his breath.

But Glazer didn't pull the gun. Instead he raised his hand and adjusted the set of his shapeless, sweat-marked Stetson, smoothed back the unshorn rusty hair that hung raggedly almost to his collar. "Guess I'll be getting on over to the Montana House," he said, still grinning, "to wait for Luke. I'll tell him you may be dropping by—all right?" Not waiting for an answer he deliberately turned his back and, with a clink of spurs, vanished into the darkness.

# AMBUSH RECKONING

## II

A MUFFLED exclamation from Sam Riggs broke the lobby's stillness. Troy Holden scarcely noticed. Anger drove him forward in the wake of the redhead; he strode directly after him, through the open door and onto the hotel veranda.

Halting at the rail, he watched Glazer move at an angle across the moonwashed street, toward the lights of the Montana House. The man skirted a pair of horses at the tie rail, mounted to the boardwalk and walked inside the saloon.

A step sounded, and Sam Riggs loomed next to Holden in the half-shadow and half-moonlight of the hotel porch. Riggs said harshly, "What the hell do you make of *that?*"

Holden found that his hands were gripping the rail until the splintered wood scored his palms. He straightened, drawing a deep breath. "I was just about to ask you! This Luke Bartell: He's really as tough as I've been hearing?"

Sam Riggs spat across the rail, into the weed-grown dirt. "He's a bad one! The past couple years since he and his gang first showed up in this western Montana country, they've done just about what they please. Rustling's their specialty, though they don't stop with that. Bartell himself has killed three men, that I know about."

"And he's allowed to get away with it? I'm to believe that he can ride openly into a place like this—even send a man ahead to announce him, and run George Lunceford out of town—and nothing at all is done?"

He caught the bitter, nearly scornful look that Riggs shot him. "Trouble with you, you think you're still in New York City," the foreman said. "You think all you got to do is holler for a policeman. Out here, things just ain't that simple."

"You're still under the law," Holden reminded him, but Riggs only shrugged.

"You've seen our law! Poor old Peters is a good enough fellow to have a drink with, but as a sheriff's deputy he don't draw a hell of a lot of water. And as far as the sheriff himself is concerned, this is a remote end of a big country. Not many votes here—a lot easier for him to close his ears to any rumors of things that go on."

"There must be more than rumors! Have you no hard evidence—no witnesses to force the sheriff to act, whether he wants to or not?"

Riggs impatiently shook his head. "I tell you, you just don't understand. It would take an army to handle Bartell's crowd, and there ain't that much money in the county treasury. And so, who's going to offer himself up as a witness, for Bartell to take care of in his own good time? No, Holden—if you stayed around you'd learn a man here has to pack his own law, in his own holster. And he leaves it there and minds his business, except when somebody forces his hand."

Scowling, Troy Holden asked, "What about Crown, in all this? Perhaps these outlaws have been making us trouble, that you've conveniently forgotten to tell me about. . . ."

"No!" the foreman answered stiffly, and Holden knew he had succeeded in making him angry. "If it had been so, I'd of told you. The fact is, Bartell has left all the valley ranches pretty much alone. It's one of the reasons he knows he can come and go, just about as he likes. A man has plenty to keep him busy with his own affairs, as long as his toes aren't stepped on."

"Mine are being stepped on," Troy Holden pointed out. "And hard! By this time I ought to have had the papers signed, and a check for Crown in my pocket. For reasons I can't begin to fathom, Bartell decided to sic his redheaded gunman on Lunceford and ruin the deal for me. I may have to do what Glazer said: If Bartell's really going to be at the Montana House, it looks as though there's no choice but to find out from him what he thinks he's up to."

The foreman's head jerked around, his eyes searching Holden's face in the dim light. "You ain't talking about trying to brace Luke Bartell! Man, use your head! He'll have his whole bunch with him—and there's only the two of us here, from Crown. They could eat us alive!"

It was Troy Holden's turn to stare. Riggs' tacit assumption of a share in any trouble involving the brand he rode for showed a loyalty that was new in Holden's experience. Frowning, he shook his head as he answered shortly, "I'm not going to get eaten alive, and I don't ask anyone else to. Not for a few acres of grass and a few hundred head of cattle. But I *do* intend to get my price out of that ranch—I don't care who tries to interfere, or for whatever reason."

"So we're back where we started!" Riggs' voice sounded heavy with resignation. "You still mean to sell. I was almost beginning to hope you might be mad enough—"

Holden cut him off. "I can't help what you may have hoped. You know my reasons for selling. I realize you put a good many years into Crown, as my father's manager and even before that; I can see you probably feel you almost own the place. . . ."

"I never said that!" Riggs exclaimed. "But it's a fine ranch—or it could be, if it'd ever been developed the way it should. Only, the kind you intend selling to—like that Lunceford dude! Hell, I heard some of the darn fool questions he asked! What does a man like that know? Why, he'll ruin it!" Sam Riggs spoke with heartfelt earnestness. "Your pa had him a dream. As it happened he never got to work it out; but I knew his plans for Crown, and they were good ones. If you could somehow just change your mind—"

"We've said all this before," Troy Holden broke in. "Nothing's changed except that I've lost time I couldn't afford, thinking I was going to do business with Lunceford. Well, there are other buyers—but I can't risk any more delays.

"I'll get some telegrams written. I want them run over to the railroad, first thing in the morning. You'll either have to send one of the hands, or take them yourself."

The foreman's shoulders settled within his brush jacket; some of the spirit seemed to go out of him. He lifted a rope-gnarled hand, and let it drop again. "Sure," he said in heavy resignation. "You write your telegrams, Holden. Me—I think maybe I'm gonna go get drunk!"

Not waiting to be dismissed, he swung away and tramped down the plank steps, and strode off through the heavy golden moonlight. Troy Holden swore to himself. Afterward, with a shake of his head, he turned and walked again into the hotel lobby.

He ignored Sid Bravender's open stare as he crossed the worn linoleum to a writing table, in a corner near the tired-looking rubber plant. Seating himself, he looked for writing materials but there were none in the desk's pigeonholes; instead he found an old envelope in his pocket and, un-capping his reservoir pen, settled to drafting a telegram.

As he worked he was already drawing up in his mind a list of prospects—men or firms that controlled the means to buy in a property like Crown ranch. But after some moments, his pen slowed, and halted. Frowning, he looked at what he had written. With an angry gesture he crumpled the envelope into a ball, and fired it at the wastebasket by the table.

Until this puzzling situation involving Luke Bartell was explained and somehow resolved, everything connected with Crown was left hanging and in doubt. The more he thought about it, the more clearly it came home to him that his hands were tied.

16

Troy Holden capped and pocketed his pen, took his narrow-brimmed hat from the table and walked out of the hotel, frustration giving a reaching length to his stride and a hard definiteness to his footsteps on the uneven sidewalk. The moon was higher now, beginning to lose its ruddy glow and turning to a frosty silver. A wind was rising, to pluck at a man's clothing and comb the street with an occasional gout of gritty dust; it brought the chill and the tang of the high timber.

The evening was tuning up. Riders passed Holden, coming in off the trails; more saddled horses stood here and there at the hitch racks. He shouldered his way past spurred and booted men upon the walk, too occupied with his own thoughts to give much attention to any of them, or to the increasing sound and activity behind the lighted windows of the town.

A man stood alone beside a wooden arcade support, half-visible in the shadow of the tin roof. Holden went past and then, as the image of the man registered with him, he paused and came around again. Halting beside the lath-lean figure that towered almost half a head above him, he said, "Peters?"

"Mr. Holden."

Byron Peters, the deputy sheriff for this end of a sprawling county, was a polite-spoken man; he had a way of taking his hat off and holding it against his chest when he talked to anyone, as though to diminish the added height a steeple-crowned Stetson gave his gaunt shape. "Anything I can do for you?"

Moonlight showed the lawman's face—a good enough face except for a rather weak chin that spoiled it, and the sag of middle age. By Peters possessed a certain vague dignity, spoiled by the smell of brandy hung about him like an aura. Facing this man, Troy Holden said, "What do you

17

think, Sheriff? Does it look to you like a quiet evening?"

The tall man peered at the night, and the activity of the town. "Why, yes. Seems normal for a Friday, with fall gather still a couple weeks off."

"I wonder if you knew there's a man named Seab Glazer in town—over there in the Montana House."

In his present sour mood, it gave him a kind of satisfaction to see the startled way the bony head swung about for a look in that direction. There was a faint catch of breath in the tall man's chest before he answered, carefully, "I can't say I keep track of everyone who rides in. . . ."

"Still, it might interest you," Holden said, "that according to him, Luke Bartell's expected before the night's over. Probably with his whole crew."

"Glazer said this?" By Peters digested the news, and it was obvious that it troubled him. But after a moment he suggested a trifle lamely, "I imagine it'll be all right. They're a tough outfit, but we've never had any trouble. They walk a pretty narrow line here in Reserve."

"Oh?" Holden felt his temper slipping. "Perhaps you hadn't heard that Seab Glazer terrorized a man this evening—a man named Lunceford, visiting in town on honest business—and ran him out on the night stage!"

"That—that's a serious charge, Mr. Holden!"

"It happens to be true! I was there!"

"I see. . . ." The lawman seemed completely taken aback. A hand crept up and fumbled at his shirtcollar. In a hoarse voice he suggested, "It still might be hard to prove, even with witnesses. A court could say that this man Lunceford simply mistook Glazer's intentions. Do you know if he intends to press the case?"

"How could he?" Holden retorted. "I told you he'd left town!" Suddenly the futility of it overwhelmed him—the indignity of standing here trying to argue legalities with a man who walked in a perpetual fog of genteel booziness. Troy Holden lifted his shoulders.

"Forget it!" he said harshly. "Forget I said a thing. I never did understand you people—but, it's your town, and your country; and I guess you like it the way it is. But I'm damned if I have to!"

The tall man bobbed his head. He sounded hurt. "Now, Mr. Holden! Wait!"

"Good night!" Troy Holden said bluntly. He turned and deliberately walked away, not waiting to hear any more.

### III

BEFORE HE HAD gone a short half block he had fairly well worked off his head of steam; but when he stopped in the faint glow of a restaurant's plate glass window, to fish up a box of tailor-made cigarettes from his coat pocket, he found his hand was still trembling slightly. He analyzed what he was feeling and decided it was very near to shame.

There was nothing to be proud of in bullying an ineffectual but well-meaning man, who had probably never asked for his job but had held it all these years because no one else wanted it. At best the pay would keep By Peters in cigars and brandy and give him walking-around money, and keep him from being a financial burden on his brother's family. Holden chose his smoke, thumbed a wooden match to life and fired up. The glow of the flame, shielded by cupped palms, was on his face when he heard his name spoken, uncertainly. "Troy? Is that you?"

He shook out the match and dropped it, turning. The girl had halted with her hand on the restaurant door-latch, about to open it when she saw him. She dropped her hand now and turned as he walked over, touching the brim of his hat to her. Callie Peters said, "I was wondering if you'd seen my father yet this evening? Or Jim Ells?"

"No, I haven't," he told her. "I only got in a few minutes ago, myself." He thought dryly that he could have added, *I was giving your Uncle By a hard time a minute ago.* He was just as glad she didn't have to know about that.

She was saying: "I've been in town since afternoon; Pa and Jim were supposed to meet me and have supper. I'm tired waiting for them—I'm getting hungry!"

Troy Holden smiled a little. He suggested, "Will I do as a substitute?"

That brought up a quick gasp, and then an embarrassed laugh. "Oh, my goodness!" she exclaimed. "I really wasn't fishing for an invitation! But I'd like it very much."

"Come along then," he said, taking her elbow, and he opened the door for them both.

The diner was about half filled, the stools at the counter and a couple of the tables with their red-checkered cloths already occupied. Troy Holden found a table at the rear of the room, seated Callie and hung his narrow-brimmed hat on a nail before he took the chair across from her. He listened, amused, as she exchanged greetings with the proprietor, a fat man with an apron tied under his armpits. She ordered solidly—steak and potatoes and the trimmings.

Holden liked Callie Peters, whose full name—Calpurnia—must have been discovered by her mother in some battered copy of Shakespeare's *Julius Caesar.* Actually he had known her a long time. All the Peters family ran to tallness, and she already had her height when he first met her. She'd lost that early, awkward coltishness, had filled out and turned into a sunny-haired, attractive young woman; but she could never disguise the fact that she was and would always be a creature of the cattle ranges, without polish or social graces.

The man in the apron joshed a moment with the girl and then looked at Holden. Holden said, "I think I'll just have some coffee. I find I'm not really hungry."

Alone, Callie looked at him anxiously. "Is anything wrong?"

"Nothing," he said quickly, but he was afraid she wasn't reassured. For a quietness descended upon her and they said little during the next few moments while Holden finished his cigarette. When his coffee was set before him, in a thick china cup, he spooned in sugar and, stirring, looked up to see that Callie hadn't touched her food.

She said suddenly, "It isn't true? You're not really selling Crown?"

"When I close the right deal." Something accusing in her eyes made him add, a little too crisply, "It's the only sensible thing to do. Crown has hardly been a working ranch at all, these years the Holdens owned it. My father bought it for an investment—Sam Riggs thinks he had ideas of making something out of the place, and finally retiring there; but his plans never worked out. Actually, I think I was the only one ever got any use from the ranch, the times when he used to ship me out here to spend a summer toughening me up."

"Those hunting trips with Pa." Callie grinned fondly at the memory. "With me tagging along like a bird dog. It's a plain wonder you never tanned my britches and sent me home!"

Troy Holden smiled. "They were good times, weren't they, Callie? But, good times end."

Her smile faded; her eyes clouded with sympathy. "I was so sorry," she exclaimed quickly, "when I heard about your pa. Wasn't there any warning?"

He shook his head. "None at all. Later, I learned there'd been an earlier attack that I wasn't told about; and, I didn't know of the troubles with his investments. In fact, I sometimes feel I never really knew my father at all. But I like to think he died the way he would have wanted—in harness."

"And now, you're to try to pick things up where he dropped them. . . ."

"Naturally. Otherwise, everything will go. That's why Crown is so important. Somehow it was overlooked when the estate was liquidated; but the title is clear, and selling it should give me the capital I need to go back into the market and try to salvage at least part of the Holden interests from ruin. If I don't end up broke, that is. . . ." Seeing her expression, he smiled and shook his head. "This is all pretty boring," he said picking up his coffee cup. "I couldn't expect it to interest you."

She watched him as he drank. She said suddenly, "I'm just wondering if it really interests *you?*"

He looked at her in puzzlement. "What do you mean?"

"Why, all this talk of big business, and big money—are you sure that's really what you want?"

"It's what I was trained for. It's always been understood I would be taking over for my father, sooner or later. What else would I want?"

"I'm sorry." She shook her head, self-consciously. "I had no right to ask. But still, I just can't seem to picture you sitting behind a desk, in one of those big buildings in New York. Not when I've always seen you on a horse, with a rifle in the saddle boot." She hesitated. "I—I just can't believe that after Crown is sold we'll none of us be seeing you any more. Ever!"

"Oh, you can't tell about that," he said. "I always liked this Montana. I'll probably be back from time to time."

"Oh, of course!" she retorted. "Just like your pa did! You'll go and get sucked into that other world and that will be the end of it."

He smiled, not letting himself be angry with her. "After all," he pointed out, turning his cup about in the saucer, "that *is* my world. Here, I was never really anything but a stranger.

My life is back there: my family and friends—the girl I'm going to marry. . . ."

The chime of her fork into her plate brought his head up quickly. Her eyes were pinned on him, her cheeks gone suddenly dead white beneath their tan. "Why, Callie!" he exclaimed, startled and feeling all at once like a clumsy and stupid fool.

"It's all right. I just—" Suddenly her mouth was trembling and she put a hand against it and abruptly turned her head away. He was sure he saw a bright flash of moisture in her eyes. He could only stare at her—stunned by a revelation, and horrified to think of the unintentional hurt he had caused.

It was not intentional that he had never told her of Bea Applegate. The thought had simply never occurred to him, that this girl might imagine she was in love with him!

He was trying to think of something to say, when a shadow fell across the table. Looking up quickly, he saw the pair who stood over them with the smells of horse and of the open night clinging to their clothing. Morgan Peters, looming a head taller than his companion, looked at his daughter's averted face and then swiftly, speculatively, at Holden. Holden saw the danger that narrowed Morgan's eyes and hollowed out his cheeks in a tight-lipped scowl. He said quickly, "Evening, Morgan."

There was a resemblance to his brother, the deputy sheriff, but the gaunt face with its beak of a nose was as strong as By Peters' was weak. Gray eyes, beneath a tangled shelf of faded brows, probed at Holden and then, not answering the greeting, the tall man looked again at his daughter. "Callie? Everything all right here?"

The girl nodded vigorously, but without raising her head. "Of course, Pa."

"You sure? I kind of thought, to look at you—"

"I—burnt my tongue on something."

23

"Oh." Peters accepted this, though he still looked doubtingly at the pair seated at the table. Then the scowl smoothed out of his features and his high, broad shoulders appeared to slacken within the flung-open windbreaker he wore. Beside him, Jim Ells—another of the Kettle Creek ranchers, a man of about thirty, with yellow hair that strong Montana suns had bleached out to cornsilk—looked on as though he had missed the undercurrents of feeling here.

Morgan Peters said, "Holden, Jim and me would like a word with you. We got a proposition to make." He glanced around the restaurant, which was well filled now with the evening's trade, and busy with talk. "Kind of noisy here. Maybe we can borrow my brother's office, if you wouldn't mind coming along with us for a few minutes."

Curious, Troy Holden hesitated as he looked across at the girl. "Will you excuse us?" She nodded, still avoiding his eyes. He pushed back his coffee cup, and brought out money to leave by his plate in payment for both their orders—though he could see that Morgan Peters didn't too much like this either. Afterward he got his hat off the hook and followed the pair of ranchers, who were already making for the door.

The office at the jail was a tiny cubicle, with barely room in it for a desk and a couple of chairs and a battered filing cabinet. There were two small windows, heavily barred, and a thick slab door opening into a single cell that was almost without light. As they turned in here, Holden and his two companions heard a sudden racket of hoof-sound breaking and growing fast; they halted where they were, to watch a body of a half dozen horsemen come spurring boldly into town.

They brought a tang of lifted dust and lathered horseflesh and oiled leather as they swept by, with a certain arrogant assurance—looking neither to right nor left, nor easing out of the rolling gait that carried them swiftly on toward the heart of the village. Troy Holden saw the glint of metal on horse trappings and holstered six-shooters and booted rifles. He saw, briefly, the features of the leader who rode straight-up in the stirrups, his head lifted so that the fully risen moon lay plainly across his face. Even that one brief glimpse was enough to hint at the power in the chiseled face, with its massive jaw and full, down-sweeping moustache.

Holden heard a grunt break from Morgan Peters, and as the riders went by and the rush of hoofbeats faded he looked at the rancher. "Who was that?" he asked, though he already guessed the answer.

"Luke Bartell," Peters said, and he made the name sound as though it tasted bad.

Young Jim Ells swore bitterly. "Damned bunch of long-riders! Why do they have to pick our town? Why can't they go somewhere else and leave us alone?"

Troy Holden might have said, *Then why don't you try doing something about it?* But he kept silent; and they entered the tiny jail, to find By Peters at the window, peering out into the street where the moon-glimmering sheet of dust was settling in the wake of the vanished riders.

The deputy sheriff turned quickly and the wall lamp touched a faint sheen of sweat on his hollow cheeks. "Was that who it looked like?"

"It was." Holden thought Morgan Peters' face held a trace of bitterness as he answered. Surely he knew his brother had been drinking—no doubt there was a half-empty bottle in a drawer of the desk, yonder.

The lawman passed a hand across his cheeks; the hand shook. He seemed to pull himself together with an effort. "I guess I better get out on the street. A Friday night—a good part of the range in town: I only hope to God nothing happens!"

"It ain't likely," Morgan assured him. "Nobody wants trouble with Luke Bartell. But if there's trouble, don't try to manage it single-handed. We're always ready to back you up."

By Peters nodded, abstractedly. He hitched up his coat, touched the wooden handle of the gun in his holster. He took his hat from a nail behind the door, and drew it on as he walked outside.

## IV

INTO THE troubled silence, Troy Holden observed, "From everything I've heard, Bartell and his outfit are rustlers and outlaws. Do they know at the county seat that men like this are riding around the country, just as it pleases them?"

He had asked Sam Riggs the same question and got the same answer. Jim Ells retorted angrily, "You have any idea how far it is to the county seat? Canada's closer. The law knows Bartell is going to be up and gone across the line before a sheriff's posse can get within hailing distance—it's already happened!"

Morgan Peters broke in, scowling with distaste. "I'm free to admit Luke Bartell is a thorn in our side," he admitted gruffly. "But as long as he lets our herds alone, we at least can live with it. Maybe he'll ride on for other ranges eventually, and leave us in peace.

"Anyway it's a local problem, Holden," he went on, bluntly changing the subject. "Not yours. I understand you're fixing to get out from under the ranch your pa left you."

Holden nodded. "You heard right."

"Well, that's why we wanted to see you. What do you say

we make ourselves comfortable?" He closed the street door as he indicated the desk and chairs that nearly filled the dingy cubicle. Frankly curious, Troy Holden brought a straight wooden chair away from the wall and took a seat, placing his hat on his knee. Jim Ells hitched himself onto a corner of the desk, a booted leg swinging; he left the only other chair, behind the desk, for Morgan Peters.

The tall man went around and dropped into it, and the ancient barrel chair creaked under his weight; he dropped his dusty, sweated Stetson onto the desktop and leaned to haul open a drawer, saying, "Ought to be a bottle and glasses here somewhere. . . ."

"Don't bother on my account," Troy Holden said. "I seldom use it."

"The hell with it, then." Peters kneed the drawer shut again. "Be a sight less trouble in the world if some of us used it less!" Holden wondered, from the bitter tone of his voice, if he wasn't possibly still thinking of his brother.

The rancher leaned his elbows on the desk and laced his fingers together—rope-burned, nicotine-yellowed. He said, "I'll get right to the point. Jim and I are here on behalf of ourselves, and of the ranches in the valley. We've done a lot of conferring, the past few days, trying to reach an agreement and an offer that we could present to you."

"An offer for Crown?" At his nod Troy Holden said promptly, "I'm ready to hear it. It makes no difference to me who I deal with, so long as I get my price."

Peters and Jim Ells exchanged a look. The older man cleared his throat uncomfortably. "You have to understand," he said gruffly, "we ain't, any of us, what you'd call rolling in ready cash. The past two winters were tough ones, and the market for beef is still shaky. The point is, even pooling all our credit, we're not in any shape to buy you out."

In the act of reaching for his cigarettes, Holden paused

and frowned in puzzlement from one to the other of the men. "Then—?"

"What we'd like to try and interest you in is a lease—for as long as you'll give us, on whatever terms we can arrange. Crown has some of the best grass in the valley. Using it for winter range, on shares, the rest of us can start thinking about building up our herds. In the end we may even be in a position where we're able to buy.

"How about it?"

Disappointment made Holden frown. He withdrew his hand, empty, from his pocket. "Sorry," he said, more bluntly than he intended. "A lease is out of the question. I'm selling—now. I thought it was understood."

"It's understood all right," Peters said. "The thing is, we were hoping you might be persuaded to consider a counter offer. But, there isn't any chance of that?"

"No chance at all, I'm afraid."

Suddenly Jim Ells was off the corner of the desk, standing over him, with a hot fury in his eyes. "By God," the blond rancher exclaimed, "you damn well better consider it! You hear me?"

"Now, Jim!" Morgan Peters exclaimed sharply.

The younger man overrode the protest; anger had been building in him and now it had broken loose, had become a storm of emotion. "Don't try to shut *me* up. It's him! What does he care about the valley, or anybody in it? It's bad enough that all these years, Crown has had to belong to people like him and his old man—strangers who never set foot on it, from one year's end to another. Now God knows who'll end up owning it. Some syndicate or other, like as not—and us valley people without a word to say in the matter!"

He left off his angry speech, fists clenched and thick chest swelling to his breathing. Troy Holden refused to rise to the baiting; during all this he had remained seated, looking up at the man, only the coldness and stiffness of his face to tell him that he must have lost color under the tongue lashing.

Now Morgan Peters placed both hands upon the desk in front of him, the palms flat. He chose his words with obvious care as he said, into the tense stillness, "Crown is his, Jim, to do with as he sees fit—and he's not accountable to you, or me, or any of us." He swung his head to stare at Holden, and his gray eyes—eyes that were very much like his daughter's—were completely cold.

"But I regret to say I'm some disappointed in you, mister. Your old man, I couldn't of expected much from. I never saw him again, after that single trip when he had his one and only look at Crown, and bought it. I knew it was nothing but a business matter with him; I can at least say he showed judgment in keeping Sam Riggs on, all these years, to manage the spread for him—since he wasn't interested enough to give it any real attention, himself.

"But you, boy! I got to admit I had a different idea about you. Seeing you from time to time, these past few years, I sort of watched you grow into a man. I sort of thought you had a feel for these mountains—that this high country out here was actually beginning to mean something to you." He sighed and shrugged. "But, stands to reason I was bound to be wrong. The way a shoot is shoved into the ground, is the direction it grows."

It seemed to Troy Holden that, at every turn he took with these people, he found himself in the position of trying to explain and justify himself. It had been that way with Sam Riggs, and with Callie Peters; and now he was growing weary of the attempt. Jim Ells' words still stung; getting to his feet, Holden drew on his hat. "If we've all had our say, it doesn't appear there's anything more to discuss, does it?"

"There might be one thing," Peters corrected him, though with a scowling reluctance. "I'd just as soon not have to bring this up. "It's my daughter Callie. When Jim and I walked into that restaurant, we could both see that she was crying. She ain't a girl that cries easy; I'm asking you if it was because of something you said or did."

There was only one answer for that. Stiffly, Troy Holden told him, "Why don't you ask her? As far as I'm concerned, anything that might have passed between Callie and me was a private matter." He would have turned and left, with that, but a hand fell on his arm and halted him. He looked around into the face of Jim Ells, thrust belligerently into his own.

Ells was red and his nostrils flared. "And that's something else you can do—stay the hell away from Callie!" the blond rancher shouted.

It was a cry, and a look, of pure mistaken jealousy. Troy Holden was both surprised and startled, but he felt in no mood just then to indulge the man. "Not because you tell me," he retorted sharply, and jerked his arm away.

He wasn't prepared for what happened next. Jim Ells swore and suddenly a hard-knuckled fist was swinging at his face. Holden tried to back away from it. It missed its target, barely grazed his jaw and struck him in the chest with a quick, exploding pain.

His legs tangled with the chair he had quit and he half fell over it, toppling it back against the wall. He twisted about and kept from falling only by colliding full tilt with the wall, catching himself there against both spread hands. As he did so, boots tramped toward him; the overturned chair was kicked out of the way and a hand struck his shoulder and yanked him bodily around.

Ells had his fist cocked and ready, but Troy Holden was not in a mood to take it. Jim Ells was rawhide and sinew, toughened by years of the hardest kind of labor; but Holden, for all his background of money and good living, not only followed the more strenuous forms of hunting but also valued an hour's workout every day in the gym of his New York club. Not knowing this, Ells was open for a surprise. He let Holden slide out from under his hand as he turned, and then a cleanly placed right caught the blond man squarely on one cheekbone.

It was the first time Holden had ever delivered a blow bare-knuckled, without the protection of a padded glove; the pain of it raced shockingly up his arm and exploded. But he saw his assailant's face wiped clean of all expression save that of complete surprise, and Jim Ells was flung backward against the edge of the desk.

Then Morgan Peters was shouting something as he came in between, towering over them both. "Cut this out!" he cried indignantly. "Jim, you should be ashamed!" He stared in rebuke at his friend, who was leaning against the desk and fingering his cheek, and panting hard as he glared at Holden in bitter, savage anger. Peters turned to Holden, then, and his face was hard, his voice crisp.

"I'll apologize for what he did," the big man said. "But at the same time I'm going to say this, Holden: I ain't the man to let anyone hurt my family. Neither my brother, of whom I ain't too proud—or my daughter that I think more of than life itself. And I got the right, even if Jim hasn't, to ask you to leave Callie alone. From now on, you keep away from her."

Troy Holden's eyes narrowed slightly. "Even assuming I had ideas about Callie," he said crisply, "don't you think that's taking quite a lot on yourself?"

"All the same," the rancher said with stern implacability, "you just see you don't forget it!"

Troy Holden could only stare at these two, outraged by this display of suspicion and—on the part of Jim Ells—of sheer jealousy. His collarbone ached where Ellis had struck him, and his knuckles felt sprung and bruised. For his part, he couldn't see that he had done anything at all to apologize for or explain, and a stubborn anger firmed his lips.

He had dropped his hat in the brief scuffle with Ells; he leaned and picked it up, brushed it with a coat sleeve. Holding it, he hesitated a moment; then, not trusting his tongue, he simply turned and walked out, into the moonbright night.

## V

HE WAS STILL trembling a little as he paused to pull on the hat, and straighten the hang of his crumpled jacket. But it was foolish to waste emotion on that scene in the jail office. Peters and Ells should not concern him; soon enough they would no longer even be his neighbors. Meanwhile, the garish spill of light and sound from the Montana House, across the way, was a reminder of a challenge he had been given.

Looking at the lights, and at the line of horses tied out front, he knew he could not afford to let the challenge go—nor was he in a mood to. He filled his lungs with the clean autumn night and let the momentum of his anger carry him deliberately across the street dust, that the moonlight turned to a dull, beaten silver.

As he drew near the saloon, a movement in the shadows near the hitch rack made him pause. At once a voice spoke his name: *"Holden?"*

"Who's there?"

"Ain't anybody—just old Yance Kegley. I been watching out for you."

The man edged out of the darkness and now Holden could

see enough to recognize him—some ancient injury had left the old man with a crippled leg, so that he moved with an odd rolling gait and, when he rode, had to use a shortened stirrup. He made a living of sorts as a wolfer; Holden remembered seeing his shack, during one of his hunting trips in the high hills—he remembered the swaybacked roof and the rotting barn, and the mountainous heap of rusting tins.

He frowned in distaste as he caught the reek of the old man's clothing, that seemed to be imbued with the poisons and chemicals Kegley used in his trade. Holden said stiffly, "You want something from me?"

The other man might have caught the irritation in his voice. "From you?" he retorted. "Not a damn thing! I was about to do you a favor, but I sure as hell don't have to."

Holden saw he could have made a mistake. There was no point in deliberately antagonizing this disreputable old man; interested now in spite of himself, he said quickly, "I never turn down a favor. What's on your mind?"

Kegley's ruffled feelings seemed mollified, for after a moment he said in a gruff tone, "Nothing much—except I been inside there, watchin' Luke Bartell and his boys. Was I you, I'd stay out of there. Bartell's waiting for you, mister!"

"So I understood."

"And you're goin' in anway?" Yance Kegley gave a grunt, moved his shoulders inside his worn denim jacket. "Well, I reckon a man has to choose his own brand of suicide! One thing, though: You might keep your eye on the one dealing solitaire, over at the side table—the Injun, with the snakeskin on his hat. He'll have one hand out of slight. Watch him!"

Troy Holden digested this. He nodded and spoke with real gratitude. "I thank you for the tip. I promise to keep it in mind."

He started up the wide steps, and as light from the door

struck him more fully he heard the old wolfer's exclamation; "You ain't even wearing a six-gun!"

"I don't own one," Holden said. He opened the door and walked inside.

The Montana House was the only saloon in town, and the one place where there were public games. So it did a fair business, though it was anything but fancy—a narrow shoe-box of a room, the long, plain bar facing the banks of felt-topped gaming tables along the opposite side wall. Toward the back were pool tables, a big space-heater sitting in a box of cinders, and an open-front mechanical piano with a bass drum attachment. At the moment, this was not working. When Troy Holden pushed the door shut behind him with his heel, the room was, all of a sudden, deathly quiet. The dry rattle of the bar dice was the last sound to cease.

Perhaps a dozen men were scattered among the card tables; which of them might be Luke Bartell's riders, Holden wasn't in a position to say. Another pair stood alone at the bar—it looked almost as though the regular customers were purposely letting them have it to themselves. For, one of these was the redheaded gunman, Seab Glazer. The dice-thrower turned his head, and again Holden saw the chiseled face, with the bulldog jaw and downsweeping moustache, that he had noticed in the van of the longriders as they swept into town.

Glazer murmured something and Bartell nodded shortly, his black eyes unmoving from Holden as he quietly set down the dice cup.

Cutting his glance sharply to the left, Holden saw—just as Yance Kegley had told him—a man who sat alone with a spread of solitaire laid out on the table in front of him. He had a narrow, hatchet-face, with something of the look of a breed. The crown of his tall black hat was punched out, without creases, the way Indians liked to wear them. And for a hatband he wore the diamond-patterned skin of a bull rattler.

He held the deck of cards in his left hand; sure enough, his right was out of view, somewhere below the table's edge. Eyes as black as obsidian held, unblinking, on the man in the doorway.

If this was the kind Luke Bartell had riding for him, Holden thought, it told all he needed to know of what he was up against.

He refused to give any sign of the alarm bells beating inside him. He walked deliberately forward, placed a hand on the wood and told the man in the apron, "I'll take Bourbon, friend, if you have it."

The bartender—actually he was the owner of the Montana House, a black Irishman named Costello, with fists like hams and a single curl of hair plastered to the center of his forehead—was plainly on edge and nervous, as though concerned about his place of business. He gave Holden almost a resentful look, then grudgingly set out a tumbler and filled it from a bottle he took from under the bar. He scooped up the coin Holden put down and, scowling, moved away. Holden drew the shot glass to him but he didn't drink. At that moment the street door opened, drawing his hasty glance. He saw Yance Kegley close the door and sidle, limping, toward a side wall, keeping discreetly out of the way. The old wolfer must have decided he didn't want to miss whatever was to happen. . . .

Luke Bartell broke the heavy stillness. "Your name's Holden?" he said; and, getting a cold stare and a nod: "Maybe you know who I am?"

"I know."

"Then we won't have to waste any words."

He came along the bar, to halt a couple of paces from Holden with Seab Glazer looming at his elbow. Thus confronted, Troy Holden stood his ground. The fingers of his right hand, resting on the bar, turned the half filled whiskey glass and made wet circles on the wood. Bartell said loudly, "I understand you're stuck with a ranch you're trying to get rid of."

Holden retorted, "You should know! I all but had it sold—before the redhead stepped in."

Seab Glazer grinned at him wickedly. Bartell merely shrugged. "Maybe it *was* kind of rough on that rabbit of a man who got run out of town tonight," the rustler admitted indifferently. "But it seemed as good a way as any to teach you a few of the facts of life."

"What facts?"

"Chiefly this one: It don't matter a damn what you *think* you're gonna do with that Crown spread. In the end, you're gonna make your deal with me."

"With *you?*" Surprise jarred the words out of him, and Holden saw those other eyes narrow and harden.

"That's what I said," Luke Bartell answered tartly. "Why— is there something so peculiar in the idea of me owning a piece of cattle range?"

Holden considered the question. "Some people I've talked to might be inclined to think so." He shrugged. "But I suppose what they'd think is neither here nor there."

"Damned right!" the rustler said, and laid the flat of a hand on the bar. It was a big hand, and powerful, with a saddle of coarse black hair across the back of each rope-scarred finger. "I've been looking over this country, careful. I've seen a lot of it I like. I like that Crown spread of yours the best of what I seen.

"So name your price, Holden. If it's fair I'll meet it, and no haggling. But, one way or another, I'm taking that spread! What happened tonight should tell you that you'll deal with me, or you won't deal at all!"

Troy Holden felt the weight of every eye, the pressure of every held and lung-trapped breath in that room. Something pulled his glance to a table toward the rear, where a man sat alone with a shot glass and a half-emptied whiskey bottle in front of him. The man lifted his head and Holden saw it was his own foreman, Sam Riggs. After that fruitless quarrel on the hotel veranda, Riggs had stomped away saying he intended to get drunk. From the flushed looseness of his features, it looked as though he was already well on the road—but he was plainly sober enough to understand what was going on in front of him.

The fate of Crown could affect every living being within a radius of miles from this valley, and every man here knew it. Suddenly, as he remembered the pressures he'd been undergoing—not only from Sam but from Morgan Peters and Jim Ells and all the others who resented him, for being different from themselves—Holden thought cynically that it would serve them right, were he to take Bartell's deal and go away and leave them a rustler for a neighbor. In that moment he could almost seem to feel again the weight of Jim Ells' crushing fists. . . .

He shook his head. "I'm afraid not, Bartell," he said flatly. "We can't make any deal."

The big man's head jerked as though in disbelief. A slow flush stained his cheeks. The big hand tightened to a fist. "And why the hell not?"

"I don't do business with crooks. And I don't take money that almost certainly has blood on it!"

The words were barely out of his mouth when they were drowned in a shout of fury from the redhead, Seab Glazer. He brushed past his chief and came bearing in—one hand reaching for Holden, the other dipping toward the cutaway holster thonged to his leg.

Timing his move, Holden waited until the man was well

37

within range before his hand came off the bar, still holding
the glass of Bourbon. He let Glazer have glass and all,
squarely in the face; then, as the redhead yelled and doubled
up, pawing at his streaming eyes, stepped forward to seize
hold of the gunman and, half turning him, propel him across
the narrow width of the room. The one with the snakeskin
hatband was starting—belatedly—to bring up the six-shooter
he had been holding in his lap. Glazer struck the table and
upended it, slamming it into the seated man, and they both
went down in a tangle of smashed wood and a spray of
spilled playing cards.

The gun popped out of the breed's fingers, hit the floor
spinning and came sliding across the boards, straight toward
Holden, who had been meaning to dive for cover around
the street-end of the bar. Now, instead, he leaned and
scooped the gun off the floor and came up with it leveled
and ready.

"I'll use this," he said tersely, "if I have to!"

Bartell must have thought he meant it, for the big rustler
froze where he stood—his right hand just brushing back the
skirt of his coat, to clear the holster strapped beneath. The
ones Holden had floored came rolling free of the table's
wreckage now, Glazer swearing furiously and pawing still
at his streaming eyes; they too caught sight of the weapon
in Holden's grasp. As they went motionless he straightened,
hoping no one could see the violent shaking of his knees
or the sweat he felt upon his face.

Keeping his voice firm he told Bartell, "I might as well
make it clear: I'm a stubborn man. I meant what I said
about no deal—and you won't change my mind, by sending
toughs like the redhead at me!"

Bartell's blocky face was a mixture of dangerous emotions.
About to speak, he turned his head sharply: Holden saw
reflected, in the bar mirror, what it was had drawn his atten-

tion—the wolfer, leaning forward where he stood against the wall and showing all his teeth in a grin of wicked delight.

You might have thought this scene was being played strictly for Yance Kegley's benefit and his amusement. But when he saw Bartell's savage stare turned on him, the grin died and the old man hastily drew back, obviously not so happy about being noticed. Luke Bartell dismissed him, then, turning back to the man who had dared to challenge him, "Holden, you may be tougher than I thought," he said grudgingly. "I won't make that mistake again. But, tough or not, you're a fool if you think you can pull a bluff on me!"

Anger began to have its way with Troy Holden, swamping the voice of caution. "How would you like to go to the devil?" he snapped. "Just stay away from me. Stay away from Crown. And after this, leave my buyers alone!"

Pure ugliness peered at him from Luke Bartell's eyes. The mouth behind the heavy moustache pulled down into a snarl. "Why, you damned dude! I'll tell you what's going to happen: There won't be no buyer. I'll take that ranch away from you—on my own terms!" Suddenly, to a flip of his thumb, a blur of gold streaked toward Holden. By reflex Holden plunked the coin out of the air, left-handed, and looked at what he held in his palm.

A gold eagle. Twenty dollars.

"There's my terms," Bartell said. "You'd best put it in your pocket; because after what just happened it's every cent you're going to get! It don't matter whether you take it or not—I'm going to run your tail clean out of this country!"

Troy Holden raised his cold stare to the outlaw's face. He looked at Seab Glazer and the breed, who had climbed to their feet and stood hating him with their eyes. He looked around at the other silent faces that filled the room with a tension that was almost like the throbbing of a pulsebeat. Without a word he flung the coin, ringing, in front of

Bartell's scuffed boots. And laying the six-gun on the bar he turned and left the Montana House. His movements were deliberate and unhurried, but the sudden cold blast that struck his body, as the glass door swung beneath his shaking hand, told him nearly every inch of him was drenched with sweat.

## VI

AT THE LIVERY BARN Troy Holden found the old hostler dozing, shook him awake and told him to fetch his horse. Waiting, he stood and looked at the village and listened to the quiet sounds of the night, while he forced his nerves to unwind.

No one came near him; there was no immediate hint of a sequel to that encounter at the Montana House. Later, he was checking the cinch and preparing to put toe in stirrup when someone came stumbling toward him up the hoof-splintered ramp. He turned quickly, and saw it was Sam Riggs.

The foreman showed the whiskey he'd been drinking. In the yellow light of a lantern on a roof prop, his face looked swollen and he swayed a little. "Here you are, Holden!" he grunted. "I been huntin' all over. Tried the hotel, but they hadn't seen you. . . ."

"I'm riding back to Crown! I'm too keyed up for bed." Making no comment on Riggs' obvious condition, he added, "What happened in the bar? After I left?"

Riggs gave a low whistle. "That was a scene! Glazer, and that breed they call Wasco—after what you done to 'em, they really wanted blood; but Bartell shut 'em up. He said—"

The foreman hesitated, then blurted it out: "He said you was nothing but blow. He said you're still just a damned dude, and he's giving odds you'll be out of the country by morning!"

Holden's tight smile was icy. "Has he had many takers?"

"Look, Mr. Holden!" Urgent feeling drew Riggs an anxious step nearer, and he lurched giddily and put a hand against a roof timber to steady himself. "What you done in there tonight—that sure wasn't blow, and it wasn't bluff! I'll say it made a liar out of *me!* I think of the things I said this evening—and the things I thought and didn't say. . . ."

"Don't bother," Holden said, cutting across his apology. "I made a stupid play to the grandstands, that could have got me killed—and it accomplished nothing."

"The point is, you stood up to Luke Bartell! I don't know another man that ever tried it! Least of all, a—a—" He fumbled for words.

"A damned dude?" Troy Holden supplied. "Let me tell you something, Sam. Where I come from, I've known crooks who make Bartell look like nothing! They're twice as tough in their own way and they're every bit as dangerous—even if they do sit behind mahogany desks, in padded chairs, and wouldn't know one end of a six-gun from the other. The Holdens have never knuckled under to men like that, and I'm not going to start with a cowcountry tough like Bartell."

"All the same," Riggs insisted, "you better watch your step with him." He added, dropping the subject, "If you're riding, give me time to get my horse and I'll go along."

Holden looked at him, smelling the whiskey on him, and shook his head. "I'm afraid I'd have to hold you in the saddle. No—you stay in town and sleep it off. Besides, I have something I want you to do for me tomorrow: Wait till the stage gets back from the railroad and if there's any mail, bring it out to the ranch."

Riggs looked at him shrewdly, and Holden knew the foreman understood he was still preoccupied with the letter which hadn't been waiting at the stage line office. Sam Riggs nodded and then said, as he remembered, "There was something too, about some telegrams you wanted sent. . . ."

Troy Holden shook his head. "They'll have to wait. I can't sell anyone a pig in a poke. Until this threat from Bartell is cleared up—one way or another—any buyer I brought in to look at Crown could be put through the same thing that happened to George Lunceford tonight. I can't allow that, not again!"

"Then I reckon we've got a job ahead of us!"

Troy Holden only nodded moodily, and swung into the saddle. Some of his own restiveness of spirit seemed to convey itself to the horse and he had to use the bit to curb it down as it swung about, shod hooves trampling the splintered floorboards. After that, Holden rode out through the wide doors, ducking his head for clearance, and down the ramp to the street. He scarcely heard Sam Riggs' anxious parting words: "If it was me, I'd keep my eyes open!"

He swung the bay into the intersection of the cross street, full into the silver wash of moonlight, and would have sent it directly on toward the junction with the north valley trail; but he saw movement on the porch of the hotel and heard Callie Peters call his name across the dust. As he reined over that way, she came out from under the roof overhang, onto the steps. Their faces were almost on a level as Holden pulled in, without dismounting.

She was breathless with concern. "Troy! What are you trying to do to yourself? Walking into that place, that way—alone! Challenging Luke Bartell and his whole outfit!"

Irritably he demanded, "How did you know?"

"Why, Sam Riggs told us—just now, when he was here looking for you. I almost died!"

"It wasn't as bad as all that. And nothing came of it."

She insisted, "But it could! They'll never let it end there! Don't you see?" Her words broke in a sound that was almost like a sob. Then, before Holden could think of any answer, they were interrupted. Big Morgan Peters emerged from the shadows of the veranda; he shaped up tall and lean against the lobby lights as he came out to stand beside his daughter.

The rancher said sharply, "Girl, ain't you being just a little silly about this?" His head swung, and Holden could almost feel the eyes boring at him from below the brim of the man's hat. "I have to admit, you got more guts than I pegged you for, Holden—even if I can't say as much for your common sense, taking the kind of chances you do!" Grudging as it was, Holden knew that was the nearest to a compliment he was going to get from the man; and it was immediately tempered by an ill-natured reminder: "All the same, I hope I don't have to repeat what I told you before."

What he meant was, his warning about staying away from Callie. Just now he wasn't even making allowance for the fact that this scene was his daughter's doing, calling Troy Holden across the street to speak to him. Stiffly Holden said, "I remember, all right. Maybe *you'll* remember what I answered!" Turning to the girl, then, he touched a finger to hatbrim and said, a trifle stiffly, "Good night, Callie. And don't worry—nothing will happen to me. You'll be seeing me again."

On that note he sent the bay ahead. He could imagine Callie's bewilderment over the cryptic exchange—and likely as not, her father's smoldering anger. And now a quick spurt of flame drew his glance to someone he hadn't noticed before, on the walk below the veranda's splintered railing. The match was carried to the bowl of a pipe; its glow revealed the face of the yellow-haired rancher, Jim Ells. His stare met Holden's above the flame as, deliberately, he sucked fire into the bowl of the pipe, his cheeks drawing in.

And Troy Holden rode on, feeling the eyes of the two men and the girl on him as he went ahead up the crooked street—wondering too, uneasily, just how many others watched him go.

That same uneasiness traveled with him, even when he had put the town at his back and there was only the night with its sharp contrasts of black and silver, and the shouldering masses of rock and pine ridges. He had been more tense than he realized—the encounter with Bartell had tapped reserves of energy, and coming on top of his other frustrations of the night it left him edgy and ill-tempered. He had never thought of this country as containing personal enemies—men who might even like to see him dead. It was a new concept and an unpleasant one, that put nagging worry at the back of his mind to grow stronger as the minutes passed.

He began to feel his aloneness and his vulnerability, so much so that an odd prickling made itself uncomfortably present along his spine. Somehow he had a sense of other riders abroad in the night. A wind had come up, raising a sound of surf in the pine tops; but once he was so certain he had heard hoofbeats striking bare rock, somewhere on the trail behind him, that taut nerves jerked the rein and made the bay horse halt and stomp in protest. Troy Holden cursed the rattle of bit chains, that interfered with his hearing. Settling the bay, he pulled into the dense shadow of a thicket while he searched the murmuring wind that blew up from the south.

Nothing—no further sound; and though he waited a good ten minutes, no horseman appeared. Nerves and imagination, he told himself. But even as he did he could think of other explanations.

If that was another horseman, following him from town, he could have guessed he'd let himself be heard; he could be waiting now for Holden to decide he was mistaken, and start on again. Or, if you assumed he knew this hill country—and whoever he was, it stood to reason he must know it better than Troy Holden—then there was no real reason for him to keep to the trail at all. The wagon trace followed the easiest grades, snaking down from that bottleneck pass where the stage road linked Kettle Creek with the outside world; on a night of such clear moonlight, a rider could easily pick a more direct route.

As his horse grew tired of standing still and turned restless under him, Holden became angry at the futile waste of time and finally put the bay into the trail again. And, riding on, he found his uneasiness giving way to other feelings.

All those people tonight—Sam Riggs and Luke Bartell and Seab Glazer; Jim Ells and Morgan Peters and the latter's drunken brother. Yes, and even Callie! He resented the way every single one of them seemed bent on involving him in matters that held no personal interest for him. He had tried to explain to Callie that this was not his world. It had no claims on him—it could do no more than delay him from getting back to those other people and affairs that were his prime concern. He shook his head, as a baffled impatience arose in him and closed off his senses to the beauty of the night—to the ridges like black cutouts, the wide sky and the milky disc of the moon whose glow blanked out the near stars. . . .

The land leveled off finally; this twisted wagon road shook free of its kinks and became a straight pencil-line that cut directly down through dense jackpine. Below, the valley lay like a half inflated sack, pointing northward within its sheltering fold of ridges. Where the trail took its final turn, a boulder the size of a small house crowded the timber. When he rounded this a nighthawk whisked by in silent but sudden flight, so close to him that he ducked involuntarily.

The bay swung its head; thinking it was the bird that had startled it, Holden spoke and tightened the reins. A bare instant later, he realized his mistake when another horse snorted, somewhere to his immediate left.

His head whipped about sharply, even as he felt the bay's barrel swell to an answering whicker. Against the shadow of the big rock he glimpsed a dark shadow that could only be a horse with a rider motionless on its back. His hand pulled the rein involuntarily just as a gun spoke, in a smash of sound and a smear of muzzleflame.

He felt the bullet spear into him. If the horse hadn't been moving away he likely would have been swept from the saddle. Instead, lurching wildly, he managed to catch at the horn. He heard his own voice yelling at the animal, and somewhere found the strength and presence of mind to drum both heels into its flanks.

The bay gave a squeal and lunged straight ahead, down that alley of moonlight descending through the trees. As it did so, either the same gun or another spoke again—behind them now, its roar battering against the face of the big rock. The blow struck solidly. It lifted Holden, slammed him forward onto the neck of his horse.

After that he knew he must be falling, but it felt rather as though he went spinning away into some black and engulfing nowhere.

## VII

HE WAS conscious of pain that was too general to be local-
ized, and an odd and unnatural sensation of motion. It
came to him that his head and limbs were without support,
and that they were dangling and swaying in a way that
vaguely alarmed him and, as it continued, filled him with
nausea.

Dull agony blocked his thought processes, but he became
enough aware to realize he lay jackknifed across a creaking
saddle, bound there, and rocking helplessly as the horse
under him picked a way over uneven and tough terrain.
When he opened his eyes he could see nothing but the
vaguest blur of dark ground sliding beneath him. He tried
to cry out in protest and lift his head, and immediately
regretted the effort it cost.

But abruptly the movement ceased, though he felt the jar
as the animal beneath him stomped restlessly a time or two.
Another horse moved up beside him, a voice he thought
he should recognize spoke somewhere harshly: "Hell's fire!
Will you take it easy? I'm doing the best I can!"

Holden tried to mutter something in answer, but he was
already sliding again into the muffling recesses of unconsciousness.

. . . He was still lying face down, but the torturing motion
had ceased. Unable to move, he had his face pressed against
some fetid-smelling material that might be dirty bedclothes;
he could breathe only poorly and it was likely some deep-
buried fear of suffocation that roused him. When he opened

the one eye that he could see with, it was to stare directly into a blazing yellow flame set only inches away. He blinked and groaned.

The light was a kerosene lamp, on a box or table beside his bed. Now a hand moved it away, and the same voice he had heard before spoke gruffly: "You pick a poor time to come around, mister! You may not know it, but you got a rifle slug in your back—pressing right against your spine. I'm just now fixing to get it out of there."

Holden saw a glint of reflected light, glancing from metal. It looked like the blade of a butcher knife. Horror roused him, actually lifting his head a trifle out of the musty blankets. "Not with that, damn you!" he tried to say, hearing only a croaking protest from his own lips. Then a bent knee came down, hard, upon his naked shoulders and pressed him flat again, and the voice said, "You're gonna hold still, you hear—if I have to set on your head to make you do it!"

There was no strength in him to struggle. He lay like that, pinned and helpless—and then the blade bit home, and Troy Holden learned to the core of his being what pain really was. He shouted, his whole body arching like a taut bow. After that, mercifully, all consciousness drained from him.

How much later he could not know, he lay unmoving and awake, all strength seemingly spent beyond recovery. There was no desire in him to move; he scarcely comprehended how long he had been aware of himself, and of the world to which he'd returned. Remembering, then, what had gone before, he sent down tentative probes of awareness—until they met a deep center of dull, throbbing ache somewhere toward the middle of his back. Hastily he withdrew them.

He must have let out a groan. Someone moved into his field of vision and this time he recognized Yance Kegley. The old wolfer said sharply, "You better take it easy, there!"

Holden's throat felt swollen, unapt for speech. When he tried to shift his head a little the muscles at the back of his neck protested. At the second effort he brought out something that sounded like, "Where am I?"

The cripple made it out, apparently. "My shack—where else?" he answered. "And in my own damn bunk!"

"How long?"

"Well, this is Sunday afternoon. In case you don't remember, it was Friday evening somebody boosted you out of the saddle with a couple of thirty-caliber slugs!"

Troy Holden groaned again. He closed his eyes again for a moment, fighting the draining lethargy and listening to the old man move about the room in his warped, crippled way. After a moment he was able to ask, "Did you manage to carve the bullet out of me? You and that butcher knife?"

At that Kegley chuckled, obviously pleased with himself. "Like prying the pit out of a cherry. Damned thing near popped up and hit me in the eye. Want a look?"

He dug in a pocket, held out a horny palm containing a battered chunk of lead. Holden focused his eye on the bullet, and grimaced. "Keep it for a souvenir!"

"I ain't no sawbones," the old man said blandly. "Still, I think I done a pretty good job, considering. Didn't have to carve you up too bad, and the hole looks clean enough. But the slug was lyin' right against your spine. Reckon the test will be when we find out if you got any life in your legs, at all."

"You may have to wait a while for that," Holden said grimly.

He felt sickened at the thought of the crude butchery that had been done on him, and at the moment felt a dread of testing the results. The drained weakness settled on him

49

again, and the world splintered and melted once more into darkness.

After that came an undetermined succession of waking and unconsciousness, that went on for he knew not how long. Once, during one of his clear moments, Troy Holden asked, "Do you have any idea who it was that ambushed me?"

There was the slightest pause before the old man answered, and Holden was to wonder afterward if perhaps he was lying when he said finally, "I never seen nobody. I was riding home and I heard the shots, not too far ahead. When I got to you, you were lying in the trail and I could hear a horseman going through the timber—like maybe I'd scared him off, coming along like that."

"It was no more than one rider? You're positive of that?"

"I listened for a long time, to make sure. Then I looked you over—thought you was dead, at first, but soon seen you wasn't. So I caught up your horse and got you across the saddle and headed for here."

"And I'm eternally grateful to you," Troy Holden said carefully. "Only—I'm wondering why you couldn't have taken me back to town instead."

"Because I wasn't goin' that direction," Kegley retorted, as though it were the most reasonable explanation in the world; and for the first time it occurred to Holden, with a faint thrill of dread, that he might be in the hands of a madman. "Besides," the old man went on, "there ain't no real sawbones hereabouts—not anybody who could of done a better job than I did. I figure, at the very best, you're gonna be laid up and pretty near helpless for quite some time to come.

"Supposing whoever wanted to murder you found he hadn't quite managed. If you was in town, or somewhere handy—what would keep him from making a second try? And what could you do but lie there and let him?"

50

That hadn't occurred to Holden, and it made a horrible kind of sense. But at once it suggested something else: "How do you know he won't find our tracks, and follow us both here?"

"He won't follow no tracks," Yance Kegley said flatly. "Don't think I'm such a fool I left any for him! That's a much traveled road. Whoever notched you ain't gonna have any luck reading sign on it. Especially after I brushed out the evidence where you fell off your horse. He may not even know for sure he got a hit.

"No—take it from me: For the time being at least, you're safe enough. . . ."

Troy Holden let himself breathe more easily. Crazy the old man might be, but plainly there was a lot of cunning craftiness to him too. Probably he'd made the whole grisly business into a game, taking a half-demented delight in outwitting the would-be assassin.

As though satisfied, some deep-seated instinct for self-preservation seemed to let go. He sank again into oblivion, but deeper than before into a nothingness that was broken only by rare moments of lucidity. Somehow he was aware that Yance Kegley was taking care of his needs—changing the dressings on his wounds, even managing now and then somehow to get food inside him. His mind was willing to have it so, while his body went about its essential work of mending the hurts that had nearly done for him.

Time, as such, meant nothing. But there came a moment when he surfaced, and realized he was more fully aware than on any such previous occasion—and, for the first time, interested in his surroundings.

He still felt more or less dead from the waist down, but he didn't let himself think of that just yet. He lay on his back, a pillow under his head, a blanket drawn over him. Above him were rafters, laid with a crude ceiling of roughadzed timbers. In one corner, cleats nailed to a pole made a ladder, rising to a square hole and a trapdoor to the loft.

Turning his head, he had a view of a crude-looking cabin that seemed to contain no more than a single room. Whatever it was let in the daylight, he judged it was not glass but more likely some kind of oiled skin. It showed him walls of chinked logs, furniture put together from split poles and rawhide—a couple of graceless straight chairs, a rickety-looking table. A fire burned in a mud and brick fireplace, with shelves nearby holding food and supplies. Odds and ends of clothing hung from pegs, and a rifle hung above the door. In one corner, partially hidden by the table, he saw a disorderly heap of what looked to be traps of various sizes.

The smell of the room was compounded pungently of grease and stale food and tobacco and dirty clothes, and something else that could be the stink of a wolfer's baits and poisons.

Suddenly the door opened—dragging the floor, on poorly hung leather hinges—and Yance Kegley entered. Looking past him Troy Holden saw, in some astonishment, a blank whiteness and a swirl of snow that followed the old man in on a blast of icy air. He had an armload of chopped wood balanced in the crook of an elbow. He worried the door shut, limped over to the fireplace and dropped his load beside it. Afterward, turning away, the old man ripped open the fastenings of his heavy coat.

The coldness he had brought in seemed to cling to him and his clothing. He took a briar pipe, had it halfway to his lips when he saw Holden looking at him.

The pipe halted in mid-air. Kegley grunted and stared at the injured man, across its unlighted bowl. "So! You decided to join the living."

"I'll let you know!" Troy Holden answered gruffly. He was eyeing with growing concern the snow that clung wetly to the old man's clothing. Suspiciously he demanded, "Just what day is this?"

Kegley cocked an eyebrow at him. "Why, it's the twenty-fourth of November. Yesterday was Thanksgiving."

"Good God! Don't tell me I've lain in this bed for five weeks!"

"Well, I'll say you ain't been doing much traveling," Kegley agreed dryly. He frowned at the hurt man. "You mean to say that you wasn't even conscious, all that time? Why, hell! You've been awake, off and on. You've talked to me."

"I must have been out of my head. But I don't think I am now."

"You do seem on the mend." The old man pulled off his coat and hat, shook the snow from them and hung them up. He shoved some more wood onto the fire, and turned back to his patient. "Still a ways to go, though," he said. "Hole in your chest ain't making any real trouble—bullet missed touching the lung, and didn't damage the ribs too much. But it's that other one. . . ." He flipped back the blanket, uncovering Holden's lower legs. He pointed a gnarled finger. "See them things down there? Them's your feet. Mister, you still got me all-fired curious to know if you can move them any. Suppose you show me!"

Holden looked down the length of his body. Suddenly, despite the chill of the room a faint sweat broke out upon his cheeks. He heard himself begin to stammer: "I—I don't—"

"Damn you!" Yance Kegley looked all at once twice his actual height, standing over the crude bunk and glaring at him in scathing anger. "You ain't even trying! I pegged you for having more gumption than this. Could be I was wrong?"

Staring back at his tormentor, Holden felt something akin to active hatred. He still had that horrible nothingness, there at the middle of his spine, and when he tried to focus his attention there he became aware of a core of pain that made him rebel against testing himself against it. But there was no escaping the cruel contempt of Yance Kegley's hypnotic stare; under its prodding, Troy Holden set his jaw and his hands drew up into fists and he watched his feet—curious objects, that seemed no part of him at all—move a few wavering inches away from each other and settle back again.

At once, old Kegley was grinning as though the triumph had been his own. "That's more like it—makes one thing, at least, you don't have to worry about any more." He rubbed hard palms together, with a faintly rasping sound. "Now, then, how about some grub?"

"Since you mention it," Troy Holden admitted, "I don't feel as though I'd ever eaten."

"Another good sign," the old man said, nodding. "I'll put something together." He turned to it.

Holden was suddenly weak with relief; he hadn't realized how deeply anxious he was, at the root of his being, over the effects of that bullet Kegley had dug out of him. Lying there, watching the old wolfer set about the chore of preparing a meal, he said suddenly, "I realize I'll never be able to repay what I owe you."

He expected Kegley to agree, with more of his acid sarcasm; instead, the old man merely looked at him most oddly. When he spoke it was to say, "I'm surprised you ain't asked me any questions about the state of your affairs, down the valley. . . ."

Thought of the people of Kettle River had frankly not occurred to him; it was more or less with indifference that he asked, "They know yet who it was shot me?"

"They don't even know you been shot!"

Kegley carried a smoke-blackened coffeepot to the door, stepped out long enough to scoop snow into it and returned to hang it over the fire. He saw the look of astonishment on Holden's face, then, and he said with some heat, "Did you think I'd let the news out—warn your enemies, so they could come up here while you were lying helpless and finish you off? And do for me at the same time, like as not?"

Holden saw the sense of this argument, but he could only shake his head. "In the Lord's name, then—what *do* people think happened to me?"

"Well, now, I reckon they think you pulled out." Kegley was turning the handle of a coffee mill, seemingly unaware of the enormity of what he was saying. "That night in the Montana House—when you stood up to Luke Bartell—he warned you not to try and stay around this country. From what I've heard folks sayin' they've all about decided you must have thought things over, and decided to do like he told you."

"They think I turned tail and ran from him?" Troy Holden groaned, aghast at the thought. He added bitterly, "That must make Bartell feel pretty pleased with himself!"

"I reckon." Kegley dumped the contents of the mill into the coffeepot. "You see, there's a trifle more I got to tell you. Luke's taken over your ranch." He nodded, to the look on Holden's face. "Yep. Something like a week after you disappeared. Him and his boys just rode into Crown, told Sam Riggs and the rest of your crew to go lose themselves, and took charge."

Holden stammered: "That's fantastic! They couldn't have!"

"Who was to stop 'em—those neighbors of yours? Morg Peters, and Jim Ells, and so on? By the time they even heard about it, the thing was done. Hell! Bartell knew he was too tough for the whole bunch of them, put together!"

"But—" He started to say, *the law!* But then he thought of By Peters and knew the answer to his question—knew he had been all over that ground before, the night he argued with Sam on the steps of the hotel in Reserve.

Kegley had guessed his thought. "Even supposing the

sheriff's man around here amounted to a damn," he pointed out, "without you who's there even to prefer charges? Luke Bartell said he'd have Crown, and it looks like he figures he can bluff it out and keep his word. And so far it looks like he's doing it!"

If there was any doubt remaining that Luke Bartell's had been the scheming mind, and the will, behind the bullets that knocked Troy Holden from the saddle that night, they were gone now. But Troy Holden said grimly, "Luke Bartell could be in for a surprise!"

"Not for a while, anyway," the old wolfer reminded him dryly, and went to fetch a mixing bowl and a sack of flour off the shelf. "With holes like them there in you, I see another couple or three months before you'll even be getting around with a cane. I been in about the same place you are now, boy," he added, slapping his gimp leg, crippled in an ancient injury. "I reckon I should know how long it takes. Meanwhile, I hope you'll remember: If Bartell *should* get wind that you're still alive, and find out where you are—it could go real bad for the both of us!"

Holden, thinking this over, saw the truth of it. But it helped not at all to fight the sudden rush of bitter impatience that surged through him and left him helpless and shaken. He lay a moment, digesting what he'd learned, scowling as he watched the old man at his work.

He said suddenly, "I want to write a letter. Independent of what happens to Crown, there are people, back East where I came from, that have been waiting too long to hear from me. Business that no one else can handle. . . ."

"Why, that's all right with me," Kegley said, with a lift of his shoulders. "Sure, you can write—all the letters you hanker to. Only, don't expect to get 'em mailed, right soon."

"Why not?"

For answer, Yance Kegley jerked his head toward the

plank door. A gust of wind, hitting the shack just then, shook its walls with staggering force. "Hell! You seen what it's like out there. This storm started day before yesterday. Rate it's building, I ain't expecting to make it into town inside a couple weeks at the least—and by then the stage roads will likely be closed for the winter.

"Still, don't let me stop you if you got the itch to do some writing. I think there's paper and pencil somewhere."

He started peering aimlessly about for them. Troy Holden sank back upon the musty pillow, defeated. "Don't bother!" he muttered, and saw the old man's face break into a cruelly mocking grin.

## VIII

IN HIS several visits to this country Troy Holden had heard tales of Montana winters, but he had never thought to experience one himself. Now, in Yance Kegley's shack in the hills above Kettle Creek range, he found himself caught up in something Kegley assured him would go down in the book.

Days on end the snow descended from a blank, swollen sky; angry winds buffeted the cabin and the pines on the white-shrouded slopes were lost in a blind smother. Kegley tied ropes from his door to barn and woodshed, so that he could manage his chores and find his way back, snow-encrusted and half-frozen, to the safety of his roof and his fireplace. And the weeks dragged on.

Of much of this, Holden was scarcely conscious. He existed in a region of pain and mending tissues, and such thoughts as he had were for that other world, a couple of thousand miles away from this storm-locked cabin, where even now his fate was being decided. He had no illusions. High finance waited on no man. The months he lay helpless here were a critical time of battles which, through his absence, he was losing by default.

It was when he thought of Bea Applegate that he ground his teeth in pure frustrated agony.

His wounds were healing—a slow process, but after all he had nothing else to do but wait it out. A day came when he ventured to try his legs, with Yance Kegley's help. Out of bed, he tottered from weakness and nearly fell; but he rallied his courage and his strength and even managed a step or two, and knew then that he was whole again. He practiced daily, hobbling about the cabin at first like an old man until wasted muscles began to regain their strength.

He had heard the old-timers speak of something called "cabin fever," and now he learned what they meant: Two men, shut up like this in a space small enough that either one, alone, might have wearied of the confinement, began to find each other's company a graveling burden. There came moments, during that long winter, when Holden really began to wonder about his companion's sanity, and to cast about for means to protect himself if the old man grew violent.

Kegley would yell at him, cursing him for taking up his bed and eating his grub and not lifting a hand to the chores. At first Holden promised that he would be paid, and paid well, for his inconvenience; eventually he merely clamped his jaws and tried to shut his ears, and refused to answer. He owed the old man his life, and he knew it. But there were times when he caught the fever, himself—when he seemed to feel the walls closing in on him and when old Kegley's ugly face, and his movements as he limped grotesquely about the dismal shack, seemed completely hateful.

He took refuge in reading. Kegley owned two books—an outdated almanac, and a dog-eared volume with its front cover ripped away which turned out to be an ancient copy of Scott's *Ivanhoe*. Holden had never been much of a reader but he went through both these volumes twice, escaping into them when he thought he would go mad if he lay any longer doing nothing. The old man, meanwhile, hunched at the table and engrossed himself in unending games of solitaire with a pack of greasy cards, wetting one splayed thumb each time he dealt a card.

One night Holden awoke and lay in the darkness, listening to an unfamiliar sound. It took him a moment to place it. There was the wind, pummeling the mud-chinked walls; but there was something else: water, dripping from the eaves. Melt water! He almost shouted to rouse Kegley where the old man lay wrapped in furs and blankets on the bare floor; then thought better of it. Let the old man sleep! He lay listening to the cheerful sound outside, not daring to believe, until it lulled him to sleep again.

"Chinook!" old Kegley told him next morning, his toothless mouth grinning. "Listen to her blow! That south wind can eat up the snow so quick that you can see the drifts shrink!" But then native cruelty made him add, grinning, "Only, don't get your hopes too high. Could be another blizzard blow in from Canada by tomorrow. Even if it don't, the stage roads ain't gonna be open for another month or better.

"So, lay back and relax. You ain't going nowhere soon!"

The wind changed. More snow fell. But at last it became evident the back of the winter was broken. The big blizzards never returned; the chinook kept blowing, and the drifts shrank in runnels flashing under the warming sun, and black earth began to appear. One day Kegley saddled up and rode out on his rawboned sorrel horse, his rifle across his knees. He came back toting the tongue and haunches cut from a buck deer—almost the first fresh meat since winter closed its iron grip on them.

Now real restlessness seized hold of Troy Holden, and set him prowling. Wearing a windbreaker the old man lent him, he went out to try his legs in the clearing where Kegley's shack stood. The feel of sun and fresh air, and solid earth under his feet, revived him wonderfully. He walked further every day; he saddled the bay for short rides into the thawing hills. He even tried his hand with the ax, splitting firewood and stacking it in the woodshed, which was itself a storehouse for all the strange agglomeration of junk the old man had scrounged in his wanderings through the hills— Holden even saw a box of dynamite sticks, the box stenciled with the name of the mining operation from which Kegley had probably stolen it.

There was agony at first, and then exhilaration, in stretching mended muscles and feeling them respond to the demands he put on them. But his return to health, and the easing of winter on this Montana high country, brought him face to face with his problem. The key to it was starkly simple: The key was Crown. It was still the only asset left him—and it was in the hands of Luke Bartell. Somehow, he must contrive to get it back—and while he was at it, he promised himself with bleak definiteness, he would repay someone for the agony of a bullet in the back, and for the terror of wondering if he would ever walk again.

He had a reckoning due him—overdue. If his enemies had thought him a dude who would break and run at the first real threat, they might learn what months of suffering could do to temper and harden a man into someone they could not ignore.

One thing—he had been taught patience. He would husband his strength, wait till he was fully ready before he made his move. Even after the breaking weather made it possible for him to leave Kegley's, he continued to bide his time. On his rides in the hills he took along Yance Kegley's six-shooter—an ancient Smith & Wesson, converted to cartridges—and a box of shells he bought from the old man. He spent time practicing with the gun, shooting at marks, learning something about a hand-gun. He had always been good with a rifle; he had a feeling that skill with a six-shooter was something he might soon find valuable.

As he rode back to the cabin at the tail end of such a day, with melt water flashing and runneling from under snowbanks, he felt that he was very nearly ready. There was still a dull center of throbbing ache low in his back, that especially bothered him when he was tired; he hoped that would go away in time. Whatever his program for striking back at his enemies, he might as well get on with it. For one thing, he'd long since worn out his welcome at Kegley's. Old Yance, he was sure, would be more than glad to see the last of him. . . .

He rode out of the mouth of a rocky draw and pulled in abruptly.

The sprawl of cabin and outbuildings lay just below him, beyond a belt of timber. The door of the horse shed stood open; Kegley was cleaning out the place, using shovel and wheelbarrow and beating a path across the muddy slop of the yard to a manure pile below the corral. What had caught Holden's attention was a pair of riders who were making their way across a boulder-strewn stretch of mountain meadow, coming toward the shack at such an angle that so far, at least, they seemed to have escaped the notice of the old man working around the horse shed.

Holden frowned, considering. He could not see those riders clearly, at this distance, but there was something about

61

one of them that reminded him sharply of one of Luke Bartell's men. The breed they called Wasco. . . .

He spoke to the horse and sent it down the slope, keeping to such cover as he could as he dropped toward the band of pine and new-leafed aspen. He lost the riders, and the buildings. He was wearing an old windbreaker Kegley had lent him, and as he rode he dug into a pocket and drew out the Smith & Wesson. Moments later, breaking through the trees, with the blind side of the shack just before him, he heard a pair of horses arriving in the muddy yard beyond.

Holden dismounted, looked about for a place to tie the reins and finally made hasty anchor to a bush that had sprung up close to the wall of the house. Gun ready, he went at a quick prowl to a forward corner where he hoped he could see what was going on.

The horsemen were just pulling rein, their animals stepping around under them in the slop and the rotten, melting rags of snowdrifts. One of them was Wasco, sure enough—Holden recognized the steeple-crowned hat with the snakeskin band, and the narrow hatchet face beneath. The other was moon-faced, button-nosed, with a mean squint and unshaven whiskers so tow-yellow they seemed no more than a whitish sheen against his cheeks. Him, too, Troy Holden remembered from that night in the Montana House, looking on while he faced Luke Bartell.

They had guns belted at their waists, in their saddle boots. They were looking down at Yance Kegley, who had just emerged from the stable with a wheelbarrow-load for the manure pile. One look, and Kegley had snatched up his rifle from where it leaned against a doorpost. He stood, head bared in the weak spring sunlight, the weapon leveled and ready.

The breed ignored the rifle. Holden heard him saying

heavily, "I see you made it through the winter, old man. Like a bear in a hole, or something."

Kegley's answer was crisp and shaking with some emotion. "Cut the palaver! I know why you come here, I guess!"

"Oh?" Wasco cocked his narrow head on one side. "There ain't all that much to know."

"That's what you say!" Kegley gave a snort, shaking his head like a baited bull. "I reckon maybe Luke Bartell didn't send the pair of you on purpose to kill me!"

At that, the towhead threw back his head and a hoot of laughter shook his shoulders. "Oh, hell!" he retorted when he could speak. "As if that's all we had to do with our time! We just seen your place, and dropped by. We was sent out to check on the grass, higher up—Luke's gonna be needing plenty of summer feed, now that he's got him a ranch and is bringing in the beef to stock it."

Wasco nodded curtly, his eyes expressionless. "That's how it is. You got no quarrel with us, old man. Put up the rifle."

"Sure!" old Yance retorted. "You'd like me to do that. Give you a chance maybe to get me in the back!"

The grin faded from the blond rider's face; an angry flush of color began to spread beneath the pale sheen of beard. "If he'd wanted you killed, do you reckon Luke Bartell would have had to send *two* of us—to take care of one half-witted cripple? Hell, I'd step on you like I would a bug!"

Goaded too far, Yance Kegley cursed and the rifle in his hands snapped up as if he meant to take a shot at the towhead. But Wasco was too quick for him. A jab of the spur sent the breed's roan horse lunging forward, directly at the man on the ground. Too late, Kegley tried to veer out of the way. A muscled shoulder struck him solidly. He lost the rifle and stumbled into the wheelbarrow of manure, toppling it as the gimp leg gave under him and he fell headlong in the mud.

The old man let out a yell. He scrambled to his feet again, but without the rifle, and stood dripping muddy ooze as he watched the horsemen warily closing in on him.

The breed said to his companion, "Put a rope on him, Starke. Looks like we might have to teach the sonofabitch a lesson."

"No!" Troy Holden spoke from where he stood a dozen feet away. "Forget the rope. Both of you—get your hands up!"

Suddenly everything stopped. The towhead, Starke, had already begun taking down the coil from his saddle; he paused and, like his companion, turned to stare at this man who had appeared out of nowhere.

Holden stared back, across the leveled barrel of the gun. He let it swing slightly, its muzzle moving from one rider to the other. "You haven't raised them!" he pointed out, in warning. Slowly, two pairs of hands groped upward.

Starke was first to find his voice, in a tone of disbelief. "It's the dude! By God, if it ain't!"

"Surprised to see me?" Holden suggested, his jaw tight. "Or just surprised to see me *alive?*"

Whatever expression had been in Wasco's dark face withdrew, now, behind a stolid mask. "We don't exactly know what that's supposed to mean, Holden."

"Don't you? You didn't have reason to think I might be lying somewhere with a bullet in my back? Or, as much of me as the wolves would have left!"

Imperturbably, Wasco retorted, "Far as anyone could have guessed, you'd took Luke Bartell's hint and decided to clear the hell out of this country—while the clearing was good. What else would we think?"

The answer Holden might have made was lost as Yance

Kegley, with a scream of rage, bent and snatched up his fallen rifle. Whirling on his crippled leg he brought the weapon up for a shot at the man who had dumped him in the mud, but just in time Holden thrust out his left hand and deflected the rifle barrel, shoving it down hard. When the gun went off the bullet plowed into the earth just in front of Wasco's horse. Both animals reacted to the roar of the rifle, acting up and raising gouts of melt water; for a moment the riders had their hands full bringing them under control.

Troy Holden was busy, too, handling the furious old man who was bawling curses and trying to wrest free of Holden's grip on his rifle. Finally Holden had no choice but to take the weapon from him; holding it by the barrel, the six-shooter in his other hand, he told Bartell's men, "I suggest the two of you get out of here. Now!"

Wasco settled his roan with a savage jerk at the spade bit. When he looked at Holden there was anger in his smoky eyes, but also a certain grudging respect. He said gruffly, "It appears we got some news for Luke. But if you got good sense, mister, you won't ride into Kettle Creek Valley. There's nothing for you there. Nothing but maybe a bullet!"

Holden's mouth twisted. "The bullet's already been tried," he answered. "And it didn't do the job. . . . Now, go on!"

Wasco looked at the six-gun pointed at his chest. He shrugged, and turned his horse. A nod to Starke, and the two of them spurred out of the yard and across the meadow. The drum of hooves echoed from rock faces as they took the dim horse track that led toward lower country.

## IX

TURNING to Kegley, Troy Holden offered him the rifle and the old man snatched it from him; he held it in both shaking hands, his body stiff and his arms trembling with thwarted rage. "Why did you do it?" he cried hoarsely. "Why'd you stop me, gaddamn you? I'd of killed that breed, wasn't for you!"

"His gun was in the holster. It would have been murder."

"What the hell do I care? No more'n he deserves. The other one, too. Called me a half-witted cripple. . . ."

The muscles of his whole face worked; his lips trembled, his eyes looked out of their sockets with a wild glitter that Holden had seen there before, and that had made him doubt the man's sanity. Holden took a slow breath and said calmly, "Go ahead and be mad at me. I owe you too much to resent it—but, I think perhaps the time has come for me to leave. I should have gone before."

"Damn right!" But having said that, Kegley calmed. He looked down at his own soaked and mudstained clothing, and said with a shrug, "Good thing for me you didn't, though, I guess—you saved me from a bad time, just now. A beating, or worse."

"It may be I only postponed it. Those two could be back."

"They'll meet a bullet, if they do—next time, I'll be ready!" The old man added, "Far as I'm concerned, anything you might have owed me is squared. But now your enemies know you're alive, I'd as soon you cleared out before they come here again looking for you."

Holden nodded. "I'll pack my belongings."

"I doubt we'll be bothered tonight." Kegley squinted at a gray cloud sheet edging across the sky, bringing a premature dusk. "Could be a storm, in that—though, it's likely not cold enough for snow. You might as well wait till morning."

"That makes sense," Troy Holden agreed. "Tomorrow, then—and I know you'll be glad to get rid of me!"

And the old man didn't offer to deny it. . . .

The storm came in, and by daylight had settled into intermittent squalls of windlashed rain, falling out of a low and slaty sky. Through this—still wearing Yance Kegley's canvas windbreaker, with the converted Smith & Wesson in his pocket—Troy Holden rode the bay horse down toward Kettle Creek. And as he rode, knowing the long period of waiting and convalescence was ended, a tightness began to swell within him. He didn't need the spot of ache low in his back, that the damp chill worked at relentlessly, to remind him what could happen to a man who rode these trails.

Still, it hardly seemed the kind of day for an ambush. Nobody in his right mind would want to be hunkered on his heels under a bush, rifle across his knees, rain dribbling off the brim of his hat and down the neck of his slicker, and turning his cigarette into a sodden mass even as he smoked it. Holden pushed on, and the bay's hide began to steam in the continuing drizzle.

Riding was tiring work, in such weather. Scudding clouds hid the upward peaks, and there was an erratic, tumbling wind that came in spurts to whip at a man's clothing and push him around in his saddle. But now he dropped into a shallow sidecanyon, carved by one of the streams that fed into Kettle Creek, and its walls shut away some of the wind. Here there was grass, and tight-rolled buds about to explode into leaf on bushes and scrub cottonwood; the willows along the stream were so bright red they nearly seemed to glow. Only a few ragged banks of snow were left melting under the rain. In the relative quiet he thought he heard cattle bawling, somewhere ahead, and he caught a whiff of woodsmoke.

Rocks and brush fell away and a flat opened in front of him, with a small holding of shag-pelted cattle feeding and horsemen working them. He saw the source of the smoke—a fire burning on the streambank, a tarp stretched over it to keep off the weather. Nearby a chuckwagon stood, its horse team staked out and tearing at the new grass. Bareheaded in the thin rain, a man was using an ax to chop a downed log into firewood. He stopped his work and straightened, scowling, as Holden rode up.

Trying to work in a wet camp would make any man savage-tempered, Holden thought. Reining in, he remarked sympathetically, "Not a very good day for it, is it?"

"Ain't nothing good about this!" the other retorted, and squinted suspiciously as a gust of wet wind swept smoke between them. If he had ever seen Holden, he plainly failed to recognize him now.

"What oufit is this?"

"Rockin' Chair," the man answered, naming Morgan Peters' brand. "And *you* don't belong to it!" Ax in hand, he sent his stare past Holden, checking to see if he had others with him or came alone. "Whoever you are," he declared flatly, "this ain't where you're supposed to be!"

Holden didn't answer. Instead, he turned his head as a trio of riders came jingling toward them from yonder where cattle were being worked and branded. It was Morgan Peters himself, in the lead; close behind him, Holden recognized the Rocking Chair foreman—a slab-lean, black-haired man named Ed Dewhurst. It almost amused him to see how Morgan Peters jerked suddenly straight in the saddle, his eyes widening in astonishment.

"Hello, Morgan," he said.

The rancher might have seen a ghost. He shook his head slowly, and put up a hand and pulled it across his face and mouth in a bewildered gesture. "*You!*" he exclaimed. "Where did you come from?" He added, scowling, "And what the hell has happened to you? You look like the devil. Thinner by twenty pounds since the last time I laid eyes on you!"

"Could be. I've fought a bout with a couple of rifle bullets, since that night last fall. And I didn't win by too wide a margin, at that."

Words started to tumble from Morgan's mouth. They turned into a bewildered stammer, and he shook his head and tried again. "Light down, and let's get out of this rain where we can be halfway comfortable. I've got to hear this from the beginning!"

They turned their horses over to the ax-handler and ducked underneath the tarp, where Dewhurst joined them. "You know my foreman, don't you?" Peters asked by way of introduction. As they hunkered by the fire, the cook brought tin cups and filled them from the big camp pot. Morg Peters produced a bottle, with which he laced the coffee, telling Holden, "The last time I offered you a drink you turned me down. But a day like this, a man can use a little something to take the chill off."

Holden was glad enough to agree. He drank, welcoming the spread of warmth the whiskey and boiling coffee put through him. And sitting crosslegged with the drizzling rain tapping its fingers on the stretched tarp overhead, he told in detail the story of his ambushing.

Morgan Peters listened with a scowl and thoughtfully pursed lips. "You never got any kind of look at whoever shot you?" he demanded. At Holden's shake of head the rancher shrugged. "Too bad—it might have made a difference. More likely not though, the way things stand." He drained the last of his coffee-and-whiskey, shook out the grounds into the fire. "How much do you know of what's been happening down here on the Creek, these past months?"

Grimly Holden said, "I heard Luke Bartell had helped himself to my ranch."

"That's exactly what he did! Simply rode in with his crew and took over. No one knew what to do about it. You'd vanished, overnight. All kinds of rumors were going around: That you'd been killed, that Bartell had scared you into running, that he'd closed a legitimate deal and held your bill of sale to prove it.

"I sent my brother down to the county seat, to talk to his boss and check the recorder's office—he could find no record of a sale or transfer of title. Still, lacking a complaint from an aggrieved party, the sheriff didn't figure there was anything for him to do. For all anybody could prove otherwise, Bartell and his crowd were your welcome guests and had every right to be there. And they *do* have possession; hereabouts, that's a good nine-tenths of such law as we've got."

Troy Holden said, "Then it's up to Kettle Creek. Just what are you people doing?"

"You can see what we're doing," Morgan Peters answered roughly. "I'm not the only rancher that's got his crew in the field, making spring gather six weeks ahead of the normal time. Jim Ells and Bob Thatcher have thrown their crews in with mine. With a man like Bartell for a neighbor, we want our herds counted and the new stuff under our own brands, as early as possible. No use laying temptation in Bartell's way!"

"He might want more from you than a few calves," Holden warned. "Yesterday a pair of his men showed up at Yance

Kegley's place and said they were checking grass. I gather that Luke Bartell is bringing in outside beef to stock Crown, now that he has possession—and that he means to help himself to as much of your summer graze as he needs, to put it on."

Morgan Peters stared as though stunned by this news. Beside him the foreman, Ed Dewhurst, swore savagely. Peters, finding his voice, exclaimed huskily, "I wonder if that's really his game—a squeeze-out! Us Kettle Creek men are willing enough to share our hill range with any reasonable neighbor. But if someone like Bartell moves onto it and starts grabbing and holding . . ." He shook his head, rubbed a rope-scarred hand across his face. Leaving the thought unfinished he said tiredly, "Well, reckon I better get back to branding."

He tossed his empty cup into the nearby wreckpan, preparing to heave himself to his feet. Troy Holden said, "Wait!" And as the older man looked at him: "There's a side to this thing that we haven't discussed—something Luke Bartell may have lost sight of."

Peters settled back, probing his face with a narrow look. "What are you getting at?"

"This." From an inner pocket he took a bulky envelope and tapped it on his knee. "I happened to have this in my coat pocket that night I was shot, since I had been expecting to meet George Lunceford in town and close a deal for Crown. It contains the deed, my identification as inheritor—every document I need to prove myself the owner of record. Without it, Luke Bartell hasn't a leg to stand on. *With* it, I can force your sheriff to move whether he wants to or not—or if he won't, then go over his head to the governor and let him know how property rights are being enforced in this part of his State!"

Peters sat a little straighter, a new interest kindled in the glance he exchanged with his foreman. "Now, there," he admitted slowly, "you might have something! Though I can't see Bartell letting a piece of paper get in his way. He'll never give in without a fight—I can promise you that."

"If things come to a fight, what about you Kettle Creek men? Will you be in it?"

The rancher didn't immediately respond. The thickets of his brows were pulled down in thought as he dug for papers and tobacco sack and expertly spun up a cigarette, seeming to concentrate more than need be on the familiar job his fingers were doing. Finally he said, "I just can't give you an easy answer, Holden. It might depend on how the fight shaped up—it might depend on a lot of things. For one, it's not realistic to expect a thirty-a-month cowhand would put his life on the line, for the sake of a mere riding job."

"Meaning, that you can't count on your crews?"

Snapping a match on his thumbnail, Morgan Peters glanced across his shoulder at a rider walking his horse toward the wagon camp through the thin rain. The rancher nodded toward him and the cigarette bobbed between his lips as he said, "Here's someone it might help for you to talk to. . . ."

There was something vaguely familiar about the man, though a rubber poncho made him shapeless and his head was tilted forward as he rode. Troy Holden ducked out from under the tarp, Peters and Dewhurst behind him. He stood waiting, and the oncoming horseman finally lifted his head and he got a view of his face. "Why, it's Sam Riggs!"

Morgan Peters confirmed it. "He's riding for me now, since the takeover at Crown. . . ."

Stepping forward, Holden reached up a hand toward the man in the saddle. "Sam! I'm glad to see you."

The ex-foreman of Crown ranch pulled to a stop. He turned and looked at Holden. And Holden got the shock of his life.

He had never seen such a change in a man. Sam Riggs had seemed, before, almost ageless; now his unshaven cheeks were slack and white-stubbled, sagging as though all the hard years had caught up with him. There were deep lines from nose to mouth corners that Holden didn't remember, and the mouth had none of its old firmness. One eye—the left one—drooped nearly shut and all he could see of it was an eerie half-moon of white.

There was, in this broken old man in the saddle, hardly any likeness to his old friend, the peppery ranch manager who had argued so fiercely against the decision to sell Crown. Not appearing to see the outstretched hand, he laid both his own upon the saddlehorn and leaned his weight on them. For a moment Holden thought the man didn't even recognize him; but then he spoke, in a dull and lifeless voice. "Holden. Thought we'd seen the last of you. Thought you'd run, for good."

Slowly, Holden let his arm fall. A surge of temper rose and quickly died, killed by his puzzlement and alarm at what he saw in that other face. Trying to spark some sign of the old fire in it, he said, "What happened to me doesn't matter. The important thing is, we're going to get Crown back."

No response in the slack features or in the dull stare of that one eye. Sam finally stirred his shoulders, in a movement that could scarcely even be called a shrug. "You think so?" he muttered. "Good luck! If you manage, I hope you get a good price for it."

He nudged the horse with a heel and sent it on to the picket line. Troy Holden pivoted slowly to watch the old fellow go. Big Morgan Peters moved up beside him.

"What in the name of God is the matter with him?" Holden demanded, aghast.

"You're looking at a whipped man," the rancher said

bluntly. "When Bartell's crowd rode onto Crown, and told your crew to pack their sougans and drift, Sam Riggs wanted to give them an argument. So they worked him over. Seab Glazer, and that breed they call Wasco—they was particularly eager. They used everything on him, including their gun barrels and their boots. When they were finished they piled him on his horse and took him to the boundaries of the ranch and set him adrift.

"One of the boys found and brought him in, and Callie took on the job of patching him together again. I didn't honestly think he'd pull through. They'd busted him up bad, inside, and they injured that one eye permanent. But the worst damage was to his spirit. You remember the man he was before; well, you've just seen what they left of him. . . .".

Troy Holden was having a hard time with his breathing; his chest felt constricted, and angry spasms shook him as he saw Sam Riggs dismounting from his horse now, with the uncertain movements of an old and beaten man.

Morgan Peters was still talking: "Callie pulled him over the worst of it—I'm real proud of her, for the time and the care she gave him. Once he was on his feet again—at least, as much as he'll ever be—I offered him a job with my crew. Hell, I couldn't do less for a man I've liked and worked with and respected for as long as I've known Sam Riggs! It's a fact he ain't really much use to me, but at least he's got his self-respect. I wouldn't want to have him turning into a barfly, in some cowtown saloon like the Montana House.

"Still, if he was meant for an object lesson, then I reckon Bartell got what he aimed for. Because, I've seen other punchers take a look at what was done to him, and it turns them mighty quiet. And you maybe can't blame them."

"And that's what you meant," Troy Holden broke in, "when

you warned me not to count on them in a fight. After seeing Sam, I can understand. I'll remember."

There seemed little more to say, and he was restless to ride on. The man who had taken his horse was sent to fetch it. In the saddle, Holden paused for a last question. "How's Callie? She and Jim Ells get married yet?"

Mention of the girl put a coolness between them, reminding of an earlier argument. Peters' thick brows lowered a little and he said carefully, "Not yet."

"Just wondered," Holden said, and reined away from the camp and headed on toward the flat, knowing Morgan Peters watched him go.

## X

SOMEHOW, as he rode on through the continuing rain, he could not erase the pathetic picture of old Sam Riggs, nor rid himself of the grinding anger that rose each time he thought of what had been done to the loyal Crown foreman. The Kettle Creek ranchers themselves—men like Morgan Peters—had good economic reasons for standing up to Luke Bartell; but Sam Riggs had acted out of nothing but blind loyalty to the brand he rode for, and he had been cruelly repaid. Having seen what had been done to him, Troy Holden knew now there could be no settlement with Bartell that didn't include some element of revenge for Sam.

For the first time, he realized, he was thinking of this business in other terms than the purely selfish one of getting back what had been stolen from him. . . .

Where this tributary he had been following broke out of the pines and rushed in a tumble of miniature rapids to

pour into Kettle Creek itself, he struck the main valley road.
It followed the creek, keeping to a bench above the water
but dropping down on occasion to ford it and reach easier
grades upon the farther bank. Perhaps it was an illusion
but spring seemed further advanced, here in the valley
itself. The cottonwoods were beginning to shake out the fresh
green of leaves; somewhere behind the leaden, weeping sky,
Holden heard a lonely music of wild geese, making north
toward Canada.

At the first of the crossings, where the creek sang over
a pebbled bottom, he let the bay walk its forefeet into the
water and have rein-length to drink. And sitting the saddle,
with rain peppering the sliding water, he all at once had an
uncanny sensation that other eyes were watching him.

Irritated with himself, he tried to shrug the feeling aside
but it persisted so strongly that he scowled and dropped a
hand into the pocket of his coat, to touch the gun he carried
there. Slowly he lifted his head and ran a look about him,
not sure what he was hunting for. He saw nothing, and
was ready to blame the tightness of his nerves when the bay
suddenly jerked up its head, water dripping in a spray as
it snorted and tossed its mane and looked in the direction
of a clump of timber on the opposite bank, a few yards
upstream.

Troy Holden glanced in that direction, and discovered
the pair of horsemen sitting motionless in the shadow of the
branches. He saw the saddle gun one of them held, its
muzzle carelessly trained on him, and he froze.

The man with the rifle was Seab Glazer; the redheaded
gunman called above the murmur of the water: "All right
Holden! Keep coming—right over here to us."

As Holden hesitated, with the reins tight-gripped until
the cold leather ground into his palm, Glazer urged his own
horse forward down the bank. A low-hung pine branch hung

in his way and he tilted his head slightly, so that the crown of his sweated range hat could clear it. Slight as the movement was, it nevertheless caused the muzzle of the rifle to swing briefly off its target. And Holden gave the bay a kick and a desperate wrench of the reins, in an effort to pull the bay around.

The swiftness of the current was his undoing. The bay tried to turn too fast and in too narrow a space; its hooves slipped and it started to go to its knees. It fought back with a great splashing and rattling of the smooth rounded stones of the creekbed. And in that wildly lunging instant the rifle on the far bank let go.

The bullet hummed past the bay's ear like an angry bee. The horse squealed in terror, rearing, and its legs swept from under it. Man and mount went down.

Holden felt the saddle go from under him and the reins slip from his hand, and icy water closed over his head. An iron shoe struck his shoulder, a numbing blow—it could have crushed his skull, just as easily. It was this terrifying thought that set him struggling to escape the peril of the frightened horse thrashing too close beside him.

He struck the shallow bottom with his shoulders, came up blinded and gasping with water streaming from nose and mouth. He slipped and almost went under again, but caught his footing. Waist-deep in the current, he mopped streaming hair out of his eyes and caught a glimpse of the bay buckjumping away from him, plunging up the farther bank.

For the moment Holden was powerless to do anything but stand doubled over, coughing the water out of his lungs. When he finally lifted his head, it was to see Glazer and the other man sitting their horses at the edge of the creek and grinning with open amusement. "By God," the redhead declared, "if that wasn't as neat a piece of saddlework as I've seen in a coon's age!"

77

"I'd of thought it was kind of a chilly day for a swim," the other Bartell man said.

"You never know about these dudes. Some of 'em are pretty tough." Abruptly, then, humor died in Glazer's face, leaving it hard and dangerous. He gestured with the barrel of the rifle. "Come out of there, bucko. Hurry up!" And to his companion: "Catch up his bronc."

While the second rider spurred off after it, Troy Holden waded to shore. The muzzle of the rifle resting on Glazer's lap followed him at every step; as he came out of the water, the redhead swung a leg over and stepped down to meet him. Holden could only submit and let the man run a hand over his streaming garments.

Glazer found the six-gun quickly enough and confiscated it, shoving it away behind his pants belt. Still searching, he discovered the manila envelope in another pocket and thumbed open the flap, while Holden tried to conceal his start of alarm. Whether or not he had any idea what it contained, Glazer apparently decided this was worth further study and he pocketed the envelope, afterward stepping back a pace to eye the prisoner narrowly.

"I didn't really know whether to believe it yesterday," he grunted, "when we heard you were still around. I thought sure we'd seen the last of you. Well, I got an idea now you're going to wish we had! After Luke's had what he wants from you, we're gonna take up the little matter of you trying to get tough with me, that night in the Montana House. . . ."

Holden made no attempt to answer. He had been wet enough before, thanks to the needling rain, and after his ducking he was soaked through. Now the cold was getting through him, to the bone. He had lost his hat and the hair was plastered to his skull; he put up a hand and shoved it back from his eyes, and then the other rider was back leading the bay by its reins.

"Mount up," Seab Glazer ordered.

"Where are you taking me?"

"Where'd you think? To Luke, of course. . . ."

And so this was his return to Crown ranch—a sodden figure, bracketed by his captors' mounts, trying to contain the spasms of shaking chill that ran through him as the wind hit with icy impact. His shoulder hurt where the bay kicked it and so did that spot of ache low in his back—his constant reminder of the rifle slug that had nearly crippled him, months ago. He looked at the rifle in Seab Glazer's saddle scabbard, and wondered if it might have been the same weapon.

They followed the river, coming at last to the feeder gulch where a wooden sign indicated the side road to Crown. By this time the rain had slacked off and nearly ceased, though the mounting wind kept the day miserable and the low clouds scudding overhead. There would be an early dusk, still a matter of hours ahead.

They took the side road, and presently passed beneath the high gateway with the brand burned on a slab of wood that swung wildly in the wind, from the crossbar. A little later, twisting past a stand of aspen mixed with pine, the familiar road brought Troy Holden and his captors in on the headquarters buildings of the ranch Luke Bartell had stolen from him.

Crown had scarcely been a working outfit, running a minimum crew and no more than a token beef herd, while waiting for Vern Holden to decide how he meant to develop it. Nevertheless Sam Riggs, as manager, had done what he could on limited funds and had taken pride in keeping the physical plant—house and barn and corrals and allied structures—in top condition: Fences taut, paint constantly renewed, shingled roofs and siding intact. Now it seemed to Holden, as they rode in, that he could already see signs of deterioration in the few months of Bartell's occupancy. The door of a tack shed, broken off its hinges and simply leaning against the opening with no attempt to repair it, was a small thing that told a great deal. Somehow it sharpened Holden's anger as much as anything he had seen yet.

The buildings lay along the foot of a rim, with tongues of pine and aspen in new leaf running up the folds of the hill behind. Someone came to the bunkhouse door and watched the three ride by, and when they were within a few yards of the main building Luke Bartell himself strode out onto the porch.

He came to the edge of the steps and halted, arms akimbo, the wind plucking at his coat and lifting the thick mop of black hair upon his head. Seab Glazer told him, "I brought you something."

"Looks like you brought me a drowned rat."

Holden found it humiliating that, despite all his efforts, he still could not prevent the shudders of chill from shaking him. Bartell saw and the heavy moustache lifted above a grin of cruel amusement, though the eyes remained agate-hard and devoid of humor. "Mister," he said, "you're a hard man to get rid of."

*And a harder one to kill,* Holden would have answered in defiance, but his lips and tongue felt too stiff to form the words. He merely stared back and Glazer said, "He wasn't too damned hard to catch."

Bartell turned away, throwing an order across his shoulder: "Fetch him in."

When he stepped down, Holden nearly went to his knees; his feet and legs were like chunks of ice, and the muscles threatened to cramp. He set his jaw, forcing life into his limbs. But then Glazer gave him a shove toward the door

Bartell had left open, and he had to grab at the frame to keep from stumbling.

Inside, welcome warmth met him—the one thing he could see at first was the roaring leap of flames in the wide stone fireplace. He walked directly to the fire and spread his hands to it, soaking up warmth, feeling it spread through the stiffness in his limbs. At once a steaming odor of wet wool began to rise from his clothing, mingling with other smells of liquor, tobacco, and sweat.

Only now did he become aware of the half dozen men scattered about the room, some sprawled comfortably in leather-slung armchairs or on the big horsehair sofa. One—it was the breed, Wasco—leaned against the wall with his arms folded and a keen interest in his narrow hatchet face as he watched Holden.

No one interfered with him. Seab Glazer was telling of the capture, and the ludicrous spectacle of the dude falling with his horse into the creek lost nothing in the way he told it; it brought contemptuous snickers from his listeners, which Holden, peering into the fire, ignored. But he turned as he heard Glazer saying, "I took this off of him, Luke. Figured it was something you'd want to see."

Bartell, seated now on a corner of the big oak center table, took the manila envelope Glazer handed him. River water had not had time to get at the contents; Bartell dug them out and leafed through them. Eyes thoughtful, he shoved he papers back and laid the envelope on the table beside him, and looked at Holden, idly swinging one booted leg.

Holden returned his stare. A lamp in a wall bracket had been lighted against the dull light of the afternoon, and it showed him what had been done to this house by its new occupants.

They hadn't been easy on it. The floor was actually littered with trash and, especially in the vicinity of the fire-place, was freely spattered with gobbets of dried tobacco juice. Some accident had happened to one of the windows; a broken pane was masked with cardboard and the curtain hung in shreds. Floor and furniture alike were generously scarred with spur marks—the man lounging in the chair by the table had now scooted around and cocked one boot upon the edge of the mahogany where he rocked it idly back and forth, spur rowel carving a trough deep into the fine wood.

Troy Holden deliberately took his eyes from this destruction.

Bartell said, "I didn't rightly know if I believed it, yesterday, when Starke and Wasco said they'd run into you up at old Yance Kegley's."

"I can understand that," Holden replied grimly. "It looks as though someone didn't quite do his job with a rifle."

A faint scowl etched its crease between the outlaw's brows. Not directly answering the charge, he said, "Well, now, most people here on the Kettle have been taking it for granted you done the smart thing and cleared out when I told you. I'm afraid you showing up again, like this, wasn't quite so smart after all."

"Smart or not, remains to be seen."

"You think so?" Cold contempt turned Bartell's voice crisp as he indicated his silently listening crew. "Look around you, mister. Do you really think there's a single damn thing you can do to me?"

Troy Holden followed the gesture, considering the menace that surrounded him. He drew a breath, and hoped he sounded more confident than he felt. "This isn't the Dark Ages. It's 1893! You can thumb your nose at law and order if you want to; but even in this forgotten part of the world, sooner or later they're going to catch up with you, Bartell!"

"Not with me," the outlaw retorted flatly. "Because, you see, I *am* a smart man! I always know just what I'm doing. If you don't think so, here's something you might take a look at."

He eased off the edge of the table, rang his spurs across the floor to a rolltop desk that stood against one wall of the room. From a pigeonhole he took a folded paper, returned with it and handed it to Holden. Curious, the latter looked it over and saw it was a bill of sale to Crown Ranch—land, stock, and buildings.

The signature was his own.

Holden stared at the writing, and his head lifted and his angry stare met Bartell's. "A forgery!" he snapped.

"And a damned good one," the outlaw agreed blandly, "if I do say it myself. Don't bother tearing it up," he added quickly, and took the paper back from Holden's fingers. "Only put me to the bother of having it to do again.

"You left me several good samples in the desk to work from," Bartell went on pleasantly. "And now you've been good enough to drop these in my lap." He picked up from the table the papers Glazer had taken from the prisoner. "This title deed, with the assignment duly made over, should give me all the legal claim I'll ever need." Smiling crookedly beneath the heavy moustache, he slipped the sheaf of papers back into the envelope. Troy Holden, with darker feeling than he would have wanted to show, watched the manila envelope disappear into an inner pocket of the outlaw's corduroy coat.

Bartell took whiskey bottle and glass from the table, poured himself a drink. Leaning his hips once more against the table's edge, he pointed the glass at Holden and said crisply, "So now you know the score—and some other people are going to learn it, too. I'm making changes around here. This ranch was never given a chance to amount to much;

but from now on there's going to be one important outfit on the Kettle, and it's gonna be Crown. And, that means Luke Bartell!"

Holden said, "I didn't really think you intended standing still. Your men told me, yesterday, you already had them out scouting summer range."

"That's right." Bartell took a drag at the whiskey, his obsidian stare considering Holden shrewdly. "As it happens I've got a thousand new head of beef on the way, should be getting in tomorrow maybe. And that's only a start."

"A start, you mean, at crowding every other brand off the hills and out of the valley!"

The outlaw shrugged. "That doesn't concern you, does it?"

"And just what do you imagine I'll be doing, while it's going on?"

"If you don't watch your step, you could be lying under a cutbank somewhere," Bartell answered bluntly. "With dirt in your face."

Holden said, "I suppose the second time, you imagine you can get the job done."

It was a long moment before Bartell answered. He finished his drink slowly while his eyes studied the prisoner above the rim of the glass, his expression veiled and unreadable. Finally Bartell set the empty glass on the table and said crisply, "I won't even pretend to know what you're talking about, mister. I do know I'm getting a little tired of you. I still got no use for dudes, and for you in particular!"

The rest of the outlaws had heard all this without any comment or interference. Now Seab Glazer shifted his boots and said gruffly, "Why waste palaver? Just tell me what you want done with him."

Bartell rubbed a thumbnail across his jaw. He said, finally, "What you did to that other stubborn fool—that Sam

Riggs—seems to have been effective. We'll try the same dose, again."

Glazer's eyes narrowed. He said doubtfully, "You sure about this? You don't want him dead?"

"Riggs was about twice the man he is, by my estimation," Bartell answered with a shrug. "It was just a fluke, him getting the best of you that night in the Montana House. And I imagine you'll see to it that by the time you get through with him now, there won't be enough left to give us any more trouble." He looked at the breed, leaning impassively against the wall. "You want a part of this?"

"Yeah." Wasco pushed to a stand, a gleam of pleasure lighting his smoky eyes. "Yeah, I want a piece. I got a little score of my own to settle."

Bartell nodded. "You know what to do. Take him to the edge of Crown grass, and give him what you gave Sam Riggs and set him adrift. Make sure he don't ever want to try coming back. . . ."

XI

THEY MUST have been inside the ranch house longer than it seemed, for when they emerged it had stopped raining. This, at least, was welcome. Holden had managed to dry out after a fashion, standing in front of the log blaze, but his clothing still held dampness and the searching wind quickly got to him. Now as he climbed stiffly to the saddle, at Glazer's curt order, and rode away from the ranch house with the redhead and the breed flanking his horse, the clouds overhead actually showed signs of breaking. A dazzle of late afternoon sunlight marbled their blank gray surface.

Glazer didn't set the same course by which they'd arrived at Crown; the main road was probably too well traveled, and he'd want more privacy for what he had in mind. Instead, the three rode directly south, over valley grass that was chopped up by tributary ravines and broken by tongues of timber. Troy Holden debated trying to make a break and hit for the cover of some of those inviting trees, but each time he gave it up; something told him his guards would be waiting for him to make such a mistake.

Seab Glazer appeared to be enjoying himself; he even struck up a tuneless whistling through his teeth that grated on the prisoner's tense nerves. Once, the redhead broke off long enough to tell Wasco, "Damn good thing you brought a rope. I forgot to."

The breed grunted something. Glazer asked the prisoner, "I reckon you know why we need a rope?"

Holden shook his head. Glazer gave a snort of laughter. "When we get through with you, and turn you loose, you ain't gonna be in any shape to set that saddle. We're gonna have to *tie* you on!" A moment later he pulled rein and told the breed, "We might as well get at this."

Wasco dismounted without comment. Seab Glazer gave Holden a command which he thought of disobeying; but he had no choice, and with reluctance he stepped down while the redhead watched him carefully. When Glazer was off, the breed took all three horses and anchored them to a fallen pine.

They stood in rank wire grass, on ground that was sodden from rain and snow melt; a multitude of tiny green toads slithered away from Glazer's boots as he walked to face the prisoner. A grin of evil pleasure lifted the man's upper lip, revealing strong white teeth; piercing blue eyes stabbing at Holden, Glazer deliberately worked the fingers of his right hand—flexing and spreading them, in anticipation.

Staring at the fist, and then at the ice-blue eyes peering at him above slanted cheekbones, Troy Holden remembered Sam Riggs as he had looked after this pair got through with him, and he knew what was in store for him; he very nearly gave way to despair. Seab Glazer took another step and set himself. Somewhere to Holden's left and rear, he could hear Wasco's boots whispering in the wire grass as he came up from tying the horses. For that one moment his enemies were separated, and with a sudden lunge Holden launched himself forward, every ounce of his will and shoulder muscle going into the swing of his fist at the jut of Seab Glazer's jaw.

Apparently the desperate move came, as he had meant it, as a complete surprise. The redhead put up no defense at all, and only at the last instant did he think to save himself by jerking back and tucking his chin under. Holden's fist missed its target but it bounced off Glazer's chest, throwing him off balance. At the same instant Holden's left hand was grabbing for the handle of Yance Kegley's six-shooter, still shoved behind the redhead's belt. His fingers managed to touch the gun. He almost got a grip on it; then Glazer stumbled backward, out of his reach, and something heavy that could only be Wasco's fist struck a clubbing blow at the point where Holden's neck joined the shoulder. Crippling pain smashed through the upper part of his body and he felt himself going down.

Somehow, dazed as he was, he knew that a boot would follow up the blow and when he lit he managed to roll, trying to escape it. So when Wasco drove the kick at his body, he felt it only in a wrench of his clothing as the heavy cowhide just missed his flesh. He was on his face in the wire grass then and he got his hands under him and started to push himself up. A shadow fell across him. He heard Seab Glazer's angry cursing and a hand grabbed his collar and he was hauled up, arms dangling helplessly. A fist smashed him in the face. The very violence of the blow tore his clothing from Glazer's grasp and dropped him onto his side; he lay there, almost as though paralyzed by the crushing blow he had taken. A taste of blood was in his mouth.

Glazer was cursing his companion. "Damn it, get the bastard on his feet and *hold* him. Give me a fair chance!"

They both had him then, dragging him upright. His arms were seized and hauled roughly behind him. For a moment he found his face pressed flat against Seab Glazer's chest; he caught the gamey smell of the man's clothing. Deliberately he jerked his head up with all the strength he could manage, felt the top of his skull make solid contact with Glazer's jaw. He heard the crunch of the man's teeth clicking together. Glazer stumbled back, letting out a howl that sounded as though he might have bitten his tongue. The thought gave Holden a moment's satisfaction, even though he knew he was likely going to pay for it.

Then hard blows were ripping at him. A cheek was laid open, a fist took him on an ear and set his whole head to ringing. Something slammed into his middle, and to the sledging pain of it the breath gusted through bleeding lips and he tried to go to his knees, both pinioned arms feeling as though they would tear from the sockets.

A gun went off, somewhere. There was a shout, and the ground carried the drumming jar of horses' hooves. Another shout; he thought a voice was saying, "Let him go, or I'll aim for somebody's leg!" Abruptly, then, his arms were freed and he sagged limply forward to the ground, onto his face.

Dazed as he was with pain and gulping for the wind that had been knocked out of him, Troy Holden nevertheless managed to raise his head, and had a look at his rescuers. To his astonishment he saw they were Jim Ells and Callie Peters. They had ridden out of the trees some hundred yards distant, the outlaws being so engrossed in what they were doing to Holden they'd let themselves be taken unawares.

Now Holden looked at the gun, still smoking in Ells' hand after the warning shot, and he thought in alarm, *You can't handle both these men!* Luckily, the yellow-haired rancher had sense enough not to try. He saw the pair, overcoming their first surprise, start to drift slightly apart like wolves separating to come at their prey from two directions for the kill. He couldn't cover them both, so he made his choice and dropped his gun muzzle squarely on Seab Glazer. He said, in a voice that shook slightly, "Tell your friend to unbuckle his gun and drop it. One funny move from him, Glazer, and by God I'll drop *you!*"

The redhead glowered, but he must have recognized that Jim Ells was frightened enough to be dangerous. His mouth twisted and he growled an order at his companion: "I guess you better do what he says." Just the same Wasco hesitated—after all, it wasn't his head the gun was pointed at. But Glazer swore at him and, with a shrug, the breed unhooked his belt buckle and let belt and holster fall.

"Now, you," Ells said, and the redhead followed suit, afterward dropping the gun he'd taken off Troy Holden. His eyes never left Jim Ells as he turned his head and spat blood on the ground from his bitten tongue; his scowl held murder.

Callie Peters leaped down from the saddle, now, ground-reining her pony. She was dressed as Holden was most often used to seeing her—in work clothes, jeans and boots and hickory shirt, with a corduroy jacket and flat-crowned riding hat. She started toward Holden as he climbed to his feet; glad as he was to see her, he waved her away as he said gruffly, "I'm all right. Just let me have one of those guns."

Yance Kegley's pistol was the nearest and Callie quickly got it and passed it to him. Ells was herding the outlaws toward the log where their horses were tied. Holden called a quick warning: "Careful! There's a rifle on one of those saddles!"

"Get rid of it," the rancher ordered. Sullenly, Glazer slid it from the scabbard and leaned it against the log; afterward, on command, both men whipped their reins free and swung into the saddles.

Glazer, cutting his hating stare back and forth, told the three of them, "You'll hear more about this!"

"I don't doubt it," Jim Ells said. To Holden he sounded resigned and apprehensive, though his manner was firm enough. "But for the time being it ends here. You can come back later to pick up your guns. Now, get out of here and leave us alone!"

Without further argument, the outlaws kicked their horses and the others watched as they rode away, finally vanishing across a shallow rise. Jim Ells looked a little white. He blew out his cheeks and the gun sagged in his hand. "They've headed toward Crown. Do you suppose they're going for help?"

"We had better not wait to find out," Holden said grimly. He added, "I can't begin to thank you for this. They were going to give me what they gave Sam Riggs!"

The rancher shrugged, and slid his gun back into the holster. "Thank Callie. Butting in was her idea." Holden could have said that didn't surprise him at all. He imagined Ells resented having to take any part in what had happened.

To an anxious question from the girl, Troy Holden said, "I'm all right, really. But let's get out of here. . . ."

He was already pocketing Kegley's six-shooter, moving stiffly to his waiting horse; his whole body ached in protest. Only after she saw him gain the saddle, would Callie Peters turn to her own.

They all rode easier once they knew they had passed the boundaries of Crown, but they kept on during another silent quarter hour. At last they drew up in a screen of timber where they had a good view of the trail they had left. There was a spring, here, born of melting snow; while Jim Ells kept a watch for pursuit, Troy Holden climbed down from the saddle. He shook his head at Callie, hovering anxiously and eager to help, and instead scooped up the icy water in his hands and bathed the cuts on his face.

His cheek stung like fire; his belly held a deep ache and his shoulder, where Wasco had clubbed him, hurt whenever he moved his arm. But the icy shock of the water helped clear his head. Holden rinsed his bleeding mouth and had a long drink, and mopped his face on a sleeve of his ruined coat. "They didn't have a chance to do the job they wanted to on me—though I still don't understand how you showed up, just when I needed you."

Jim Ells explained briefly. "We learned that you'd been at the roundup fire, and left on the road to Reserve. Callie insisted on riding after you, and at the crossing we saw sign that looked like you might have run into trouble. The tracks led to Crown. We were watching the house when they brought you outside."

"It wouldn't have gone well," Holden said, "if you'd been caught."

Ells shrugged and looked away. It occurred to Holden that, as it had worked out, to all intents and purposes they *had* been caught. Bartell's men would not forget this afternoon. "I'm sorry as the devil that the two of you had to get involved," he said. "But it was one of the luckiest things ever happened to me!"

Callie stood close beside him, looking up into his face. The horses had fallen to cropping at the thin grass near the spring. There seemed no indication that anyone had followed them from Crown; the late afternoon quiet could hardly have been more peaceful.

All except for the black scowl on Jim Ells face as he watched the girl saying, "Troy, you don't know how we've wondered—and worried—since that night last fall when you disappeared!" Holden knew Ells' look; he had seen it on the blond rancher before. It was pure, naked jealousy.

Feeling she didn't have his attention, Callie put her hand on Holden's sleeve. "Pa told me someone tried to—*kill* you!"

"They didn't quite manage." He looked at her and smiled, though a trifle bleakly.

"You think it was one of Luke Bartell's crowd?" Jim Ells asked.

"That seems rather obvious, doesn't it? When you see who's now sitting on my ranch!"

"Morg says you have the papers to fight him in court, if it comes to that. . . ."

That reminded Holden of his loss, and he half raised a hand to his empty pocket and let it fall again. "There were papers," he said, "but Bartell has them now. On top of that, he turns out to be a first class forger! He showed me a bill of sale for Crown, that I would have sworn I had signed myself! Now that he holds the deed and everything else, he can fix things so that fighting him is going to be a very tricky business."

Callie said fiercely, "But you're not going to quit!"

"Oh, I'll fight him," Holden promised, his voice hard. "But I don't know just at the moment, what with. . . ."

They talked a while longer, comparing notes and conjectures, accomplishing little. Finally Holden turned to his horse and checked the cinch and, with one hand on the pommel, said, "If anyone wants me, I'm riding on to Reserve. It appears I've got some hard thinking to do. There's one other thing," he added, remembering; and he told them what Luke Bartell had boasted—of a thousand head of seed stock on its way to Kettle Creek, due to arrive perhaps tomorrow. From their expressions, he knew they both saw the seriousness of this.

He said, "I told Morgan Peters I'd got wind of some such thing; now I have it direct from Bartell himself. It's my guess this herd will only be the first. He's got unlimited sources of stolen cattle—covered by forced bills of sale, of course! He can keep bringing them in, loading the range down with them and pushing his neighbors until something gives way. There's no reason to think he'll quit until he's taken everything in sight."

The girl seemed shocked beyond speech. Jim Ells, his face thunderous, blurted out, "But—*why?* What does scum like Bartell want with a ranch and grazing rights? Him and that cutthroat gang of his have never been anything but longriders!"

Troy Holden shrugged. "Perhaps that's just the point. It could be there's a side to such a man that nobody ever guesses. Perhaps he's decided, all at once, that now he wants respectability."

"Yeah!" Ells grunted. He drew a breath. "Well, I'll pass this word—though what anyone can do, is a little more than I see just at the moment. Kettle Creek men ain't ever been called on to do a hell of a lot of fighting."

"I'm afraid they'll fight now, or they'll end up where I am—with nothing at all!" Holden swung into the saddle. There seemed nothing more to say. He nodded to them both, and turned his horse in the direction of the valley road.

## XII .

A FULL MOON was rising behind banks of broken cloud as he came into Reserve, making him think of the night last fall when he had ridden into this town with Sam Riggs, to keep his aborted appointment with a buyer for Crown. He felt infinitely older, scarred and bone-weary and wiser to the ways of this land—he thought of how detached and superior he had felt then, to the local people and their problems and knew he had only been naïve.

Luke Bartell had been an education.

Just as on that other night, a stagecoach was making up for its run to railhead. Melcher, the agent, stood talking to the driver and he recognized Holden instantly, as Troy put his horse to the tie rail before the station. Melcher seemed not at all surprised, from which Holden judged that news of his reappearance had preceded him, likely carried by someone from Morgan Peters' roundup camp. "I got mail for you," Melcher said, and Holden followed him inside the station where the agent opened a desk drawer and took out a bundle of nearly a dozen envelopes tied with string.

"Some of these came last fall," he said, "after you—uh—disappeared. I hadn't made up my mind yet whether to return them, when the passes closed. The rest have been piling up at railhead, all winter long, waiting for the first coach to bring them in."

Nearly all, Holden saw on thumbing through the envelopes, were from his New York attorney. One or two were marked "Urgent!" He merely stuffed them into a pocket, thanked the man, and left.

Before anything else, just now, he needed dry clothing. Luckily the store was still open; having given a boy a dollar to take his horse to the livery barn, he went in and bought everything new, from the skin out, settling for whatever the merchant had available—sturdy-looking jeans, flannel shirt, a jacket and hat. He changed in the store's back room, noticing in a mirror that the cuts and swellings resulting from his fight with Glazer and Wasco, while nasty enough, had not left his face in too bad shape after all. Afterward he crossed the street to the restaurant where he ordered dinner and then, having lighted up the first from a new box of tailormades, settled back at last for a look at his mail.

He arranged the letters chronologically, by their postmarks, and ripped open the envelopes and stolidly read his way through the record of a winter of disaster. He found nothing in it that he could not have foreseen, and hadn't already taken for granted. Yet there was a grim finality about seeing everything in black and white. The lawyer had done all he could to protect an absent client's interests; still, with no word from Troy Holden despite his constant letters and his repeated pleas for advice, there had been little enough he could do. And so, slowly at first and then in a sucking rush, everything had gone. While Troy Holden lay on that musty bed in Yance Kegley's cabin, the last of the Holden possessions had been sold from under him.

Except for his horse, the new clothes on his back, the few dollars left in his wallet—and title to a ranch that he was no longer sure he could prove—there was simply nothing. He was a ruined man.

He stubbed out his cigarette and took up the one remaining envelope. It bore no return, nothing but a New York postmark ten days old. It felt too thin to contain a letter. He ripped it open, and a newspaper clipping fell upon the table cloth.

He sat and looked at it, his stare floundering down the narrow column of print: "The wedding of Beatrice Applegate and Charles Frederick . . . The bride, daughter of socially prominent . . . The groom is a member of the New Haven shipping family, graduate of Yale in the class of . . ." It was all there, down to the last details of the wedding gown and the flowers in the ushers' buttonholes, and yet for a stunned moment Holden was unable to take it in.

Bea—and a man he had not even known was in her circle of friends! Was it something that had been going on all the time, without his hearing a word of it? Or, had it begun only since he left the East, coming to a head during long winter months when she had no word of him? What about all the letters he had written, last fall, and the ones from her he'd waited for so impatiently and never received? Could it be that, even then—?

It didn't matter. It didn't matter a damn!

The waiter brought his plate, just then, and set it before him. Holden looked at the food, and with a shake of his head pushed it aside. He gathered up his mail, crammed it into a pocket; he left money beside the plate, got his hat and stumbled out into the early night. Still dazed, he stood blinking, seeing nothing; then the lights of the Montana House caught his eye. He headed that way, at a long angle across the empty street.

He scarcely bothered to notice if there was anyone else in the big room, blind even to the danger from Luke Bartell's men. Hardly responding to Costello's greeting or noticing the curious look the man gave his battered face, he called for a bottle. He poured a drink, tossed it off and, ignoring the pitcher of water the Irishman set out for him, immediately poured a second shot without a chaser. He scarcely noticed how it stung in the cuts on the inside of his cheek.

Costello said mildly, "I'd go easy on that stuff, Holden. It's got a kick."

"Fine," Holden grunted, and drank and poured again. But then the revulsion of a system untrained to the brutal assault of so much raw alcohol, taken so quickly, hit him and he put the glass down with a shudder.

Seeing this, Costello nodded in sympathy. "That's better. I heard about what was done to you—I guess the whole town's heard, by now. It's enough to make a man tie one on. But that won't lick Bartell."

Irritated, Holden moved a hand in a curt dismissal. Costello meant well but he had no idea what he was talking about. He didn't know about Bea Applegate, and Holden wasn't going to discuss her with a bartender; he hadn't hit *that* low.

But enough hard common sense remained to tell him that drinking himself into a stupor would not solve his problem. Angrily he shoved the glass away, so hard that it overturned and rolled across the polished wood. With no more than a reproachful look, Costello righted the glass and used his bar rag to mop up the spilled whiskey.

"Sorry," Holden grunted, and turned to look at the room.

It was early yet and he was Costello's only customer; but the saloon could have been filled with Bartell riders, and in his blind emotion he would not have seen the danger. Shuddering a little at his own careless stupidity, he drew a breath and forced a grip on himself; but the sense of abysmal emptiness—and the crawling burn of the whiskey—filled him and for a moment he felt he might be sick.

That passed. With clearer thought came a question which, he thought, only Costello might be able to answer. He took another of his machine-rolled cigarettes and lighted it, fighting to keep his hand from trembling, as he shaped his words.

"I take it you have no real love for Bartell," he said carefully. "Will you tell me something I want to know—if I promise it won't go any farther, and you won't be held to account for it, ever?"

The Irishman's eyes narrowed. He rubbed the bar with his cloth, as he considered. "Try me."

Holden said, "This is probably asking too much—there's no reason you should remember the night, last fall, when I had my encounter here with Luke Bartell. Still, I'm wondering if by any chance you can tell me which one of Bartell's men might have left soon after I did, that night. Because that had to the one that followed me, and shot me in the back!"

Costello regarded him for a long moment as though weighing his answer. He shook his head. "I see your thinking, but I'm afraid you got it wrong. It wasn't any of them."

Holden stared. "You must be mistaken!"

"Not a chance. When I got Bartell and his crowd in my place, I don't lose track of them for a minute! There was eight of them here that night, and I particularly remember, after the way you roughed Seab Glazer, I was leery Glazer might take his mad out on my place of business. But nothing much happened. They hung around, drinking and playing poker, till nearly two in the morning; and when they left, they all left together. And in that time, none of that crowd was out of my sight for longer than ten minutes or so at a stretch—mostly, to use the privy out back. I know for certain, it wasn't long enough to have had anything to do with bushwhacking you."

"But—!" The protest died in a stammer; Troy Holden scowled fiercely at the man, wondering if the two drinks he had taken could have befuddled his thinking.

If not Luke Bartell—or Glazer, or the breed, or any of those others—then it appeared his whole line of thinking on the subject of the ambush was dead wrong. And who, then? It simply didn't make sense!

He remembered suddenly Bartell, and Glazer too, both insisting today they knew nothing about the attempt on his life; it looked as though they could have been telling the truth! But who else did it leave? All at once, like a cold finger touching his spine, the memory came back of Morgan Peters warning him to stay away from Callie; of Jim Ells and his jealous rage, that fateful night, and their short and indecisive battle in the jail office.

Yet this very afternoon, Jim Ells had saved him from a beating, or worse. And as for Morgan Peters, he surely wouldn't shoot any man in the back! Or, was that really so certain? Now that they thought Holden might be useful to them in their own fight with Bartell, they could have decided it made sense to change their policy and try to keep him alive. . . .

Costello was peering at him curiously. "From the look of you, I'd say I just blowed you clean out of the pond!"

"I won't deny it," Troy Holden said shortly. "But I have to thank you for the information." For a moment he wondered if Costello could be the one who was lying, then for some reason decided otherwise. He had a strong feeling that the Irishman, even if forced to remain more or less neutral, had no use at all for Luke Bartell. Completely bewildered, he shrugged and dug up a bill and dropped it on the counter. "For the drinks," he said. "Including the one I spilled. Whatever I need right now, it plainly isn't liquor. A good night's sleep, maybe."

Moving rather like a man in a daze, he turned and walked out into the spring evening.

He woke in a hotel bed and lay for a long time staring at

the ceiling, where a reflection of morning sun on a rain-puddle in the street below danced and shimmered. All that he had learned, and all that had happened to him yesterday since he rode down from Kegley's shack in the hills, came over him afresh and brought a hopeless feeling of muddle and confusion. The lawyer's letters, and that damned news-paper clipping, lay on a table beside the bed, mocking him with their message of total loss.

When he moved to rise, his whole body seemed a solid ache of protest. Seab Glazer and the breed had been stopped before they could give him the beating they intended to, but they had done well enough.

The reflection of his swollen face in the mirror showed the evidence. Holden fingered his beardstubbled cheek and hoped the barber in this town possessed a gentle hand. He moved about the room, easing some of the soreness out of his muscles, taking his time with dressing. And as he but-toned his shirt he stepped to the window for a look into the street, and thus saw the three riders jogging up the street toward the intersection where the hotel stood.

His hands went suddenly still. He recognized the coni-cal crown and the snakeskin band of Wasco's hat, first of all; then another of the foreshortened figures identified it-self as Seab Glazer, and he decided the third looked some-thing like the towhead, Starke, who had been with Wasco at Kegley's place two days ago. He saw them pull rein near the street's opposite corner, catty-cornered from the hotel; he saw them conferring, still in the saddle, and he noticed how they continued to look in his direction.

Holden drew back from the window, not liking this.

He finished dressing quickly, stowed his belongings in his pockets, took the jacket and hat he'd bought last evening and, finally, picked up the converted Smith & Wesson. Weigh-ing it thoughtfully in his hand, he had another look through the window and this time failed to see any of Bartell's men.

It would be hard to say why he felt so strongly their presence in town this morning had something to do with himself. Still, the alarm bells were beating inside him as he left his room, locking the door behind him, and traveled down the faded carpet of the corridor toward the lobby stairs. The gun was in his pocket, but so was his hand.

Starting to descend the steps, he caught the sound of voices and something prompted him to caution. Halting, he dropped to a crouch and now could look down into the lobby, and just make out the one who stood at the desk talking to Sid Bravender. Right enough—it was Starke. He had the desk register turned toward him and he tapped the page with one forefinger while Holden heard him say, too quietly, "Next time, friend, don't lie to me. Not when I can read for myself!" Bravender stared back, a frightened look on him. Starke pushed the book away and strode out of Holden's line of vision, but his voice rose clearly as he called to someone beyond the street door: "We were right. He's here. . . ."

A step creaked under Holden's weight. Bravender, behind the desk, glanced toward the stairs; when he saw Holden a look of horror seized his face. He flung a pointing hand toward the invisible Starke, while he shook his head in frantic warning. Holden, nodding, simply straightened and faded up the steps; in the upper hall he hesitated, debating his moves. A slight, cold sweat broke out upon his face.

There could be no doubt of it now: Whether actually sent by Luke Bartell, or merely turned loose to settle scores for themselves, the three of them were after Holden, and arrogant enough to come directly into town to find him. If they laid hands on him, he felt, this time they would not settle for a beating.

Voices below, again. It sounded like two men, crossing the lobby in long strides—so, perhaps the third remained outside on the street, in case they might be mistaken and the dude wasn't in his room. Holden retreated before them, moving back through the dim hall. At the rear end of the corridor daylight showed through the glass of an outside door, that opened upon the head of a flight of wooden steps angling toward an alley below. Fortunately the door wasn't locked. He wrenched it open and darted through, just as the tread of heavy boots hit the forward end of the corridor. He could only hope his enemies failed to see the door closing, or catch his shadow silhouetted against the pebbled glass.

He went down the ladder-like steps as swiftly and silently as he could, and now the gun was in his hand.

## XIII

Troy Holden could only wonder about the third man, the one who hadn't entered the hotel. As he dropped down the steps he could feel every muscle tighten and the juices dry out of his mouth, at thought of Seab Glazer—or the breed, perhaps—down there somewhere with a gun already trained on him, dead center, letting him walk into it. But he reached the alley without a challenge. Beyond this rear corner of the hotel lay a cross street, and here he paused for a look to his left, toward the junction with Main.

At once he saw Seab Glazer.

The redhead had taken a stance in the middle of the intersection, where he could watch not only the hotel but the livery barn opposite, as well as the approaches along both arteries. That way he could prevent any chance of Holden's getting to his horse; all he had to do was wait there he was while the pair he had sent into the hotel flushed his quarry out to him.

Holden lifted his gun, wondering if he could get a shot at Glazer. In that same instant, there was the sound behind him of a door violently thrown open. Jerking about, he saw Wasco and the towhead, Starke, emerge at the head of the outside stairs, and he knew he had never fooled them at all. One of the pair gave a shout and a gun's roar filled the alleyway. The bullet missed. Desperately Holden threw a shot up the stairway, hoping to delay his enemies; after that he turned and burst at a run into the open street.

Out in the intersection fifty yards to his left, Seab Glazer had been alerted by the shot. If he had been content to stand his ground he would have made easy work of picking Holden off. Instead, in his eagerness, he started running even before he fired, and the bullet chopped into muddy ooze just behind the fugitive. Too late Glazer saw his mistake. Before he could plow to a halt, for better aim, Troy Holden had gained the other side of the street and plunged straight on into the alley.

Here a high board fence gave him momentary cover and he hugged it close as he sprinted over mud and cinders. To his left rose the rear walls of the business buildings that faced on Main Street; on the other hand were backyards and residences, mostly complete with fences and vegetable plots and chicken runs, woodsheds and privies. In one yard was a woman hanging clothes on a line, and a brindle dog on a chain that leaped and bayed in a thwarted frenzy to get at him.

He knew he had only seconds. Where a good-sized bush in new leaf grew beside a shed standing flush with the alley, he dropped into cover. Crouched there, with a shoulder against the rough boards and gun in hand, he almost at once heard hurried footsteps. Starke and Wasco came by

**103**

at a jog trot. He wondered about Glazer, then guessed that he must be staying on the main street, beyond the row of business houses; these two were keeping pace with him, checking the slot between each pair of buildings to make sure their quarry didn't try to slip free by ducking into one of them. Confirming this, he watched the men pause briefly at the corner of the drygoods store opposite his hiding place, heard one of them shout something. Then they jogged on, out of sight, while he debated his next move.

As though to give him the answer, a shod hoof struck wooden flooring suddenly within the shed at his elbow. A horse! This was some townsman's private stable—and here was the chance, thrown in his lap, to saddle and take off across lots leaving his enemies vainly searching the town for him. But even as he came to his feet, something made him pause.

He thought, *By God, no!*

He had taken too much. He had been shot at, beaten, robbed, humiliated in every possible way. He had lost everything he owned and even the girl he meant to marry. To lose his pride, now, by running away from these enemies would be the final defeat. Somehow he couldn't do it.

Yet a man who was no gunfighter had no business against a trio like those who were hunting him now. Troy Holden was afraid; it took a physical effort to keep from giving way to the muscular spasms that threatened to seize his whole body, and set his hands to trembling. He checked the loads of the Smith & Wesson—five bullets. Five shots, against the guns and the filled shell belts of three of Luke Bartell's killers. . . .

Drawing a breath, he crossed to the rear of Fossen's dry-goods store and up the three plank steps. The door was unlocked; he entered a dimly lit storeroom and groped his way forward, through a second door and past the curtained fitting room where he'd tried on his new clothes last evening. In the main room beyond, the merchant, Bert Fossen, and another man stood at the front window peering intently into the street. They turned as he came toward them along the aisle between counters piled high with yard goods and clothing.

The second man was By Peters; they both stared at Holden in a way that told they knew exactly what was going on—more than likely the whole town knew by now. Partly amused and partly irritated, he said, "I hope nobody minds my coming through the back way. . . ."

The deputy sheriff found his tongue. "Holden!" he exclaimed, and could get no further. Shouldering between the pair, Troy Holden started for the street door.

A strangled sound broke from the storekeeper. "You're not going out there? Mister, this town's full of Bartell men—and they sound to me like they're after your hide!"

"Is that a fact?" he muttered sourly.

Even as he spoke, boots tramped the loose sidewalk boards outside. Seab Glazer appeared beyond the plate glass and halted there, his head turning restlessly. He had a baffled, angy look about him, as though the search was going badly and he failed to understand what could have become of his quarry. He lifted his gun, rubbed his jaw thoughtfully with the muzzle. And then Troy Holden sucked in his breath and held it, as he saw Glazer turn and look at the door beside him—almost as though some vagrant suspicion had crossed his mind. He actually put out a hand and laid it on the china knob.

The three within the store stood frozen, Holden himself falling into a crouch with the gun clutched tightly. Then, just as the knob began to turn, a cry sounded faintly somewhere down the street. Glazer's head whipped around. At once he whirled and was sprinting away, the warped boards carrying the thump of his running boots. And trapped breath whistled through the storekeeper's gaping jaws.

By Peters exclaimed softly, "My God, I thought for a minute—"

"You thought what?" Troy Holden snapped. "That there'd be a shooting, and you might have to do something about it? Well, you may still not be out of the woods! This thing isn't ended."

The deputy raised a hand jerkily. Before he could manage a reply, Troy Holden was already striding to the door and wrenching it open.

Main Street lay entirely empty, but Holden felt certain the whole town was watching him from behind doors and windows. He tried to ignore this sensation as he waited, for long minutes, with his back pressed to the rough wall of the drygoods store and his eyes searching the street.

He could see no sign of the men he knew were hunting him. He switched the gun to his left hand while he rubbed the palm of his right along his pantleg. Then, feeling more alone and exposed to danger than he ever had, he started walking in the direction Seab Glazer had taken.

Staying close to the wall not only made him a less conspicuous target, but enabled him to raise less noise from the loose-laid planking. At each building corner he cautiously checked the alleyway beyond, before crossing to the next. By the time he had traveled a dozen yards, the sweat was flowing freely down his ribs. Somewhere in the town, someone was working a pump with a squeaky handle; the rhythmic sound drifted across the stillness and presently stopped. In the livery, across the street, a horse whickered and went through a brief flurry of stomping, momentarily drawing Holden's attention and sharply tightening his nerves before he placed the sound.

Under the tin arcade fronting a harnessmaker's shop,

a display of fancy saddles was racked either side of the open doorway. It was here that Holden suddenly caught the sound of a boot striking wood, behind him, and he halted and spun in midstride.

The towhead, Starke, was just stepping up onto the boardwalk. Scarcely thinking, Holden went to one knee behind the rack that held one of those saddles; Starke fired in the same instant and lead chewed a sliver of wood from the window frame above his head. Holden dropped his forearm upon the saddle, bracing his wrist there; the smell of new, oiled leather mingled with exploding powder as he worked the trigger, aiming at a balloon of smoke from the gun in front of Starke's belt buckle. To the mingling of the shots, Starke jackknifed; bent double by the bullet's impact he stumbled back, struck an arcade support and went spiraling around it to land, rolling, in the mud of the street.

For a moment Troy Holden could do no more than stare at the first man he had ever killed.

He thought he had never seen such stillness as there was in the grotesque and terrible sprawl of that body—the head to one side, face pressed in the dirt; an arm bent crookedly under it, one spurred and booted leg canted across the edge of the walk. Slowly he straightened to his feet. And in the very next breath he was whirling to fade through the open door, into the dim interior of the harness shop.

The hurrying steps that had given him warning drew quickly nearer. Suddenly here was Seab Glazer with the breed, Wasco, at his heels. They halted by the body of Starke, breathing hard from their run; Glazer looked, and started to swear in a steady, monotonous undertone.

Troy Holden forced himself to step from the shadowed doorway. With all their attention on the dead man, the two seemed unaware of him and he was about to speak a challenge, when the sharp ears of the breed must have caught some sound. The man turned; smoky eyes, filled with a pure malevolence, met his and the man started to raise his gun.

Holden kept coming. The Smith & Wesson's barrel swept in a chopping arc against the side of the breed's skull. As the hat with the snakeskin band popped from his head, Wasco's eyelids fluttered and his knees broke and he dropped without a sound, and Holden's gun muzzle fell to point directly at Seab Glazer's chest.

"You can join them, if you want to," Holden said bluntly. "It's up to you!"

The redhead's chest swelled. For a moment, seeing the hatred in his narrow face, Holden didn't know what to expect; but then with a grimace Glazer dropped the gun into his holster and let his hand fall away from it. Between tight lips he said, "You win this time, dude. But not again—not ever!"

The street, that had been empty and silent a moment before, was beginning to come to life. Doors slammed, men appeared but still hung back—perhaps they weren't convinced it was really over, and safe enough to satisfy their curiosity without danger of becoming involved. Now from the direction of the drygoods store came Fossen, the merchant, with By Peters' loose-hung shape towering over him. Holden nodded to them; he said coldly, "A dead man for you, Sheriff. And a couple of prisoners, if you want them. . . ."

"You're pushing your luck, Holden!" Seab Glazer grunted. He turned to the lawman then, and as their eyes met Holden saw By's face drain of color. "What about it, Sheriff?" Glazer's words were coldly taunting. "You want to try arresting me, maybe?"

By Peters looked at him; his stare touched on the redhead's holstered gun and slid hastily away again. A muscle at the corner of his mouth quirked, pulling his mouth out of shape;

he wet his lips. Troy Holden could imagine the consuming longing for the brandy bottle in his desk drawer.

Obviously he was on the edge of panic. Just as obviously Glazer knew it.

The whole thing was all at once a farce and Troy Holden had had all he wanted. It was battle enough to avoid showing the aftermath of high tension that left him shaken. He kept his voice level as he said, "So far as I'm concerned, I'm satisfied if they know now I'm not to be got rid of as easily as they might have been led to think."

"Oh?" The redhead's eyes locked with his, in a look of mutual, naked hostility.

During this the breed, Wasco, had been recovering from the blow of Holden's gunbarrel. It had broken a crimson trickle of blood down the side of his face; Wasco had pushed to a sitting position but his head hung groggily forward. Now Seab Glazer leaned, hooked his friend under an arm and hauled him to his feet.

"Come on!" he grunted. "Pull yourself together. We're riding." He picked up the hat with the snakeskin band and jammed it on the breed's head, retrieved his gun and shoved it in the holster. He pointed the man toward the place where their horses stood.

Holden said sharply, "Wait a minute!" He indicated the body of Starke. "What about him?"

Briefly Glazer had turned back for a look at the dead man. He lifted his eyes to Holden and they were devoid of any feeling at all. "You killed him," he said. "You can bury him!" But he was the one who broke gaze, and not a man there failed to notice it. With a shrug, he turned away; in dead silence, they watched him walk to his horse, give the unsteady Wasco a peremptory boost into the saddle, and mounting, take the reins of Starke's animal.

They rode north, toward the valley trail, with Wasco bobbing unsteadily over the saddlehorn, and the dead man's horse trailing. They neither one looked back.

## XIV

FOR THE next hour Troy Holden tried to empty his head of thought; since his problems appeared insoluble anyway, he put them out of his mind while he had a shave and used the tin bathtub in the barber shop's back room, and then went down the street for a meal at the restaurant. It was still short of midmorning when he stepped outside and saw a bunch of riders approaching.

There were Jim Ells, Morgan Peters and his foreman Ed Dewhurst, and another Kettle Creek cowman named Thacher. Something told Holden they were looking for him, even before they caught sight of him and with one accord reined over. From the saddle, Morgan Peters spoke. "We want to see you, Holden."

Still bothered by dark suspicions put in his head by Costello the saloonkeeper, Holden said shortly, "Maybe I don't want to see you!"

He caught the quick hostility in Jim Ells' windwhipped face—even if he had saved Holden from a beating, yesterday, jealousy over Callie Peters would always be his overriding sentiment. Big Morgan Peters scowled and answered, in a tone of puzzlement, "Holden, I don't get it! Yesterday, at my camp, you were looking for help from the Creek ranchers in the struggle with Luke Bartell. We're here, now, with what we thought you'd call good news. What's changed you?"

Troy Holden was in a mood to say that a great deal had

happened to change him. But despite his almost sure conviction that one of these men had used the rifle that nearly killed him, something in the looks of them made him pause. Curiosity won out. He nodded shortly and said, "All right. I was just going back to the hotel. Meet me there."

Peters nodded, and the four pulled abruptly away.

Holden took his own time, following. When he passed the spot where Starke had died he tried not to look too closely; a dark stain of blood remained, though Deputy Sheriff Peters had had the body moved to the back room of the furniture store where a coffin was being nailed together for it, and someone else had tried to douse the boardwalk clean with a bucket of water.

However many times he might walk that street, Holden knew, he would think of it as the place where he had killed his first man.

The horses were tied before the hotel and their owners were waiting in the lobby when he got there. They had the dingy room to themselves, with its tacky furniture and wilted rubber plant; Morgan Peters began the talking, without preliminary: "We thought you'd like to know things are stirring along the Creek—mainly because of you, Holden. Jim Ells, here, and Callie, started it when they brought us word of what happened to you, after you left my camp."

Troy Holden nodded. "I could have ended up in the same shape as poor Sam Riggs, except for Ells puttting a stop to it. A lucky break for me."

"I tried to tell you," the blond man said curtly, "that it was Callie's doing I stepped in—or that I was even there. I got no reason to go out of my way to do you a favor. Or to look for trouble with Seab Glazer."

Holden gave him a look. "That's all right. You made it clear enough."

Morgan Peters had waited out the interruption. "You told

Callie and Jim," he went on, "that Bartell admitted he has a thousand head of beef cattle heading for the valley. I understand you said they might even be reaching here sometime today."

"According to Bartell. Yes."

Peters drummed the arm of the sofa with rope-toughened fingers. "Believe me, it puts a whole new complexion on things. Nobody's been anxious to make a fight with that outfit; but some of us ain't ready to stand by and let something like this happen, either. A thousand head of new cattle, suddenly dumped onto this range, could be a real threat.

"Of course, the first thing is to make sure the threat is real. If Bartell's bringing in a herd, I figure he'll cut across a corner of the Blackfeet Reservation and then straight south, up the creek. Accordingly I sent a rider, at first light, to do some scouting and report back."

"Meanwhile," Ed Dewhurst said, "we're out going the rounds—seeing everybody. Thacher, here, has already thrown in with us; there'll be others. And their crews!"

"That's right," Peters seconded his foreman. "Naturally, there's some who try to argue that Luke's got a right to stock the ranch he bought from you, any way he sees fit. They don't want to face the proof that he stole Crown, and that he's out to steal the rest of this range the same way!"

Frowning, Holden looked at the tailormade cigarette he had taken from its box. He said slowly, "I'm wondering if Jim Ells, or Callie, remembered to tell you that I've lost the deed to Crown? Once Luke Bartell forges my name and registers transfer of title at the county seat, I won't have a thing to fight with!"

Morgan Peters leaned forward in his chair, to lay a forefinger on the other man's knee. "One thing you ain't," he said, "is a quitter. That's why we came to you. And no sooner do we hit town," he added, "than my brother and a whole bunch of other people meet us with word of Bartell's men trying for you this morning—and you killing one, and sending the others packing. Damned if it didn't take you to show us it can be done!" The tall rancher wagged his head. "No question, we need someone like that on our side. Throw in with us and maybe we can help get your deed and your ranch back for you."

Holden looked at him sourly, not answering at once, remembering that this was the same man who once had scornfully given orders to stay away from his daughter. The man's attitude had changed since then—since yesterday, even, when Holden had got a turndown from him at the roundup camp. Now positions were reversed, and these men wanted his help.

He snapped a match and got the cigarette alight. And at that moment boots struck the veranda outside and a man who looked as though he had ridden hard came bursting into the lobby. As he looked hastily around, Morgan Peters lifted a hand and said, "Over here, Charlie." Charlie came ringing his spurs across the worn linoleum.

"I seen the broncs outside," he exclaimed, a little breathless. "Figured you must be here. . . . Boss, Milt Spurrier came back from the reservation, hell for leather. I volunteered to bring you the word."

"And that is?" the rancher prodded.

"There's a herd coming, all right. Milt used the glasses on 'em—figures not much less than a thousand head, and at least six riders pushing them. They're pointed straight for the creek."

Excitement galvanized his hearers. Morgan Peters demanded, "When will they hit it?"

"He thinks, sometime toward midafternoon."

"Then there's time. We can stop them!"

"By God, yes!" Peters slapped both hands on his thighs and swung impetuously to his feet. "We'll see whether Kettle Creek's to be had for the taking! We'll stop this herd and turn it back, before Bartell can so much as lay hands on it!"

Still seated, Holden peered up at the rancher through the smoke of his cigarette. "You really think you have the men for the job?"

"The men, and the place! Squawhead, just above the rapids where the canyon narrows in. We can dig in there, if we have to—put in a stopper they can never get past, even were there twice the cattle and three times the crew to push them!"

Holden frowned thoughtfully. He knew the place and had to concede it could make a good defense—a tough granite spur, creating a bottleneck past which Kettle Creek forced its way in a boiling chain of cataracts and minor whitewater rapids. At the base of the spur, whose characteristic shape gave Squawhead its name, there were fallen boulders where armed men could hole up and do a job of fending off anyone trying to move up the canyon past them.

And yet something about this whole business seemed somehow, vaguely wrong, and trying to put a name to it kept Holden where he was while the rest of these men stood by waiting impatiently for his answer. Morgan Peters prodded him: "Well? What about it, Holden? We'd admire to have you along."

Then Jim Ells suggested, with a trace of a sneer, "Maybe the affair this morning with them three Bartell riders was nothing but an accident. He's been talking a good fight against the ones that took his ranch away from him—but he don't appear to care much about getting into the showdown!"

That lifted Holden's head with a jerk. His eyes pinned

the blond man's, as he got slowly to his feet. He said crisply, "You can look for me at Squawhead. I have another piece of business I've got to attend to before I can join you—but don't worry: I'll join you."

From Ells' look, he was pretty sure the blond rancher only half believed him. Peters, however, appeared satisfied. The big man nodded. "Good!" he said, and he turned across the dingy lobby, the others following. Holden watched them go tramping hurriedly outside to their waiting horses; after that, he turned toward the stairs and climbed quickly to his room.

He wanted to give those others time to leave town ahead of him, and so he took his time. Having checked the reloaded Smith & Wesson, and pocketed it together with what remained of the shells he'd bought from Yance Kegley, he delayed a little longer before picking his hat off the brass bedpost and walking back down through the hotel building. At the livery, across the intersection, he put the gear on his bay horse and led him outside—to discover Callie Peters in the saddle of her favorite pony, waiting for him.

She grinned as she saw his expression. "I'll bet you didn't expect *me*." But instantly she sobered. "Are you all right, Troy? Oh, your face!"

He touched a swollen cheek. "Still a little sore. But it's nothing really. Nothing for you to worry about."

"How can I help but worry?" she began, but Holden was already lifting into the saddle, anxious to be off, and he scarcely heard her. Any other time he would have enjoyed a chance for her company; now, he simply could not afford it.

Fortunately, she appeared not to have heard of his shooting scrape with the Bartell riders, for she said nothing about it. Her mind was on other things. "Have you any idea what Pa's up to?" she demanded, reining her pony closer. "And

Jim, and the others? I saw them riding out, just now, but they wouldn't tell me. They were in such a lather to be going—and now you, too. I *know* something's wrong!"

Holden looked at the appeal in her eyes. Her anxiety touched him, but he shook his head. "I'm sorry."

"Meaning, you know but you won't tell me, either!"

"I'm sorry," he repeated. "Right now I've got to be going."

The girl's jaw settled. "Go ahead, then. But you should know, from the old days, you don't get rid of me that easy. If you won't tell me what's happening I'll just tag along and find out!"

"Callie! No!" But then he sighed, recognizing an unbeatable stubborn streak in her; he shrugged. "If I were your father I could warm your britches and send you home. Since you're too big for that, I suppose it's hopeless!" Instantly she was grinning again, and she put her horse alongside his as he kicked the bay into motion down the muddy, puddled street.

"Where are we going?"

He was too angry with her to answer.

A thin pencil line of smoke rose from Yance Kegley's mud-and-slab stovepipe chimney, and the old man's horse was in the corral, but at first Holden could see nothing of the hermit himself. He hailed the shack but got no answer. Since it was close to noon, he reasoned Kegley must be somewhere close. Callie Peters stayed in the saddle, watching in silence as he stepped down and stood looking around and slapping the reins into his palm impatiently.

He could feel the pressure of time, and also the nagging ache of the healed bullet wound in his back, aggravated now by hours of steady riding; both horses were heated and blowing, from the stiff pace he'd set over the hill trails. . . .

Then Yance Kegley came in sight through the scrub pine,

following the path from the spring with a bucket of water at the end of one arm and throwing that bad leg in his limping gait. The old man set his pail down. He eyed the marks on Holden's face and said, "Well! What happened to you? Looks like you ran into trouble, after you left yesterday. I could have told you!"

Holden admitted it with a nod. "And there's more on the way."

"Bartell?"

He nodded again. "I was hoping you could help."

"Me?" Kegley looked narrowly from one to the other of his visitors. "I somehow didn't think the two of you had dropped in for dinner. . . . What is it you want from me this time?"

"Something I remember seeing in the shed. Come along and I'll fill you in."

Callie wasn't included in the invitation. Troy Holden was still put out with her, for insisting on coming after he had asked her not to; but stronger than this emotion, he realized, was one of concern over what might happen to her. Somehow he had never understood that he could feel quite so protective toward this girl whom he'd almost watched grow up, during the intervals of their acquaintance.

Now he left her with the horses and he and Yance Kegley walked over to the shed, Holden explaining in a few words what was building between Bartell and the valley ranchers, and what he had in mind. The old wolfer listened with scowling intentness, finally nodding. "It might be something to see!" he admitted, beginning to show his yellowed teeth in a wicked grin. "Hell, yes! But—you ever used this stuff?"

"No."

"I thought likely. Then you'll need a hand with it." Kegley pawed at the beard stubble that bristled his jaws, and nodded as he reached a decision. "Reckon I'll just throw leather on my bronc and ride along with you. Don't worry—I won't hold you up none. And I got an idea this is something I wouldn't want to miss. . . ."

Shortly they were in the saddle and making for the valley floor again, at the point where Kettle Creek broke through the narrow gap at Squawhead. Despite his bad leg, Kegley was no mean horseman and he knew every deer trail and shortcut. But as they rode, munching cold meat sandwiches the old man had prepared, Troy Holden watched the movement of the sun overhead and worried about the inexorably passing time.

The long detour by way of Kegley's shack had eaten up more of the day than he had anticipated. More and more he began to wonder if they could hope to reach their goal before real trouble hit.

And when a shift of wind into their faces brought the faint rattling of gunfire, somewhere ahead, he knew he had failed and that they were too late.

## XV

A HAND caught at Holden's sleeve. Callie Peters' face tilted anxiously toward his. "That's Pa, isn't it?" Her voice broke. "What's he up to? You've *got* to tell me now!"

"It sounds as though he's up to his ears in trouble," Holden answered shortly, jerking free. "We'll find out soon enough." Yance Kegley was pushing unerringly ahead. With the others close behind, he led the way along a steep ridge where they had to double forward in their saddles to avoid the low-growing pine branches, then into a ravine and up across the adjoining ridge. Here a sharp twist to the right plunged them into a descending draw that was choked with brush and scrub growth.

It was treacherous work and the horses were tiring fast. They went down in single file, fighting not to overrun one another, the riders praying against missed footing in the treacherous spill of rubble. And abruptly they dropped out of the timber, and there was a view of what lay below.

Kettle Creek came flashing and tumbling in white water through the narrows of Squawhead, with scarcely enough level room on its far bank to contain the wagon road. Below the narrows, the canyon walls funneled out again; and it was here the Kettle Creek ranchers led by Morgan Peters had taken their position, in talus that skirted the base of Squawhead spur. So situated, they could have turned back any herd, or even a small army if one had tried to move past them. Anyone could see at a glance that Callie's father had used sound strategy.

But good as it was, it had failed him. Those boulders were little protection from the guns that had been planted on the timbered flank of the spur itself. Now the guns were taking a toll; what should have been an easy victory for the Kettle Creek men had been turned into a furious and nearly one-sided battle. Seeing how badly they were pinned down, listening to the confused mingling of six-gun and rifle fire, Troy Holden could only groan as he recognized at last the thought that had been gnawing and troubling him all along.

He said in bitter self-accusation, "Damn it, I should have seen Luke Bartell was only spreading bait, when he let me know he had a herd coming! He was counting on me to pass the news. He knew if Morgan Peters decided on an effort to turn them back, this would have to be the spot. By placing his own guns on the ridge, he'd have them like sitting ducks!"

Yance Kegley said suddenly, "Look yonder. . . ."

Downstream, the burnished smear of sunlight on creek surface caused a man to squint; but Holden could see now the strung-out formation of the trail cattle, coming slowly up the far bank. The riders didn't seem to be pushing them hard; probably their instructions were to hang back until Bartell had a way cleared. The cattle, moving easily and almost under their own momentum, were still a good many minutes away.

An anguished cry broke from Callie Peters, and brought Holden's eyes to her to see the tears upon her face. "Can't we do anything?"

"If we do it will have to be quick!" he answered bluntly. "Dug in where he is, there's no chance in the world of getting Bartell—but just possibly he can be drawn off." He turned to Kegley. "I'm going to ask you to see that this girl stays right here out of trouble. Don't let her do anything foolish."

"Oh, hell!" The old man shook his shaggy head. "Let her look out for her own self! I come this far, Holden—I'm gonna be in at the end. I got my reasons." And he kicked his horse and started it on down the draw. Holden appealed to the girl with an exasperated look; but there was no time to reason with her and, turning away, he sent the bay plummeting in the old man's wake.

They came down onto level ground without a spill and spurred ahead, pushing the tired horses to the limit. Where Kettle Creek slowed down again below the rapids, they hit the water in a high, reckless splashing. Pulling out under the farther bank, they were conscious of the sporadic working of guns at the narrows; but now, also, above the murmur of the water they could hear a first rumbling of the approaching herd.

Yance Kegley opened the gunnysack he had carried tied to his saddlehorn and brought out the dynamite sticks, already capped and fused. "You light 'em, count two, and throw—*hard!* If you count three, no use to bother about throwing. . . ."

Gingerly, Holden put one stick in his coat pocket and dug out a match, holding it ready as they rode forward at a walk toward the approaching herd. Presently he said, "Close enough!" and they both pulled rein.

Holden popped the match on a thumbnail. He held it while they lighted their fuses, and then let the match fall and stood in stirrups listening to Kegley count aloud in a voice that was high-pitched with excitement. They threw precisely together; the sticks lobbed end for end, trailing sparks, and struck the earth well ahead of the point animals. And instinctively both men ducked their heads between their shoulders, as red fire and powder blast seemed to rip the canyon apart.

The ground shook mightily; the horses squealed and reared. Stunned by shock waves, Holden brought the bay under control and peered into a screen of smoke as debris began to patter down around him. The massive sound pulsed and rolled away between the shouldering ridges, and his numbed ears began to be aware of other things—the sudden bawling of terrified cattle, the rumble of hooves lunging into motion.

If gunfire still raged behind them at the narrows, he no longer heard it. He caught sight of Yance Kegley and swung his arm forward, shouting, "Keep after it!"

They rode into the smoke, picking their way among debris and past the crater the dynamite had blasted. Holden dug the second stick from his pocket, with a hand that shook. The smoke pall began to shred out; he saw what had become a tangled mass of cattle trying to turn on itself and break into a stampede, heard terror in the sounds lifting from hundreds of throats. If stopping the herd had been the one purpose, they had already accomplished it; but Holden wasn't satisfied. He pulled close beside Kegley and yelled above the uproar, "Let's give them another round—just in case Bartell didn't hear that one!"

Again the fuses were lighted, the sticks went arcing, and Holden pulled in behind a solitary pine for such protection as it could give when the blast struck. Kegley had thrown harder and farther than his companion; Holden distinctly saw one dark form hurled high, grotesquely spinning. And now real, blind panic hit the herd and tore it apart, to plunge headlong into the waters of the creek or scatter senselessly across the open flats. Ears still ringing, blinded by smoke and powder flash, Holden heard a horse scream shrilly and cringed at the thought of a rider going down before that tide of hooves and meat and horns.

A little sickened, he turned back. He had lost Yance Kegley in the confusion and the drifting smoke; meanwhile, it seemed to him the racket of gunplay had ceased, yonder at the narrows. He took the Smith & Wesson from his pocket and held it in his lap as he kicked the bay in that direction, to find out if his strategy with the dynamite had paid off the way he hoped. He was vaguely aware that shooting had broken out again at the narrows.

Suddenly he was aware of a drum of running horses, dead ahead and drawing nearer. Two riders came bursting around a point of rock and timber, and they were Bartell and Glazer; as they saw him in the middle of the road, they hauled in so sharply that Seab Glazer's nervous mount danced about under him in a complete circle. Luke Bartell shouted, "By God, Holden, is this your doing?"

"Every bit of it!" Holden answered. "You won't turn that stampede this side of Canada!" And in spite of the odds there was all at once no fear in him at all—only the exultation of facing his enemy, and knowing that he had finally managed to hit the man where it hurt.

For now Bartell was cursing him, his face distorted with black fury. And in the next breath a gun rose in his hand and the outlaw fired, point blank.

The saddle of a nervous horse was a poor base for shooting. The bullet came nowhere near close; neither did the one that Holden fired hurriedly, in reply. Seab Glazer, he saw, had a gun and was trying to get a shot at him, but Bartell's horse backed into his and for that moment the redhead had all he could do to settle it. The leader, cursing foully, leveled for another shot.

A rifle spoke, somewhere at Holden's right. Bartell's whole body shook to the impact of a bullet. His head jerked forward, the reins slipped from his hand. As the outlaw started to double forward, Troy Holden twisted for a look.

He had known the rifleman must be Yance Kegley, even before he heard the old man's yell of triumph and saw the unholy glee on his face. With a smoothly practiced move Kegley flipped the rifle, to crank the lever, and dropped its barrel across his forearm again, hunting for Seab Glazer. In the same instant Glazer fired. The slug struck old Kegley square; it sent the rifle flying from his grasp as it picked him off his saddle. He slammed to the ground and his momentum carried him, rolling, over the edge of the cutbank and down the sharp drop to the creek.

Then Troy Holden, taking careful aim down the whole length of his arm, brought the redhead into his sights and worked the trigger, and somehow knew the shot was good even as a burst of powdersmoke blurred his vision.

In the shocked aftermath of the mingled weapons, he realized he was the only one left in a saddle, still unhurt. Slowly he lowered his gun, too numbed for the moment to do more than look at the crumpled figures of Bartell and Glazer lying in the road. Seab Glazer's frenzied horse, out of its head with panic, spun wildly and one hoof struck its owner's body, causing it to give limply. Then the animal went galloping away, reins and stirrups flopping.

The other horses had already begun to settle. Troy Holden took a long breath, filling his lungs with the stink of burnt powder, and reined over to look at Yance Kegley.

Kegley sprawled at the creek's edge, an arm and part of his torso bobbing in the water. Holden stepped hurriedly from saddle, keeping hold of the reins as he took the shallow drop sliding on his heels. Crouched there, the sound of a galloping horse made him freeze and lift his gun as a Bartell rider swept suddenly into view.

The man was bareheaded, bent forward in the saddle and frantically whipping up his horse with the ends of the reins. Holden saw him discover the bodies of his dead leaders; he didn't even pause to look at them. A sidelong, almost indifferent glance flicked over Holden, in passing, and then the man was gone.

And Troy Holden deliberately lowered the hammer of the gun and dropped it into his coat pocket, having seen enough to convince him he no longer needed it.

Yance Kegley's blood was beginning to stain the water of the creek. Holden went down on one knee and pulled the man up onto the bank, and propped his head at a better angle. His mouth tightened as he saw the hole Glazer's bullet had drilled in the old man's chest.

Kegley stirred. His eyes came open and discovered Holden bending over him. He tried and found speech: "Bartell?"

"He's dead. You killed him."

"So!" The word was a grunt of satisfaction. "So this time I made it!"

"This time?" Troy Holden echoed, and suddenly had a premonition of what he was about to hear.

The old man actually tried to laugh shortly, but it ended in a cough and a grimace of pain. "Hell!" he muttered. "It was him I was trying for, the night I put that bullet in your back. . . ."

"*You?*"

"You never guessed, did you? And damned if I was going to admit I'd made such a damned fool mistake. But you had to come along the trail just the wrong time, that night. I thought you was Luke Bartell—and there I'd been waiting, a dozen years, to even my score with him!

"You ever wonder," he demanded, forcing the words from a chest wracked by contractions of pain, "where I got this gimp leg of mine? It was down at Billings—twelve years ago. I drove the wagon in from my homestead ranch, one day, just as Bartell and a gang hit the bank and got driven off empty handed. Bartell was killing mad, shooting at everything in sight. He seen me on the wagon seat. He couldn't help but see I didn't have no gun, but that never stopped him. For pure devilment he threw a bullet at me as he went past. It took me in the hip, knocked me off the wagon. The leg never healed right. By time I got out of the hospital I'd lost my ranch, lost everything. Couldn't even hold a riding job. And all these years since, I just been bidin' my time—waiting. . . ."

Sweat stood in huge drops on the old man's leathery face. "That night in the Montana House, Bartell looked straight in my face and I was sure he remembered me. Later I heard somebody behind me on the road and I thought he'd followed me, to finish me off before I could finish him. Wasn't till after I'd shot that I seen my mistake. Wasn't nothing I could do then, but fetch you home and try to—"

The tortured words broke off in a last spasm. Yance Kegley fought for breath. A hand caught at Holden's sleeve and tightened on it, a shaking grip. Then the blood poured from his mouth and he fell back limp, and Holden let him down.

Shaking, he could only stare at the dead man who—he knew now, beyond any question—must have been deranged from years of pain, and loneliness, and a festering hatred for the one who had crippled him. Only a crazy man would have thought that Bartell would remember him, a dozen years later—after a single glance, and a casual shooting. Or that, even having recognized him, Luke Bartell would have been bothered about completing the job.

Only a crazy man would have left Holden in the dark about the ambush, letting him read all kinds of meaning into what had been, after all, no more than a simple accident. . . .

More riders approaching brought him quickly to his feet then, to see Morgan Peters, and Callie beside him. Not until now did he realize that all the shooting had stopped; with Bartell's cattle stampeded down the valley, out of sight and hearing, a strange silence lay upon the land. He could hear the lapping of Kettle Creek, a twittering of birds flitting through the new-leafed brush along the bank.

Callie and her father reined in, to stare at the bodies of the dead men. Then Callie slipped from the saddle and came running to Holden; her face was white and her voice tremulous as she cried: "Troy! You're not hurt? Oh, please don't be!"

"None at all," he assured her, and saw relief flood warm color into her cheeks. She was in his arms, then, her face against his chest, and almost of their own volition his arms closed about her and it seemed entirely natural she should be there. All at once it was as though Bea Applegate was someone he had known in some other world—someone whose face he could not even clearly remember.

He lifted his eyes to find Morgan Peters staring at the two of them, with an unreadable expression. "So it's like that, is it?"

"I'm afraid it is," Holden said; his words were mild but his answering look held defiance. "Whether you like it or not, Morgan."

"Uh-huh." The rancher shifted his weight in the saddle and pushed the back of a hand across his mouth. When he spoke again his voice was gruff but it didn't sound really angry. "Jim Ells is the one who ain't going to like it! Still, Jim's a reasonable man—when he sees he's got no choice but to be. Besides, even he has to admit that you pulled the lot of us out of a real bad hole, today." The gaunt head nodded solemnly. "Callie tells me using the dynamite was your idea. Man, man! You could have blown yourself to pieces!"

"But I didn't."

"No. And it worked! When Bartell pulled his men down off the ridge to see what the hell was happening to his cattle, we were able to catch them on the flank. Only a few got away. Luke Bartell was one." He looked at the bodies of the outlaws. "I see he didn't get past you."

"It was Yance Kegley that killed him," Holden said quickly, for the record. He added, "What about yourself? Did you lose any men?"

"One of my boys is dead, a couple wounded. Bob Thacher took a bad one in the arm, but he'll recover. Thanks to you, it was no worse than that." Peters was grinning suddenly. "You ought to see Sam Riggs! He got that breed—that Wasco, that beat him up so bad. I think it done him good.

He's holding his head up again—as if he'd suddenly took a new lease on life!"

His arm around Callie, Holden said, "Tell Sam I'm going to want to talk to him. If he'd like a job at Crown, there'll be one waiting."

Peters looked at him keenly. "What does that mean? Sounds to me you're saying you aim to take Crown over—to run it." And at Holden's nod: "You're *not* going to sell?"

"A lot of things can happen," Troy Holden said. "A man can change. Something you've fought for can suddenly appear a lot more valuable than you ever knew.

"Somehow, it never occurred to me that I could come to think of myself as a part of this valley, or this Montana country. Now all at once I don't want to belong anywhere else."

The rancher gave him a probing look; slowly he nodded; and there was satisfaction in the way he answered, "I'm glad to hear that. Damned glad! I used to think Vern Holden had missed the big chance of his life, when he failed to realize just how much this country had to offer—besides a mere business investment. But maybe his son has found out in time. I hope so. I'd be glad to have you for a neighbor."

"Perhaps something more than a neighbor," Troy Holden said, and his arm tightened about the girl. Suddenly he felt not only frightened of the mistakes he had nearly made, but humbly grateful too. True, he had lost much; but he began to suspect he had gained infinitely more.

# HELLBENT FOR A HANGROPE

## A note from the author:

Here's the data concerning factual elements in my novel.

"For my descriptions of locale—Catoosa, Fort Smith, Younger's Bend, and Robbers' Cave—I relied on personal observation, on correspondence, and on interviews with people who could remember Belle's cabin as it looked when it was in existence. For historical background and the character of Belle Starr, I'm not unnaturally indebted almost entirely to her biographer, Burton Rascoe *(Belle Starr,* Random House, 1941).

"Besides Belle, Parker, and Bat Masterson, the historical characters consist of: Belle's children, Ed and Pearl; the Indians, Sam Starr (a worthless fellow—Fort Smith Weekly *Elevator),* Jim July, and Frank West; and the obscure and unlamented outlaw called 'Blue Duck' (of whom Rascoe can offer little more than a photograph and the information that he was 'killed by unknown party, Indian Territory, July, 1886').

"The only historical happening portrayed is the mutual killing of Sam Starr and Frank West. The conjecture that Sam was responsible for John Middleton's death is Rascoe's suggestion. All else is fiction, except for certain historical facts that are merely alluded to, as background for the story."

# I

THIS rain that comes spinning from a darkening sky is cold, and there is wind behind it to run and flatten the grasses of the Indian Nations. The boisterous wind has found an abandoned camp wagon and whips the mud-streaked canvas cover in a fluttering roll of gunshots, snaps the slickers of the men grouped nearby.

Rain scores bleak faces and chapped knuckles; it gutters from lowered hatbrims as these men stand and stare at what lies upon the ground. The flanks of a clot of saddle horses, held by one of them, throw off a faint, steaming mist.

From compassion, someone has knelt with a blanket to shelter the face of the man who is dying. Spears of rain drum soddenly against the cloth. Nothing, however, remains to be done for the others whose bodies clutter this wet, hoof-chopped earth — a half-dozen of them, lying face down in rain-pocked puddles, or with dead eyes open to the weeping sky. The callous leavings of murder.

They, at least, are beyond the storm's chill discomfort. But suddenly a cry is raised.

"Mark! Another one here — and alive!"

The leader, bearded, hard-grained, lifts his head sharply. "Can you get him on his feet? Bring him over — hurry it!"

Yes, the man can walk, with help to support his weakness. There is blood on him, the glaze of shock still in his eyes. He murmurs again and again, in an anxious demanding, "My horse! I got to find my horse. A buckskin —"

"The whole blamed remuda's gone!" the bearded man informs him. "Looks like you came through luckier than the

131

rest of this Stirrup outfit — nothing worse than a clout on the head. I'm afraid, though, you haven't much time if you want a last word with your boss."

But from the ground the dying man speaks suddenly, his voice terrible in the agony of the effort. "He ain't — of my crew! He belongs with them that done this — "

"What are you saying, Cass!"

It is already too late. A convulsion has stiffened Cass Dumont, lifting him up onto a shoulder with head arched violently backward. When he drops flat again, the slackened features tell their final story.

For a moment, no one says anything, or moves. Then, slowly, every eye turns upon the stranger. A look of bewilderment — perhaps real, perhaps feigned — crosses his bloodied face. "Wait! It's not true!"

The bearded cowman prods him, "No? Then who are you? What's your name?"

"Craddock — Owen Craddock. I own the Diamond C brand, in the Llano Valley in Texas. It ain't big, but people down there will vouch for me."

"This ain't the Llano!" Mark Stroud, the bearded man, puts a questioning stare over the angry circle of men. He squints as a sudden gust of wind lifts the needling rain against him. "Any of you boys know that country? Ever hear of a Diamond C?"

There is an exchange of looks, and then slowly heads shake in solemn and ominous reply. The herd boss reads their temper accurately. But being a leader he shapes his own decision.

He tells the crew firmly, "This thing ain't for our settlement. We're no court of law, to condemn or execute a man. All we can do is take him in to Dodge with us, let the authorities handle it. Is that clear to everybody?"

There is no answer. The prisoner alone makes protest in a dazed whisper, "A buckskin with a cropped ear. Thirty thousand in his saddlebags. I tell you I got to find them!"

Only the drumming of the rain answers him.

IN THE marshal's office in Dodge City, a sharp-eyed old man with white hair and a face gaunted below the cheek bones glanced up across the match flame he held to the bowl of his pipe. He scowled. Three strangers had entered — three cowmen in rain-shiny oilskin slickers, bringing some of the cold with them from the wet autumn dusk.

"I'm Mark Stroud," the solid, bearded one in the lead told him. "Of the Tomahawk drive. I sent one of my men on ahead with — "

"Oh, yeah." At once interested, the jailer shook out his match and tossed it in the general direction of the stove that roared away in a corner of the room. The pipe he snatched from his mouth to hold engulfed in a knobby-knuckled hand.

"The Dumont wagon, and them poor bastards that was massacred. Yeah, it got in yestiddy." His look sharpened as it moved over the two men with Stroud. "Feller said you was bringing a prisoner."

"This is him," said Stroud.

At the jerk of his head the jailer turned to peer closely at the one who stood next to the Tomahawk boss. He was a man of medium height, in the plain garb of a working cowman, with light-gray eyes that looked pale and angry against the mahogany mask of a hard-planed, tight-lipped face.

Stroud said, "McGee there brought his belongings — what there is of them."

The old jailer gave no more than a glance as the puncher called McGee stepped forward to deposit a blanket roll upon the desk. His whole attention was for the prisoner.

"Bat's likely over on Front Street," he volunteered. "Sizing up the shape of the evening. This town is pretty well set on its ear over this whole thing, I can tell you. About everybody must have known Cass Dumont." He looked again at the prisoner. "How about hearing your side of the story?"

The man who called himself Owen Craddock returned the look coldly. "Why? Why waste it on you? I'll wait for the marshal!"

"Well, damn you!"

Stroud said, "Oh, he's salty all right — even with his neck in danger!"

"Nobody's going to stretch my neck!" the prisoner retorted. "I can prove who I am. Besides, I've lost a horse and thirty thousand dollars, and any chance I had of getting them back grows less with every minute you hold me here. Am I supposed to like that?"

The jailer and Mark Stroud exchanged looks. The ancient lifted bony shoulders and turned back to the desk. He shoved his pipe between yellowed teeth with a click.

"Might as well be shet of that raincoat, Craddock," he grunted. "Looks like you could be here a while."

A smell of steaming woolens had begun to fill the little office. With suppressed fury the prisoner stripped out of his oilskin slicker and flung it onto the desk. Divested of it he shaped up as long-waisted and narrow at the hips, with no spare weight on him.

An uneasy, waiting silence was unbroken except for the chatter of a tin clock upon a shelf. Craddock looked around. He saw, besides the scarred desk, three barrel chairs whose yielding timbers someone had reinforced indifferently with wire; a wooden cabinet; a standing rack that held two rifles and a wicked-looking, double-snouted shotgun. Just above this, on a board studded with nails, hung a truly amazing conglomeration of small arms.

There were six-shooters of every make and caliber, from ancient horse pistols down to a modern, snub-nosed Bullog. There were guns with rubber butts, and one that looked like a presentation piece — all silver and pearl, and encrusted with floral chasings along its barrel. There was one with a cherry-wood handle that was fairly saw-toothed with a badman's tally notches. Finally, Craddock noticed a brace of pepperboxes and one single-chambered midget that must surely have been designed to strap to a lady's calf, beneath her petticoats.

It would have been an interesting sidelight on this place called Dodge City, if it had been possible to trace the story behind those guns and know how each had come to have its place on that board in the marshal's office. But Owen Craddock's only thought was to wish he could get his hands on one of them — and find it loaded.

Then the puncher, McGee, at the window, sang out, "Hey! Here comes the marshal!" Boots struck the sill and the office door was thrown open. Craddock swung about impatiently.

He did not look like the manbreaker he was reputed to be. He seemed to be not much older than Craddock himself — around thirty, perhaps. Under his slicker he was dressed like any dandy in checkered suit and waistcoat, with a pearl stickpin thrust precisely in his four-in-hand. He wore extravagant sideburns and a drooping mustache, and a bowler set jauntily on the back of his head. Tucked under his arm he carried a gold-handled walking stick.

But his eyes were stern and his manner direct, and he was taking command of things before the door had closed behind him.

"All right," he said crisply, pulling off the slicker and snaring it on a wall hook. "You're Stroud." He nodded to the Tomahawk boss. "I think I saw you around town a year ago." He put his glance on the prisoner, then assessed him in a brief, keen probing. "And you say your name is Craddock?"

"That's right. If you'll just send a wire — "

"All in good time!" Masterson interrupted, waggling a hand for silence. "Just calm down for a minute and let's have the story. Might as well sit." Without looking, he swept a space clear and hitched himself onto a corner of the desk, leaning forearm on thigh, swinging a polished boot.

Craddock's fists were knotted hard and a tight muscle fluttered at one corner of his angry mouth.

"Damn it!" he burst out. "You tell me to wait! I've already lost two days, letting this Stroud hombre drag me all the way up here with him when I could have been on the trail of my money!"

"A fire-eater!" murmured the lawman, his eyes narrowing a little. "Well, we'll get this thing over with as fast as possible. I'm a busy man my ownself." Suddenly the head of Masterson's walking stick was pointing at Craddock and the marshal said sternly, "Right behind you. A chair. Sit down in it!"

It was a command which the prisoner studied during a hostile moment. Finally, hooking a toe around the chair leg, he hauled it forward and dropped into it.

"You've had this man tied up?" the lawman demanded suddenly, turning a surprised look at Stroud. He had noticed the marks of the rope on Craddock's wrists.

"Damn right! He tried a break last night — almost got away. I took no more chances."

Masterson accepted this without comment. "Well, keep talking. Let's hear the rest."

"It was a couple of days ago and a few miles below the Strip," Mark Stroud said. "Me and the boys happened along a few hours after somebody jumped Cass Dumont's trail camp. Cass was a good friend of mine," he added, his tone roughening. "I don't reckon I'll ever get it out of my head — the sight of what those raiders did."

"And they left this behind them, eh?" Bat Masterson swung his attention to the prisoner. "Mind telling us what you were doing in that camp — er — Craddock?"

"Of course not. I'd just dropped in on it. I'd sold some cattle and was heading home down the Chisholm — "

The marshal interrupted, "Alone? In that country, with saddlebags stuffed full of beef money?"

"Why not? I can take care of myself — and I was in a hurry and traveling light, not carrying much in the way of grub. Game is pretty well thinned out down there so late in season. When I saw that horse herd camped and the chuck wagon, I naturally rode in and introduced myself and got a bid to stay and eat."

Masterson gently tapped his chin with the gold head of the walking stick. "How many head of horses would you say Cass had with him?"

"Better'n a hundred. I knew Dumont by reputation, of course, as a large-scale operator. He told me he'd sent two big herds north this year and these were the combined cavvies he and a skeleton crew were trailing home. Good stock, too."

Stroud put in, "Cass was a proud man when it came to mounting his outfit. A hundred horses that carried the Stirrup brand would make a fine haul for those Indian Territory horse thieves."

Masterson nodded thoughtfully. Then he sat straighter, dropped the point of his walking stick on the floor.

"So this raid happened. Go on from there."

"Well, we'd finished eating," Craddock said. "I was putting the saddle and stuff back on my horse when the raiders came at us out of a creek bosque. There was no chance to make a fight of it. First I saw, the camp was swarming with horsemen and Dumont's men were going down. I couldn't say how many the raiders had with them, but it was a massacre!"

"And what did you do?"

"That ain't exactly clear. I pulled my gun, of course, and I remember that Dumont was there. I started to yell something. Then I don't remember much of anything until Stroud's men were pouring whisky into me and my head felt as though it had split open."

Masterson turned a raised eyebrow to Craddock's accuser. "That sounds like a pretty straight story."

"But damn it, it don't gibe with what Cass Dumont told us!"

"Dumont made a mistake," Craddock answered. "He was all worked up. When he saw the gun in my hand it must have struck him that I'd been posted in camp as a lookout and he used his gun barrel on me without asking questions. Judging from what happened to the others, maybe that's the one thing saved my life!"

Stroud shrugged heavily. "The man's lying!" he told Masterson, swinging to his feet. "But he's your problem now and if you want to turn him loose I guess there's no way I can stop you!"

Bat Masterson let this go unanswered. "About the horses," he wanted to know. "You make any effort to trace them?"

"No use. It was near dusk before we found the camp, and the trail pointed east — straight for the jacks. You savvy that timber country north of the Canadian? Even if I'd had men to spare from handling cattle in a steady downpour, there'd have been no trail we could follow for long."

The marshal nodded, satisfied, and came off the desk.

"All right, Stroud." He put out a hand. "Thanks for taking this trouble. I'd appreciate it if you don't say any more than you have to outside the office. This is a touchy kind of business — one for the Federal court to settle, it looks like."

"Sure." The Tomahawk boss shook with him. He gave his puncher a signal and they headed for the door. With his hand on the knob, Stroud hesitated long enough for a last cold look at the prisoner and a warning. "Don't take no chances with him."

They were gone then, in a gust of chill wind, through the briefly opened door.

II

MASTERSON swung away from the desk, took a tour about the office that brought him to a window where he paused for a look outside.

"Rain's stopped," he commented to no one in particular. "Might be breaking up." Then abruptly he was back at his place on the desk.

"Let's get down to cases," he told Craddock. "You a family man?"

"No. No time for it."

"Who is there could help us prove your identity, then?"

"I tried to tell you when you first came in to send off a wire to Art Humbird. He owns the Big H in Kimball County, Texas."

Masterson shook his head. "Nobody nearer than that?" Nevertheless he jotted down the name. "It could take days," he pointed out, dissatisfied. "Isn't there anyone you know here in Dodge?"

"No."

"Never been in town before?"

"Sure. I made a hand on trail drives a time or two before I got to building my own ranch." He added with heavy sarcasm, "But since I saved my pay instead of blowing it in the saloons, I guess there's nobody'd be apt to remember me!"

"What about these cattle you say you just brought up from Texas? Where were they disposed of?"

"Caldwell. Or rather, to a man I ran into a little south of there. He was looking for a herd of stockers to take to Montana and he bought my outfit, chuck wagon, and remuda, and signed up my entire crew. He paid cash, and I pocketed it and headed south."

"Without even a look at the town, I suppose? After three months on the trail?"

Craddock lifted his shoulders. "Time's short enough without wasting it in these track town saloons. It's taken me fifteen years, day and night, to build myself the makings of a ranch." His mouth twisted bitterly. "And now it's gone!"

"How do you mean?"

"Why, I mortgaged clear to the hilt, putting that trail herd together. If I lose the money, I lose everything! Do you wonder I'm concerned about it?"

There was a little silence while the yammer of the battered clock announced its presence, measuring out the wastage of minutes crowding by. Finally taking up the pencil, Bat Masterson scribbled a brief message. He tore the sheet off the scratch pad, glanced over what he had written and flipped it to the jailer.

"Run this over to the station and get this on the wire for Texas. Say it has to go right out."

The old man nodded and pushed himself up from his chair, with a complaining nod of aged joints. From a peg he got his hat and a corduroy jacket that was worn slick at the elbows. He drew these on, moving with an exasperating slowness, folded the paper carefully, placed it with exactitude in a pocket and buttoned it in. Only then did he start an unhurried progress toward the door.

Craddock gritted his teeth, but said nothing until the door had finally closed. Then he tried a different line of persuasion.

"Hasn't it occurred to you that if those raiders were friends of mine they'd never have ridden off and left me? Even supposing they figured I was dead?"

"You got a good argument there," the marshal admitted slowly. "Yet, as I told Stroud, it isn't my decision. Only the Federal court at Fort Smith has jurisdiction over happenings in the Indian Nations. And even so, the judge likely won't want to take action until he's consulted with Cass Dumont's heirs."

"Do you mean you expect me to rot in jail until the Dumont clan get together in their own good time and decide whether to hang me or let me go?"

Masterson rubbed his neck with the cane handle. "They cast a long shadow. With all the money Cass piled up for them, even Hangin' Judge Parker would hardly go against anything they wanted, let alone a small-fry cowtown peace officer like me. As it happens, one of the daughters is here in Dodge right now with old Bud Tipton. They've been in the office half a dozen times since yesterday. Bud, in particular, is ready to eat fire. He rode top hand for Cass a good thirty years — since away back before the War — and I can tell you, if he gets his say — " The marshal broke off with a grunt. "Speak of the devil!"

The door had swung open. A woman stood in the opening, and behind her loomed the spare, hard figure of a cowman past his prime.

"Miss Dumont," murmured Bat Masterson, as he came off the corner of the desk. Craddock rose more slowly,

Yes, she was a Dumont, all right — The resemblance to the murdered man was past mistaking, in the set of her head and the rounded, rather stubborn jaw. She was younger than Craddock would have expected — the baby of the family, then? Her hair was a ripe corn yellow, worn brushed back above her ears and tied at the nape of the neck with a black satin ribbon. She had a pretty, imperious face with gray eyes and winged eyebrows.

Right now it was plain that she had been weeping. And her manner as she stared at Craddock and then turned questioningly to the marshal held the after-effects of extreme shock.

"Is . . . this the man?"

"Yes," said Masterson. "I'm still investigating. I haven't anything to tell you for certain."

Craddock found his initial hostility a little shaken before the signs of this young woman's grief. Something moved him toward her a step.

"Miss Dumont! I don't know what you've heard, but it ain't true — I mean that I had anything to do with the killing of your father. I'm honestly sorry for what happened."

He couldn't tell if she believed him. The man with her answered, in his voice an edge of hoarseness for which time and long exposure to raw weather of all sorts must have been responsible.

"You're a liar! Vinnie and I have been talking to Stroud, and what we heard was plenty enough to — "

"Bud, stay out of this!"

But the old cowman ignored Masterson's warning. He shouldered between Vinnie Dumont and the prisoner.

It was evident the long, tough years had cured more than they aged Bud Tipton. His face had the texture of tanned leather. In repose it showed few wrinkles, but at any movement the skin fell into a score of deep creases that furrowed his cheeks and made a webbing about deep-set, fierce blue eyes. He was scowling now as he confronted Craddock.

"All them fine boys!" he exclaimed. "And old Cass — cold and murdered. And you standing here, damn you, convicted with the old man's last breath!"

"Just because he was dying," Craddock pointed out stonily, "doesn't mean he was right!"

It was the wrong thing to tell Cass Dumont's top hand just then. Bud Tipton's face warped with rage. The next moment, without warning, he had flung himself headlong at the prisoner.

Craddock was hurled backward by the unexpectedness of the attack. He caught a muffled scream from the girl, heard Bat Masterson's oath, then he was slammed into a corner of the filing cabinet. The old man's hands had found his throat — amazing strength in those fingers.

Craddock lashed out and, feeling the scrape of beard stubble, hit again. His blow must have hurt. At once Tipton's hands broke away and Craddock himself fell back against the side of the cabinet, gasping for air. Bat Masterson had managed to grab the old cowman and was trying to shout sense into him. Vinnie Dumont had both hands pressed against her face and was sobbing with fright and near-hysteria.

Somehow more terrible than any curses was the deadly implacable silence with which Bud Tipton writhed and struggled to break loose, while his eyes held their venomous stare on Craddock's face.

Then the girl was crying, "Bud! Oh, stop it — please!"

The words seemed to break through to him. Slowly the fury went out of Tipton. He ceased his struggling.

Bat Masterson grunted, "That's better!" and turned him loose.

Tipton jerked his head to shake back long, tawny hair that had fallen about his hollow cheeks. He accepted the hat Masterson picked up from the floor and handed him. Craddock felt of the muscles of his throat, trying to keep a hold upon his temper.

Carefully straightening the hang of his coat, Bat Master-

son said, "I'll have no more of that sort of thing — not in my
office. You hear me?"

"Let him alone," grunted Craddock. "It's not worth an
argument."

Bud Tipton, not answering either of them, turned his back
and went directly to the weeping girl and placed a com-
forting arm around her shoulders. "Sorry, Vinnie. I never
meant to make a row and get you more upset."

She had already recovered from the brief storm caused by
nerves strung too taut with grief. She nodded, and turned
to Craddock. "I apologize for Bud," she said stiffly. "He just
lost his head for a minute. He and my dad were always . . .
very close."

"Why couldn't it of been me?" the old man groaned, lashing himself in a tone of bitter self-reproach. "Why'd I ever
let him start for Texas without me along? Better if I'd taken
the outfit home myself, so he could have stayed and gone
back with you on the cars! All through the years I stuck
close to him, and then at the very last — " He choked, shaking his head blind with misery. The hat he held was crushed
between rope-scarred fingers.

"Now, I've told you I won't have you blaming yourself!"

"Yes, Vinnie." He turned away, carefully shaping his
crumpled hat, putting his whole methodical attention to the
job.

Despite her lack of years, Craddock decided in surprise
that there was a real strength in this girl. With the intoler-
ance of the unprivileged for inherited wealth, he had been
prepared to find her weak and thoroughly spoiled. Her
clothing certainly looked expensive enough: the little gray
jacket and skirt that accented the curves of her figure while
artfully seeming to conceal them; the exaggerated fullness
of her bustle that was probably in the latest Eastern fashion;
the lacy jabot and the cameo pinned at her throat.

Yet with it all she had the unmistakable, healthy coloring
of a ranch girl, and she carried herself in a way that told of
experience at bracing to the sway and roll of a saddle. Craddock thought it likely she had spent many hours on horse-

back beside her father as he rode about the business of the sprawling Stirrup ranch in Texas. If that were so, it would have made them closer than most fathers and their daughters.

He told her, "I accept the apology. In return I just hope you'll try to believe that this is all a mistake, that I didn't kill Cass Dumont!"

Vinnie Dumont met his glance squarely for a long minute, a troubled frown shaping itself between her brows. She said finally, "I . . . don't know. I just don't know." She turned away and faced Masterson. "Is there anything you want us to do?"

"Not a thing," the marshal answered. "You see, this is a matter the law will have to handle. Believe me!"

"All right." She seemed a little bewildered still. The shock of her father's passing was not yet lifted from her. She touched the old cowman's sleeve and said gently, "Come on, Bud. Let's go."

Without a word he followed her to the door.

She had left a small umbrella in the seat of a chair. Masterson spied it and, halting Tipton at the last moment, handed it to him. He also took the occasion to give the old puncher some sound advice.

"What you ought to do is take that girl straight home to her folks!"

Tipton shook his head. "You don't know Vinnie! She'd never go — not at a time like this. She wants old Cass buried proper, and she's determined she's going to see this whole business to a finish. Besides she ain't alone. She's got me to take care of her."

"But no relatives? No womenfolks she can lean on?"

"What does she need with such? There's the aunt she was visiting in St. Louis, the one that brought her to join us out here, but she's already gone back. Don't worry! I can look after Vinnie all right. I've taught her to look after her ownself pretty damn good!"

Bat Masterson made a gesture of defeat. "I just hope you both know what you're doing. The girl's young — not old enough to have much sense. And I doubt that you ever had any. So try to keep her out of trouble!"

Tipton's only answer was a grunt, as his gaze moved away and touched on Owen Craddock. Instantly the veined lids narrowed down, the whole gaunt face fell into uncompromising lines. Craddock returned his look, without expression, for the space of a half-dozen ticks from the tin clock.

Then Bud Tipton had whirled and strode with cougarish grace into the dusk to join his young employer. And Bat Masterson closed the door. As an afterthought he rammed the bolt home.

"Well, what do you think?" he said, turning.

He froze, face gone hard. At the desk, where he had moved soundlessly, Craddock stood with the gold-headed walking stick lifted clublike. For a long count of three they faced each other without moving, and then Masterson's hand darted into his clothing. When it came out it had a Colt six-shooter leveled.

"Put it down!" he snapped. "Drop it!"

### III

OWEN CRADDOCK felt his jaw muscles working. He opened his fingers, let the improvised weapon fall to the desk and at a gesture of the marshal's gun-muzzle backed silently away from it.

"So!" grunted Masterson. "Another second and I suppose you'd have brained me with that — or taken a bullet trying it! Stroud warned me to look out for a trick!"

"You should have listened!" The prisoner's tone was heavy.
"Because I aim to take any chance I see. Turn your back
and I'll probably try it again!"

"Yes, I think you would! Pretty damn tough, aren't you?"

The marshal waggled his gun barrel at the chair Craddock had vacated. Only after the prisoner sat down again
did Masterson leave the door. The six-gun had disappeared
in his shoulder holster. He dropped into the desk chair,
lifted a polished boot against the edge of the desk and laced
his fingers across the front of his checkered waistcoat.

"Now we can finish our talk," he said.

Craddock was kneading rope-marked wrists. "What's there
left to talk about?"

"A lot of things, maybe — if we're going to get to the bottom of this business and clear you."

Owen Craddock lifted a slow look at the officer. Astonishment rimmed his voice. "You don't mean that after what just
happened you actually believe what I been telling you!"

"Have I said I didn't? As a matter of fact, I think I do believe you. Don't ask me why — just call it a sort of hunch. I
been around long enough that I've found it pays to play my
hunches about men. And I don't think you're any murderer.
I got you pegged otherwise."

"How?"

Masterson took his boot down and, leaning forward,
opened a box on the desk and took out a cigar. He toyed
with it, scowling thoughtfully, bit off an end and spat it into
a handy spittoon.

"You're an ambitious man, Craddock. And a hot-headed
one. Anything or anybody that gets between you and your
goal, you kick them out of the way — or break a toe trying.
And once in a spot where you aren't able to turn a hand or
solve your own problems, you get sullen and rebellious and
nobody can do a damned thing for you."

Craddock's smile was crooked and faintly cynical. "Go
ahead. What else?"

"Why, that's about it. Except I wonder if you're actually
quite as tough as you make yourself out. I was watching

while you talked to that girl just now. There's a soft streak in you, Craddock, but something's pushing you pretty hard. What is it?"

The younger man shrugged. "You claim to know."

"Not entirely. There's a part of the story nobody but you could fill in. And I'm curious. You were born in Texas?"

"That's right."

"And, let's see. You'd have been how old, when the War ended?"

Craddock pulled his head back, eyes narrowing. "All right," he said harshly, "if you're asking. I was ten that spring. My dad never got back after Appomattox. I guess my mother just didn't care much about outliving him — "

"Go on."

"What's the use? It's the same story any lone youngster could have told in those days. The carpetbaggers swarmed in like locusts and we watched them strip Texas clean. My folks' Diamond C iron down with the rest, naturally — just as though it had never been."

"And what did a ten-year-old kid do with himself the years when that was going on?"

"Anything to weather out the storm. Stole and begged. Swamped in saloons and shined shoes and helped load freight wagons, and did a thousand other things to stay alive. Finally when I was big enough I got a riding job, and after that it was easier. But always there was just one aim in life — to make the Diamond C a living brand again! I did it, too. And now I guess I've lost it all, for sure!"

The marshal studied him thoughtfully. "You're a young man yet. What you accomplished once you could a second time. I haven't any doubt you will. But I admit it's not the chore a man could be expected to tackle of his own free choice!"

The marshal had fished a match from his waistcoat pocket. He snapped it to life against his thumbnail and carefully got the cigar to burning just as he liked it. Shaking out the match, he said:

"So, just assuming you got out of jail? You'd be heading

straight down into the Indian Nations, I suppose. With nothing but a gun and your own nerve, bent on getting your hard money back in spite of all the outlaws in the Territory!"

"I'd sure as hell make the effort."

"That's what I thought. And you know what your chances would be, too."

He drew deeply on the cigar, rubbed his chin thoughtfully with the ball of his thumb as he let the blue smoke stream from his nostrils, then went on:

"I admit I don't know that country any too well, myself — not many white men do, outside of outlaws and a handful of Federal marshals, and the ranchers in the Strip. It occurs to me, though, that if I were hunting a prime bunch of stolen horses I'd be inclined to start my looking over at a place called Catoosa. You've heard of it?"

Craddock frowned. "Seems like I have. Where does it lie?"

"In the Cherokee Nation." Masterson picked up a pencil, began tracing a sketchy map. "Near a bend of the Verdigris, where a couple of old trails cross. You can spot it by a long, low hill the redmen call Gi-Tu-Zi — Place of the People of Light. I understand they held sun dances up there a long time ago. The Frisco goes through the town. There used to be some cattle shipped out before the railroad built its line on the Tulsa, fifteen miles west."

"And what makes you think the Stirrup horses would be there?"

Bat Masterson spread his hands. "Just a guess. Still, it would take a good fence to dispose of that large a haul — and Catoosa has some of the choicest. It's one tough town! The Jameses and the Youngers used to hang out there, but they didn't make much of a dent in it. That whole country is a setup for white outlaws, the nearest Federal court being a hundred miles away at Fort Smith. Things are plenty primitive still, even though the Indians have had twenty years or so to rebuild what was left after Stand Watie and the Ross faction got through fighting it out during the War Between the States.

"As you likely know, war among the Cherokees has a history that reaches clear back to the days of the Removal, with Watie and John Ross jockeying for power in the tribal assemblies, and old Tom Starr and his sons feuding and murdering anybody they didn't happen to like. It's all quieted down now, of course, but it ruined the Cherokees — and it's turned their Nation into a sinkhole for any Border tough who cares to hide out there."

The marshal nodded thoughtfully at what his pencil point had drawn. "Yes, that town would be as good a place as any to begin looking. Though I wouldn't want to ask too many questions. They'd likely keep a close eye on any stranger who might be one of Hangin' Judge Parker's marshals with a warrant in his hat. And wherever the trail led, he could be pretty sure the word would be running ahead of him."

"You figure they're pretty well organized?" asked the Texan.

"You can count on it! There's always one or two, in a bunch of outlaws like that, who'll be tough enough and smart enough to line up the rest and take tribute from them. As a matter of fact — " he hesitated over the incongruity of what he was about to say — "if you can believe the legends, these Indian Nations outlaws have got their boss, all right — a woman! Yes, that's right!" He nodded again, seeing Craddock's unbelieving look. "The white woman who married one of the sons of that old murderer, Tom Starr."

"You must mean Belle Starr!"

"Oh, then I guess you've heard the stories. About Younger's Bend, this hidden stronghold she's supposed to have somewhere along the Canadian, and the gang of horse thieves that take orders from her." Masterson shrugged. "Well, who can say what strange things go on down in that country? Belle was here in town a few months back, with her current lover — a fantastic character who likes to call himself Blue Duck. She's a gun-toter, all right. And she's served at least one prison term for horse stealing. For all I know, maybe there's something in the stories."

Craddock grunted, "What difference? If the trail led to Younger's Bend, or wherever, damned if I wouldn't follow it.

But of one thing I'm pretty sure — it was a man who led the gang that ran off Dumont's horse herd."

Masterson gave him a sharp look. "You saw him?"

"I . . . think so. I don't know for certain." He shook his head, frowning at elusive memories. "I've been trying to decide whether I just imagined it or whether, lying there half-conscious, I actually did see and hear this hombre, sitting his horse right near me and yelling orders at the rest of them."

"What did he look like?"

"His face? Somehow I can't remember that, or much of anything else clearly except — he had a gun in one hand, and it seemed to me there was something wrong about his hands."

"Wrong?"

"I don't really know what I'm trying to tell you! It's all vague, like a dream. It must have been no more than that, and yet it keeps coming back, dimly. The gun and the hand holding it, and something horribly wrong about them both."

He relinquished the struggle with half-memories. "But what's the difference? Here I sit and my money — and the Stirrup horses, too — will have been scattered in a hundred directions before I manage to convince the Dumonts they've got the wrong man, and talk myself out of this jail!"

For a thoughtful moment Bat Masterson said nothing, while he considered the cigar between his fingers. Then, with a sigh of decision, he tossed it away and, rising, walked to the window. He drew the shade on the darkness outside, complete now with the full coming of night. The marshal went then and opened the stove, estimated the height of the flames. Taking some chunks of cottonwood from a box he dropped them into the stove, closed the lid and adjusted the draft.

Mystified, Craddock watched him move around behind the desk, take the comfortable padded chair and bring it out beside the stove, shoving aside one of the hard barrel chairs to make room for it. He placed it precisely. At the desk again he opened a drawer and removed something that glinted in the lamplight. Handcuffs — two sets of them. Deliberately, unhurried, Bat Masterson proceeded to snap one to each of his own wrists.

"Now," he said, "if you'll help with the rest of the details — "

But Craddock could only stare in slow understanding, as the marshal returned to the chair beside the stove and, seating himself, proceeded to snap the free links of the handcuffs, one after the other, to its arms.

The prisoner stumbled to his feet. "What the devil is this?"

"Why, it's supposed to look like a jailbreak. Do you think we can get away with it? I'm afraid it's the best I can manage under the circumstances. But I don't suppose you mind too much leaving town under a cloud, if you can just get on the trail of your money. The word from Texas, when it comes, should eventually clear all the charges against you."

"But what will this do to you? Suppose you're making a mistake, and I did kill that old man? With all the power the Dumonts have — "

The marshal shrugged. "I'll have to take my chances. I got a sound enough reputation, I guess, to survive letting myself be tricked by a desperate criminal. Just once, anyway. It'll be up to you, of course, to see to it you aren't caught a second time."

"You needn't worry about that!"

"I hardly thought so — Your stuff is in that pile on the desk. You'll find a piece of rope in the cabinet yonder to tie my legs with. For a gag, there's the handkerchief out of my pocket — a clean one, I'm glad to say! You can take the horse and saddle from the shed out back. Though I suppose that means I'll have to add another charge — one of horse stealing."

Craddock was at the desk, quickly slinging six-gun and belt around his waist and buckling them, finding confidence in the familiar feel as he setled the holster into place. He folded the crude map Masterson had drawn, pocketed it.

He asked crisply, "How much time have I got?"

"Say, fifteen minutes. That's all I can promise before the night jailer will be coming in. I hope I won't have to sit here much longer than that. Especially if that pesky stove starts smoking."

There was almost feverish haste in Craddock now, but he forced carefulness into his movements. The knots fastening the marshal to his chair must be genuine, the whole appearance of a surprise attack and jailbreak thoroughly convincing. Finally, standing above the lawman with the gag ready to slip into his mouth, Craddock hesitated, hunting speech.

"I never been in debt to any man. I don't think I like it much. If there was only some way — "

"You'll do better to save your talk," Masterson told him gruffly. "You need every minute of time you've got."

Craddock slipped the handkerchief into place and tied it. "That feel all right?"

Getting a grunt and a nod for answer, he turned to the locked door. He pulled the bolt, cracked the heavy panel open to test the early night outside. The street appeared empty. Craddock glanced back at the bound figure, stiff and motionless, sitting beside the crackling stove.

He said, "Well, then — " and couldn't finish it.

Instead, he slipped through into chill, damp darkness and quietly pulled the big door closed.

# IV

SUNLIGHT, glittering from metal pinned to the coat of one of a pair of riders just ahead, struck Owen Craddock's eyes. The next instant, without thinking, he had reined and kicked his weary horse into thick brush that choked the trail. At once he wished he hadn't. In these last two days, hiding and dodging had become instinctive, but surely he was deep enough into the Nations by this time to be beyond the orbit of manhunt.

Nevertheless, having pulled out of the trail he had no choice but to stay hidden until the riders had passed. He watched them through the filtering of leaves. They wore the peaked campaign hats, the blue tunics, tan breeches, and metal badges of the Indian Police. One wore a corporal's stripes on his sleeve.

Craddock caught a glimpse of bronzed, stolid faces and of shoulder-length black braids. Then the two had cantered past and there was silence again in the brush. As he waited until the hoofbeats in the muddy trail had faded, he ran a palm across his jaw and felt the scrape of beard.

The rains that had come to end the summer's long drought seemed over now, leaving a clean blue sky and a world made new and sparkling. Some of the trees already showed the first yellow of the season's decay. A dead leaf came twisting silently down, and through the woods sounded a hushed pattering of ripened nuts. It was as though the chill of fall lay waiting deep within the ground, to climb sluggishly nearer and nearer the surface as time drew on, and finally lay its withering breath over the whole, rain-freshened earth.

In saddle again, following this trail that had brought him
south and eastward across the sparsely settled Indian Territory, Craddock judged he had not a great deal more distance to travel. And in fact, another hour found him out of
the scrub oak timber, and the rolling prairie lay about him.

Old cattle trails began to shape up, hinting at the nearness
of a railroad and of a station which, during its short season,
served as shipping point for Texas herds. Presently he
sighted just ahead, against the horizon, the low, sprawling
hill that was marked on the map Bat Masterson had sketched
for him.

Beyond gleamed the Frisco tracks, spearing in from the
north. A single wide street struck across them, centering an
unlovely scatter of buildings. This, then, would be the village
of Catoosa. Craddock looked the place over from behind
narrowed lids.

Small as were the chances of his running into the men he
was seeking here, it could still be risky riding openly into
such a place when he knew nothing at all about it. Still, he
reasoned that the killers were not apt to remember one face
out of the whole Stirrup crew that they had indiscriminately
slaughtered.

Craddock held back for only a moment. Then, despite a
queasy tightening inside him, he touched steel to his tired
horse and sent him on into the shadow of the barren hill,
across a hollow, up a slanting rise to the railroad right-of-
way.

Cinders spurted under the gray's hoofs, and an iron shoe
clanged on steel as he made the crossing. Near the tracks
stood a depot, and the old cattle pens were falling into ruin
now. The town's score or so of buildings were crudely con-
structed of rough green lumber and logs, many roofed with
sod. Others had false lifts and an occasional awning of wood
or of dirty, sagging canvas.

There were no sidewalks. At intervals down the center of
the wide street stood the inevitable wooden fire barrels filled
with rainwater.

Selling liquor in Indian Territory was, of course, a serious criminal offense. But this apparently laid no hampering restrictions on the village saloons which, along with the brothels and gambling joints, seemed to comprise most of the business houses. Besides these, Craddock saw some stores of poor description, a few private homes, a blacksmith's shop with corral adjoining. Scrubby horses stood here and there, tied to awning posts and hitching rails.

Everything appeared quiet enough.

There was a scattering of Indians in braids and moccasins and cheap homespuns. Of the few whites he saw, he suspected that none had any legal business in the Nations. Some of course would be cowhands, strayed here from the long trail or from one or another of the cattle outfits that ranged on leased graze up on the Cherokee Outlet. But others were of a more sinister cut — whisky runners who brought their illicit rotgut on flatboats up the Arkansas; outlaws and Border toughs.

Himself unshaven, his clothing rumpled and soiled, Craddock thought he probably fitted in well enough to avoid being conspicuous. He dismounted and tied, taking his time about it while he explored the street from beneath a pulled-down hat brim. A tobacconist's sign reminded him he was short of smoking materials, so he stepped across the split-log threshold of the shop. It was a dark cubbyhole, and the scent of the weed was strong.

On a high stool behind the counter, a German of tremendous build was rolling cigars: bunching a wad of fillers, trimming it with the flash of a steel blade, spinning it into the wrapper between broad, swift palms. But when he spat on it to seal the head, Craddock vetoed the idea of buying any of the pile of finished product.

He said instead, "I'll take some rough cut and papers."

The German twisted on his stool to reach them without getting up. He had bulging, sweaty cheeks and an eye that held the stranger with shrewd interest.

Craddock took out his wallet, removed a twenty-dollar gold piece and laid it on the counter. The other shrugged, not touching the bill.

"Is too big," he said with heavy accent. "You got it nothing smaller?"

Craddock set a fingertip on the money. "I'm looking for a horse I lost. A buckskin with one cropped ear. He had a Heart on the left shoulder, a Diamond C on the flank."

There was a heartbeat of silence. The sweaty face did not change expression, but the pale eyes somehow seemed to turn colder. By nothing else did the man show any sign that he had heard the question.

Expressionless, he shoved the money back across the counter. "I got no change for this."

Craddock silently withdrew the coin and dug up silver with which to pay. The cold pale stare was still following him as he went out again into the street.

He thought, *You'll have to do better than this!*

He was somehow certain that the German was a fence. And, should he rouse the suspicions of one such, the word would spread quickly and turn the whole place against him. It was precisely of this, he realized now, that Bat Masterson had tried to warn him, cautioning him against the rash recklessness that could lead him to some blundering move and ruin all of his chances.

Impatience rose high in Craddock. He went back to his horse and took the reins, but he did not jerk the anchoring knot free. After all, this was the only lead he had. If any hope remained of recovering his lost money, he would have to find the way to it here or nowhere. But above everything else he must remember to use caution.

He left the marshal's horse tied where it was and, crossing the expanse of mud, headed for a sprawling building on the corner opposite. Over westward, he noted that the sun was dropping lower toward the barren hill that stood against the sky there.

An Osage buck lay sprawled against the wall of the saloon, sodden and snoring, whisky-smell mingling with his own greasy odors. The same sour tang greeted Craddock as he walked into the barroom. Never much of a drinking man himself, he felt the distasteful quivering of his nostrils. But he went directly to the bar that filled one side of the narrow room and set an elbow on it.

The saloon was a dark and dirty pigsty of a place, its only decoration some pictures of nudes that had been cut out of magazines and nailed around the bare, unplastered walls. One other customer stood at the far end of the counter, idly rolling the bar dice across a felt-covered board while he drank beer out of a bottle.

Craddock ordered a drink, then let it stand while he helped himself to the free lunch. The food was stale but he was hungry enough not to be particular.

He caught the bartender's suspicious eye and motioned him over. "You know anyone interested in a horse trade?" he asked. "I got a bronc I'd as soon not use any longer. A good one. I'd give boot for a fast mount with good bottom."

The look he got was the same closed, cautious stare he had previously encountered at the tobacconist's, across the street. But there was thoughtful appraisal behind it, and Craddock believed he could almost read the busy turning of questions in the other's mind.

"Is there a bill of sale for this animal?"

"Lost it."

Letting this sink in, the man gave his attention to turning the bar rag inside out. "I'll let you know," he grunted finally.

The customer nodded shortly and turned back to his drink. But over the rim of the whisky glass he saw the bartender wiping his way down the counter toward the dice thrower. When Craddock looked again the two had their heads together, leaning across the polished wood in a secret exchange of talk. Their eyes flicked more than once in his direction, and though he pretended to pay no attention Craddock knew a sudden lift of exhilaration.

Presently the dice player set down his leather cup and moved along the bar toward him. Craddock stepped aside to give him room, as he halted at the free lunch and began to build a sandwich with nervous movements.

The man said, without looking at him, "You wanted to get rid of a horse?"

"I said I had one to trade."

This was a distinction the fellow shrugged aside. "Where is it?"

"Out there."

He followed Craddock's glance through the door. They could see Bat Masterson's gray gelding switching its tail in sunlight across the street. It was an animal with few tell-tale markings, a fact that should commend it to a Catoosa horse trader. But this one only grunted and tore off a mouthful of meat and bread.

He was a round-faced, sallow individual, with staring blue eyes and a mustache he had waxed to turn upward at the ends. Coarse, straight hair showed under the brim of the hat set at the back of his round head. He wore an ill-fitting suit, with a gun and belt strapped about his middle. His shirt was buttoned to the throat but he had no tie or collar.

He said, chewing busily, "I got some broncs that might be for sale. Still, I don't know. A horse like that one of yours might not be worth much to me. Where'd you pick him up?"

"Kansas. Western half."

The man ran his tongue about his teeth, wiped his mouth on the inside of a wrist. "You mentioned boot?"

"I said I might be willing. It would depend on what you had to trade."

"Damned fine broncs, I can tell you that much." A decision quickly made, he turned to give instructions to the bartender. "I'm going out with this gent for a while. If Kinney shows up, ask him to wait."

"All right, Blue Duck," the man promised. "I'll do that."

The bizarre name jarred through Craddock as he turned to follow to the door, trying to remember exactly what it was Bat Masterson had told him. He suddenly realized that this must be the man who was Belle Starr's current lover.

They walked outside to where their mounts were tied. The outlaw's was a good-enough-looking sorrel. As he rode over to join Craddock his stare went over the gray, tallying its points, but his only comment was, "Looks gaunted."

"He's been ridden hard," said Craddock. "There's nothing wrong with him outside of that."

Blue Duck grunted and gave the sorrel's ribs a kick. Craddock fell in beside him, and in a moment they had put the dingy village at their backs. Craddock was glad enough to be out of it, though he still kept up a wary caution since he had no trust for the man beside him. He knew that only the hope of picking up some quick money, without having to let a fence in on the deal, had persuaded Blue Duck to lower the bars even by this much.

They rode in silence, following a trail across the rolls of the prairie bottom. The light of the late sun had a golden patina, and shadows were beginning to creep from the hollows. Except for themselves, no one seemed to be abroad.

Presently, at the bosque of the Verdigris, the way dipped. In a swale stood what remained of a brush-roofed dugout. Poplars rose about it, throwing dappled shadows across the remnant of a neglected garden plot and a cedar-pole stock pen where horses were stirring. The roof of the dugout had collapsed and the doorway gaped blackly.

Craddock judged that Blue Duck had simply appropriated this abandoned home site as a place to leave his horses, while he went into town and made contact with a fence. Nevertheless, he asked casually as they descended into the swale:

"Your place?"

The outlaw snorted. "Hell, no! White men can't own Cherokee land. Even an Injun don't call none of it his except the improvements, and those revert back to the tribe once he stops using them — like whoever built this and walked off and left it. Sometimes I figure maybe Virg Hoyt had the right idea."

"Hoyt?" repeated Craddock. "Don't know him. What did he do?"

"Married a Cherokee. It gives a man advantages, Virg says. Puts him under Cherokee law for one thing, which means he can thumb his nose at any Federal marshal he runs across, so long of course as he don't get mixed up in a homicide."

"But that Cherokee law — isn't it pretty rough?"

"Well, that's how I look at it. You know what a damned Injun is! Cherokee Police catch you with just one bronc you can't show title to and it's fifty lashes. A hundred, the second time. Third offense, they shoot you." Blue Duck shook his head. "I don't know. You take your choice which you want to dodge — them, or Hangin' Judge Parker's marshals. I ain't made up my mind for sure, so for the time being Blue Duck stays single." He cast his companion a sideward look. "You got a name?"

Craddock had already considered the matter of an alias and rejected it. His own name was unknown here and therefore safe enough, and never having gone under a false one he disliked the risk of a slip that using it might involve. So he answered truthfully and watched the man's eyes narrow as he tested the name for associations and found none.

Circling the abandoned dugout, they came to a halt before the sagging stock pen. Under the deepening shadow of the poplars a half-dozen nondescript animals milled within the bars. The first glance was enough to convince Craddock these were none of the stolen Stirrup cavvy.

"All prime stock," declared Blue Duck, around the forefinger he had thrust into his mouth to dislodge food from between his teeth. "I'd need a pretty good boot, under the circumstances. Make your choice."

"Well, I — " The words stuck in Craddock's throat. All at once he felt the hammer stroke of the pulse in his forehead, and heat was rising into his face as a shifting of the horses in the pen showed him one that had stood, unnoticed until now, against the far panel.

The buckskin with the cropped ear!

He saw the animal lift its head in his direction, during a long moment. Then it shook its mane and came single-footing gracefully across the pen. Without looking, Craddock could imagine he felt Blue Duck's stare boring into him, holding a sudden suspicion as the buckskin walked up to the fence and silently stretched its long neck across the top bar.

But the outlaw merely said, casually enough, "How about the buckskin, now? There's a sound piece of horseflesh."

"I don't know. Don't look to me he's got the barrel to hold up for any distance under a stock saddle and a rider."

"What the hell you talking about? When have you seen a deeper chest or a likelier set of legs?"

Ignoring the argument, Craddock swung to point out another animal. "Personally, I like the looks of this roan."

It was at this precise moment that a voice spoke somewhere behind them.

"All right, Blue Duck!"

Both turned their heads with a start as a rider came edging out of the leaf shadows. He crossed a shaft of slanting light. In his hand the barrel of a carbine flashed and was answered by the deputy marshal's badge pinned to his shirtfront.

"Stay just the way you are!" he ordered, his voice dangerous in the stillness. "Keep your hands in sight!"

A cry was wrung from the outlaw. Recklessly he jerked the sorrel about — only to confront another rider closing in on him from that direction. Too late, Blue Duck saw the shape of the trap, that there was no escape. And it turned him in cold, mistaken fury on the man beside him.

"Why, damn you, I should of guessed — "

A gun was in his hand. As Craddock saw its barrel lifting he knew he hadn't time to clear his own weapon, and there was no hope of the lawmen intervening. He staked everything on a quick and desperate grab across the space that separated their horses. His hand found the barrel of the gun and he twisted it violently aside.

It went off. Craddock felt the jolting rush of the explosion, but the bullet ripped harmlessly into branches overhead. And in that moment, he managed to wrest the six-shooter from Blue Duck's hand and throw it on the ground.

By that time, the Federal men were upon them. Blue Duck subsided under the menace of their leveled guns.

# V

THE deputies were hard-eyed, bronzed men whose mouths showed no tolerance of lawbreakers. The one who had first spoken turned and called across a shoulder:

"You can come on down now, Standing Bear. Claim your property."

Craddock, steadying his mount, turned to look. As two more horsemen rode out of the brush, he did not fail to catch the sudden strangled sound that broke from Blue Duck. One of the approaching riders was a Cherokee — a solid figure who dwarfed the white man beside him. But it was this white, Craddock thought, who had drawn the outlaw's startled exclamation. He was a puny-looking creature with a narrow chest and a face burnt brick-red beneath the brim of a hat that appeared to be too large for him.

Standing Bear, the Cherokee, had drawn rein and with a thrusting finger he pointed out four horses in the corral.

"Them are the ones was stole from my feed pen."

"Absolutely sure, are you?"

"I know my own horses."

The officer lifted his shoulders, a satisfied look on him. "There you are, Blue Duck! The judge has been waiting for a clear case against you, ever since you beat that murder charge two years ago. Looks like we finally got what we want."

"We'll see!" cried the outlaw. "By hell, we'll see all right!" He was almost incoherent with rage as he turned on Standing Bear's white companion. "You, Rufe Sago! For turning me in, I'll —"

"That'll be enough!" snapped the lawman.

Sago's nervous grin broadened when he saw that Blue Duck was going to be kept away from him. At least, Craddock was thinking, Blue Duck seemed to have corrected his first erroneous suspicions. One glance at Rufe Sago must have been enough to settle in his mind who had betrayed him.

The deputy was regarding Craddock with a cold scrutiny. "Who are you?" he demanded. "How do you figure in this?"

"I don't," Craddock told him. "I rode from town to look over some horses. I didn't know who they belonged to, never even saw this fellow —" he indicated Blue Duck with a jerk of the head — "up to an hour ago."

Plainly disbelieving, the lawman turned to Sago. "What about it?"

The informer met Craddock's look uneasily. He reached a hand inside his open shirt collar to scratch at a red-burnt throat.

"Reckon it could be so," he muttered. "Blue Duck was alone when I watched him putting them broncs in the pen. Of course I didn't stay around. They looked like Standing Bear's hosses and I wanted to get word to him."

Blue Duck's voice had sunk to a bitter rasp. "You wait!" he told Sago. "I'll have your hide, damn you! They can't hold me! Sooner or later —"

The deputy said impatiently to his companion, "Let's start moving. We'll need the horses and Standing Bear's testimony."

"What about the rest of the broncs?"

"Those, too. Hell, they were all stolen from one place or another. Maybe there's warrants out on them."

He had put away his gun. Handcuffs came clinking from a hip pocket as he kneed his horse closer to Blue Duck's.

The horse thief tried to balk but it was useless. The lawman made short work of seizing his wrists one after the other and clicking the steel into place. Blue Duck looked at the cuffs, and his mouth began trembling under the points of his waxed mustache.

"I want to send a message. You got to let me do that much!"

The deputies exchanged looks. "To Belle Starr?" one said flatly. "Nothing doing! This is one time you don't take that harridan into court with you to get you off free!"

"But I tell you — "

Blue Duck subsided into sullen despair. He swung a look around at the faces of his captors, then at Craddock's. It clung there a moment. And slowly, slightly, Craddock nodded.

That was all, yet it seemed enough to pacify Blue Duck and to iron some of the anguish out of him. He settled back into saddle, in apparent resignation. But at the promise he had read in Craddock's nod, a renewed confidence was already building in his face.

No one appeared to have any further interest in Craddock, to his relief. He watched without comment as the Cherokee and the Federal men dropped the bars of the pen, ran the horses out of it and got them bunched and moving. He sat his saddle for minutes after the cavalcade had vanished into the bosque, with Blue Duck's reins anchored to the pommel of one of the deputies.

Glancing down, he saw the prisoner's six-gun where it lay in the leaf mold, forgotten. He swung to earth, got it, and put it in a pocket of his coat. Then he looked about for Rufe Sago. The informer was walking his horse toward the rise that led to the town trail.

He called sharply, "Just a minute, you!" and started after him, leading the gray.

Sago hauled rein, peering back. His red-burnt face, under the floppy hat, held puzzlement, then perhaps the beginning of fear as Craddock told him, "Come down. I want to talk to you." When the man failed to move Craddock simply reached and grabbed him by his clothing and without effort hauled him from the saddle. "I said come down!"

The man hit the earth. He lost his balance and staggered so that Craddock had to steady him. Still holding him pinioned by a tight handful of shirtfront, Craddock said:

"Now I want to know the truth!"

"Let go!" cried Sago, writhing helplessly. "I got nothing to do with you!"

"I'll decide that. You just answer questions."

"But you already heard all I told them marshals!"

"I heard a mess of lies. I have an idea you stole them broncs from Standing Bear yourself!"

"No!"

"And then Blue Duck took them away from you, and you didn't have the guts to try and get them back again. So you just turned the law on him. Is that about the way it happened?"

"You go straight to — "

Craddock's palm swung up and smacked the man's narrow jowls, right and left. Moisture came off on his fingers. Rufe Sago turned limp at the knees, eyes glazing. From him issued the sour odor of sweat and fear.

"What the hell is it to you?" he whined. "I heard you say you never even seen Blue Duck before!"

Craddock's hand was poised for another blow and the man cringed away from it, eyelids fluttering.

"I asked you a question. Is that the way it happened or isn't it?"

Sago's mouth worked. He tried to speak but could only stammer. He managed a nod instead, jerkily.

Craddock dropped his hand. "And how about the ones you didn't get from Standing Bear? That buckskin. What did you do with the saddle off of him and the gear?"

Whatever reaction he had expected, all he got was an empty stare, a quick babbling protest. "But that one I never stole, I swear it! I found him."

"Where?"

"Running loose on the prairie. He had a headstall but nothing else — no saddle. No way of telling who he belonged to, so I just picked him up. Nothing wrong with that, is there?" His voice was growing louder with injured virtue. "What the hell, a man finds a horse running loose, I reckon he has a right to — "

Rufe Sago faltered, as though smothered by quick terror of what he saw in Craddock's face. But actually the Texan's thoughts were far from him just then. For somehow Sago's hysterical babbling had the ring of truth, and the realization sank a numbing shaft through Craddock.

If he could believe this, then any hope he'd held of getting back his saddlebags and their contents seemed to go glimmering. Even finding the buckskin meant nothing. It could lead him nowhere, since neither Rufe Sago nor Blue Duck had the money.

A deep and angry bitterness filled him. And in that moment Sago must have felt a laxness in the grip that held him, for he made his bid for liberty.

When a knee came up hard into Craddock's groin he doubled over in a rushing agony. His hands fell away from his captive and Sago backed off, free. Before Craddock, sick with nausea, could make any effort to recover, the sharp toe of a boot swung against his head. It found his temple, dropped him face downward to the loamy earth.

Not unconscious, he was dimly aware of what happened, of Rufe Sago's cursing his startled horse as he scrambled astride. Then Sago was spurring up the bank toward the town road in panic. The pulse of hoofbeats that the ground carried to Craddock gradually subsided to a tremor and was gone.

He lay there in the stillness beside the abandoned dugout. For a long time he made no effort at all to move. Retching shook him, left its miserable aftertaste. The whole side of his head throbbed from the kick of Sago's boot. But nearby the river murmured, rain-swollen, and he got up finally, stumbling over to it, and flung himself prone upon the bank.

The water was muddy and foul but he dipped it with his hands and drenched his head to clear his fogged senses. There was some blood where his scalp had been torn. He washed this carefully. As lagging strength returned under the cold dash of the water he rose again, steadier now. He went to where his hat had fallen, picked it up, knocked shape into it and put it on.

Now what?

Bat Masterson's gray stood waiting, pulling at the grass. Eying it Craddock wondered if the moment hadn't come to accept defeat, before he wasted more time and strength on a thing that looked hopeless. He had to credit Rufe Sago's story of finding the buckskin without saddle, bags or gear. Which meant that almost anything could have happened to them.

During the shooting and confusion of the raid, he supposed, the horse must have bolted and wandered free for miles. The saddle, insecurely cinched, could have dropped from its back anywhere on the limitless prairie. Or perhaps someone had caught the horse and stripped off the saddle.

Either way, he might as well admit that the contents of the saddlebags were gone for good. He might as well ride on to Texas and begin the slow, heartbreaking business of starting over from nothing.

And what about Cass Dumont's murderers, the men who had stolen the fine Stirrup horses? The image of Vinnie Dumont's grief-stricken face rose before him and he put it angrily away. Was that his concern, and would there be any thanks coming to him for making it so? There was as little chance of recovering the Stirrup stock as there was of getting back his lost money or, for that matter, of bringing life back into the slaughtered Dumont crew.

The pain in him was a good deal lessened now. Craddock lifted the gray's stirrup fender, undid the latigo and tightened it to a fresh knot. His hand was on the pommel to lift himself up when the reaction hit him.

Be damned to logic! There was still a chance. What if the raiders themselves, having discovered what the buckskin's saddlebags held, had decided to turn the mount loose figuring that with its markings, the animal could be too easy to trace, too dangerous even to have around? It was a slim possibility, but as long as any hope remained at all —

He felt better at once. Perhaps a part of his physical illness had been revulsion against the thought of quitting. Head instantly clearer, the nausea gone, he swung to saddle.

And when he spurred the gray, it was to head into the trail leading back toward Catoosa.

The road was empty. The grouping of hoofprints in mud showed that Rufe Sago, coming this way before him, had held to a wild gallop that had slackened only a little as panic left him. When Craddock once more picked up the cluttered buildings of the village he found them in shadow, a spray of gleaming sunset fanning up behind the blackly etched hill low against the western skyline.

An engine, hauling a short string of freight cars and a single coach, was just pulling from sight along the Frisco tracks. The throb of its drive wheels died and the plume of trailing smoke dissolved in golden wisps where sunset touched it. A few lights showed in town, though dusk was still some minutes away.

Almost the first thing Craddock sighted, riding into town, was Rufe Sago's lathered horse racked in front of the saloon where he had met Blue Duck. Quickly he swung down and tied. He stood under the awning a moment searching the dusky street before he turned and shouldered inside.

A couple of smoky lamps made the saloon even more murky and dismal than it had seemed by daylight. Trade had picked up, however. Craddock cast a glance at the men he saw at the bar and around the scattered, round-topped tables, and quickly found the face he was looking for.

A side door opened onto a shadow-filled alley. At a table near it, a man had scrambled hastily to his feet, his knee catching the table leg and jarring it with a screech across the floor boards. A half-filled glass, overturning, rolled from side to side leaking a dribble of spilled whisky. The man was Rufe Sago. There was only this glimpse of him, and then he was bolting frantically toward that handy side entrance.

Craddock let out a shout that brought every eye upon him. Shaking his gun from its holster into his hand, he crossed that room in a few quick strides. He slipped through the open door and swiftly placed his back against the rough outer wall beside it.

Half-dried mud made a poor sounding board for running feet, and for a time he was completely confused, trying to decide which direction Sago had taken. Then, at the rear of this shadowed narrow space between buildings, there was a sharp splintering sound as a boot struck against an empty bottle and sent it crashing into a wall.

Craddock pushed away from the clapboards and started toward the sound. A high fence blocked the end of the alley. He heard the thud and scrape of a man hurling himself at it and scrambling over. He had a brief look at the fugitive silhouetted on the top of it before Sago dropped from sight.

In seconds Craddock reached the fence and hauled himself up, to hang straddling it while he searched the space beyond. There was brush and the backs of adjoining buildings. But there was no sign of Rufe Sago at all, and no way of telling where he had gone into hiding.

Craddock was not foolish enough to go looking blindly for him and invite a shot from the shadows. Reluctantly he dropped down off the fence and shoved his gun again into holster. He waited a moment longer, thinking some sound from beyond the fence might betray Sago to him, but the man was too wary and not that easily smoked out.

So he turned and walked back through the alley. Re-entering the bar, he passed through a sudden dead silence to lay a hand upon the edge of the counter.

The same bartender was on duty. He met Craddock's eye with a guarded, narrow look.

"Your friend Blue Duck is in trouble," Craddock told him in a voice he made no effort to keep down. "That lobo I just chased out of here had a couple of marshals laying in wait for him, and they picked him up and started him off to jail at Fort Smith." When he got no answer he went on, "I promised Blue Duck I'd send a call for help down to Younger's Bend. You know anyone who'd oblige me?"

Even as he spoke it occurred to him that these men might all be better friends of Sago's than of the man Sago had betrayed, which could mean he was talking himself into a bad situation. For a moment he thought the bartender did not intend to answer. The man sent his stare over the faces of the listening men, brought it back to Craddock. At last he said, reluctantly:

"There's Jim July. He's in town some place. He might go."

"How would I know him?"

"He's an Indian. Good-looking young buck."

Craddock grimaced. "These Cherokees all look alike to me. Well, thanks — I'll look around. If you see this July, tell him about Blue Duck. And if Sago comes back, let him know I'm hunting for his hide!"

There was no answer. Craddock turned, walked outside and paused beneath the canvas awning.

In theory it should not be hard to locate someone in a village of this size. Actually, for a stranger to go poking about the cribs and deadfalls of Catoosa would be the worst sort of folly. As he weighed his next move, the old, characteristic impatience at anything blocking his path began to have its way with him.

Another saloon attracted his notice, across the way and just beyond a weed-grown space that separated the darkened general store of Reynolds and Company from its neighbors. The racket of a tinny piano came from there, joining the medley of raucous sounds that seemed to swell louder momently as night drew in upon Catoosa.

Craddock chose this saloon for his next stop. He left the shadow of the arcade and went at an angle across the muddy, hoof-churned street.

It was not entirely dark yet. With the fading of sunset the sky had tempered to a sheet of steel. It would hang like that above the land for some moments of deceptive half-light, then the last of the glow would drain out of the sky, the stars would pinpoint it, and night would rush down to smother the earth. In this moment poised between night and day, the crunch of Craddock's boots seemed alarmingly sharp and clear. Every sound was magnified, every shape and outline keen-edged, yet a little distorted, a little unreal.

But there was nothing unreal in the gunshot that all at once slapped along this street, or in the bullet that split the air a foot from Craddock's body.

## VI

CAUGHT so, trapped in the very middle of that open space, Craddock halted while his glance searched and quickly located the origin of the shot. It had been fired by one of two men he saw on the shadowed veranda of the Reynolds store. A single glimpse was enough to give him the picture.

Rufe Sago, it appeared, had recruited a champion for himself. The big man standing next to him had fired, for smoke trailed from the mouth of his six-gun. His face, under the shadow of a wide-brimmed hat, was not distinct in that half-dusk. But everything about his stance and the set of the gun in his hand indicated that he meant to make a second try, the first having missed.

The nearest cover was one of the wooden fire barrels in the center of the street. Craddock made a lunge for it. He dropped into its meager protection, somehow managing to beat out the shot. It shocked through the echoes of the first one, but the bullet was lost somewhere above his head. And as Craddock shook his own Colt loose from the holster, he could hear Rufe Sago screaming:

"Oh, damn you! Kill him — kill him!"

There was the beginning of cold, nervous sweat on Craddock's body, and his hand felt slippery squeezing the six-gun's butt plates. Yet his principal emotion was less that of fear

than of a harsh and uncompromising anger as, with mouth
drawn hard at the corners, he quickly reared and fired across
the barrel's wooden cover.

He did not hit either of the men on the store veranda. Yet
he came so close that they broke away in violent haste, the
big one stepping backward against the wall where he made
a poorer target, Rufe Sago hurling himself prone to the
boards of the floor. The next instant Craddock felt and heard
the solid chunking of lead strike the barrel which shielded
him.

The barrel was well filled after recent rains. The head of
water within it killed the bullet's force so that it was spent
before it could reach the opposite staves. But a trickle of
water began spilling and gurgling from the hole the bullet
had made.

Along the street, Craddock could hear the town's reaction
to this outbreak of violence. Men were crowding at doors and
windows, shouting hoarse questions. A woman's voice could
be heard making the same exclamation over and over, with
hysterical monotony. And another near bullet decided Craddock it was time to settle this business.

He came to his feet and started forward, shooting once
as he went. He reached a building corner, and in the open
space beyond wet weeds whipped at his boot tops. He circled wide into the vacant lot, to put himself out of line of
the store front while he was moving into close range.

And suddenly, at the store corner, his antagonists faced
him across a distance of a mere dozen feet. The big man had
left the wall and run out to the veranda railing where he
stood with one hand gripping a support post, the other
holding his gun. For what seemed a timeless instant these
two who had never faced one another before, who had no
personal quarrel, shared a direct and searching stare. Then
the big man remembered to fire, but Craddock's reflexes had
kicked the trigger back a second sooner.

He saw the big fellow sent back hard. His body weight
seemed suddenly to drag him earthward. His head fell forward, he bent at waist and knee, his gun arm sagged so

that the discharge of his own weapon went harmlessly into the ground. But his other hand kept its grip on the post. When he fell it was a last convulsive contraction of this arm that pulled him onto the rail and across it, and sent him toppling slowly to strike the dirt on the flat of his back with lifeless arms and legs thrown wide.

This left Rufe Sago exposed, still lying prone upon the veranda floor. With head raised he showed Craddock a face wet with sweat and twisted by utter terror.

"Sago!" Craddock ordered sharply. "Do you hear me? Throw away your gun! I aim to get a confession out of you!" Instead, the man had begun scrambling backward in a frantic crawl, belly-flat. And when he came against a post of the veranda which stopped him, the look of a trapped animal was in his eyes as he began firing wildly.

Craddock had tried to avoid killing the man. But his only payment was the sudden hot stab of pain as a bullet creased his left forearm. He fired through the wide-spaced pickets of the veranda and saw Rufe Sago's body contract like that of a stepped-on spider. The gun thudded from Sago's hand to the flooring, and that was the end of it.

Slowly Craddock moved forward to the body that lay in the dust, stooped long enough to make certain that no life remained. He went on to where Rufe Sago sprawled at the edge of the veranda. He did not have to look closely, even in the thickening dusk, to see the work his bullet had done. He lifted a stare toward the shadowy figures of men who watched in silence.

"Is there anyone else?" Craddock demanded harshly. "He was a yellow dog. He didn't have the guts to settle his own score. He sent Federal men after Blue Duck and set this other one, a man I never saw before, to take care of me. If there's any other friend of Sago's wants to pick it up, then let him do it now instead of laying for me in some alley!"

He waited again, feeling the constraint of hard will that made him stand and make this challenge. Finally, as it passed unmet, he eased the trapped air from his lungs, returned the gun to holster.

"All right!" he grunted. "Now maybe one of you can tell me where I'll find a man named Jim July."

"That's me."

A tall man detached himself from the group in the saloon doorway. Light from inside showed his face — the broad, roughly-chiseled bronze of an Indian. As Craddock walked over to meet him he sensed the cautious reserve in the man.

He said, "Somebody told me you're a friend of Blue Duck's, that you'd be willing to do him a favor."

"I might," the Cherokee answered carefully. "What's this I hear you say about the Federals?"

But a slight wave of giddiness had washed through Craddock, induced by the aftermath of danger and the pain of his arm. Because he needed its strengthening, he said:

"Let's have a drink, first!"

This saloon was bigger than the one across the street. It had an adequate display of gambling devices, and its bar was a gaudy piece of furniture, with a mirror that must have been a difficult job to haul in from Fort Smith or some other river port. But beneath its garish surface lay a vicious tawdriness that the glare of oil lamps and the mechanical pounding of the nickelodeon did nothing to disguise.

Jim July said as they walked in, "You been hit!"

Craddock looked down at his arm. The sleeve was soaked, and a warm red thread of blood trickled across the back of the hand and dripped from the knuckles.

He said gruffly, "Sago burned me a little. Get a bottle and glasses, will you?"

He indicated an unused card table with a jerk of his head. The Cherokee nodded and headed for the bar. Craddock walked to the table, pulled out a chair, dropped his hat onto the table as he slacked into the chair and unbuttoned the shirt sleeve, carefully rolled it back.

Fortunately the bullet scratch along his forearm could have been much more serious as well as more painful. The slow oozing of blood had already nearly ceased. His shirt was ruined but except for a sore arm he had little other ill effects to reckon with.

When Jim July came from the bar with liquor and glasses, Craddock was trying awkwardly, one-handed, to wrap a handkerchief about his arm. He let this job go while he poured a drink and downed it in a quick toss, waiting for the jolt to work its way through him and clear his senses. The Indian seated himself opposite, watching in silence. He was a young fellow, in his twenties, with a look of guarded intelligence in his smoky eyes. He studied Craddock carefully and thoroughly.

No one approached this table, though Craddock caught the open stares of men who had drifted back inside the building after the shooting. He thought he recognized in them a grudging respect, and once through the other talk he heard some words of comment, "That Rufe Sago didn't count for nothing, but Bland Colvin, now there sure was a hell of a fast — "

Suddenly it occurred to him that he had simply walked away from the bodies of his victims without a second glance. He shrugged. Let someone else have the grisly chore of disposing of them. A seeming disregard for killing was most likely a help to him, in this dangerous role he had undertaken.

"I want to get to Younger's Bend," he announced flatly, watching the Cherokee's eyes. "And I don't know how. Somebody said you could show me."

Jim July's only answer was a grunt, deep within his chest. In his expression was no change.

"Of course, if you don't care what happens to your friend Blue Duck — "

"What about him?"

"He's on his way to Fort Smith with a pair of Federal marshals and the horses he lifted from Rufe Sago. If I could have taken Sago and made him talk I would have been able to clear Blue Duck. But now that that's out of the question, I want to get help for him."

The Cherokee considered this. "A long ride to the Bend," he finally said. "Better we go after them. We take Blue Duck away from a couple of marshals easy."

Craddock knew a quick alarm. This was a suggestion he

hadn't anticipated, and July was plainly in earnest about it. Apparently, murdering a couple of officers concerned the Cherokee not at all. But Craddock, appalled, had to find an excuse to stop him somehow.

"They've already had a long start on us."

July was blandly confident. "Oh, we catch up with them once they make camp." He nodded, liking his thoughts. The coarse black hair, chopped off at shoulder length, gleamed dully in the light from the wagon-wheel chandeliers overhead. "I get some of the boys together. We take care of this."

Craddock reached for the bottle, hand trembling a little despite the best effort he could make to steady it. His mind, groping for argument, found only a blank as he heard the screech of the Indian's chair being pushed back in rising.

At that very moment a hard-ridden horse was pulled to a stand in the dark outside. Quick boots struck the wide steps. One of the saloon crowd sang out coarsely:

"Hey! Look at this! Here's Belle!"

Craddock jerked around, his hand almost upsetting the whisky bottle. A woman slapped open the swinging half-doors and entered in a stride that was unhampered by a divided riding skirt.

She was only medium tall, but with the well-developed figure of a woman in her middle thirties. The swell of her breasts and hips was accented by the white chiffon waist and tight black jacket she wore. On her dark hair was a man's stetson, with its wide brim rolled back and an ostrich plume thrust into the black plush band. About her waist was slung a cartridge belt and holster, with a full-size Colt pistol snugged against her thigh.

She was acclaimed with loud greetings to which she returned only a careless, unattending shake of head. Obviously a more important matter was on her mind. She paused to send a restless black-eyed stare probing about the room. The next minute she was heading, with her swift, wide-pacing swagger, directly toward Craddock and Jim July.

Courtesy might have brought Craddock to his feet, but Belle Starr's way was too direct to invite such refinement of manners. Before he could move she was already standing before them, knuckles on hips. Her quick stare encompassed Jim July, then darted to the stranger's face.

"I guess you're the man," she said. "I no sooner hit town than I hear that some stranger has killed Rufe Sago and Bland Colvin, and that he says he wants to get to Younger's Bend — likely to see me about something, I reckon. They tell me the law has Blue Duck."

Craddock nodded. "That's how it is. If you're Belle Starr, then I promised I'd see that you heard the details. Not in so many words, of course, but — "

"Well, I'm ready to listen!"

She pulled a chair out for herself and dropped into it without grace, crossing spurred riding boots. She reached for a glass and poured whisky from the bottle with practiced ease, but let the drink stand at her elbow.

She said again, "Well?"

In a few words he told her of Blue Duck's capture by Federal officers. As she listened Belle picked up the whisky she had poured and drank about half of it. Her keen black eyes never left Craddock's face. She was no beauty — rather coarsely plain than otherwise, with a mouth that tended to sternness. But no man could have denied the compelling intelligence in her sharp black eyes.

"The horses," she interrupted impatiently. "The ones that didn't come out of Standing Bear's feed pen — what did they look like? Pretty good stock, were they? Notice any fresh brands?"

Craddock shook his head. "Far as I could see, they were nothing but scrubs." He watched a look pass between Belle and Jim July, a look he interpreted as plain relief.

"I guess it's all right, Belle," the Indian muttered. "I was thinking Virgil Hoyt might have given Sago some of that Stirrup stuff to handle — "

The sting of excitement that shocked through Craddock was almost more than he could keep from turning into a physical trembling. At last he had his tie-in!

Virgil Hoyt. Where had he come across that name? He

remembered then that it was one Blue Duck had mentioned.

Suddenly he found Belle's stare pinned on him. He read suspicion in it. "I'm a little curious about you, mister. Who are you? What caused you to buy into this trouble of Blue Duck's?"

He knew just how dangerous a question this was. On the answer might rest the success or failure of his whole attempt to work deep into the pattern of Indian Territory outlawry.

"My name's Craddock," he said coolly. "Likely a new one to you. A little better known up around the Dakotas. I've had a long trail down here, and it was no pleasure running into a pair of Federal marshals at the end of it. I don't like the breed. Nor do I like the kind of a man who would sell another out to them!"

He thought she appeared satisfied. Her attention shifted suddenly to his wounded forearm, that he had kept unobtrusively in his lap. "What have you got there?"

He lifted the arm for an indifferent look. "I should have shot faster. Sago got one over too quick for me."

"Let's see."

"It's nothing."

But when Belle's mouth showed beginning impatience, he shrugged and placed his arm on the table. She gave a grunt of disapproval at the awkward job of bandaging he had done.

"That ain't no way to treat a bullet scratch, even if it don't amount to much. Hey, Aprons!" she yelled over her shoulder, above the racket of the saloon. "You got a clean towel or something?"

The bartender said, "Coming up, Belle."

"Go fetch it," she ordered Jim July.

As he left the table, Belle was rolling Craddock's bloodstained sleeve higher, out of her way. As she leaned toward him, one of her breasts pressed by chance against the back of his hand. He would have drawn back if he could, but Belle seemed unconscious of the contact or at least not embarrassed by it.

"Always pays to be careful with any kind of gunshot," she was saying. She had unwrapped the handkerchief and shook her head over the shallow bullet groove. "That better be cleaned out." She dipped a corner of Craddock's handkerchief into her whisky glass. "As good as anything," she explained. "I ought to know what's in it — it come out of my own still!"

The raw stuff burnt like fury, but Craddock maintained his silence while she dabbed the bullet wound to suit herself. She took the cloth Jim July brought, ripped it and made a deft bandaging job. By the time she finished, a considerable ring of men had left their drinks and their poker playing to watch.

"Thanks," Craddock told her finally, moving and twisting the arm, flexing his fingers and feeling the stretch and sting of the hurt. "That ought to take care of it."

"Get yourself a clean shirt. Looks like there's blood in your hair, too."

He fingered his scalp above his ear. "I got kicked. More of Rufe Sago's doings. It's nothing."

He did not want this woman working over him. His hand still retained its impression of that brief contact; he found it vaguely disturbing.

Jim July had been drinking alone. Craddock did not know how many jolts of the cheap moonshine brew the Cherokee had poured into himself, but suddenly he struck the table top with his fist, a blow that set the whisky glasses leaping.

"Don't we do anything about Blue Duck?" he demanded harshly. "We let them marshals tote him to court? They got a long lead, but the horses will slow them down. And they have to make camp somewhere."

Belle Starr shook her head firmly. "It ain't my way of doing things. We'll ride on in to Fort Smith ourselves. They can't bring him into court before Monday, and then it'll be no more than to arraign him in front of the judge and set bond. I'll raise that fast enough."

"But there'll be a trial. Hangin' Judge Parker will go plenty hard on him."

"I can make a monkey out of Parker. Nothing I like better after the year he gave me weaving chair bottoms in the Detroit pen. I ain't entirely through settling for that. We'll leave in the morning!"

Craddock had held a quick, silent debate with himself. He didn't at all like the idea of showing himself in Fort Smith where warrants bearing his description must already be in circulation. But he could not relinquish such a hard-won gain as this.

He said, "I'll ride with you if it's all right. I buy into a thing, I like to see the finish of it."

There was a silence. Belle and the young Cherokee looked at him, holding him in a long scrutiny that touched him with the cold thought that he had overplayed his hand.

It was the woman who finally said, "That's a two-day jaunt to take for nothing."

He shrugged. "I've nothing better to do. There's a horse that has to be got rid of — I was about to make a deal with Blue Duck when we run into the law. Once that's taken care of, I'm pretty much at loose ends."

"Yeah?" He could see a slow interest building in her eyes. This man, this stranger who had ridden in from nowhere and killed a pair as dangerous as Sago and Brand Colvin might be someone worth keeping in sight. But all she said was, "Suit yourself. As for the bronc, tomorrow I can get you your pick of a score of good ones. It's a matter of knowing who to deal with."

"Thanks." Craddock pushed back his chair and rose, getting his hat. Holding it, he looked down at the woman. "And for fixing up the arm."

"Forget it."

He felt her look follow him as he walked from the room. But even as the door swung to behind him, he could hear her boisterous shout of, "Who's interested in a hand of show-down poker?" and the quick response of half a dozen male voices.

The bodies of the men Craddock had killed had been removed and he tried to avoid looking at the place of the shooting as he passed it. The gray still stood where it had been left. Craddock untied and rode around to a public stable, where he put the horse into a stall. The stableman let him have a basin of water to wash off some of his blood and grime. He would have to wait until tomorrow to buy a new shirt.

Just now he was exhausted from days of grueling saddle work, and nearly starved. A meal and a night's sleep, if he could find accommodations, would take care of that. Underneath was satisfaction in what he had already accomplished. He felt that he was beginning to get somewhere at last.

Heading back upstreet, hunting a place to eat, he heard raucous singing inside the saloon he had left and the pounding of the piano. He stopped a moment to look in.

A circle of tough-looking men were crowded around the old out-of-tune music box that had cracked keys. and one broken leg raised on a chunk of wood. Belle, on the piano stool, was beating out an accompaniment to a bawdy saloon ballad, her shrill soprano lifting above the rest of the voices. The ostrich plume bobbed grotesquely above her head.

## VII

ACROSS from the remodeled army barracks that housed the Federal Court of Western Arkansas stood a gruesome stout-timbered structure. It held Craddock's attention as he and Jim July rode up through morning sunshine. The Cherokee caught his look.

"Room for twelve on that gallows."

Craddock had heard the stories. Now the actual sight of the thing filled him with a kind of fascinated revulsion.

He asked, "They actually do have hangings in such job lots?"

"Six at one time, I know for sure. They say twenty-one men in a day. But I'm not around to see that."

They swung down and tied their horses, and it gave Craddock a certain grim amusement to reflect that it was a stolen mount — the roan gelding, acquired with Belle Starr's help before they left Catoosa — that he left at the hitching-pole directly opposite the jail. He had chosen the animal carefully, in order to get one of neutral markings that would be difficult for even a former owner to recognize.

His face he could not disguise. But however many warrants might be out for him, and whatever sum the Dumonts might have placed on his head, he thought no one was likely to think of finding him here in Fort Smith — in Judge Parker's own courtroom.

He said, "No sign of Belle."

"She be along. She's got lawyers and bondsmen to look up this morning. We go on in."

Craddock and Jim July picked their way across the drying mud through busy traffic. Fort Smith was booming, as the wooded hills and fertile valleys here at the edge of the Indian Nations filled with an influx of farmers. The population was well on its way to tripling within a ten-year period, and the crisp September morning was busy with the song of hammer and saw.

But none of this pulse of activity reached within the dark and musty room where District Court was now in session. They let themselves in and took places unobtrusively on one of the hard benches at the rear. The jury box was empty, a handful of idlers the only other spectators. No trial appeared to be in progress. Instead, Judge Ike Parker was cleaning up various odds and ends of judicial business.

He appeared almost dwarfed by the tall desk before him, the black leather chair that nearly engulfed his slight figure. Craddock saw a man not yet fifty, his beard just tinged with the first gray of advancing age. He sat with steepled hands propped before him, lower lip pinched between extended forefingers as he listened thoughtfully to the lawyers grouped about his bench. He looked, Craddock thought, more like a seedy schoolmaster than the blood-thirsty hanging judge whose black shadow stretched far across the wild territories westward.

But he it was whose two hundred appointed deputy marshals carried such white man's law as was ever seen in the Indian lands. Before this bar, in ten years, had paraded hundreds of the worst criminals who ran wild along the frontier. Scores of times, from this box, juries handpicked by the judge himself had pronounced the verdict, "Guilty as charged." A verdict from which there was virtually no appeal, and which almost never brought any other sentence than death on the mammoth gallows across the street.

The drone of voices ran on. A couple of attorneys were protesting something to the judge apparently, arguing with the prosecution officials. Parker let them talk, listening behind the droop of half-closed eyelids. But as the undistinguished drone built to a sudden climax, the bearded head lifted and Parker's sharp rejoinder came.

"Motion denied!"

"But Your Honor — "

The gavel was in the jurist's hand instantly, falling with a sharp finality.

"May I remind the attorney that if he wishes to be debarred from this court, all he has to do is continue contradicting me?"

In the sudden quiet, the words stung. The rebuked lawyer turned stone white, then slowly reddened to the ears, but he made no further protest. Judge Parker waited, head cocked sideward. Finally satisfied, he nodded and his bearded lips quirked into a thin smile that he quickly ironed out.

"That's better!" he said. "The prisoner has already been tried and found guilty, and your arguments are entirely out of place. It remains only to pass sentence. John Eagle!"

An Indian in the dock lifted his head. Craddock thought he could see the stiffening set of his shoulders, as against an expected blow.

"You probably know the penalty this court exacts for the crime of murder. Critics have accused this court of undue severity. If they had ever for one day shouldered its responsibilities, their easy carpings might sound a little different to them. John Eagle, you are hereby remanded to the custody of Deputy Marshal Maledon. You will return to your cell, on October fifteenth next to be conducted to the gallows and there hanged by the neck until you are dead. And may God have mercy on your soul!"

The gavel crashed again, a grim punctuation to the solemn ritual. Craddock saw the prisoner's body sag.

"Next case!" rapped the judge.

A whiskered skeleton of a man moved forward, placed a hand on the shoulder of the condemned man. "Come along," said George Maledon, the hangman.

With the efficiency of a stage set being shifted, the grouping at the bar changed. As John Eagle was led away through a door to the jail and his angry lawyers moved, scowling, up the aisle and out of the courtroom, a clerk stepped forward and laid a folder of papers before the judge. The brief stir of talk that ran through the few spectators quieted again as a new prisoner was marched through the narrow doorway, in the custody of a deputy marshal, and placed before the bar.

It was Blue Duck. At sight of him Judge Parker stiffened. His bearded head jerked back and his hands spread flat upon the papers lying on his desk.

"You!"

"Me, Judge," said the prisoner, in a voice that held audacity and little fear. "Been a while since we met, ain't it?"

The judge picked up a paper, laid it down again because his hands were suddenly trembling.

Craddock, at the rear of the courtroom, heard Jim July grunt, "He's going to load everything on this one. You don't reverse one of Parker's decisions and make him like it."

" 'Blue Duck,' " Parker read from the sheet of paper, his tone and expression heavily underscoring the weird alias.

His eyes lifted, stabbed the prisoner. "Haven't you got a better name than that?"

"If it suits me, why should it bother you, Judge?"

Someone in the courtroom snickered. Parker sent a glance probing the musty room before he returned to the man in front of him.

"Just keep talking," he said bleakly, "if you want to end up with a citation for contempt of court!"

Blue Duck had turned an amused glance toward the courtroom audience, but this warning ironed the smirk off his sallow, wax-mustached face and brought him around to face the bench again meekly enough.

Judge Parker was scanning the previous record of convictions.

"'Horse stealing, served sixty days; introducing whisky to Indian Territory, served thirty days; selling whisky without a license, served thirty days; murder, sentenced to death by hanging, verdict—'" his voice trembled and choked—"'appealed, commuted to life imprisonment at Menard, Illinois. Released after serving one year of sentence.'"

Drawing a slow breath, the jurist leaned back against the padded black leather of his chair. He rocked the chair slightly from side to side, eyeing Blue Duck over the steeple of his joined hands. In his look was a controlled anticipation.

"And this time what is the charge?"

The clerk read it off in a tired drone that hummed about the half-empty room and almost drained the legal verbiage of all meaning. Judge Parker elaborately studied the nails of one hand, polished them on his legal robe, examined them again.

The saga of George Standing Bear's stolen horses having been reduced to the law's dry jargon, the judge stared into a corner of the ceiling as he said in a bored tone, "And the prisoner pleads?"

"Not guilty!"

"Put his case on the docket," Parker instructed the clerk. His cold stare returned to Blue Duck, holding a malevolent satisfaction. "You'll have three weeks or so to sweat it out. And this time, I think perhaps we're going to hang the goods on you." He gave the deputy a meaningful nod.

"What about bail?" cried Blue Duck, suddenly losing all his cool assurance as the officer's hand fell upon his shoulder. "You can't make me roost in that cell until trial, without bail!"

"The bond I'd set in this case," Judge Parker told him heavily, "is more than you'd be likely to raise. Take him out."

"Just a minute!"

No one had noticed the opening of the twin doors at the rear of the courtroom. Every head turned now, as Belle Starr came sweeping in, a pair of lawyers in her train. Craddock, looking at Judge Parker, saw him stiffen again, saw his face darken. In a quick knotting of dramatic tension, Belle paraded down the aisle with her legal aides in tow, and in her hand was a sheaf of greenbacks.

"Here's your money!" she challenged, her coarse, loud voice filling the room. "Enough for any bail you want to name!" She plopped it onto the high desk, under the nose of the judge. "But you better go easy! There's something in the Constitution about that. Article Eight of the Bill of Rights, ain't it?" She appealed to her attorney for confirmation and he nodded.

"'Unreasonable bail.' That's correct, Your Honor."

"You don't have to tell me!" snapped the judge. Despite himself he couldn't deny a kind of grudging respect. "This woman knows more law than half the tinhorns that plead before this court, especially the ins and outs and the loopholes!"

Belle tossed her head, bridling. "And why not? One year at Detroit was enough for me. You'll never get me again, Judge — or none of my friends either, if there's any way I can stop you. Especially when you start measuring them for that thing out there!"

She flung a hand dramatically toward the window, and the stark and ugly gallows. Someone in the room gave a gasp. Down came the gavel.

Judge Parker was on his feet, drawn to his full height in the seedy black legal robe, his face furious. "Court is adjourned," he snapped. To the clerk he said, "Take care of the bond." He turned abruptly toward the door leading into chambers.

Belle laughed harshly. "One thing more, Judge. You think you're going to hang this charge on Blue Duck, don't you? You ain't got a case. There was just one lying witness to claim he put them horses in that corral, and that witness is dead. You'll waste time and money if you insist on holding a trial."

She spoke only to the jurist's retreating back. Stiffly he passed through the door and it closed behind him. And Craddock, weary of the musty smell of the courtroom, got up himself and went into the clean freshness of the morning.

He left Belle and her lawyers in a huddle with the court clerk over the setting of Blue Duck's bond. Waiting beside his horse in warm sunshine across the street, he thoughtfully built a cigarette and thrust it into the corner of his flat lips, wiped a match alight for it against his jeans.

To avoid the grisly sight of the gallows he let his glance move over the town and on to the sun-smear of the Arkansas River directly below. North and east, beyond the river and reaching toward the Boston Mountains, lay a crumpled country that already showed the touch of early frost. Crimson oak and yellow maple flaunted their first colors; a cottonwood that stood nearby shook down paper-dry and yellow leaves, and a quick wind picked them up to skid them, whirling and rattling, across the hard earth at Craddock's feet.

So far he thought he was not doing at all badly, considering the blind start he had made. Somewhere out in Indian Territory an outlaw, Virgil Hoyt, was holding Cass Dumont's Stirrup horses, rebranding them and feeding them a few at a time into the stream of traffic in stolen stock. Through Belle Starr, if there was any hope at all, Craddock meant to get in touch with that man, and if luck were with him, perhaps even yet manage to lay hands on his lost saddlebags.

If luck were with him.

He turned as Belle came toward him across the street, flanked by Blue Duck and the tall, handsome Cherokee. She seemed jubilant over her performance in the courtroom, but her companions were unsmiling. Craddock wondered a little. In Jim July's striking dark features, with their frame of shoulder-length black hair, was the Indian's unreadable stolidity, but it was the other one who puzzled him.

Blue Duck failed to show the pleasure which might be expected in a man just released from jail, with every likelihood of the charges against him eventually being quashed. He greeted Craddock with a nod that held little friendliness.

Without preliminary he said, "I understand you went and killed that skunk, Rufe Sago. Thanks for the favor!" But his words and tone were so surly that Craddock did not bother to reply.

The next moment Blue Duck had turned and was walking away through the traffic of the street. Craddock watched him go, frowning.

"What's eating him?" he demanded.

"Aw, he'll be all right," Belle told him. "Too long without a drink is all his trouble. Couple of snorts will make him human again."

Craddock accepted this explanation with a shrug. He told the woman, "That was a fine showing you made in there."

"You thought so?" She tipped her head back with a whoop of laughter that echoed along the street. "I told you I could make a monkey out of old Parker. I'll do it any chance he gives me. It makes that year at Detroit taste a little better, every time I see him squirm."

"Then you figure Blue Duck won't have any trouble?"

"None at all. They got no witnesses now — no way in the world to prove who put the broncs into that corral. Minute the trial opens I'll have our lawyers move for a dismissal. Parker will bust a blood vessel, but he can't do a thing but grant it."

Her own saddle horse was tied near Craddock's, at the hitching-rail, a handsome black with an expensive saddle and with her brand, "BS," on the left shoulder. Belle went

and took the reins, and as Craddock turned to test his own
cinch he tried to think of what the next ticklish step should
be, now that the business of Blue Duck was ended.

She spared him the trouble.

"What's your program, Owen?"

He looked at her in some surprise. She had never before
called him by his first name. She was standing near his
roan's shoulder, hand on hip, head tilted to one side, as she
looked up at him, eyes squinted a little against the direct
beat of the sun in her face.

"I don't know," said Craddock, turning back to his work.
The horse grunted and shifted its feet as he yanked the
cinch strap tight and made it fast. "I said before, I'm at
loose ends right now."

"Need money?"

He hesitated for just a breath of time. "Who don't?" He
smoothed down the saddle fender. "You got a suggestion?"

"Maybe. I been watching you. Whoever you are you're a
cool sort — had to be to polish off Sago and Brand Colvin
the way you done. Why not come down to Younger's Bend
with us?"

He appeared to think the matter over. "Why, I reckon
that sounds all right," he decided without hurry. "I was thinking I might drift toward Texas, now that Kansas has got a
little hot for me. But I had nothing in the fire down there.
Sure, I'll ride along with you. Thanks."

She brushed this aside. "I got more business with them
lawyers, will likely be tied up here the rest of the morning.
I told the boys to meet me about two o'clock at that fleabag
hotel, and we'd start back."

"I'll be around."

Covertly he watched her return to her black mare — Venus,
the name was. She stepped up with the easy assurance of a
born rider. As she put the horse to a canter, Craddock had
to admit that her erect, full-breasted figure made a good appearance on the back of a horse.

Remembering Jim July then, he looked for him but the
Cherokee had managed somehow to get his horse from the

place at the rack next to his own, and slip away unnoticed.
Well, that was the way of an Indian. Craddock quickly forgot him. He told himself with satisfaction, *well, you got your
invite to Younger's Bend.* He had expected a bad moment
or two before he managed this. It appeared, for the time
being at any rate, as though things were still working out
and might continue that way for some time.

## VIII

IN THE early afternoon, on the stroke of two, after some
hours of tedious time-killing, Owen Craddock rode around
to the hotel only to find that the others had not yet arrived.
He tied his horse and walked inside the lobby, a dingy place
with sunlight beating in through plate glass on a frayed carpet, a few shapeless leather-upholstered chairs, a dusty
rubber tree in a pot.

He picked a corner chair, out of the too-bright sun, and
settled into it to wait, taking up a day-old copy of the Fort
Smith *Elevator.* As he turned the pages, a black headline
leaped out at him:

**CASS DUMONT MURDERED**
Well-known Texas Drover
and Entire Crew Killed

Hastily he read the story beneath it:

From Dodge City comes news of one of the most shock-
ing crimes perpetrated in this region in many years. The

body of Cass Dumont, wealthy and popular Texas cattleman whose Stirrup brand is widely known throughout the
West, and the bodies of six members of his trail crew have
been found on the trail, victims of outlaws who drove off
the fine remuda of saddle horses with which the party was
returning to the home ranch near Denison, Texas.

Mark Stroud, foreman of a trail drive whose members
found the bodies and discovered the evidence of the crime,
states that —

Craddock skimmed through the rest of the story in feverish
haste, looking for reference to himself. Yes, there it was —
near the bottom of the half-column of print. According to
William Barkley Masterson, Dodge City marshal, a man had
been brought in from the scene of the crime for questioning
but had managed to escape on a horse stolen from the jail
corral. The heirs of Dumont had posted a reward for his re-
capture, or for information leading to the apprehension of
those responsible for the murders and theft of the Stirrup
remuda.

The name of the escaped prisoner was not included, nor
was there any description of him or of the horse he had
stolen. Craddock marked this with satisfaction. Bat Masterson was as good as his word. He was giving out to the press
no more information than he could help, so that Craddock
might have every possible chance to recover his money.

He folded the paper and shoved it deep into the crack
beside the chair cushion, as his eyes sought the banjo clock
ticking above the desk. It was drawing on to half-past two. In
a vague alarm, he came to his feet and was heading for the
street door when it opened and Belle stepped into the lobby.

Her black eyes hunted quickly past Craddock, returned to
his face.

"Where are the others?"

"Haven't showed up."

She frowned in irritation and he followed her out onto the
sidewalk where she stood peering along the street, arms
folded beneath her generous bosom, one boot toe beginning
to tap impatiently. She could be a half hour late herself,

Craddock observed with dry amusement, but she would not be kept waiting.

"The hell with them both!" she exclaimed finally, shrugging her shoulders within the tight jacket. "I'm not going to go hunting that pair through every whisky mill in Fort Smith. They can come on by themselves when they've sobered up. Let's ride!"

"Suits me."

As far as Craddock was concerned, the sooner they were quit of this town the better. The newspaper account might be sketchy, but in Masterson's official report to the Federal authorities he would have had to give more complete details. Too many people at Dodge, including the Dumont girl and the old puncher, Bud Tipton, knew what Owen Craddock looked like and could supply the law with a complete word-picture and the name of the wanted man.

He gave Belle a hand up to her saddle, a courtesy that seemed wasted. He mounted the roan and they took the river road westward into the winding Arkansas bottoms. It was a fine fall day, the horizons narrowed by encroaching hills that bore the first scant touches of autumn crimson. Walnut, ash, cottonwood shadowed the trail that was no more than a well-worn wagon track.

Here south of the river was Choctaw country, the invisible boundary line separating it from Arkansas and white man's law having been crossed a mile westward of the garrison town and river port of Fort Smith. They began to pass the cabins of the Indians, each with its small acreage in sweet corn, okra, beans, potatoes and the other staples of backwoods life. They saw copper-skinned men and women working in their fields, and an occasional white — one who had married into the tribe, perhaps, or was living among the Choctaws on permit, or simply squatting illegally.

And there were others with skins so dark as to serve as a reminder of the extent to which all the civilized tribes, except the Osages, had in times past intermingled their blood with that of Negro slaves.

Craddock had only a vague conception of the distance to the bend of the Canadian River for which they were headed. From the pace Belle set, however, he judged she did not expect to make it in one stretch, but planned to stop somewhere overnight, as she had done during the trek from Catoosa to Fort Smith. They rode in silence mostly, Craddock dropping back whenever the trail narrowed, requiring them to travel single file. But a mood for talking seemed to have been growing upon Belle and suddenly she turned to him, holding Venus until his own mount had come even with hers.

She said, "Begins to feel like I was coming home again. I tell you, I'm always damned glad to get back after even a day or two in town."

He grunted something noncommittal and discovered her sharp black eyes turned on him in a sidelong scrutiny.

"Maybe you're wondering why I live like this, in a wild country with nobody but Indians and no-good white squatters for neighbors? Maybe you think I have to? Or that I've never known anything better?"

"I hadn't thought about it at all. It's your business, not mine."

"Well, I'll have you understand it's my choice. I've seen too damned much of towns and the people that live in 'em ever since I was a girl. Since I was plain Myra Belle Shirley. I grew up back in Carthage, Missouri, and later I lived in Dallas. That's where I met my first husband, Ed Reed.

"Ed got himself mixed up in a stage holdup and the law killed him, and the good ladies of Dallas run me and my little boy and girl right out of town. That was enough for me! I come up here and I married Sam Starr who ain't too bright, but at least he's steady. And if people will let me alone I'm satisfied to stay at Younger's Bend till I die. That's the Lord's truth!"

He was at a loss to explain this spate of autobiography, and more at a loss to find an answer to it. But he didn't have to, for there was more to come.

"Oh, I know the name that newspaper fellow put on me

at the trial a couple of years ago. The Bandit Queen! That's just talk. Though I'm free to admit I got a lot of friends among the boys, and any time a friend of mine needs a place to hole in for a day or two, the latchstring of my cabin at the Bend is always out to him. What's more, if he needs a hand in dealing with the court I'll do anything I can for him. What the hell else is a friend for?"

"I don't know," said Craddock and frowned.

Beneath the maudlin sentiment he was struck by a grain of truth in this crude woman's words. Whatever else might be said of her, he had to credit Belle Starr at least with a capacity for friendship — which was something he could not say for himself, through the hard and ambitious years.

The afternoon dragged out. The sun, swinging lower, made the sky ahead a smear of brightness against which autumn leaves showed as dazzling, transparent flakes of red and yellow. The horses began to show the strain of constant travel.

Craddock was glad enough when Belle told him, "Here's where we'll put up tonight."

It was a place no different from others they had passed: a log cabin, the walls calked with clay, and around it the inevitable patch of corn and smaller fields of root crops in the ground. There was a milk cow grazing at tether, chickens and pigs, a dog or two.

The owner was a wrinkled squaw with straggling gray hair and a shapeless body, and a corncob pipe that never left her toothless gums. Apparently she lived here alone and did all the work with her own old hands, that bad circulation had swollen to the thickness of bundles of sausages. She greeted Belle with a curt nod and had no more than a single stabbing stare for the man with her. Then she waddled back to her stove and began extra fixings for supper.

Craddock tended to the horses and took some of the stiffness out of his shoulders by using an axe at the woodpile and bringing in a double armload of cottonwood chunks, as payment for his meal. This, when it was ready, consisted of the usual cornpone and salt pork and turnips. They ate in silence by the light of home-dipped candles. Belle seemed to have lost her garrulous streak and the Indian woman had no curiosity, making no more than monosyllabic replies to any question.

Early, Craddock left the one-room cabin for the pole hay shed behind it, where he was to sleep. The moon had come up a white, bright disk, so he needed no light. He had his blanket spread in loose hay and was seated, pulling off a boot, when the noise of a footstep outside plucked at his nerves as at a taut fiddle string.

He slapped the boot back onto his heel and, coming quickly to his feet, reached for the gun he had hung to a peg on a roof support. He set his back against this post, and the gun was ready in his hand as the cautious step sounded again, nearer. Someone moved into the open doorway, blocking out the moon.

The gun lowered as he recognized the silhouette of Belle Starr.

"Oh, it's you!" he grunted. "Another minute and you might have had a slug in you!"

"Sorry." Belle's voice held a trace of mockery. "I didn't figure you'd scare so easy."

Angered, Craddock turned and hung the weapon back in its holster on the peg. When he looked about, Belle had left the opening and was lost in the shed's dense shadows that the moonlight made even blacker. But he heard the rustle of her skirt, the crackling of straw under her boots. Then her white blouse gathered a few nebulous hints of reflected light.

"Did you want anything?" he asked gruffly.

"No. I wondered if you did. If you had everything you needed?"

"I'll get by, I reckon. This hay will make a good enough bed."

"You sure there's nothing, Owen?"

Her breath touched his face, so unexpectedly close that he would have drawn away a step only the post at his back prevented him. And then, as he stood there, her whole body came against his and he felt her hands move up to his shoulders.

Astounded, Craddock lifted his own hands, involuntarily. They touched her waist, and through the clothing discovered the suppleness of her body. Her fingers had crept behind his head and were pulling his face down toward her own.

Even as a remnant of cooler wisdom tried to stay him, he felt the beginning of a pulse throbbing in his throat. His arms tightened. There was a kind of brutal anger in the way he swept her to him.

But then reason returned and with it, in a blinding clarity, realization of the way Belle Starr had staged this and elected him, unasking, for his role. He remembered Blue Duck's sullenness that morning, wondered, and instantly was sure that the outlaw and Jim July hadn't simply failed to make that rendezvous at two o'clock but had been ordered not to. Blue Duck's sullen manner had been that of a man told by his mistress to stand aside when a new lover attracts her eye.

Passion quickly chilled, Craddock released her and reached up to free himself from the hands that pulled his head down. Belle spoke in protest, shaking her head, her lips still hard against his. But his strength was greater and firmly he took her hands away and straightened.

Her hard, quick breathing filled the darkness that made their faces invisible.

"You — dirty dog!" she said in a whisper.

He could not afford to enrage her. Searching quickly for a way to put her off, he could only manage what sounded even to his own ears, like a lame answer.

"Sorry, Belle! But this ain't my way of doing things."

"What ain't?"

"I don't think too much of myself, but I never been one to go behind a man's back when I had nothing against him. Especially one I'd never even laid eyes on!"

Her breathing had stilled; she was silent for a minute and he realized she was trying to puzzle out his meaning. That, he thought wryly, ought to have been obvious to anyone but Belle.

"You ain't talking about Sam?" she finally asked in surprise.

"All I'm saying is, I oughtn't to have done this. I apologize." Dropping her wrists he walked past her and placed himself in the doorway with a forearm lifted against the jamb, leaning there to look out upon the silvered surface of the night.

"But — " She had followed him to the door. She laid a hand against his shoulder, then dropped it again. He could guess her confusion, and a sense of relief and satisfaction flooded him.

Mention of her husband, he thought, should tie her hand. Surely she wouldn't put herself in a worse light by arguing against his scruples in the matter.

"Sam Starr," she began again, "is just — just — "

And then she gave it up. He thought he heard a sharp oath, under her breath. She walked stiffly past him, went through the door and turned again so that the moonlight lay full upon her.

"We'll try to git started early." Her voice was heavy, sullen. "It's a good distance yet."

"All right, Belle. And I meant what I said — I'm sorry for what I done."

"Oh — " She threw out her hand, in a gesture that could have meant anything but was most probably acute exasperation. Without another word she turned and strode back toward the darkened cabin, and she made no sign of hearing the "Good night" that Craddock sent after her.

He stood as he was for some time when she had gone. He lifted a hand, ran the back of it thoughtfully across his mouth. Who would have thought the woman had such fire in her, could do that to a man?

He would need to watch his step now, even more carefully. The trail he followed was perilous enough without this fused dynamite that she had hurled in front of him.

# IX

BY MIDDAY the wagon road bent northward toward the bluffs lying along the Canadian, and came at last to a fording that was swollen and muddy from the late rains. Craddock and Belle Starr took this and crossed the boundary separating the Choctaw and Cherokee lands.

The north bank was a broken, rolling country of ravines and steeply timbered hills, which frost had not yet colored. The Indian cabins were perhaps more isolated here, more confined in their own small clearings set among the hills of scrub oak and mahogany. Craddock supposed it was long anticipation, and the uncertainty and importance of what might be ahead that lifted a high tension in him. There was, after all, no obvious danger in these quiet woods and open, sun-struck glades.

They came at last along a broad ravine lying athwart a region of high spurs and ridges. A branch trail led them up from the wagon road to a flat-crowned hill where, amid timber and a little tilled land, a cabin stood alone. And Belle Starr reined in and looked at Craddock.

"Well, we're here," she said.

His face must have showed some of the thoughts that crossed his mind, for she laughed a little shortly.

"What's the matter? You been reading them newspapers, maybe, about Belle Starr's outlaw mansion on the Canadian? Take a look!" She flung out an arm, pointing through the trees to the broad, sweeping arc of the river gleaming under yonder bluffs across the valley to the south. "Younger's Bend. I named it that myself — and none of your business why! I got a good view from this point. I can watch the trails. I like to see people come and go. I like it when some of the boys stop by. We're crowded — only one room, you see — but we can generally put a friend up for a night or two."

"A place as open as this," Craddock observed, "what about the law coming in here to look for these friends of yours?"

Belle shrugged. "Hell, there's marshals poking around all the time. I keep out of trouble, and they don't bother me much. Generally, we can spot them quick enough that anybody who don't want company can head for the hill in back of us and lend a hand with the still. The law wouldn't think of touching that still of mine — it turns out the best moonshine in the Territory.

"Most of our neighbors are Starrs. Yonder a mile or two the West clan starts. They're cousins, after a fashion, but we been having bad blood since a skunk named Frank West gave the evidence that put me and Sam in prison. Then there's a scatter of other people, whites and Cherokees. Old Hi Early's place up on the hill to the northwest — Hi puts all his strength into growing peaches, so he don't bother us none. Gets prizes at fairs with them peaches."

The utter quiet of the backwoods, broken only by the quarreling of squirrels up and down a nut tree branch overhead, lay upon this hill top. The warm sun swept the rich leaf loam with the swaying shadows of the tree heads; a breath of wind brought the dark river scent and the faint pungency of the year's decay. Far down the flats a crow went flapping away, briefly stitching his dark cries into the hem of the day's stillness.

Belle handed her black mare's reins to Craddock and stepped down. "Horse pen's around behind the house," she said. "Give Venus some grain. Don't let her drink much."

He nodded and rode on to take care of both horses, finding a shed for stowing the saddles and a place to spread the sweaty blankets. He saw a small persimmon tree with a few late-hanging fruits still on it and went and plucked one of them. He had tasted sweeter, but he ate it slowly, leaning against the tree and giving his surroundings a more careful surveyal.

There had been no other saddle horses in the trap — only a scrubby work nag. An ancient farm wagon stood behind the shed. He and Belle were alone here, apparently, as utterly isolated from the world as they had seemed to be when they had first ridden up to the cabin. It was so foreign from his preconceptions that he could not help a certain sagging sense of anticlimax.

His glance swung to the shouldering ridges. So this was Younger's Bend! And did he really hope to find anything here of any use to him?

There could be nothing for it now but wait and keep his eyes open, though waiting was always, for him, the hardest of all chores. Craddock spat out a persimmon seed and wiped his fingers on his jeans as he walked back to the cabin.

It was nothing like the legends — a construction of cedar logs, maybe sixteen feet long and not quite as wide, and with a stone chimney and a single door hung ingeniously on twists of hickory bark. Its one room had a packed clay floor and no ceiling other than the peaked rafters of the roof. The furnishings were as crude as any he had seen in the Indian cabins.

There were bunk beds around the walls, a curtained sleeping space at one end.

Belle hadn't changed from her riding clothes, but she had removed her hat and jacket and rolled up her sleeves, and was busying herself about the fireplace. As Craddock's shadow came into the doorway, she turned with an irritable gesture at an empty wooden bucket on the table.

"That boy, Ed, went and forgot to fetch the water again."

He remembered a spring at the foot of the hill, as they came up the ravine trail from the river. "I'll bring it."

It was a long walk for water and promised a harder climb back to the cabin with the heavy weight of a filled water bucket. Craddock let the bucket stand while he took the plank lid from the boxed-up spring, scooped a dipperful and drank. Cold, sweet water. He submerged the bucket, brought it up dripping. He had replaced the lid and was stooping for the bucket before any instinct warned him that he was not alone.

He froze. Slowly, turning only his head, he looked at the figure in overalls that, having come up on him with unbelievable stealth, was hunkered on splayed bare feet in the sun shadows a couple of yards away — an Indian, but more nearly like an image graven from stone in his unmoving stillness. The heavy features, the unwinking black eyes pinned on Craddock's face held nothing readable. But the meaning of the shotgun whose twin muzzles held him, unwaveringly, was past mistaking.

Craddock was the first to move. Straightening, without the bucket, he let go of the breath that had started to cramp his lungs in a long and soundless sigh. He was careful to keep his arm far wide of the six-shooter in his belt holster, as he came around to face the squatting Cherokee.

"Hello!"

"You're her new one, ain't you?" said the Indian in a dead, guttural voice. "Blue Duck was by and told me she'd be bringing you with her. I've had my gun loaded and ready just waiting for you."

Realization struck Craddock, hard. "You're Sam Starr!"

The Indian's head tilted in a nod. "Uh huh, old Sam. Belle's old hound dog, that any man can kick!" His mouth had thinned hard at the corners, the muddy skin puckered across his flat cheek bones.

Craddock could put a name to the ugly look in Sam Starr's eyes now. It was jealousy, and a long-nourished, inwardly consuming resentment.

"They all think they can laugh in old Sam's face, and him too dumb to know it," the Cherokee went on in his toneless voice. "Like that lawyer man, the time I was tried and sent to prison, makin' fun of me because I couldn't read or write my name, or answer him proper with all them people staring. The way folks laugh because they know why Belle called this place of ours Younger's Bend, and why her kid wears the name of Pearl Younger. The way you think you can laugh at Sam, now!"

Craddock knew he could not afford to show any fear. He said coldly, "Whatever Blue Duck told you about me and Belle, he was mistaken. Maybe he's just hoping to set you against me, being jealous and scared to tackle me himself. Hell, if half what I've heard is true he's the one you should be using that shotgun on. Don't you know that?"

The head with long, greasy hair wagged from side to side. "Old Sam ain't as big a fool as you take him to be. There's just one thing I want — my woman! And Belle, she ain't ever going to leave me for the likes of him. She wants to keep all this."

He indicated, with a toss of his head, the Bend, the cabin on the hill, the slumbering woods, the shoulders of timbered ridges that reached down toward the looping river.

"She's a white woman and by tribal law she can hold onto this only as long as she shares her bed with me. No sense, then, to kill Blue Duck. Everybody'd know who done it. Old Sam would just end up on that Fort Smith gallows. And would be any better off?"

A bitter wisdom was behind this philosophy. A shoddy compromise, perhaps, yet if Sam knew these were the best terms he could get —

Craddock shook his head, in a kind of sympathy for the illiterate, half-savage Indian who squatted before him in the mud.

What he said was, "If you let Blue Duck get away with it, then there don't seem much sense throwing that shotgun onto me."

For a long moment the opaque stare held him. "You ain't Blue Duck. Your type's a cut above the others she's brought in here. Yes, I kind of think she'd take you and leave the Bend, if you was to ask her."

"But I ain't asking her!"

The Cherokee seemed not even to have heard. "You listen and I tell you a little story. There was this man they found floating in the river last spring — drowned. The buzzards been working on his face."

Sam lifted a knobby hand, ran it thoughtfully down across his own flat features. They held no expression, but his eyes seemed to warm to a pale gleam at his recollections.

"The lawmen found out his name — John Middleton. They found out he'd been here at the Bend while I was away on a scout. What the marshals never knew was that this Middleton had talked Belle into running away with him, leaving old Sam and going off to meet him somewheres in Arkansas. And they never got around to thinking that a load of buckshot in a man's face can do worse things to it than any buzzard."

A cold finger traced Craddock's spine, sickeningly. And now, with a single smooth movement, Sam Starr had risen to his feet. The tunnel-mouths of the shotgun tubes never wavered as he paced silently forward until the barrels were set against the third button of Craddock's shirt.

Sam Starr plucked the gun from Craddock's holster and tossed it away into the brush. He said, "Now, you turn around and walk where I tell you."

Craddock could feel the spasmodic, uncontrollable leaping of a nerve in the muscle that edged his jaw. This inability to conceal fear was almost harder to bear than the near menace of the shotgun's tubes, the icy trickle of sweat that had begun worming its course down his ribs.

"How you going to explain to Belle?" he asked.

"I guess Belle won't need no explaining. She's smart enough to figure it out for herself when you don't come back, so soon after John Middleton. She'll learn maybe that Sam ain't as easy as she thought, for her and her men to get around him."

"For the last time, will you let me tell you — ?"

The shotgun pressed against his chest, hard. "You turn around and walk ahead of me!"

They moved along the trail through the ravine, down toward the muddy, swollen, rushing river. Sam stayed a yard behind, where there would be little risk of the prisoner suddenly turning on him.

Sickening thoughts of a body floating faceless and fouled

in the reeds of the muddy shallows rose within Craddock. He listened for sound of the man he knew was close at his back. But if Sam's bare feet made any noise, the crunching of his own boots and the rasp of his own breathing surely covered it.

Once, with the eerie sensation of being alone, he even paused, half turning — but the Cherokee was there, sure enough, and the shotgun muzzle lifted dangerously. Sam did not have to say anything.

They must both have caught the sound of approaching riders at the same instant — the indecipherable drift of voices, the muffled thud of hoofs coming up from the ford. Sam Starr gave a grunt that had surprise and fear in it.

Craddock, halting, demanded sharply, "Could that be someone looking for you?"

He got no answer but when he glanced at Sam he found the Indian casting around, anxiously, hunting quick cover. In another second the riders would be on them, and there was no hiding place except a scrubby pit of plum thicket that would hardly give any concealment.

Craddock said sharply, "Get into that and lie low. Maybe I can keep their attention away from you!"

He saw the look of astonishment Sam Starr flashed him. But the rapid nearing of the horsemen allowed no time for questioning. Sam was making for the slight shelter of that brush clump as Craddock swung around again to face the pair of riders who swept into sight.

They were lawmen, all right. One wore a deputy marshal's badge. The other, a half-breed, was a lieutenant of Indian Police. It was not easy to meet their cold scrutiny, knowing they must be ticking off every feature, every detail, down to the holster that held no gun. They would believe, finding him here at Younger's Bend, that he must be an outlaw himself, and they'd be trying to identify him. Perhaps, in that wad of papers he could see bulging the deputy's shirt pocket, there was a reward dodger with his description on it.

No one had looked at him much during the few hours spent in Fort Smith; but he was being looked at now, and hard.

Nevertheless, he met the looks boldly as the lawmen came toward him up the trail, the horses of both of them shining wet from crossing the river.

If his face struck any responsive chord in either of the horsemen there was nothing to show it. For an instant he thought the deputy intended reining in, but they both went on past. He stood there and watched them turn into the hill trail leading directly up to Belle Starr's cabin.

Experience must have taught them that: in order to serve a warrant at Younger's Bend they had to get in fast and nab their man before he had time to take to his heels. So they could not afford to dally.

He watched until they were out of sight in the trees about Belle's cabin, and the silence had returned.

He said then, "Well, Sam, I reckon they didn't see you," and looked toward the bush where Sam Starr had taken cover. The Cherokee was gone.

There was no sign of him anywhere on the open floor of the ravine. Craddock shook his head, marveling at the Indian's uncanny ability to come and go without sound. He realized suddenly that his throat was tight and dry and aching for a smoke — the aftereffects of the tense strain he had just been under. His hands still trembled a little as he brought out the makings, fashioned a cigarette, and got it lighted.

He took his time with the smoke, letting some of the jumpiness in him settle. Satisfied then, he walked back to find his six-gun that Sam Starr had thrown into the dirt. He wiped it off with his bandanna and returned it to holster, then on second thought transferred it instead to his waistband, underneath his shirt, leaving a button unfastened so that he could get to it quickly.

To all appearances still unarmed, he took up the bucket of water and started up the hill with it to the cabin.

## X

WITH arms akimbo Belle stood in the door, shouting furiously at the lawmen who were remounting their horses, their faces red and angry.

"Take your papers and get out of here!" Craddock heard her ranting. "You damned manhunters! I'm sick of you dropping in every time I turn around. Ain't you got nothing better to do than spread lies about an honest woman that's trying to raise her family in peace?"

"Aw, go on!" the deputy snapped back as she paused for breath. "We know all about you, woman! Every outlaw since Jesse James has used this hideout at one time or another. As for that husband of yours, we want him and the Indian Police want him. And some day, by hell, we're bound to get our hands on him!"

She started in again, cursing them. But the deputy simply turned his back and spurred away toward the river trail, and the half-breed lieutenant followed. They gave Craddock no more than a glance as they passed him, going at a clatter down the hill. They were out of hearing by the time he reached the cabin and walked in to place his bucket on the table.

Belle's fury, it seemed, had been mostly put on for the lawmen's benefit. She appeared quite pleased with herself as she commented, "Well, I gave them an earful!"

"They were after your husband?"

"I know damn well it was Frank West give 'em word he'd be here! They got a post office stickup charge against Sam, and the Creek Nation's holding a claim against him for cleaning out their treasury. It's a matter of which lays hands on him first. I reckon at that he'd do better to give himself up to the marshals, rather than take a chance on what the Cherokee Council might do. Apt to get his hide stripped off, should the Council find him guilty."

"Why the trouble with West?" Craddock wanted to know. "You said it was him put you in the pen, that time. He's a cousin of Sam's, ain't he?"

She shrugged. "Every Indian in this country is related to everybody else, about. The Starrs, though, have always been a little too much for the rest of 'em. I got a notion Frank West hankers to lay hands on this property — that's what he's really after. Well, I reckon Sam can look out for himself."

Craddock was entirely of the same opinion, but he kept silent. He had made up his mind to say nothing at all of what had happened at the spring. Instead, he went out to the horse pen, saddled, and put his mount in the direction of the timbered ridge that lifted some thousand yards to the north.

If Belle had wanted to know his intentions, he would have thought of something to tell her. He was relieved, however, that she seemed to pay no heed to his comings and goings about the place.

A dim trail took him down into the damp hollows, then up the lift of the rocky hill. He brought out his six-shooter and carried it, his hand lying along his thigh, while his moving glance kept up a careful scout of the shadows and the shifting pattern of the trees and undergrowth and rocks.

Once or twice he stopped his horse and called softly, "Sam! Oh, Sam!" But there was no answer.

Finding the whisky still was a matter of following his nose; a sour, fermented odor led him to it. It was a big one, a homemade contraption, crudely patched together of odds and ends, except for the bright copper screw. There was a litter of broken equipment, of dead campfires, and refuse. The smell of the place stung Craddock's nostrils, and he felt the keen edge of disappointment as he looked about.

If his saddlebags were hidden anywhere on this hillside,

it would take a month of searching to unearth them among this mass of rocks and trees and scrub growth. Any notion he might have had of stumbling across his money he could just as well forget. It was not going to be that simple.

A flit of movement in the trees brought him around quickly, gun barrel lifting.

"Sam?" he called again.

There was no answer — only the dead silence of the hillside and the tingling expectancy, at any moment, of a shotgun's blast to come tearing suddenly through the leaves and branches, the blinding flash and the impact of bird shot. He felt his eyelids quivering, every muscle of his face strained and tight to take the charge.

Then out of the trees, Sam Starr came walking and the ugly weapon was slung harmless across his arm. Slowly Craddock let the tension out of him. He even lowered his six-gun, slid it back into holster.

"They're gone," he said. "Belle got rid of them. They wanted you all right, but it's one time at least they didn't get you."

The Indian only grunted. There was nothing in his dark face — no friendliness, no gratitude, even, for the white man's aid in holding those lawmen from him. Yet somehow Craddock understood that Sam Starr was drawing a line of truce between them. And he believed the truce would be respected.

Still without saying a word Sam turned and went striding away into the lengthening shadows. Craddock watched for a long time after his broad, stocky figure had gone from sight. He spoke to the roan, finally, and gave it a nudge with the steel that started it back down the steep trail toward the clearing.

The day was thinning out, turning faintly hazy as barred tree shadows stretched longer and the dank smell of deep woods rose from the earth. Smoke spiraled lazily above the cabin chimney to drift away in thin layers upon the still, heavy air.

The sun was a swollen ball low over timbered ridges, gilding the sweep of the river and the even ranks of peach trees growing on Hi Early's mountain, when a couple of youngsters came riding in astride a flop-eared old mule. One was a girl, about twelve years old. She might have been pretty except for a certain heavy, sullen cast to her features. Craddock looked with curiosity on this girl that rumor made the illegitimate offspring of Belle and the outlaw, Cole Younger.

Her half-brother, Ed Reed, was a few years her junior. Both accepted the presence of a stranger at the cabin as though they were used to the comings and goings of men they had never seen before, and were likely never to set eyes on again.

Pearl Younger, it turned out, was full of another matter that she found a good deal more exciting than any visitor. An Indian stomp dance was in progress at Aunt Lucy Surratt's across the river. Her mother seemed disinterested at first. Craddock would have thought that after these long days of riding, anything in the nature of a dance would be about the farthest from a woman's mind.

However, as they sat down to supper at the cabin's crude trestle table, Belle asked Craddock, "You ever seen one of them things?"

He told her he never had. They were quite a doings, she conceded — one of the few occasions left to the Indian for letting off steam, for getting good and drunk and shaking free the constraining shackles of a borrowed civilization. No trouble to anybody — just a rousing hell of a good time.

Maybe he'd like to take one in?

Craddock only shrugged, not at all sure any of this appealed to him or, for that matter, that it was the kind of thing suitable for a girl of Pearl Younger's tender age. But Belle was interested herself now, so it was finally decided that they all would ride down to Surratt's for an hour or two — the boy and Sam, as well. And Craddock could think of no excuse to decline the invitation.

They took the wagon, with the mule and the work horse on the pole for a team. Sam handled the lines; Belle, beside him on the seat, had changed her riding clothes for a high-

necked, long-sleeved dress of stiff black wool, with a locket
at her throat and gold rings in her ears, and on her head the
hat with the ostrich feather. The children rode in the back
of the wagon. Craddock, on his saddle horse, followed.

Just before they left the cabin, Sam Starr brought out a
whisky jug and deposited it under the seat. When they were
creaking through the dusky silence of the river trail, he fished
it up and Craddock heard the *pung* of the cork being drawn,
the gurgle of the liquor as Sam tilted the jug across a bent
elbow and drank from its neck.

Belle took it from him, swigged the stuff down with a
gusto that fully matched her husband's. Then the jug was
handed back across the seat and the half-grown Pearl had a
go at it. Even little Ed had to take his turn, the rest enjoying his choking and sputtering when the fiery moonshine
proved too much for him. So they rolled on, in high good
spirits, while Craddock rode behind in crawling disgust.

Belle's children were certainly getting an early start at
their education, along certain lines at any rate. He saw no
evidence that they had had any actual schooling — he
doubted they could read and write their own names. Ed, he
supposed, would grow up to an early apprenticeship in petty
thievery, would be in and out of jails before he was twenty,
and likely as not end with a bullet in him or a horse-thief's
noose around his neck.

And Pearl? He closed his mind. Thought of the life she
was training for, when her young good looks ripened and
her heritage asserted itself, was too unpleasant to dwell on.

He declined the whisky jug, so Sam took it back and had
a second jolt. Sam had no better skill at holding his liquor
than any other Indian. Already he reeled a little on the
wagon seat.

The moon, pushing up through the tangled branches of the
deep woods, laid a shimmering path of brightness toward
them down the black course of the river as they took the
crossing, with the wagon's wheels grinding in rocks and sand
and the animals working to breast the swollen current. The
moon's white disk was well into the sky, swallowing the

stars in its surrounding milky aura, when at last they sighted their destination.

Fire glow etched the thinning pattern of the trees, black shadows crossing and recrossing it in an aimless, ceaseless shifting. Better than a mile away, they had become conscious of the overtone of yelling voices across the normal night sounds. This swelled mightily, became a bedlam, a screeching, yipping uproar. And as the wagon broke through the last fringe of trees and the clearing lay about them, all this racket seemed to engulf them.

Craddock tightened his grip on the reins, spoke to settle his horse that had been made uneasy by the noise and the Indian smell. The Texan had never seen anything like this. Before the Surratt cabin a tremendous bonfire writhed and crackled, streaming golden sparks toward sky and circling tree heads as the rising wind whipped at it. The space around the fire seemed full of reeling, drunken Indians.

Craddock saw sprawled and shapeless figures that lay where stupor had overcome them, to be trampled indifferently by those who still managed to keep their feet. He saw a pair of men fighting in a dreadful, silent intentness.

Craddock glanced at Belle, wanting to ask her how much of this she found entertaining to watch. She was climbing down from the wagon seat. The children already had scrambled out and Sam Starr was groping, half-drunk, to set foot on the wheel hub.

Craddock shrugged and took his time about dismounting. He tied his horse to a tree trunk, waited while Sam hitched the wagon team. Then, with misgivings, he followed over to where Belle stood.

He heard Sam's sudden exclamation, almost stumbled into him as the man halted dead in his tracks.

Belle said, "What is it?"

"There — by the fire!"

Her gaze followed Sam's pointing hand. Craddock saw a man seated on the ground and heard the name she gave him.

"It's Frank West!"

"I was just hoping!" Sam flipped aside the denim jacket

and dragged out the hogleg revolver he had thrust into his waistband. "It's as good a time as any to square with him!"

"Frank's dangerous," Belle warned him. "Don't take no chances."

Sam grunted, "I don't mean to!" And he began moving forward.

Craddock pulled his gun halfway out of holster, then as firmly rammed it back. This was none of his mix, at all. He turned as Pearl Younger started past him, intending to join her mother.

"Pearl!" he exclaimed sharply. When she did not look at him he reached and seized her by a round, firm arm. "You better stay out of this!" he told her. "I don't know what's going to happen — "

Belle had joined her husband now and they were walking slowly, directly toward the unsuspecting Frank West. Just as they reached the circle of the fire glow the man looked up, saw them. They halted and quickly Belle moved in front of Sam to keep West from seeing the six-shooter Sam held ready and· leveled.

But West had seen something and he came at once to his feet. A castoff army overcoat was wrapped about him against the chill of the fall night, so that the shadow he threw was grotesque. Even at this distance Craddock could see the wariness in his copper-skinned face that the fire wash turned ruddy and formless.

He demanded, "You want something with me?"

Sam Starr answered him. In the ceaseless hubbub Craddock was able to catch only an occasional word of what he said, but it was enough to guess that Sam was tongue-lashing his enemy, reviling him with every term of abuse the Cherokee could dredge out of his dark mind, whipping himself to the pitch of killing.

Few of those within the clearing seemd to be aware of what was happening. But Owen Craddock waited in a tense expectancy, one hand clamped tight on gunbutt and Pearl pressed close against his arm.

Watching Frank West he saw the Indian draw into a

crouch, his head lowering, his body grotesque in the floppy overcoat. Then, apparently at a signal, Belle stepped aside out of her husband's way — and the gun in Sam's fist roared.

At that point-blank range he could not miss. Frank West was driven backward, crumpling. Someone screamed — it was like the stroke of a knife-blade, the way it cut across the other noise and focused that entire scene on the events beside the fire. The rhythmic pulsing of hand-clapping and shuffling feet, abruptly ceasing, left emptiness — a sudden hush.

Frank West was down. A groping hand lifted convulsively and pawed aside the front of the overcoat to reveal the red gushing blood that fouled his cotton shirt front. No man so wounded could last more than seconds at most, and already Sam Starr was straightening, looking about for any further challenge.

Suddenly Craddock felt the swelling of a warning cry, but it came too late. He could do no more than stare as, for an instant, firelight flickered on the gun the dying Indian had managed to drag from overcoat pocket. With what must have been the last of hs strength, Frank West drew his bead on the head of Sam Starr and forced the trigger.

Sam dropped his smoking gun. He staggered backward, both hands rising to clutch at his face as though he wished to shut away the glare of the fire. He spun clear around and went down, a limp, ugly heap.

It was over as quickly as that. No one could have told for certain which of the two men was first to die.

# XI

DRIVING slowly back to Younger's Bend, Craddock handled the team with the utmost caution, doing his best to avoid the buried stones and the deep wheel ruts that caused an eerie sliding and thumping in the wagon box. The last hundred yards of trail up the hill to Belle's door yard was the most unpleasant. A breath of relief escaped him when this had been maneuvered and he could pull the oddly-matched team to a halt, and set a boot upon the brake.

For a moment he sat listening to the night stillness and the sough of wind in dark branches. He turned finally to look at the woman, faintly visible on the seat beside him.

"Well? What do you want done with him?"

"Leave him in the wagon. He'll be safe there as any place — and I couldn't sleep in a house with a corpse." Her tone seemed hard and callous, or had the shock of death put heaviness in her voice?

He suggested tentatively, "You said he'd be buried at his father's place? We could take him there."

"Too far. They'll send someone out tomorrow. Unhook the team."

"All right."

Craddock saw she had made up her mind that this was how she wanted it. And after all she was right that Sam would be as well off as anywhere, in the high wagon-box.

The children were at Surratt's, left in care of the woman whom everyone called, indiscriminately, "Aunt Lucy." Craddock waited while Belle got down from the wagon, then drove it over to the pen. He unhitched the mule and the

work nag and unsaddled his roan which was tied to the
wagon tailgate. He put them into the pen with Belle's black
Venus, hung up the harness. He took a moment to adjust the
canvas that covered Sam Starr's body, fastening it so that the
night wind, rising, would not dislodge it.

He lingered a moment beside the wagon. There was little
reason to waste sympathy on a man like Sam Starr — a murderer and a thief. Yet he could not be indifferent to death in
any form, and there had been something oddly pathetic about
this illiterate Cherokee, with his dogged, jealous passion for
a woman who patently had but little use for him.

"Take it easy, Sam!" he muttered and turned toward the
house.

Belle had a lamp lighted. She had dropped new fuel onto
the glowing coals of the fireplace and had hung the smoke-
blackened coffeepot on the crane. As Craddock entered she
was unpinning her shawl.

She told him, "Coffee won't take long to heat up. I could
use some."

"Same here."

He watched her disappear behind the curtain, carrying the
shawl and her hat. Then he proceeded to get down thick
china cups and saucers from the utensil shelves and put them
on the table along with a couple of unmatched spoons and
the jar of "long sweetenin'," the molasses that was used when
brown sugar — "short sweetenin'" — was not available.

Belle was slow in returning. The scent of the strong brew
began to fill the cabin, and he had taken down the big pot
and was pouring from it when she pushed aside the curtain.

She had been working on her hair which had gotten
somewhat out of place during the hour since the tragedy at
Surratt's. It was hardly a time for vanity, Craddock should
have thought, but Belle was no ordinary woman and he had
long since ceased attempting to predict her moods. How,
indeed, would a man explain a woman who, barely an hour
past, had deliberately aided her husband in a murder by
shielding his drawn gun with her own body, and who could

now sit calmly sipping black coffee without any trace of emotion in the mask of her cold, tight-lipped features?

They sat for a time in silence, and the curling ribbons of steam above their cups gradually thinned to nothing. After the first few swallows of coffee, Craddock found that his stomach revolted against more and he pushed it away from him and looked across at Belle. She sat leaning forward, elbows on the table, coffee cup lifted in both hands while her black eyes looked abstractedly into a corner of the room.

Craddock asked her, "What'll you do now, Belle?" The stare she lifted to him held a cold question and he explained, "You won't be able to keep Younger's Bend, will you, with Sam gone? You no longer have a share in the tribal lands."

Belle put down her cup and her voice was hard. "Let 'em try and get it from me!"

"You think you can go to war with the whole Cherokee Nation? Like old Starr himself?"

Her only answer was a shrug and Craddock let the subject drop.

He fashioned a cigarette and lighted it. Neither spoke for a long time. The stillness of the night and the river and the circling hills crept in and claimed this room, to be broken only by the roar of the fireplace or a spent limb's breaking in a shower of guttering sparks.

A sense of their aloneness came upon Craddock suddenly, filled him with a vague discomfort. He shifted a little and his voice sounded startlingly loud to him as he asked:

"What about the children — Pearl and Eddie? This is pretty tough for them."

"Sam wasn't their pa."

"I knew that. But they saw him killed. That's no sight for any youngster — and this is no place for them to grow up. Surely you realize it, Belle?"

"Do I?"

He shrugged. "All right, so it's none of my business."

Not answering, Belle rose from her chair, taking her half-empty cup with her. He heard her moving about outside his line of vision, emptying the dregs into a bucket of slops, poking up the fire and shoving on another length of saw wood.

Craddock took a final drag at his cigarette and dropped it in his cup where it sizzled out. He had pushed his chair away from the table, was about to rise when, with a rustle of skirts, Belle suddenly came and plopped herself into his lap.

His moment of astonishment, quickly spent, left a cold revulsion. Only last night he had embraced this woman passionately — this uncouth and homely creature whose breath against his face still carried the taint of the corn liquor she had drunk. There was no passion in him now. Without gentleness, he pushed her away from him and came to his feet.

For a moment they stood like that.

"You told me — I thought — " Belle's black eyes were wide, her face drained of color and holding an astonished blankness.

Craddock knew what she meant to say. Last night he'd let her think it was only respect for Sam Starr, her husband, that kept him from her arms. And now Sam lay dead, in a wagon not a hundred feet from where they stood and apparently Belle, with her peculiar sense of scruples, believed that this should make everything right between them.

"I'm afraid you thought wrong!" he told her bluntly, because with Sam's death things had reached a state where only plain talk would serve. "I got no time for women, Belle — any woman at all. I travel too damned fast to be tied."

Slowly the color returned to her face, except for a thin, white line about her tightened lips. And in her eyes was the fury of a woman spurned.

"Then get out!" she whispered. And in a sudden shout, "Get the hell out of my house!"

Appalled, he realized what he had done. In one moment he had thrown away all he had so far gained. But there was nothing else for it how. Without a word he turned and picking up his hat from a corner of the table, walked directly to the door.

His hand on the latch, he heard her footsteps behind him but he did not look back. He flung open the door, stepped through, and it was there, just where lamplight edged into the frosty glow of moon, that he received a lash across his shoulders.

He staggered a little as the horsewhip thong curled about his chest and was yanked savagely free. In turning he took a second blow, felt the sharp pain of the rawhide flicking his throat and drawing blood. He could see Belle's face now, could see her arm lifted as the whip circled and came darting toward him again, with all her strength and fury behind it.

Owen Craddock ducked, throwing up a hand. He managed to catch the blow against his forearm. He let the leather coil. Then, before Belle could haul it back, gave a swift, twisting jerk. His hand clamped upon the taut lash and Belle Starr was pulled forcibly against him, losing her hold on the stock of the whip.

He shook his arm to free it of the coils and flung the whip aside. Her fists hit out blindly, taking him in the chest, the face — hard.

"You hellcat!" he gritted. "Stop it!"

He caught one of her hands, chased the other until he managed to trap it, and held her like that clamped against him, both of them breathing hard. Craddock felt sweat on his face and stinging in the bloody welt the whiplash had raised along the side of his neck.

Suddenly she had begun cursing him, in such a stream of invective as he had never heard from a woman's lips. He let the abuse fall away, taking no effect. And when Belle finally had to stop long enough to draw breath, he warned her quickly:

"Hold it a minute, will you? There's someone on the trail!"

She ceased her struggling at once, to listen. The thud of shod hoofs came plainly, up from the river road and drawing quickly nearer. They took the last steep pitch of the climb to the cabin hilltop. A call drifted across the moon shadows.

"Anybody home?"

A man's voice, a voice, Craddock thought, that sounded oddly familiar, almost as if once heard in a dream, though he could not place it.

He had dropped Belle's wrists and was already fading back against the rough wall, just at one side of the doorway. Belle appeared to have forgotten him. She stood unmoving, staring in the direction of the trail, and as the shape of a horseman became visible she called out:

"Who is it?"

"Virg Hoyt."

The rider pulled his horse to a restless stand. Lamplight smeared brightness on metal trappings as the animal tossed its head. The man in the saddle was a dim and formless figure, but to Craddock he seemed tall and solidly built. He could distinguish no more of him than that.

"Evening, Belle," said that naggingly familiar voice — and suddenly Craddock knew exactly where he had heard it before!

He was seized by a sudden trembling, waves of cold excitement running through him as he stood in darkness with a hand lifted to the butt of his holstered gun.

Virgil Hoyt seemed not to have discovered him. Without making a move to dismount, he sat looking at the woman who stood fully revealed in the lighted doorway.

He asked, "Is Sam around? I need a man for a chore, and I thought maybe he'd like to fill in."

Belle had calmed. "He's around," she answered in a leaden voice. "Over by the corral. Look for yourself."

Hoyt must have caught something strange in her manner. He stared at her a moment, then grunted, "Thanks," and touched up his horse with the spur.

It was a high-strung animal and lunged sideward away from the steel prod before it straightened out and took its rider around the corner of the house and out of sight. The man and the woman remained just as they were. It was only minutes before they heard Virgil Hoyt returning, afoot now and moving fast.

On the ground, he did indeed shape up tall, with a massive

structure of muscle and bone. He towered over Belle as he demanded:

"When did this happen? Who killed him?"

"Frank West. We ran into him this evening at Surratt's, and they shot it out."

"The hell you say!"

He sounded genuinely shocked. But before he could say anything further he must suddenly have seen the dim shape of the man who stood unmoving in shadows by the door. Instantly he was whirling, his head jerking back. Lamplight fell full across him. At last Craddock had a clear look at him — and beyond any question of a doubt, recognized him!

The face beneath the pushed-back hat brim was the same — broad and square and unshaven — the mouth a sour one dragged down hard at its corners. The nose had been broken, and above it suspicious eyes squinted beneath a matting of shaggy brows.

It was a face Craddock remembered with startling clearness from a moment of pain-shot delirium, a moment when the ground had spun beneath him like a vast turntable, and the black curtains of unconsciousness had trembled and parted briefly.

But there had been something else —

Lowering his glance from the angry face, Craddock let it travel downward, seeking out the man's right hand. The arm was bent, thrusting aside the skirt of Hoyt's denim jacket, to clear the holstered gun beneath. And, looking at that hand and gun, Craddock felt stirring within him the faintest echo of what he had felt that other time — a nauseous sensation of something wrong, something somehow evil.

Only now he knew the reason for it.

What he saw was simply a grotesque and clawlike stump. At some time in the past something had cost Virgil Hoyt a couple of his fingers. In order to accommodate this wreck of a hand, the cherrywood grips of the gun above which it hovered had been cropped and cut down to fit the mutilated palm. Little wonder, then, if to Craddock's dazed senses both hand and gun had appeared foreshortened, wrong; no wonder they had stamped their impression so vividly on him.

The outlaw demanded, "Who is this? Damn him, let him speak up!"

"He's a new one," Belle answered. "Name of Craddock."

"Oh?" Virgil Hoyt nodded a little, but he did not relax any of his taut wariness. "The same that did for Sago and Colvin up at Catoosa? Yeah, I been hearing about him — from Blue Duck and some others. Supposed to be pretty fast with a gun, I understand."

Craddock answered him. "Not too slow, maybe." And he added with reckless audacity. "What were you after Sam for? If you got a job that needs an extra man, I might fill in."

Silence met his offer. He could sense both of them staring at him. After that scene with Belle, he could have expected almost any kind of outburst, but she said nothing at all. As for Hoyt, he stood there in the faint spread of lamplight, and something about his scowl reminded Craddock, too late, that it wasn't entirely impossible that the outlaw was himself remembering the Dumont camp.

Some men, after all, possessed phenomenal memories — even for the anonymous faces of dead men, shot down and left lying in the rain.

He was quickly reassured, however, when Hoyt lifted wide shoulders and said, "No reason we couldn't use you, I guess. It wouldn't hurt to have another gun, in case we should run into trouble. You got a horse?"

"In the pen."

"Saddle him."

Within ten minutes of Hoyt's coming to Younger's Bend, the two of them were mounted and striking for the river trail, heading out.

Belle still stood in front of the cabin. But as they cantered past, Craddock saw her turn and walk inside. The door swung shut behind her.

The riders dropped on down the hill trail into the silent ravine. The night was growing colder and a damp breath blew up from the curving river to meet them. Opposite, the bluffs across the channel lay black against the stars and the westward-swinging moon.

Neither had much to say as they took the river crossing, then turned toward other wooded hills that lay to west and south. The outlaw set the pace. Following him over the dim trails that threaded this scrub timber, Craddock saw plenty of opportunities when he could have pulled a gun and taken Virg Hoyt by surprise.

It was a strong temptation, now before they got to where Hoyt's men were waiting and the odds would be piled against him. But Hoyt did not strike him as a man it would be easy to break, and he didn't see that it would gain him anything. Better to play this thing out as he was doing, and watch his chances.

The country they traversed became wilder and the going more obscure, so that Craddock marveled at his companion's ability to find a way at all. The moon had set. They seemed to have left the trails entirely, and there were times when the Texan could only blindly follow the sounds the other horse made in the opaque darkness. Branches whipped at his face; he rode with head bent and arm lifted to ward them off.

At last, in the throat of a deep, tree-clogged ravine, a campfire appeared. The trees thinned out and they were at the edge of a boulder-strewn pocket of grass. There were no buildings — nothing but the wooded hills lifting tall and close, and overhead the faint pattern of the stars.

But Craddock knew they must have reached their destination.

VIRGIL HOYT sang out and at once the forms of two sleeping men exploded from blanket rolls near the fire, bolting for the denser shadows. The outlaw's laughter followed them as they tried to shake the sleep out of their eyes.

"It's me, boys!" he called as he spurred ahead. "And a recruit. Come on back!"

The two came, a little sheepishly. Craddock, halting his mount beside Hoyt's, at once recognized the sallow face, the protuberant blue eyes and waxed mustache of Blue Duck. The other man was a stranger to him.

Blue Duck stared at him without welcome. "You brought him?"

"Why not?" Hoyt demanded, dismounting. "I thought he was a friend of yours after that doings in Catoosa."

Blue Duck merely scowled and turned to throw more limb-wood on the fire. Virg Hoyt looked at Craddock, an eyebrow lifted, and spread his maimed hand in a gesture, as much as to say, Maybe you understand him — I don't!

He indicated the other man saying, "Prentiss, this here is Owen Craddock. You've heard of him."

Prentiss was a stringy, unintelligent-looking man, typical of the scum of small-time outlawry that hung out here in the Nations. He gave Craddock a grudging, unfriendly nod. This was the full extent of the formalities.

As Craddock also dismounted, Hoyt tossed his reins to Prentiss and said, "Take care of 'em." Without a word the man reached to take Craddock's bridle.

The Texan shook his head. "I'll look after my own."

As he followed Prentiss into the darkness he caught Blue Duck's question drifting after them, "Where's Sam Starr?" The answer didn't carry, but Craddock supposed Hoyt was breaking the news of the Cherokee's passing. The death of a man he had cuckolded was not likely to grieve Blue Duck, to any noticeable extent.

Craddock stripped the roan, turned it loose to fall to grazing. He stood a moment and studied, through narrowed eyes, the dense shadows where the ravine drew in. Horses were moving behind a stretched rope barrier — a good-sized bunch.

The glow of the fire reached them but faintly, so there was no thought of reading brands or of making out anything more than the occasional outline of a lighter-colored animal or the flash of an eyeball reflecting light. Even so, he knew beyond any doubt what horses these were. The remnant of Cass Dumont's remuda!

Back at the camp, when he walked in carrying his gear, Blue Duck was hunkered down beside the crackling fire shivering and complaining of the cold.

"This is no time of year to be sleeping out with a blanket," he protested. "Damn it, there's going to be frost in here by morning. I'm froze stiff!"

Hoyt had his blankets spread and was pulling off his boots. "Quit bellyaching," he growled, without looking up. "And go back to sleep!"

Blue Duck subsided. The leader rolled into his blankets, and the last that was visible of him was that maimed claw of a hand pulling the covers closer about his body.

Craddock dumped saddle and roll to the earth, not quite within the reach of the firelight's circle, and cleared a spot of sticks and rocks before undoing his bed. The night was cold, and the chill of the earth came to him through the thickness of blankets as he seated himself. He stood his boots within handy reach, unhooked belt and holster. After a moment's indecision, he slid the gun from its pouch and placed it inside his hat, where its handle would be conveniently within reach.

Craddock felt the hardening of his mouth as he looked at these sleeping companions of his, these men who had been among the raiders who had massacred the Stirrup trail crew. He slid into his blankets, wrapping them about him with the deft movements of long experience. He was tired enough that the cold of the ground and the danger of his circumstances could not have kept sleep from him for long once his body relaxed and invited it. . . .

It was still dark when he awoke, and he lay for a minute or two wondering why he should have roused. The night seemed colder still, though his body had built its own warmth within the blankets. When he lifted his head from the saddle and looked over at the fire, his breath was a silver mist before his face.

Lacking fuel, the fire had died to a seething pool of coals, and its circle of warmth and light had contracted until only the faintest glow spread from it. The moon was long since gone, the stars gave not much in the way of light. But as he looked over the camp, Craddock could see well enough to make out that Virgil Hoyt's blankets seemed strangely flattened — empty.

Quickly he reached and closed his fingers about the handle of his gun. From the other two men the heavy sounds of sleep were unmistakable, but Hoyt had vanished. Craddock thought now that it must have been some slight noise the outlaw made that had reached him through the fog of sleep and brought him awake.

He slipped out of his blankets, moving with caution. The ground was hard and shockingly cold without his boots. Suddenly motionless, he waited as Blue Duck mumbled and stirred, then settled again.

Craddock stole soundlessly to the missing outlaw's bed and knelt to touch the blankets. They felt warm. Virgil Hoyt could have left them only minutes before.

A night breeze fanned the coals; the fire brightened. The thought struck him suddenly that the outlaw might be somewhere in the near darkness, watching, and this was enough

to send him scurrying beyond the reach of the light. There
he straightened slowly, gun ready, and probed for a clue to
Virgil Hoyt's whereabouts.

He supposed it need have been nothing more than a dis-
turbance in the corral that had drawn the outlaw leader from
his bed, to take a look perhaps and make certain all was
well with the horses.

Then off to his left, Craddock heard the sound of footsteps. He swung quickly in that direction and began prowling forward, cautious and alert. Hoyt must be confident he'd
got away from the fire undetected, for he was making little
effort now at secrecy. It was fairly easy for Craddock to pace
him, keeping a distance between them as he stalked the man
across the black ravine.

A branch swept Craddock's face and he stopped, groping,
to find he had narrowly avoided stumbling headlong into a
tree trunk. He had crossed the clearing and was in the band
of scrub growth that edged this ravine's steep wall. He heard
a crashing of brush just ahead, then a subdued crackling of
loose stones. This ended after a moment, giving place to a
new and deeper silence.

Setting a palm against the tree's rough bark, Craddock
waited. He did not want to go further, since the brush and
rubble were all too apt to give him away. Apparently, though,
Hoyt had halted, and Craddock asked himself what the outlaw could possibly be up to now?

Wind that poured along the ravine rose suddenly in a
harder gust. It swept through leafless trees and buckbrush,
baffling his ears as he stood shivering with the chill that
worked up through sock feet, and tried to listen.

He was rewarded by a faint, surreptitious scraping of
stone on stone. The outlaw must be moving rock for some
reason. The sounds ceased, after a little. He was still puzzling over their meaning when a renewed trampling of boots
over loose stone warned him suddenly that Virgil Hoyt was
retracing his steps.

At once Craddock turned and was running, on silent feet,
back to the fire. He came in cautiously, but the two men

rolled in their blankets were still asleep. Ghostlike Craddock crept into his own bed. He kept his hold on the gun, beneath the blankets, as he lay and watched for Hoyt to come.

He was barely settled when he heard the outlaw's stealthy approach, so close behind him it seemed impossible Hoyt could have failed to see or hear some movement. And apparently he had. He walked into the fire glow and stood for a long moment looking down at the sleeping figures. Craddock could vaguely make out the bulk of him, and he felt the butt plates of his gun grind into the fingers that held it.

But nothing happened. Hoyt turned finally and leaned for fuel which he thrust into the fire. It stirred, golden sparks streamed into the wind, and the circle of wavering light widened. In the dancing shadows, Craddock saw Virgil Hoyt stand above the fire and spread his hands to its warmth — the whole one and the other with its fingers grotesquely missing. The upward wash of flames made the outlaw's craggy face appear flat and shapeless, put a shadow across the smashed nose. Watching him, unseen, Craddock wondered at the thoughts behind that face and those small, wicked eyes.

Then Virgil Hoyt was swinging from the fire, returning to his blankets. He did not bother about removing his boots. Almost instantly his snores were mingling with those of the other sleeping men.

Craddock lay long awake, his thoughts at work on what he had just seen. And before he slept he believed he knew exactly what Hoyt had been up to so secretly, out there in the darkness.

Blue Duck had been right about the frost. By daylight the ground was whitened with it. Their blankets crackled stiffly when they crawled out into the raw chill of dawn. Blue Duck shivered and cursed weakly, hunting fuel to rebuild the fire which was now no more than a handful of ashes and charred sticks. His complaining finally irritated Virgil Hoyt into silencing him with a sharp command.

By the time a new fire had been got to burning, the sun was gilding the tree heads atop the ridges that pocketed this hollow. But it would be some time before its warming rays poured down here and dispelled the mists and thawed the white blanket of hoarfrost.

They were a tough-looking lot of unshaven men as they hunkered shivering beside their fire and cooked bacon and coffee and passed around a can of beans. Craddock felt of his own beard stubble and knew he made no better appearance than the rest — which suited him perfectly. He ate his breakfast in silence, listening to the talk and waiting for a cue.

The man named Prentiss scraped out the last of the beans and chucked the empty can aside, saying, "We-uns had better get them broncs on the trail, huh? It's a long piece to where we're going."

"We'll keep pushing them." Hoyt wiped greasy hands on the legs of his jeans. "Too bad we was caught shorthanded when this thing came up, but four should be enough to handle the horses without too much trouble. Sanderson will pay two thousand for the lot — and that'll be the last of this Stirrup cavvy."

Craddock did some quick figuring and shook his head over the results. There must be nearly seventy of the stolen horses still remaining, the rest having been disposed of piecemeal through tortuous channels. The price Virgil Hoyt expected to get for them was a mere fraction of their actual value. The fence, Sanderson, would pocket the difference, while the money collected would have to be split among the dozen or so who had had a part in the raid.

A paltry payment, surely, for the enormous risks taken. And when one considered that, instead of the fine Dumont breed of horses, the most these men usually were able to deal in would be a few head of rustled longhorns, a scrubby Indian pony or two, the petty economics of Territory outlawry became obvious.

It was on such small pickings as this that the thieves who gravitated about Belle Starr's cabin at Younger's Bend kept themselves alive. But that didn't mean they were not dangerous. They were just the sort that would slit a man's throat for a five-dollar gold piece.

Breaking camp was a simple matter of dousing the fire, catching up the saddle stock, strapping gear and bed rolls into place. At last the rope corral was struck, and yells and a brandishing of hats got the Dumont horses started. They came pouring out in a swift tide, manes streaming and heads tossing, a sight to make any man who could feel the good, wild thrill of fine horseflesh running free catch his breath. They tried to mill and scatter at first, but the riders came in on their flank and scooped them up into a solid, compact mass.

"Now stretch 'em out!" Virgil Hoyt shouted. "Get 'em rolling!"

Spurred by the yelling and by the fierce, high spirits engendered of the brisk morning and their release, the animals strung out quickly along the ravine. Timbered ridges echoed back the drum-roll of many hoofs. When Craddock looked behind him, he saw the wide, dark track they beat into the silver spread of frost that lay across the grass, where sunlight spilling down the rims had not yet reached.

He meant to imprint the picture of this site in his mind, beyond forgetting. He would be back!

They struck south and west. The hills opened up and the rolling prairies of the Choctaw Nation lay before them, tawny with sun-cured grass. Morning's chill ended, and as the day took on warmth the riders shed coats and jackets, fastened them behind their saddles.

It was a remote and primitive region, its emptiness unbroken now even by scattered Indian cabins. Antelope ranged the distances. Once as they dipped to the crossing of a shallow watercouse, a band of wild turkeys roosting in some cottonwoods took off and went flopping away through the tall grass.

For all the country's isolation, Virgil Hoyt showed no inclination to lose time crossing it. He kept the herd moving, kept yelling at his men whenever they showed signs of easing up the pressure and letting the horses drop back or attempt to graze. He was, Craddock realized suddenly, a frightened man, actually terrified of the risks he was taking.

Why, then, did he choose to run the horses in broad daylight? It must be because the outlaws were not sure enough of the country, or of their ability to manage so many head of stock if they had no better light than the moon to help them.

As it was, they were forced to watch the rims constantly, hunting for the first hint of danger. And the high nervousness of these shabby, desperate-looking men warned Craddock he would have no easy time of it, should he take it in his head to try sneaking away before the job was ended. He could see them eyeing him narrowly. They were already suspicious enough, and any move they didn't like could start them reaching for six-shooters and saddle guns. His chances would not be good against three of them.

So he bided his time. He was curious, after all, to learn more about the workings of this horse-stealing organization. He gathered from talk he heard that the destination was a trading post operated by a fence named Sanderson. There, the horses would be picked up by other men and shuttled farther westward. At their ultimate goal — New Mexico, perhaps — the brand-vented stock would eventually be sold, and for good profit, to small mountain ranches whose owners were not particular about bills of sale when they could buy fine horseflesh at bargain prices.

Morning grew older. The horses moved at a steady, easy running walk that could be maintained unbroken and untiring for hours at a stretch and make little work for the riders. Presently, in a boggy meadow where many small pools of seep water reflected the bright sky, Virgil Hoyt called for a rest to let the horses drink.

While they drifted about the edge of the herd, letting their own mounts have rein length so they could crop at the marshy grass, the leader ordered Prentiss up onto a rise for a look at their backtrail and the surrounding country.

Blue Duck, swabbing sweat from face and throat with a soiled bandanna, wanted to know, "How much farther?"

Hoyt squinted at the sun. "A half-hour maybe. We've made good time. We can take things a little easier."

He swung his big body to the ground to examine the

cinches of his saddle. His horse was a big, tough-jawed sorrel, its mouth and flanks scarred by use of bit and spur. To carry Hoyt's weight it had to have the heavy frame and solid muscle of a plowhorse, but by a cruel discipline he kept it on the taut, nervous edge more to be expected of fine-limbed, hot-blooded stock. It was a wonder, Craddock thought, that the horse kept its sanity.

Craddock shifted his weight in the saddle, glanced over in the direction of the hill. He straightened suddenly.

"I think Prentiss has seen something!"

Hoyt jerked around to look. Prentiss was standing in the stirrups, his hat off, and was wigwagging frantically. Faintly they heard his shout. Virgil Hoyt swore and with a quickness that showed the strain he was under threw himself into saddle. He jabbed his unhappy mount viciously. The sorrel spraddled like a frightened cat, then leaped forward.

A sound of alarm came from Blue Duck as he and Craddock sat and watched Hoyt weave his way through the scattered horse herd, and up the slope. They saw him join Prentiss, saw the outlaw pointing off beyond the hill toward the east. There was brief and serious talk while tense minutes ticked by. Then both the riders were coming back, taking the slope in reckless haste.

"I knew it!" groaned Blue Duck. "Trouble, for sure!"

Craddock saved his breath until the riders were within hearing. "Well, what is it?" he demanded. "What did you see?"

"Cavalry — a couple squads of them — from Fort Reno!" Virgil Hoyt sounded bitter. "And making straight for here."

Blue Duck cried, "They seen us!"

"No, I don't reckon so. Looks more like they're just heading thisaway for water. But once they spot our tracks, it won't take 'em but one guess to know what horses these are!"

Blue Duck already had the reins in his hands. "Then the hell with the broncs! Get caught with them on our hands and no power on earth can keep us off'n that scaffold at Fort Smith. We best split and start laying trail!"

"It's already too late! They're close enough they could

track us easy and pick us off piecemeal!" Virgil Hoyt ran a palm downward across his ugly, battered face. "Oh, damn the luck anyhow! Damn it all to hell!"

Craddock had listened to all this in alarm. His eyes narrowed as a sudden thought struck him. "Just a minute!" he said sharply. "How far to Sanderson's?"

Hoyt's glance leaped at him. "Not very far."

Craddock knew then from his look that he had caught the shape of the same idea that was in his own mind. All at once the outlaw leader was nodding, teeth beginning to show in a crooked grin.

"Hey!" he breathed. "Why not? Yeah, you got something that just might work!"

Then he was jerking the reins, bringing the sorrel up onto its haunches as it pivoted.

"Listen to me! We're going to bunch these horses and start 'em moving — fast!"

"But Virg!" cried Blue Duck, the sallow skin of his face gone a sickly color.

"You heard your orders!" Virgil Hoyt thundered at him. "Get busy! With Craddock along to do our thinking for us we'll beat this game yet!"

## XIII

FRIGHTENED as they were, neither Blue Duck nor Prentis had courage enough to refuse a direct order from their chief. With a whoop and a shout they spurred at the horses that tried to dally long enough for a last lap at the water, a las pull at the grass, before they yielded with a toss of their heads and went streaming away.

Hoofs splashed fountains from the boggy pools. Then the riders had them caught up and pointed again the way they wanted them to go. And this time they applied a hard pressure that would not let the horses settle out of a dead run.

Off they went in a roll of thunder that set the ground to trembling. They were pushing the distance behind them now at an astonishing rate, the wind strong against their faces. Craddock could only hope the roan would prove a sure-footed runner, or that if it struck a bad chuckhole and went down he would have time to free himself from the stirrups before they hit.

He was of the same opinion as the outlaws themselves, that the military was bound to take a sharp and immediate interest in any large-sized band of horses being hard pushed through the Indian Nations. It was horse-thief country, and the call was out for these stolen Dumont horses.

As they flowed up across a sudden high swell of land he hipped about for a brief glance behind them. What he saw was enough to settle any doubts.

The cavalry was still so far away they made only a crawling blue clot against the tawny prairie, but they were coming on, and the ragged shape of their line indicated how it was stretched out for speed. Virgil Hoyt had seen, too, but strangely enough he was curbing his mount, the cruel bit making it dance as he pulled around.

Then a hand was lifted to cup his mouth and Craddock heard him shouting.

"Ease up on 'em! Ease up! We're just about there!"

The long rise lifting under them served as a brake for the tired horses. As the riders began to rein back, the running herd automatically slowed its headlong rush. The cavalcade crested the hill and below the riders saw a ribbon of wagon road that came out of timber and ran southward, to be swallowed up among low hills.

It appeared to be a long-traveled emigrant road leading

to Texas. And it was beside this trail Cal Sanderson had built his trading post. A sod-walled, sod-roofed building seemed to melt into the surrounding prairie browned by early frosts. There was a barn of the same material, some smaller sheds, a wagon or two awaiting repairs. There were also corrals of peeled timber construction. Some saddled horses were tied to the corral bars and to a sagging hitching-pole beside the store.

All this Craddock made out as the herd went spilling down the slope in a varicolored tide of flowing backs and graceful, arching heads. Below, men left the buildings to stand watching them come. Two of them were already running across the hard-packed turnaround that countless wagon wheels and hoofs had beaten in front of the store, to swing wide the gate of a corral — a big one, capable of holding this entire herd, and with a wing trap to facilitate shunting the lead animals into the opening.

Amid the whooping and hat-waving of the trading-post men, the Stirrup horses were pushed straight on toward this corral, and in.

For a minute or two there was only confusion and noise and no time to give attention to much else than the work of getting the horses corraled. When the gate had finally swung closed and the sweat-dark horses were milling in the crowded pen, Craddock reined away, swabbing at his face with a sleeve. The cloth caught on the spiky stubble of his beard.

Instinctively he raised a glance toward the hill rim. Nothing showed there yet. He looked for Virgil Hoyt, and saw him leaning from saddle and talking to a man he picked for the trader and fence, Sanderson. Craddock rode slowly toward them.

He had come to know Hoyt well enough to recognize the signs of high anxiety in him. He saw it now in the shine of sweat across the man's broad features, the too-bright glitter of his eyes.

Hoyt was saying, in a voice he tried to keep calm, "Well, we had a deal, Sanderson. Cash on delivery."

Sanderson was a short, unimpressive figure in shirt sleeves

and tight trousers and black string tie. He unhooked a thumb from waistcoat pocket and removed a slim cheroot from his mouth. He eyed the soggy end, leaned forward to spit into the mud in front of his polished boots.

He said coldly, "Look at the sweat on them broncs! What have you been trying to do — run all the fat off 'em?"

"What the hell! They ain't cattle — you ain't buying 'em by the pound! How about paying off, so we can get started back?" As he spoke Hoyt turned his head a little and Craddock saw him flick a look toward the empty hill rim to the east.

Sanderson took his time answering. He didn't seem the least afraid of Virgil Hoyt's crop-handled six-shooter, though no weapon showed on his own person. Perhaps he found safety in the superior numbers of his men or perhaps it was a cool, native assurance.

He had thin sandy hair and brows, and a face that slanted oddly to the point of a forward thrusting lantern-jaw. His eyes slanted, too, his mouth was V-shaped, and straggly Dundreary whiskers ran down to the sharp point of his long chin. It was his eyes, Craddock decided — pale blue, incisive — that held you.

Sanderson asked, "How many in the lot?"

"Seventy-two."

"That's right, Cal," one of Sanderson's men quickly confirmed. "I tallied them as they went into the pen."

"Go tally them again!" snapped the fence. A boot heel grinding as he turned, he jerked a head at Hoyt and walked through the door of the post.

Craddock saw Hoyt's crippled hand tighten. This was shaving it pretty fine! It would be wiser, no doubt, to forget about the money and take their leave of this place while they could. But greed held Virgil Hoyt, brought him down from saddle to hand his reins to Craddock.

"Tie 'em," he muttered. "Keep a lookout."

Nodding, Craddock dismounted and snubbed both horses to the hitching-pole, then swung underneath and followed Hoyt toward the sod building. Over his shoulder he could see

Prentiss and Blue Duck riding up from the corral, and he could read alarm in their faces over this new delay.

He walked inside the store and halted just at the entrance where he could watch the rim. He placed his shoulders against the crude plank door frame, pretending to busy himself with the shaping of a cigarette.

Sanderson's post was a cool, dark building that appeared at first glance a mere clutter of miscellaneous stuff piled to the rafter poles. Further consideration discovered that Sanderson's iron will had imposed system and discipline on all this jumble. There was a truly amazing variety of merchandise, from dry goods to harness — anything that an Indian or a passing pilgrim on the Texas road might need.

An old Choctaw woman who apparently acted as Sanderson's clerk was moving about in the gloomy rear of the room, moccasins whispering on the rammed clay floor.

Near the front was a counter which doubled as a bar. Sanderson lifted the drop-leaf to move around behind and set out a couple of glasses and an unlabeled bottle of Territory moonshine. He filled both glasses and shoved one toward Virgil Hoyt. The horse thief was about to refuse, when instead he seized the liquor and drained it off in a quick toss.

Sanderson let his own glass stand, while he thoughtfully rubbed his long chin with the thumb of the hand which held his cheroot.

He said softly, "You spoke about a deal. Now, I didn't recollect that we'd come as far as talking terms."

Hoyt's eyes hardened. "There was a deal, and you know it. Two thousand for the lot."

"It's too high." The trader shook his head and laid his cheroot on the edge of the wood. "Too high by a long ways. My men still have the risk of getting these broncs out of the Territory, and with the alarm there is out for them, that will take some doing. They ain't worth that much to me, and they'll be worth even less, the longer I'm stuck with them."

"How much then?" Hoyt's tone was rimmed with ill-suppressed fury.

"Say, fifteen hundred."

"Why, damn you!"

"That's my figure. Either take it, or get those broncs the hell away from here. Make up your mind. Which way do you want it?"

For a long count of three, their eyes met. Sanderson's utter lack of fear did not cease to amaze Craddock. And he well knew that, with the cruel pressures on him, Virgil Hoyt would be forced to back down. He saw a muscle leap and flutter beneath the beard stubble on the outlaw's broad cheek.

"All right!" Hoyt cried hoarsely. "But I want cash. Lay it right here on the wood in front of me! Get it up!"

The trader did not move. His look had narrowed, gone suspicious. "Why so much steam, Virg? What the hell's bothering you?"

He got his answer in a shout of warning from the yard. And Craddock, jerking about saw through the door the body of horsemen that had suddenly blackened the hill rim, and now came pouring down across it.

A sound of rage broke from Sanderson as he understood. "So, that's it, damn you! Trying to unload — "

His pointed face had gone livid. Suddenly his hand was rising and in it was the wicked, snub-nosed derringer that he'd had in the pocket of his vest.

Hoyt made no attempt to beat the draw. Instead, his three-fingered hand had moved and caught up the whisky bottle. He hurled it at the trader. In an amber spray of whisky, the bottle caught Sanderson squarely in the chest, driving him backward. Then Virgil Hoyt was following Craddock as the Texan made a fast run toward the horses.

The roan shied from Craddock's approach, and for a moment had him hopping on one leg, his other foot trapped in stirrup, before he was able to lift himself to saddle. Virgil Hoyt was already up, and turning his mount with a vicious yank at the spade bit, sending it forward to a solid stab of

the spur. Craddock, close at his heels, had to swerve to avoid
riding down one of Sanderson's men who came running
blindly past, unlimbering a six-gun.

A confused yelling had broken out, and someone opened
fire at the nearing blue line. If anything had been wanting to
turn it into a fight, that did it. The riders at once spread out,
halting their advance. A second gun cracked flatly at the
trading post. A blue-clad horseman spilled from his saddle.
And then on both sides a steady rattle of guns began.

But none of the four who had brought this about had any
intention of staying to take part in it. Prentiss and Blue Duck
quickly fell in beside the other two. The wagon road lay
open to the south and they spurred for it as gunfire built up
solidly behind them.

With a sudden cry, Prentiss stiffened and sprawled forward onto the neck of his running horse. Craddock glimpsed
the round black hole in the back of the man's sweaty shirt,
even as the motion of the horn dislodged him and he slid off,
limply, rolling once when his body hit the ground.

Involuntarily, Craddock looked behind him. In the doorway of the trading post stood Cal Sanderson, a rifle in his
hand, and firing after them as rapidly as he could work the
lever. Craddock thought he could almost see the frenzy of
betrayal in the man's narrow face.

The rifle blossomed and he heard the shriek of a bullet.
Virgil Hoyt's mount shouldered into his, straightening him
around in saddle.

Hoyt shouted at him, "The hell with Prentiss! We got to
get out of this!"

Seconds later they had rounded the pen containing the
Dumont horses, that were squealing and making the poles
tremble as they circled and kicked in their fear of the guns.
Then Sanderson's was left behind them, and nothing remained in their way.

Hoofs drummed on the wheel ruts and the sound of shooting quickly thinned. Presently a dip and curve of the trail
took them out of hearing entirely, and into a still and breath-

less heat that shimmered on the dead bushes and leaf-stripped trees. Here they reined in a moment.

Blue Duck ran the back of a shaking hand across his face that was colorless and shone with a film of sweat. "God!" he panted. "That was too close!"

"We almost made it pay, though," said Virgil Hoyt. "Another five minutes and we'd have had the money out of Sanderson. Well, at least he's stuck with the broncs!"

There could not have been any love lost between the fence and Hoyt. The outlaw actually seemed delighted with the trick he had pulled, and the way he had put danger off himself and onto the men at the trading post.

"But we lost Prentiss."

Hoyt shrugged. "Yeah, tough," he grunted indifferently. He took the reins again. "Come on."

They kept pushing, laying distance behind them, and gradually Virgil Hoyt led them in a wide swing to the east, then northward again, back toward the distant Canadian. Now at last, Craddock supposed, he could have made an opportunity if he wanted it to break away on one excuse or another. But knowing nothing of the country, he decided it would be wiser — and time-saving, likely enough — if he stuck a little longer. At least, until they got into land that he recognized.

Meanwhile the day was dragging out. Perhaps he could find that ravine by himself after dark; perhaps not.

Silence was on all of them, and their bodies slumped hard against the swells of their saddle pommels, limp with fatigue and the aftermath of the day's tensions and of the debacle at Sanderson's. After all, they had been in saddle since daybreak, and now the sun was swinging westward and the autumn chill was already destroying the heat that had ridden them so hard.

Coats and jackets were donned again, and the thin-blooded Blue Duck was soon shivering and cursing the cold. The country began to rough up as they came in toward the river.

The sun sank and gray dusk flowed out of the hollows like a mist.

Once, when they paused to water their jaded horses, Blue Duck spoke into the heavy hush of twilight that made their faces uncertain and shapeless. His voice sounded charged with bitterness.

"Right out of our fingers — all that prime horseflesh — the finest haul any of us ever laid a hand on. The rest of the boys ain't going to like it when they hear!"

"The hell with what they like or don't like!" Virgil Hoyt retorted. "We just didn't get the breaks. We might have expected it would turn out too big a proposition."

Yes, they might have, Craddock thought bleakly. And so the senseless waste of Cass Dumont and his crew need never have happened. But probably that was a reflection not apt to occur to men like Blue Duck and Virgil Hoyt.

The wind stiffened, became a strong, invisible hand that pummeled them and forced them to hold their tired bodies firm against its steady mauling. When the moon showed in the eastern sky it was smeared and milky behind a thin scum of cloud that coming of night had drawn like a curtain across the sky.

Sooner than he expected, Craddock all at once found himself in hills whose contours seemed familiar. Then the river lay before them, sliding and murmuring between its banks of reeds and mud.

They took the fording and presently their weary horses were climbing the hill trail, and the lights of Belle Starr's cabin beckoned to them from among the trees.

# XIV

YOUNGER'S BEND seemed to be a place of considerable activity. Saddle horses were tied around the cabin, and a rumble of voices sounded through the mud-chinked walls. Sparks streaming from the chimney told of a roaring blaze in the fireplace, to hold the damp chill of the night at bay. As the weary horsemen rode up, the door was suddenly flung open. A man, framed blackly in the open, said:

"It's them."

Virgil Hoyt lifted a hand in perfunctory greeting and they rode on, to dismount stiffly beside the horse pen and tie. Craddock loosened his cinch and gave the heavy saddle a shake to ease the galling weight of it on his horse's shoulders. He did not mean to stay here longer than he could help.

Hoyt and Blue Duck had already preceded him to the cabin. Just before he reached the door, the rumble of talk within broke off and he entered a strange silence.

At first glance he could have imagined he had walked in on a conclave of all the petty outlaws of the Indian Nations. Word must have gone out along the grapevine that Hoyt had arranged disposal of the Dumont horses, and they had drifted in here to Belle's and were waiting to divide the take. They lounged on the bunks, lined the long table with the wreckage of a meal scattered in front of them. The air was blue from their smoking.

Craddock saw Jim July and one or two others whose faces he thought he remembered from the saloons in Catoosa. Belle, herself, stood near the blazing fireplace with a whisky jug in her hands. Like the rest, she was staring at big Virgil

241

Hoyt who held the center of the floor and all of their shocked attention as he briefly told what had happened.

"The hell, Virg!" someone cried hoarsely. "You don't mean we lost 'em all! We don't get a cent?"

"I talk English, I reckon!" Hoyt shot back. "I think I talk it pretty plain." He pulled off his shapeless hat, tossed it aside. "What is there to eat? My gut's starved."

He strode to the table, leaning across a couple of men while he seized bread and salt pork, folded this into a sandwich and started to wolf it down.

"How about pouring me a slug of that?" he said, indicating the jug in Belle's hand.

She looked at it, set it heavily on the table. "Pour your own!" she grunted sourly.

The mood of this room had become suddenly dangerous, with the disappointment of profit come to nothing. The man who had questioned Virgil Hoyt turned on Blue Duck for confirmation.

"You tell us what happened."

"Ain't you heard enough?" grumbled Blue Duck. "I'm only glad to be standing here instead of laying out at Sanderson's with a bullet in my back, like happened to Prentiss."

There was more grumbling, but Craddock decided that after the first cruel shock they were of a mind to accept the bad news. Their lives were chancy, anyhow, compounded of ups and downs and abrupt changes of fortune.

"Craddock!" The Cherokee, Jim July, who saw Craddock by the door, brought the attention of the room centering on him. "Good thing you're here. Maybe now you tell us who these people are that say they know you?"

"What people?"

Belle was coming toward him around the table and his glance switched to her.

"The old man and the kid," she told him. "Just as it got dusk tonight, we caught 'em snooping. All they'll say is that they're friends of yours. What about it?"

Her black eyes moved to a corner of the cabin behind him. In bewilderment Craddock turned.

They were seated on the floor, backs to the logs. Only slowly did they lift their heads. The younger of the pair, he was certain at first he had never laid eyes on — a mere beardless youngster, yellow-headed, his immature body engulfed in a short padded jacket and worn jeans that looked too big. Craddock passed him over and went on to the leathery-skinned old man seated next to him.

Fierce blue eyes met his own, eyes filled with challenge and with hate. And recognition smote Owen Craddock with such a jolt that he felt almost physically staggered. For a wild second the very walls of the cabin seemed to reel before they settled again.

As from a great distance, Belle's prodding question reached him. "Well, you know them or not?"

Slowly he nodded. "Yeah. Yeah, I know them."

Astonishment had given place in him to a cold anger. He could feel his face harden to a stiff mask. "You fools!" he grunted at them. "Whatever put it in your heads to follow me?"

They had climbed to a stand now but seemed incapable of speech. The old man's face had gone ashen and he touched tongue to his lips.

Belle Starr demanded, "Who are they? What do they want with you?"

Craddock shook his head. "A personal matter. If you don't mind, I'd like to talk to one of them — alone. Just keep an eye on the old man for me. I'll take the kid outside and — "

"No!" cried Bud Tipton and started for him.

The click of a gun hammer halted the old foreman and he turned to see the gun Jim July held leveled.

"Stay put," the Cherokee warned him. "Go ahead, Craddock. I hold him here!"

The shine of the gun-barrel sent the old puncher stumbling backward, until the rough wall pressed against his shoulders. Sweat stood on his leathery, wrinkled face, and the hands he held a little in front of him had begun to tremble. While the room watched in silence, Craddock turned and walked directly to the door and threw it open. He gave a stern and commanding motion of his head.

The old man and his youthful companion shared a frightened look. Then, at a nod from Bud Tipton, the kid moved slowly to obey the summons, sidling along the wall to the door where Craddock waited. They stepped through and he closed it after him, shutting away the light.

At once Vinnie Dumont tried to bolt but Craddock was expecting this, and his hand clamped hard on her arm through the thick sleeve of the quilted jacket.

"Stop that!" he gritted. "And don't open your mouth until we're out of hearing! Do you want that crowd to know what they've got?"

She subsided and, still keeping a tight grip on her arm, Craddock hustled her away from the cabin and into the dark trees. The strong, cold wind pushed and pulled at them and whipped leaves down from the branches that rocked against the milky sky. Presently Craddock halted and swung the girl around to face him.

Her pale features, topped by the ruin of short-cropped yellow hair, were faintly visible in the diffused light from the sky.

"Now!" Craddock said between tight lips. "What foolishness is this, anyway? How did you ever manage to track me down?"

"It wasn't hard. Anyone could have followed the trail you left!" Her voice was tremulous but she stood up to him defiantly. "Word got back to Dodge that some outlaw answering to your name and description had killed two men at Catoosa. There, we learned you'd been seen riding off with Belle Starr, so it was just a matter of finding someone who'd sell us information on how to get to Younger's Bend."

"And once you found me, what good would it do? If I was really the monster you think I am?" He shook his head, appalled. "I knew Bud Tipton was a fool, but something tells me coming here must have been your own idea. Something you talked him into. And this disguise — "

He shot out a hand and ran his fingers through what was

left of her hair. Vinnie jerked angrily away but he felt the fine corn-silk featheriness, and then the smooth curve of her cheek. And, despite himself, he found the sensation so oddly exciting that for a moment he could only stand and stare at her in the darkness, his hand raised before him. Then he dropped it and when he spoke he deliberately roughened his voice.

"What am I supposed to do with you? What will happen when those people find out you're Cass Dumont's girl?"

"You're not fooling me," she answered. "I know you're one of them. If I had any doubts I lost them, listening to that talk inside the cabin. Why, you've even been helping to deliver the horses you stole from my father!"

Craddock gave a groan of exasperation. "Will you listen to reason? The Army has your horses by now, or most of them. They'll be returned. And if you'll keep your mouths shut and do as I tell you, maybe I can get you and Bud free of the mess you've walked into. I don't promise. They're damned suspicious of anybody that rides in uninvited, and any minute somebody is apt to guess the truth. But I'll do what I can."

She started to turn away. "I want no favors from you!" Craddock seized her by the arm and hauled her back.

"For your own good — "

"Let go!" cried Vinnie Dumont.

She tried to fight him. When struggling failed to free her of his grip, she swung wildly with her unhampered fist, a blow that he scarcely felt, but which surprised him almost into releasing her. Instead he reached and hauled her to him — and all at once found himself shaking her, as though this could somehow knock sense into her pretty, mistaken head. When he stopped they were both panting.

"Vinnie, for God's sake — "

From behind him, he heard Virgil Hoyt's mocking voice: "She giving you trouble, Craddock?"

Craddock released the girl, who stumbled away from him with a little cry. He came whirling about, pawing at the skirt of his jacket. He had no chance, however, to clear the holstered gun. Hoyt, a solid bulk in the milky half-dark, was holding his own weapon leveled — the crop-handled six-shooter in the mutilated ruin of a hand.

The outlaw said, "You wouldn't be that big a fool, Craddock! Now, keep away from that gun and stand still!"

After Craddock's revolver had been taken from him, Virgil Hoyt turned his attention to the girl. She started to draw back. "Don't touch me!" she cried breathlessly.

"Hold your ground, damn you!" In a stride he reached her and quickly slapped at the side pockets of her jacket, pawed the skirts of the garment aside to show that no holster belt was strapped to her slender waist.

Craddock said hoarsely, "You're making a mistake. Let the girl alone. She and the old man have nothing to do with you or any of the others."

"No?" murmured Hoyt. "I kind of think different. After what I just got through listening to. And you, Craddock! I been trying to get you pegged, ever since I first laid eyes on you. Who the hell are you, anyway? What sort of a game are you playing around here?"

"My business! Put that gun up and give me back mine. Don't ever get the idea for a minute, Hoyt, that I'm afraid of you."

This was blunt talk. It put the outlaw's stare on him and held it there for a long moment, during which none of them spoke and the rushing wind tore through the trees above their heads.

Then Virgil Hoyt said roughly, "You sound tough. Maybe you are. Right now, though, we're going to do what I say." He nodded toward the cabin. "Inside!"

Craddock would have argued if he had seen any use in it. Having lost his gun he was at a hopeless disadvantage. He shrugged and turned to the girl, but was not surprised when she drew back from the hand he offered her.

He was sorry for Vinnie Dumont just then. A good many frightening things were happening to her in horribly quick succession, even if she had foolishly brought them on herself. Craddock could hear her stumbling over windfall branches as they moved off through the dark with Hoyt directly behind them. He did not try again to help her. She would not have welcomed his touch.

On command he pulled open the door and Virgil Hoyt took it out of his hand. A murmur of talk broke off sharply. Dead silence and the impact of staring eyes met them as they walked inside.

The room was precisely as they had left it. Over against the wall Bud Tipton showed them a face that was ashy and held a sweaty sheen. Belle Starr leaned a palm on the edge of the table, watching them across the litter of dirty dishes.

Elbowing the door shut, Virgil Hoyt placed both shoulders against the panel and looked around with a keen and wicked triumph. He had the look of a huge, satisfied cat.

"The luck ain't run out of this outfit yet," he said, grinning. "You'd never guess in a million tries what we've stumbled into!"

"What?" demanded Blue Duck.

"Something to make the broncs we lost look like small stuff, I'll tell you that! Something that should have that Dumont clan forking over any amount we say!"

"You mean, this kid? What in hell would he mean to the Dumonts?"

Instead of answering, Virgil Hoyt reached over and, seizing Vinnie's jacket and shirt, gave them a jerk that staggered her. There was a gasp from someone, then Hoyt was turning to confront a rush from Bud Tipton, who came lunging blindly from the wall.

Hoyt swung his six-gun and when Bud was a half-dozen paces away he fired, coolly and deliberately. Bud was stopped in his tracks. His gaunt old shoulders hunched forward as the bullet struck him in the chest. Then he pivoted, a leg giving away under him and letting him fall heavily.

For a moment, as the crash of the shot died and the smoke drifted up from Hoyt's six-gun, no one made any move at all. Then Craddock, the first to jar loose of the shock of this killing, cursed and started forward. He pulled up quickly enough when gun metal flickered in lamplight and he saw Blue Duck's revolver trained squarely on him.

After that he could not have moved, for with a sob of terror Vinnie Dumont had thrown herself against his chest. Craddock lifted an arm protectingly about her.

Belle's angry cry rang through the cabin then, and she came striding to shove Jim July aside and confront the big outlaw leader.

"Damn you, Virg Hoyt! Not in my own cabin! I got neighbors to think about." She added harshly, "Killing comes just too easy for you lately, seems to me, ever since you slaughtered them Dumont riders."

The crop-handled gun, still dribbling smoke, hung slackly at the end of Hoyt's long arm. Head drawn back, eyes puckered until they almost disappeared behind their shaggy brows, he returned Belle's look. Craddock, watching, knew that this was a clash of wills of major importance to himself and to the girl.

It was Hoyt who gave way, but only by a little. He shrugged thick shoulders and his crippled hand slowly slid the gun into holster.

"Maybe I was a speck sudden," he admitted gruffly. "But he tried to jump me."

"An old man like that?" Belle wasn't satisfied. She swung her angry stare on all these tough outlaws, and it was interesting to see how they backed water before her. "I been letting you boys git away with too much around here. Just because you can ride in for a meal and a bed on occasion, you got the notion Younger's Bend is open territory for any damn thing!" Not waiting to let anyone answer her, she turned again to the crumpled shape of Bud Tipton. "Is he dead?"

One of the outlaws had knelt to examine the downed man. He looked up, nodding soberly. "Sure is, Belle. Dead as a mackerel."

Craddock felt the convulsive sob that shook Vinnie Dumont and his arm tightened about her shoulders.

Blue Duck said, "I think you better do some explaining, Hoyt. Who is this gal?"

"Who?" Hoyt looked around arrogantly, timing the detonation of his bombshell. "Why, she's Cass Dumont's daughter, that's all! Both her and this Craddock have come here to look for them Stirrup horses!"

"Craddock?" Astonishment caused Blue Duck's whole face to sag.

Craddock glanced at him, then over at Belle. This news, as well as the sight of him holding the girl in his arms, must have hit her a hard jolt. Her head lifted; a white line compressed the corners of her mouth.

And Virgil Hoyt, seeing this, remarked with cruel pleasure, "I guess he sort of put one over on you, Belle. That business at Catoosa — killing Sago and all — it was just plain trickery, meant to catch your eye and, through you, get him a chance at the rest of us!"

## XV

JUST for once, Belle Starr had nothing to say.

Jim July demanded, "You certain what you tell us, Hoyt?"

"I got ears and out there just now I heard plenty." He indicated with a jerk of his head the dark outside where night wind was stripping the branches of the trees, tearing the leaves from them. "The girl's name is Vinnie Dumont. Just stop a minute and figure how much wealth there is in that Dumont clan — and how much they'd be willing to shell out to get her back."

"You don't know what you're saying!" Craddock shouted. "You ain't smart enough to handle a thing this size. You try holding this girl and the whole Indian Territory will be too small to hide you."

Fury swept through Virgil Hoyt. "You shut up!" Beside himself, the outlaw stepped across, tore the girl from Craddock's arms and reached for a fistful of his shirt front. "We done had all we're going to from you!"

Craddock would not show fear. Contemptuously taking Hoyt's wrist he plucked the crippled hand loose — and at once felt the sharp jab of Blue Duck's six-gun barrel thrust hard against him, just below the ribs. It straightened him, breath sucking in as he stood with both of them crowding him like that — Blue Duck's harsh breathing in his ear and Hoyt glaring with eyes that promised violence.

Belle ended that moment. "Stop it, you hear? This is still my cabin and I won't have such goings on!"

As Virgil Hoyt slowly backed away from Craddock, though with mouth working furiously, Belle moved to the girl and took her by an elbow. Vinnie had the dazed look of shock. She stared from one to another of the people about her.

"You better set before you go and faint on us," Belle told her, not without kindness.

Vinnie let herself be led to a chair by the table. She dropped into it, a crushed figure. Over her head, Belle caught Jim July's attention and indicated the body of Bud Tipton with an imperious nod.

The Cherokee understood and spoke to one of the others. Together they leaned and picked up old Bud. He was not heavy but the limpness of death made him an awkward load. His head wobbled on his chest and one of his hands trailed in the dirt as they got the door opened and carried him outside, grunting with the effort.

"I don't want any part of this business." Belle was saying to Hoyt and the others. "This ain't picking up a few head of stock and running 'em off. What you're talking about can get us all in bad trouble!"

"But look at the money."

"I'm looking at the last deal you led these boys into. If I was them I'd want to be a little more careful, after that Dumont thing."

Hoyt's thick chest lifted. "Don't bait me. This is a different proposition. We just hold onto the girl long enough to get word to her kin and arrange for paying the ransom. Then we take her to Texas and set her loose. What's wrong with that?"

"And supposing the Dumonts won't pay? I figure they're more apt to send the whole U. S. Army in here, looking for her."

The man shook his head. "If they got any notion of seeing her again, they won't. That'll be made plain in the note we send 'em. The place I got in mind to take her, they wouldn't have a chance in hell of finding it."

"They won't have to find it." she retorted. "All they have to do is come here to Younger's Bend and start putting the pressure on me. You think I'll let you make me party to a kidnapping?"

"Belle, I don't ask you to have any part in it at all, if you'll just write the ransom note for us. After all, you had more schooling than the rest of us did."

She snorted scornfully. "Quit bragging. There can't a one of you so much as spell his own name. That's why you're asking me to do it." She swung away and took a few brisk paces across the floor and back again. Turning suddenly, she placed a hip against the edge of the table, and frowned at the circle of waiting men. "Well, is that it? Have you all made up your minds you want to go through with this foolishness?"

They exchanged looks. Craddock, studying their faces, never had a moment's doubt. Virgil Hoyt was their leader and these men held a still unshaken respect for his schemes and his promises. Hoyt, too, read the same answer and a grin of triumph split his wide mouth.

"I reckon you see, Belle, you can't do nothing about it."

"No, I reckon not."

Craddock had never seen her bested, but he read defeat in

her now, the admission that she was, after all, a woman and not the equal of this bunch of determined men.

There were misgivings in the slow shake of her head, but she said gruffly, "All right — it's your necks. Since you're determined, there's no use my arguing. I'll get pencil and paper."

Virgil Hoyt watched her cross the room and disappear behind the curtain. At once he turned to the men who were guarding Craddock.

"Quick! Take him out of here."

"What do we do with him?" Jim July wanted to know.

Blue Duck showed a cruel satisfaction. "Leave that to me," he grunted. "It's me he made a fool of in Catoosa!"

"Suit yourself," Hoyt said, indifferently.

The pressure of the gun started Craddock for the door that July threw open, but before he stepped through he held back for a last look at Vinnie Dumont. She had half-risen, knuckles of one hand pressed against her mouth, her face showing horror and understanding of what Craddock was being led away to. He tried to put assurance into the look he gave her, but knew it fell short of conviction.

Then he was outside and the door had closed, and in the windy darkness the two outlaws were crowding him hard.

"Just walk slow," Blue Duck warned him, "so I can keep touchin' you with the end of this six-shooter. Straight toward where we left our horses."

Craddock gave them no argument. At the pen an order halted him and Blue Duck gave Jim July instructions to bind the prisoner's hands with his own saddle rope — a job the Cherokee did swiftly, working by touch since there was not enough light in the milky sky to see what he was doing.

Craddock said suddenly, half pleading, "Listen, Jim! About the girl. I figure you a better man than the others. Will you keep an eye on them? Try not to let any of those tough no-goods take it into their heads to make things even worse for her?"

He didn't get an answer. As July finished and stepped

back, Blue Duck was there to test the lashings. He seemed satisfied.

"All right," he grunted. "I'll take over now. Up on your horse, Craddock!"

Catching the saddle-horn with his bound hands, Craddock groped until he got a toe into stirrup and lifted himself. Blue Duck was up a moment later, holding the reins of both mounts. To Jim July he said, "You can tell Virg I won't be gone long." He set out with Craddock, striking for the river trail.

The horses picked a way slowly over the uncertain footing, hoofs dislodging stones from the muddy hillside and the riders braced against the stirrups until they had leveled out on the broad ravine below. Belle's cabin was lost in the trees. There was no sound to be heard now but the creaking of their own saddles, the thud of hoofs, and the rush of wind through the branches overhead.

Could it really be little more than twenty-four hours ago, Craddock found himself wondering, that he had walked this path with Sam Starr's twin-barreled shotgun at his back? Then, the chance interference of a couple of lawmen had saved him from ending a faceless corpse, floating in the shallows of the Canadian. He could not count on anything like that happening a second time.

Suddenly the river lay just before them, slipping black and silent between its reed-grown and tangled banks. Craddock's horse felt the tug at its reins as Blue Duck pulled in, and it halted, tossing its head and stamping in weeds. Craddock shifted his stiff length in the saddle.

He said, "Isn't this a little close to Belle's? A shot would carry in these hills at night."

"You think it matters to me if she hears it?"

"I wouldn't think you'd want to get in bad with her. You ain't been making out so well there, lately!"

"And why else do you suppose I'm doing this now?" Blue Duck's voice was savage with jealousy. "Since that day in Fort Smith there's nothing I've wanted more, but it wasn't so easy, after you'd done me the favor of fetching help and

taking care of Rufe Sago. Now that we've found out all
about you I figure there's nothing holding my hand."

It came then, the sharp click of the gun going to full
cock. Craddock's strung nerves leaped at the sound. Blue
Duck's snicker came to him.

"Ain't you got nothing to say? Whyn't you try begging me
a little?"

"I wouldn't give you the pleasure." Craddock heard the
tight edge in his own voice. And he made the plunge, knowing it was the only card left him to play. "A business proposition, Blue Duck. Thirty thousand dollars for my life!"

"Thir — That's crazy!"

"It ain't to me. It ain't a cent too much."

The outlaw gave a snort. "What foolishness are you talking? I suppose I just turn you loose and then some day you
mail me a check?"

"You'll have the cash tonight to take it in your hands and
count it, and then decide whether I'm hoorawing you or
making you a fair proposition. What's your answer?"

Blue Duck evidently wasn't sure. There was a stillness
while the black river whispered past them, gurgling in the
shallows. Finally the outlaw said hoarsely, "Let's hear a
little more! What do I have to do — rob the Cherokee
treasury?"

"This is money I lost during the Stirrup raid, and the real
reason I'm down here in this God-forsaken country. You left
me for dead and run my bronc off with all the others. The
thirty thousand was in his saddlebags."

"Like hell! I never seen no saddlebags!"

"But you had the bronc — that buckskin you tried to sell
me at Catoosa. Remember? And I can tell you who did get
the bags and the money. I can show you just where he buried
both, aiming to cut the rest of you out of a share."

"And who was that?"

"Virg Hoyt, of course!"

There was another silence. When Blue Duck spoke again
his voice was quiet and dangerous. "I see through you now,

Craddock. You're just trying to poison my mind with such talk."

"You mean, you don't think he'd do it? Might as well go ahead and pull that trigger then and dump me in the river. There's no hope for you. Let Hoyt have his money and his laugh at you and all the rest who are stupid enough to trust him."

He gathered himself, waiting for Blue Duck's answer and wondering what the chances would be of throwing himself sideward out of saddle to hunt protection in the brush. He felt helpless; his wrists were so securely tied that he knew, after many minutes of working on the knots, that he had no hope of loosening them.

Blue Duck said, "I figure you're lying in your teeth, Craddock. But — where do you want to take me?"

"I'm afraid you'll have to do the taking." Craddock tried to keep his utter, unnerving relief from showing. "I'd never find the place again in the dark. It's that ravine where we held the horses last night."

The outlaw cursed softly. "A long ride for a wild goose chase. Mister, I swear if you're trying to trick me — "

"One way to find out."

"Yeah." Saddle leather creaked as Blue Duck straightened, taking the reins. "All right. We'll go have a look. But this had sure better be on the level."

Evidently he was not as familiar with the trail as Virgil Hoyt had been, or perhaps the wind and the night's moonless opacity confused him. They made a fumbling ride of it, one that seemed to lag endlessly in futile starts and stoppings. Craddock listened to Blue Duck's mutterings and felt the utter weariness that dragged him down and the sick hollowness of his starved body.

Craddock's thoughts moved constantly back to the cabin at Younger's Bend, seeing Vinnie Dumont a prisoner in that crowd of men, and trying to picture what she must be enduring. He hoped he had pegged Jim July right, as one who would have the decency and the nerve to stand between her and the rest. And, after all, there was Belle. He supposed she could be trusted to allow nothing of that sort to go on. Perhaps he had better be worrying about his own predicament.

Blue Duck cursed suddenly and pulled to a dead halt. "Damn it, now I'm lost. Ought to be a trail here and there ain't."

Craddock, leaning far over in saddle, peered ahead and thought he saw a break in the black mass of the trees. "Bear north a little," he said. "This looks familiar."

The outlaw still grumbled but he kicked his tired mount forward, Craddock's animal trailing. Within minutes more the thick wall of growth had fallen away, and as quickly as that they found themselves at the site of last night's camp.

Blue Duck brought the horses to a stand while they listened a moment to the stillness of this hollow where the booming wind did not reach them.

"Well?" said Blue Duck, meaningfully.

Craddock told him, "We need a torch or something."

"There ought to be a lantern cached with the camp stuff."

Blue Duck ordered his prisoner down, then dismounted himself and led the horses to a sapling and tied them. Craddock heard him pawing through the goods the outlaws had left here beneath a tarpaulin. Moving in that direction on stiffened legs, he saw the flash of a match. Blue Duck was silhouetted, on his knees, jacking up the chimney of an old barn lantern and adjusting its wick.

The flame took hold and steadied; the lantern's rusty bail squealed as Blue Duck rose and turned to face Craddock. He had laid his gun aside for a moment but it was in his hand again now.

He said gruffly, "I'm ready to see this money."

"It's agreed, is it, that you're to give me my bronc and turn me loose?"

Blue Duck jerked his head impatiently. "All right — all right. The money!"

The wash of the lantern lay upon them both, putting strange shadows across them. Looking at Blue Duck's poorly colored face, with its bulging eyes, and the petulant mouth beneath the waxed mustache, Craddock knew the man had no intention of keeping any promise. But he gave no sign.

He told Blue Duck. "The stuff is buried over in the rocks, close to the wall. I watched Hoyt last night after you and Prentiss were asleep. I saw him sneak away, and I followed him. I figure he either got some of the money or was making sure it hadn't been touched."

"You saw where it was hid?"

"No. But I should come pretty close."

The outlaw gave a grunt. "You better. Understand, I still think this is a trick."

"Come along." said Craddock. "I'll show you it ain't."

Craddock took the lead. The lantern, swinging in the hand of the man behind him, set the shapes and shadows of the night to dancing weirdly. Hampered by its shifting light he stumbled time and again in the deep growth underfoot and had to keep his bound arms lifted to ward off the limbs and tall brush continually lashing at his face.

Then he had shoved through the last of the brush and the pile-up of rubble lay ahead. Blue Duck, crowding behind him, nearly caused him to take a tumble.

The outlaw said, "Well?"

"Hold it higher." Craddock studied the talus heapings, not quite knowing what to look for, and pointed suddenly with both bound arms. "Appears to me like somebody had been piling up rock, yonder!"

Blue Duck saw the place. All at once he had caught fire with excitement.

"Move, damn you!" he exclaimed, his breath against Craddock's neck.

Slipping and scrambling, Craddock had a hard time going fast enough to satisfy him. Once he fell and wrenched an elbow badly trying to catch his weight against it and avoid landing on his face. Loose stone rattled and twisted underfoot. They came to a stop, panting.

"Look!" said Craddock. "He put up a stick to mark it."

Blue Duck had already set his lantern on a boulder. He grabbed the stick, a good stout limb. He thrust an end into a crevice and put all his weight upon it. Levered like that, a big chunk of rock slowly lifted, moved aside. Blue Duck grunted. He caught a rough edge and, finding it unyielding, laid his gun aside to free his other hand.

Then, thinking he caught a suspicious movement by his prisoner, he quickly darted a hand back to lay it upon the gun butt. Half bent, head twisted to look at Craddock, he ordered harshly, "You get back from me a little!"

Only when he was satisfied with Craddock's new position did he bend again to the resistant slab of stone. He put both hands to it and gave a heave that brought it suddenly from its place with a shower of rock dust. He nearly fell but caught himself. And Craddock heard his quick exclamation.

One hand of the outlaw plunged into the hole he had made and found something there. He took a good grip and hauled it free, the scuffed leather of the weighted saddlebags scraping stone as he brought them into the lantern light.

The sound that came out of Blue Duck then was scarcely a human one as he threw himself upon his trophy, flopping it over so that he could get at one of the bulging pouches. His trembling fingers were working with the flap when, almost too late, he remembered his prisoner. It must have been the crackling of stone that warned him.

He turned and saw Owen Craddock almost upon him.

Blue Duck gave a yell and scrambled frantically aside. Craddock, off-balanced, landed heavily in the rubble and his bound hands were unable to break his fall. With an effort he rolled onto an elbow, then to his knees. The outlaw was screaming with rage and fear as he tried to get his feet under him, seemingly unable to manage them. But his hand, scrabbling about, closed by chance upon the rubber handle of his gun.

Triumphant, he grabbed and swept it up, shooting wildly. The bullet merely kicked up rock dust while the sound of the gun went rocketing off through the ravine. Still groping blindly for a target, Blue Duck pulled the trigger a second time. Craddock, on his knees, lifted both bound hands above his head and brought them forward, letting go the heavy chunk of stone he had seized.

Across a space of half a dozen feet it drove straight at Blue Duck's head. It seemed to crash right in!

## XVI

AFTER the first reaction had passed, Craddock took the dead man's gun, then made a gingerly search of Blue Duck's pockets for a knife which he failed to find. There might be one in the outlaws' cache, however. He managed to get the saddlebags looped across one arm and took the lantern by its bail.

He looked for a moment at the dead man, sprawled half across the hole he had made in the rocks, a gruesome object that repelled his glance. It made him glad to swing the circle of lanternlight away to guide him back out of the talus rubble and the brush.

It was awkward going, cumbered as he was by both the heavy leather pouches and the lantern. He stumbled a time or two, and once a branch came unexpectedly out of the blackness and scored his face, bringing blood. When he reached the camp clearing, he set down his burdens and went immediately to work hunting through the stuff under the tarpaulin.

There, fortunately, he discovered a bowie knife in a leather sheath. Seated on the ground with the blade propped between his knees, he sawed the rope across it. Although the knife's edge was dull, he managed in short order to cut through his bonds and shake loose of them. Freed, he sat for minutes with forearms on knees and head hanging, too utterly drugged by tiredness and by the aftereffects of what he had been through to move.

At last, though, he had to become aware of the chill that came out of the earth and sent long spasms of shivering through him, shaking him the way a dog might do to a bone. The emptiness of his belly was also beginning to make its clamoring known.

He rose unsteadily and began gathering materials for a fire. When it was burning well and putting its warmth and brightness into the gloom of the clearing, he blew out the lantern and proceeded to rummage through the outlaws' supplies until he located the makings of a meal.

Despite his nausea, he felt better when he had eaten. He felt better still after he had built a cigarette, had smoked it down and flicked the butt into the coals of his fire.

Blue Duck's six-shooter was the same caliber as the one Virgil Hoyt had taken away from the Texan. Craddock brought it out and tested the action and balance, replaced the spent shells with new ones from his holster belt.

He thought of the body lying in the rocks. He supposed he ought to do something about it, but he lacked the will or the strength — or even the inclination. Blue Duck could be the concern of his friends and Craddock had not even had time as yet to examine the saddlebags.

He hauled them to him and unbuckled the pouches. Packets of greenbacks met his searching hands. A quick estimate indicated that the bulk of his money was there, although when he got around to taking a count he supposed he would find that Virgil Hoyt had managed to make away with some of it. But there was little enough he could have spent it on, here in the Nations, and Hoyt would not dare rouse the suspicions of his men by appearing all at once too heavily loaded with cash.

Craddock closed the leather flaps, satisfied — and a little overwhelmed at the odds that had been against him, yet had not prevented him doing what he had set out so blindly to accomplish.

Only — then he remembered that this was not the end of the job. Because there was the girl.

Craddock cursed and ran a palm wearily across his face. Perhaps it was what Bat Masterson had been talking about on an evening that now seemed long ago, when he had said, "There's a soft streak in you, Craddock!"

Perhaps Bat was right. Otherwise, why should he have trouble persuading himself to call it quits, to take his money and strike out for Texas while he had the opportunity? The outlaws would hardly dare risk harming Vinnie Dumont, and once the ransom was paid they would let her go.

Yet apparently the soft streak was there, underlying his cynicism, for Craddock knew he could not leave Vinnie Dumont in their hands. Just what any one man could do to save her was past his power to see at the moment. But this was because fatigue and the weight of warm food in his stomach had dulled his mind beyond thinking.

Whatever he might decide, his body could not go longer without rest. And he remembered he had not even taken care of the horses.

Moving in a lethargy of utter exhaustion, he stumbled to his feet and went to where both animals were tied and stripped them of gear. He tended to the fire and shook out his bedroll. Later, lying in his blankets, he had a momentary vision of Blue Duck's corpse sprawled there in the rocks only a few hundred yards from him, but even this was not enough to hold off the tide of darkness that rolled in upon him and quickly dragged him down.

He slept without movement, without dreams, yet his mind was well enough disciplined that he could wake himself before the sky had begun to pale. At once he was throwing back his cover and groping in the chill darkness to find his boots. . . .

Over Younger's Bend was an air of desertion, under a sky that was still overcast to the color of beaten silver. None of the saddle horses that last night had been tied around Belle's cabin were there this morning. Even the work nag and the mule were missing from the horse pen. No smoke drifted above the chimney. The only sound Craddock heard was the tinkle of a cowbell drifting off Hi Early Mountain — a lonely musical pulse of sound that made the feeling of desertion stronger than ever.

Trailing Blue Duck's sorrel, Craddock rode up to the cabin and halted, scowling. The door stood ajar. Insecurely latched, no doubt, it had been blown open by the gusty wind. Everyone was gone, then, and no telling where he could hope to find Vinnie Dumont.

Still, Craddock dismounted and walked over, pushed the door wide and looked in on an interior which held the litter of the crowd that had been here the night before. Dirty dishes cluttered the table; there was the wreckage of one that had fallen to the floor and shattered. There was the smell of whisky and of stale tobacco smoke.

Craddock looked and then, convinced, turned away. The door was nearly shut behind him when the sound of his own name called made him halt, surprised, and come about.

Belle Starr had pushed aside the curtain and stood looking at him. She wore a shapeless cotton nightgown, with a high buttoned neck and long sleeves, and her feet were bare. Her hair, loosened, hung about her shoulders. Her defenses against encroaching middle age were completely down, and the signs were stamped upon her harsh mouth, in the sagging of her throat, in the black hollows about her eyes. She leaned her shoulders against the wall and stared at him, with the unmistakable scowl of one suffering the miseries of morning-after.

"You, Craddock." she exclaimed heavily. "You must have killed Blue Duck, then. I knew it." She wagged her head at him. "I knew when they said they'd turned you over to him and when he never come back. You been nothing but bad news for me — for all of us. Virg Hoyt was a fool not to have made sure of you when he had his hands on you."

Craddock moved toward her. She watched him come, her head dropped forward, her black eyes peering up at him, her

mouth warped with bitterness. She seemed totally uncon-
cerned about her appearance.

"Look, Belle," Craddock told her firmly. "I don't blame you
for thinking small of me after the way I came here under
false colors. But I never meant you any harm. I don't now."

"Then why don't you let me alone?"

"Because I can't. Not while they've got Vinnie Dumont
prisoner."

"Vinnie Dumont." Her mouth shaped the name scornfully.
"I thought as much! A pretty face — and a fortune to go with
it. I know what's on your mind."

He said sharply, "You're wrong, but we won't go into that.
I just want to know where she's been taken to."

"A long way from here — and that's as much as you'll get
out of me. I told 'em I'd have no part in a kidnapping."

"Maybe you think you could convince Hangin' Judge
Parker of that? He knows that gang has virtually made its
headquarters here at Younger's Bend. To save your own neck,
Belle, you better think twice about this."

She shook her head, the uncombed hair dragging across
her shoulders. "I got nothing to say to you, Craddock. Go on
— get out!"

Craddock felt the tightening of the muscles of his chest,
and the hard conviction that this woman's mistaken loyalty
had him beaten. Her will was as strong as his own; he knew
he could not force from her anything she did not want to
tell him.

He was close to giving it up then, to turning on his heel
and walking out of that cabin and away from his only prob-
able chance of finding Vinnie Dumont. But a last argument
struck him, one that he did not like to use and did use only
with reluctance.

"All right," he said. "If that's how you want it. But let
me remind you of one thing. Sam told me about that fellow,
Middleton. Now you've lost Sam and even Blue Duck. That's
whittling them down, Belle. And the rest are hiding out somewhere with that girl. It's like you said yourself. She's damned
good to look at. And young."

It was cruel and he felt shame as soon as he saw it strike her. Her breast lifted within the shapeless cotton garment, pain shaping itself in her plain features. Then she turned from him, both hands lifting to push back the stringy hair from her forehead.

"I got a hell of a headache," she said dully. "Will you see if there's anything left in that jug on the table?"

"Sure."

Quickly he got the jug, poured a little whisky into a cup. Belle Starr took it, not looking at him, and drank. She shuddered at the bite of the stuff, then said in a heavy voice, as she stared into the cup:

"You know where the Cave is?"

"No."

"You'd never find it without help."

She turned to face him again, and in her eyes now was a cold resentment toward this man who had forced her to admit she could not afford the intrusion into the male world she dominated of a younger and handsomer face.

She said, "All right, I'll take you to the Cave. It's where they're holding the Dumont girl. After that it'll be up to you. I reckon I'd just as soon they killed you. But if you can manage it, take her and get the hell out of this country. Don't let me see either of you again."

"A fair bargain," Craddock said.

"Then, while I'm getting dressed and fixing myself something to eat, you go saddle Venus for me."

The sun was a greasy smear behind the clouds above the eastern hills when Belle came outside, secured the cabin door behind her, and stepped into saddle. The dreary turn of the weather seemed to have done nothing for her mood. Even after Craddock passed her the reins she sat motionless, staring darkly at an open spot among the trees just in front of the cabin.

She said suddenly, "When my time comes, that's where I want they should put me!"

"A little morbid, ain't it, looking that far ahead? Who knows where they'll be by then?"

Belle shrugged within the heavy man's jacket she had donned against the chill. "Sometimes I get a feeling the day ain't too far off. And I know I ain't ever going far from the Bend."

"You've got it figured out, then, how you'll make the Cherokee Council let you keep this land?"

She did not explain. Venus obeyed the touch of the reins and Craddock fell in behind the black mare. As on the day they had come here he followed Belle down the steep hill trail into the ravine and along this to the river fording.

They crossed the Fort Smith trail and headed directly south into a region of rugged sandstone hills, heavily timbered in pine and cedar and walnut. It was Choctaw country, but within an hour they had lost any sign of habitation.

This was as wild a country as Craddock had seen, given over to the coyote, the wolf and the cougar. Deer flitted through the close ranks of woods that were gloomy with overcast, and through which the trail that Belle Starr seemed to know by heart was a dim trace, tortured and twisting.

Once as they stopped to rest their horses they could hear the crying of wild geese spearing southward overhead, out of sight beyond the clouds whose dark bellies the pine tops seemed to scrape as the wind swung them. Craddock searched the vagrant sound across the blank gray sky until it faded, then lowered his glance to Belle and saw her watching him with a kind of bitter mockery in her dark eyes.

She said, "Could you have found your way around this country?"

He shook his head. "I doubt if any army could."

"Oh, they've tried. Yanks and Confederates used to hunt each other through these woods. Since the War the Jameses and the Youngers and a lot of others have used the trail and the Cave. But in twenty years no outsider has been showed the way in here — not until today. I hope you appreciate that."

"I do, Belle," he assured her.

"And just how are you figuring to do what you've come for, after I've showed you?"

Craddock lifted his shoulders. "I couldn't say. I'll just have to work it out as I go. But I mean to take that girl out of here."

She looked at him strangely. "You must love her a hell of a lot."

"What?" The words startled him, then turned him scornful. "That sort of thing's got nothing to do with it. It just ain't right for any girl to be left in the hands of a crowd of scum."

"They ain't much, I suppose," Belle admitted. "They're ignorant and maybe not too bright, most of them, or they wouldn't be where they are, taking the small pickings of this kind of a life and letting a lobo like Virg Hoyt run them around. Still they're my friends, most of them. If I thought I was turning something loose on them — "

"I won't start trouble. That's a promise. Except maybe when it comes to Virgil Hoyt. He needs a killing."

She scowled. "You're welcome to that one. Better for the rest if they'd never had anything to do with him."

They rode on with no more talk for a stretch of many miles. The day grew older; toward noon the wind lessened and silence lay upon this tumbled land except for the call of a jay, or the quick, intermittent drum of a woodpecker running through the quiet of the woods.

Craddock estimated they might have ridden thirty-five or forty miles since crossing the Canadian, though in this up-and-down country it was hard to judge. It was a trek hard on both mount and rider, dulling the mind and setting muscles to aching with the constant shift and balance in the saddle.

Sandstone scarps broke folded hills that now were thick-grown with yellow pine. A clear rushing mountain stream flanked their trail and presently Belle stopped to indicate it and say:

"The Fourché Maline. We're pretty close." He could read a beginning tension in her.

"We'll keep going," he said.

"I warn you, their lookout will have us spotted. There ain't any way to get near without them seeing."

"That's all right. I don't figure sneaking is the way to do this job. You can get me into the Cave, I suppose?"

She sounded a little dubious. "I suppose. Depends on who's holding down the gate."

"Try it. We'll just walk in, then see what they want to make of it."

They sent their horses ahead. The land tilted. Below them, for miles of blue distance, spreading hills lay beneath the overcast. Beside the trail the mountain stream ran gray and frothy.

And then Belle was saying, "All right, Craddock. Better look sharp. This is what you said you wanted."

## XVII

CRADDOCK looked for a cave but could see nothing more than a jumble of great boulders and sandstone shelves, and above these the hillside reaching steeply into timber. He saw a barren slant of slickrock just below these trees, which he took to be the lookout point, and which he had to admit must give a matchless and uninterrupted view of the approaches to the hideout.

He glanced at Belle as she turned Venus directly up the slope. After a moment's hesitation he reined after her.

Slabs of weathered, tumbled sandstone rose just above them, and what he saw now was a boulder-stream and roofless crack making a natural passage to whatever lay just beyond the first screen of rocks. It was toward this opening that

Belle sent her horse, and Craddock thought he saw the shape
of a man watching from within.

She had seen too and as Craddock moved to follow her
she turned her head and told him, "Better hold up a second.
I can handle this."

For just an instant, suspicion clogged in Craddock's mind
and narrowed his eyes. Then, although he supposed he had
no reason to trust this woman, he nodded and watched her
jog Venus up toward the rocks. The man stepped into sight
to meet her. It was Jim July, both thumbs stuck into his belt
and a rifle in the crook of an elbow.

Belle leaned from the saddle and they talked for a minute.
Finally she turned and motioned, and Craddock rode slowly
forward. Jim July stood and watched him come, a hard and
undecipherable look on his dark face. But he made no move
to cover the horseman with the rifle he held. His smoky eyes
touched the gun in Craddock's holster. Perhaps he recognized it as belonging to Blue Duck. Even if Belle had not told
him of the killing he must have guessed for himself.

Yet he said nothing at all. He stepped back with a jerk of
his long-maned head that indicated the way through the gate
lay clear. Craddock looked at Belle and caught her nod. She
sent Venus into the opening, and after the briefest hesitation
he urged his own horse after her, though it meant putting
the Cherokee at his back.

The space between these rugged, house-size blocks of
sandstone was only a few yards wide and so rough-floored
that only a narrow and twisting path, beaten hard by many
hoofs, threaded it. At one point a mass of rock had split, to
lean against the opposing wall, and here Craddock found
himself ducking his head into his shoulders as he rode under.
Then he was through the gateway and in a steep pocket
surrounded by more boulders, with a tree or two growing out
of the hillside.

His horse scrambled on the poor footing. Ahead, the way
dipped past a shoulder and as he cautiously followed Belle's
lead he found himself in another pocket flanked by rock faces
twenty feet or more in height. It was a natural corral, and

nearly a score of horses milled here, muzzling hay that had
been dumped for them. What appeared to be a second exit
was closed off with stretched rope.

Belle was already dismounting. "From here, we hoof it,"
she told him.

He frowned, not much liking this, but having no choice
he swung down and dropped the reins. He looked at the
saddlebags. On a quick decision he pulled them off the roan
and slung them across his shoulder.

Belle was looking at him curiously. But little as he liked
taking the bags with him, Craddock had no intention of
leaving them out of his sight and letting Jim July or some
other go through them for whatever they could find.

"Where now?" he demanded.

"This way."

She led him back out of the corral, among the boulders
and over the rough slants where heeled boots made for awkward going. Craddock caught her elbow a time or two, while
a bent arm kept the heavy saddlebags clamped in place
across his shoulder. They went down along another crack, so
narrow a horse would not have managed it. Below this they
came upon a spring, bubbling out to fill a natural run-off
basin.

Craddock began to see now the advantages of this hideout. It was no wonder outlaws had been using it since the
time of the Jameses and the Youngers. It had isolation, a far
view of distances, shelter for the horses, even a constantly
fresh supply of water. In this maze of boulders, a hunted
man could hide indefinitely and hold off an attacking force
of nearly any size.

They climbed again into another narrow crevice with
steep, high walls. Presently a down draft brought Craddock
a whiff of pinesmoke and he quickly raised his head. Just
above them was the Cave.

It was a fairly large, open-faced recess beneath a slabby
sandstone roof, its slanted sides pinching in at such an angle
as to cut the floor space to a mere corridor piercing the
shadows beneath the overhang. At the back the Cave seemed

to funnel down to nothing. The fire had been built well forward, and around it men stood and watched in silence as the man and woman came climbing up to them.

Craddock felt the tightening of his facial muscles and hoped they did not betray the queasiness inside him. Once when Belle stumbled and nearly fell against him he made no attempt to help her. One of his hands was occupied in keeping a strong grip on the precious saddlebags; the other hand, he wanted free.

His eyes searched for Virgil Hoyt. He did not immediately see him or Vinnie. This alarmed him until he happened to notice, at the back, a dark shadow that could be an opening into farther reaches. He had a careful eye on this as rock faces echoed back their footsteps, and he and Belle walked at last into the Cave's entrance.

For a moment after they halted there was no sound, no movement. The pitchpine smell of the fire and the rich odor of brewing coffee was about them. Finally one of the outlaws lifted a dirty paw and scrubbed the back of it across his mouth.

He said in a high nasal whine, "Belle, how the hell did this feller get in here?"

"Jim July let him through, Clem," she answered. "At my orders."

"I don't get it!"

"Well, don't work at it too hard." Belle told him scornfully. "Where's Hoyt?"

"He went looking for squirrel," Clem told her in a surly tone. "We-uns is running short of fresh meat."

Now Craddock had found the girl, picking her out with difficulty from among the dozen others in this gloomy, low-roofed recess. Vinnie Dumont stood in shadows near the back, staring at him. An outsize coat was pulled tight about her for warmth.

In a dangerous stillness, with every eye on him, Craddock walked deliberately toward her. One by one the men stepped aside to make way for him, pivoting slowly as Craddock moved past. Halting before Vinnie, he looked anxiously into the face she lifted — a face that showed the marks of sleep-lessness and strain.

He demanded, "They done anything to hurt you?"

She shook her head, her eyes on his face. She lifted a hand to touch his sleeve, almost as though she did not believe he could really be standing here.

She stammered, "Then you aren't — I thought — "

"I'm still in one piece," he assured her. "And I'm going to take you out of this somehow!"

"You shouldn't have tried it," she exclaimed miserably. "With so many against you!"

"Don't worry. You just don't worry." He slipped the sad-dlebags off his arm, dropped them to the rocks between them. "Keep an eye on that," he told her and turned again to face the outlaws.

The lot of them were watching him with a careful intent-ness, but he knew he had them baffled. They could not un-derstand the courage it would take for a man to walk into the midst of his enemies, and what they did not understand they secretly feared. It gave Craddock an advantage he did not mean to let go.

He came over to the fire and, stooping, picked up the blackened coffeepot, sloshed the liquid around in it and took off the lid to peer inside.

"Smells good," he told Belle. "Want some?"

"Why not?" She came over to accept the tin cup he took from a stack and filled for her. "I'm hungry enough to — " Under her breath she said, taunting him, "Well, now what?"

"I'll know," he answered gruffly, "when the time comes. Is there another way out of this place?"

"Back there," said Belle, nodding toward the rear of the cavern.

He turned to glance at the dark hole he had already no-ticed, considering it for a moment above the rim of his cup as he drank. Then a movement from one of the outlaws brought him around. The man had half drawn a holstered gun, but as Craddock looked at him his face twitched with indecision and he slid the weapon back again.

Still watching him, Craddock finished drinking, unhurriedly, wiped a sleeve across his mouth, flipped the dregs from his cup and tossed it onto the pile. He was about to say something when he heard Belle's sudden gasp of warning.

A man was squeezing through that narrow hole at the back of the Cave. The opening was so small that Virgil Hoyt had nearly to double himself in order to clear it. He carried a rifle but apparently had not got any squirrels. He leaned the rifle against the rock and came forward, his three-fingered hand brushing dust from his shoulders.

Only then he seemed to notice something wrong and he froze, his raised arm slowly lowering, as he stared at the two visitors beside the fire. Hoyt's ugly face was a study in bafflement and suffused with a slowly burning rage.

"Howdy, Virg," said Craddock.

Hoyt's mouth screwed down tight. "How did you manage, Craddock?" he demanded savagely. "Getting rid of Blue Duck and then talking his woman into fetching you down here — that's pretty smart work, ain't it? Too smart, maybe. What do you figure you're going to do now?"

"Why, I figure I'm going to take the Dumont girl away from you and back to her people. Try to stop me and you'll get what I gave Blue Duck."

The outlaw snorted. "Ringy, ain't you? Well, this is once you've bit off too big of a chunk." He looked at Belle. "Reckon we-uns should ought to be sore at you for leading a stranger in here, Belle. But that's all right, seeing as he likely made you do it. We'll take care of him — and settle for Blue Duck while we're at it."

Belle shrugged. "Nobody makes me do anything. I brought him of my own free will. I tried to tell you once, the game you're after this time is bigger'n you can pot. Ain't too late to come to your senses. Let Craddock have the girl."

"Seems to me I told you I ain't letting you or nobody else interfere with the way I run this outfit. Clem!" He jerked his head at the nearest of the outlaws. "Step over here and lift this feller's gun."

"One minute!" snapped Craddock, on a swift decision.

"Before any of you makes the mistake of taking one more order from this man, it's about time you were finding out what kind of a skunk you've let boss you. He'd sell you all out in a minute if he saw a way to profit by it. He's done it already — as I can prove!"

He looked over the faces of the outlaws, reading bewilderment and not too much understanding.

"You don't believe me?" He turned to the girl. "Bring me those saddlebags, Vinnie."

They lay at her feet where he had placed them. As she stooped and got them, Virgil Hoyt gave a start and a hoarse cry came from him.

"Oh, you recognize them?" grunted Craddock. "You want me to tell the boys where they came from, maybe — and why you've been hiding them? Maybe you'd like me to open the pouches and give them all a look inside?"

He saw Hoyt's broad face redden. "Put them bags down!"

"Bring 'em here, Vinnie."

It was a crisis that hung fire as she hesitated between her terror of the outlaw and her confidence in Craddock. Belle and the others could only stare, not having any idea of what was at issue. Hoyt himself must have realized he had already said too much, but if the others should get even a glimpse of what those saddlebags contained, his hopes of keeping it all for himself would be over.

Greed decided him. "Don't touch them flaps, damn you!" he shouted and his maimed right hand pulled the crop-handled gun out of its holster.

Craddock had been waiting for this, knowing it would come, and praying that sight of the leather bags would have the man's mind just enough divided to slow him a trifle.

The instant he saw Hoyt's arm jerk, his own hand was moving with such speed as he could muster. The Colt hung in holster for a fraction of a second, then pulled free. The sight of Hoyt's gun muzzle rising toward him made him fire before he was ready.

Even so the shot was good. Hoyt's gun exploded futilely in front of his boots, and then he was stumbling backward, striking heavily against the slick slant of rock behind him. Craddock, with the deafening roar of the shots reverberating about him, stood and watched him slide down — as dead as Cass Dumont, Bud Tipton and who knew how many others whose finish Virgil Hoyt had caused.

There was a moment of uncertain length in which ears rung to the close concussion of the guns. Craddock looked at the weapon smoking in his hand, then at the girl. Vinnie was trembling in spasms that shook her slender body. Her hands, clutching the leather saddlebags, showed tight white knuckles. Craddock stepped to her.

"Be ready to travel," he warned. "We're getting out of here."

A choked cry stopped and turned him. Clem had already got over the first shock of his leaders' death. One hand was wrapped about his holstered. gun and the other flung in Craddock's direction.

"Damn you!" he shouted. "What's in them bags?"

It was a bitter moment. Craddock had staked everything on the gamble that Hoyt's fall would hold the rest long enough to give him the time he needed. Now he saw that the gamble had failed, for he had reckoned without their curiosity and greed. Already guns were coming into the open and he could not beat them all. A look at Belle Starr told him she also saw the hopelessness of his predicament.

Craddock's jaw ached with tightness. But his mind was suddenly clear.

"All right!" he cried, harshly. "You want to see what Virg Hoyt died for?"

With his unencumbered hand he ripped open one of the bulky leather pouches, drew out a fistful of greenbacks neatly bundled in paper wrappers. "There!" he shouted and flung them at the group of men. One of the paper bands broke in midair and bills scattered like green leaves. "Have some more!" He grabbed a second handful and sent it after the first.

Then, despite Vinnie's cry of protest, he seized the bags from her and let them go flapping end for end.

"Take it all!" he yelled, as packets of money spilled into hands that were suddenly fighting to claim them.

He did not wait. He had the girl's arm and was shoving her toward the narrow opening at the rear of the Cave.

"We've got a chance!" he told her. "Quick! We take the back way!"

## XVIII

NOW it was only a step, a moment's effort to squeeze through, as behind them rose the fierce babble of men fighting savagely among themselves. Beyond lay a second, darker chamber through which they had to grope their way. Then gray daylight glimmered, and unexpectedly they were in the open again, in the pine cover of the steep hillside.

Craddock said, "I don't know how much time we can figure on. Let's keep moving."

But he heard a sob that made him turn and look at Vinnie, and discover in amazement that she was crying, tear streaks shining on her face.

"Your money." she wailed. "You deliberately threw it away — just to save me — and after I'd been so stupid."

"It was my own neck, too," he reminded her gruffly. "I couldn't shoot it out with the whole crowd of them. We'd both have been killed for sure."

"But except for me, you'd never have got into such a spot."

Craddock's voice was roughened by his own sour thoughts, "If we don't keep moving, we may not be out of it even now."

The impact of his money's loss would hit him fully later on; right now he could not let himself think about it. The sacrifice had bought him, perhaps, a few minutes' grace. He had to use them for as much as they were worth.

First of all, they would need horses.

"The corral should be around this way," he muttered, pointing.

She followed him blindly, stumbling over rocks and windfalls. He thought she was still crying, apparently too grief-stricken at Craddock's loss to care greatly what happened to her or where she was led. He was not sure himself of directions, but he supposed that following the bulge of the hill and cutting obliquely downward should bring them out about where the big chunks of sandstone formed a natural horsepen.

There would be Jim July to cope with, then. But he had an idea he could handle the Cherokee, if it came to gunplay.

A pair of revolver shots broke, one close on the heels of the other. Craddock halted involuntarily, felt the girl's body come against him and the clutch of her hand upon his arm.

"What — what was that?"

"Couldn't you tell?" Craddock showed her a tight, hard grin. Obviously those muffled explosions had occurred within the Cave itself. "The boys are busy splitting up the loot," he told her. "Let's hope they keep busy like that for maybe five more minutes."

They went ahead, brush and timber making a shifting screen through which the high sandstone bulwark of the lookout now showed close above them. It served to remind him of another danger. He came to an abrupt halt and without warning pulled Vinnie down beside him to the cold, needle-littered earth.

Crouching there, an arm tight about the girl's shoulders, he was aware of her blue eyes staring up at him. Her breath warmed his throat as she stammered a frightened question.

A frown and shake of head silenced her while he scanned the eroded edge of sandstone that knifed the gray sky. No movement there, however, though he waited out a long minute. At last Craddock drew in a deep breath.

"Too careful, I guess," he muttered. "Whoever was on

lookout would naturally have been pulled off as soon as he heard shooting in the Cave. Come on!"

He helped Vinnie up, angry about the precious time that had been wasted.

Then out of the jumble of rock forming the corral, below them, a couple of riders broke suddenly into view. The first he recognized as Jim July; after him came Belle Starr, mounted on Venus and leading a pair of saddled horses by their reins. She pulled up, the black mare dancing under her.

"Craddock!" she called. "Hey, Craddock, where the hell are you?"

Overcoming surprise long enough to shout an answer, he took Vinnie's arm.

"Quick! There's help!"

He didn't try to explain but hurried her, running and stumbling and sliding, down through trees and brush until they reached the place where Belle was waiting.

The woman said, impatiently, "Hurry up and mount! I grabbed a couple horses — wasn't time to be particular."

Craddock grunted his thanks and lifted Vinnie onto one of the horses, took the reins from Belle and passed them up to her. Then he was in the other saddle. As he settled himself there, Jim July was calling, "This way!" and at once the Cherokee struck off at a hard gallop.

Craddock whipped his hat from his head and slapped Vinnie's mount to a run, then he himself dropped in at the tail of the line. He took a look back, but there was no movement at the hideout rocks, no evidence of pursuit. After that the trees came between them and the ground was wheeling and blurring under running hoofs.

They crossed the rock-bottomed Fourché Maline in flashing fountains of spray and ran on, following some dim course that Jim July knew. The Cherokee's part in this escape completely puzzled Craddock, except that he knew Belle must have had something to do with it. July did not appear to him a man who would betray his friends, so it must mean that Belle had some stronger hold over him than did all the other members of the gang.

Belle ordered a halt, finally. They reined their horses at the center of a trail that was carpeted with leaf mold and shadowed deeply by the barren branches crowding overhead. The day was darkening with the spent hours of afternoon, and the clouds rushed before a cold wind that cruised the leaden sky.

"No need to run any farther," Belle said. "In another hour it'll start getting dark — too dark for that crowd to think about chasing you." She turned a bitter look on Craddock. "You certainly fixed them. They're cutting themselves to pieces, back there. If I'd knowed what you were going to do to them, I wouldn't have brung you in."

He shrugged. "It sure as hell wasn't what I intended, either. But I wasn't left with any choice."

"It was a high price," Belle agreed. She looked from Craddock to the girl, and back. She added shrewdly, "You talk pretty hard, but you didn't throw away that much money for nothing. I'm holding to what I said earlier this afternoon."

"What was that?"

"You remember it, I reckon!" Belle turned from him, pointing down the darkening aisle leading southward through the woods. "That's the trail to Texas. I don't reckon you'll have any more trouble."

"We'll make out," Craddock agreed, nodding.

She would have reined away then, but Vinnie Dumont spoke her name and Belle paused to put her cold stare on the younger and prettier woman.

"I don't know how to say it," Vinnie told her. "But if there's any way I can repay you — "

"You don't owe me nothing," Belle Starr told her bluntly, but there was a little more of warmth in her voice as she added, "I'm glad those roughnecks never hurt you none, honey. Hope they didn't give you too bad a time."

She lifted her hand in a final brief salute that included them both. Craddock would have spoken but she was already gone, the last he saw of her the small, straight figure erect in saddle, the ostrich plume streaming from her hat, the sleek black hide of Venus shining with a rippling of muscles, before shadows swallowed them both.

Jim July was already turning his bony horse. Craddock asked him, "Any hard feelings between us, Jim?"

The Cherokee considered this, then shook his long-maned head briefly. "None I know of, Craddock. That bunch, they was going bad since the Stirrup job. Something I hadn't no part in, Miss Dumont," he added with a quick flash of his dark eyes toward the girl. "A good thing maybe they got broke up and Hoyt done away with."

"I'm glad you see it that way," Craddock said.

"And the old man — the one Virg Hoyt killed at Belle's cabin. Don't worry. I see to it he's taken care of. Me, I'm moving in at Younger's Bend."

Craddock stared. "You're what?"

The Indian showed his teeth in a wide grin. "A fact. Belle and me fixed it up between us this afternoon."

"Well — congratulations!"

Craddock couldn't keep the dryness out of his tone, thinking of Belle and looking at the young Cherokee. He wondered about the difference in their ages. Fifteen years, or close to it. But it seemed that the Indian didn't worry about that, and Belle at least had found the way to outwit the Cherokee Nation and retain her claim to Younger's Bend.

Craddock said, "Then it'll be Belle July after today?"

"Not quite. We settled that, too. Belle say she don't want to go changing her name again."

"So?"

The Cherokee's grin turned slightly sheepish. He struck a thumb against his chest. "I am Jim Starr now!"

He kicked up his horse and rode from sight into the trees. Craddock, shaking his head, gave an astonished grunt. "Well, leave it to Belle."

"What was it she told you?"

He looked at her in the renewed and windy stillness. "When?"

"This afternoon. She said you remembered."

"Oh, that!" He shrugged, his mouth gone angry. "It was

nothing." And, reining his horse around, he pointed opposite
to the way the other two had vanished. "The trail to Texas,"
he said, changing the subject abruptly. "There's nothing to
stop us taking it. We're quit of that tough bunch at the Cave,
and the bulk of your stolen horses will be turned back by the
military."

"But your money!" she cried, her eyes searching his hard
face. "My family will make it up to you, Craddock. They'll
be more than glad — "

He said angrily, "What I did wasn't for no reward!"

But for what, then? Belle Starr had thought she knew. He
remembered, all right, what she had said that afternoon, *You
must love her a hell of a lot!* But that was foolish. What feeling could he have for anyone who had showed so little wisdom and caused him so much trouble and loss?

He said, "Just forget it. It ain't important."

And strangely, suddenly, it wasn't — not the money, or
what it stood for; not any of the frantic and hard ambition
that had been all the meaning of his years. These seemed far
from him and of no moment, contrasted with the new and
unfamiliar feelings stirring in him now.

"Owen!" she cried. "That's your name, isn't it?"

"Yes."

Her hand touched his sleeve, reaching across the space
between them. "Please don't hate me. I'm not worth much,
not near what I've cost you. I know I'm just a brat and I've
ruined everything. But I think I'd die if you — "

"Vinnie!"

Their horses stood head and tail, and it was the simplest
thing to lean and put his arm about her and draw her up to
him.

Somewhere off beyond the trees a wedge of geese, southward flying, laid their busy chorus upon the wind.

# THE LURKING GUN

# CAST OF CHARACTERS

### Jim Gary
He was running for his life when he found shelter in a mantrap town.

### Matt Winship
This old fighter was ready to give up until they burned the ground out from under him.

### Tracy Bannister
She was the target of vicious rumors.

### Paul Keating
What he thought was a way out turned out to be a dead-end road.

### Fern Keating
Her fiery hair signaled the burning rage of her ambition.

### Webb Toland
His six-guns weren't as deadly as his line of slick double-talk.

### Pete Dunn
He had to get off his deathbed in order to die.

## I

IT WAS the storm that finally stopped Jim Gary. It came blowing in after him, as the long trail brought him into this nameless Nevada town at an hour past midnight. Lightning flickered with an eye-punishing steadiness. When his tired Swallowfork buckskin carried him across the bridge at the north end of the settlement, its hoofs thudding hollowly on the plankings, the wind swelled suddenly to pummel the trees that lined the shallow wash below. Gary stopped in the middle of the bridge, and turned in his saddle for a long look into the uneasy darkness at his back.

No rain, yet, but it was bound to let go in a matter of minutes. The town had battened down against the coming weather; its doors and windows were shut and showed few lights. He had a feeling of being the only living thing abroad in this night of sound and wind fury, and the thought filled him with a great weariness. Yet, as he stared with burning eyes back along the trail, he knew well enough that the Planks were only hours behind him.

That day a high shoulder had given him a long rearward view and showed the pair of them, black dots moving against the tawny sweep of trail. Jim Gary knew they'd seen him too, of course. After a week of running he still had no wider lead on them than that. Boyd and Asa Plank were not the kind to let the mere threat of a storm hold them back now. They were possessed of a dogged incentive, that would keep them going as long as he found the strength to lead them on.

Feeling the pressure, Gary straightened around again and kicked the buckskin forward. It obeyed reluctantly. He knew its legs were trembling under it with last, spent effort.

Nothing moved on the main street as they drifted through, with sheets of street dust whipping and stinging about the buckskin's legs. They passed a closed saloon, and another that seemed to be open but doing no business at this late hour. A signboard creaking over the dim-lit entrance of a hotel drew the briefest of glances; thought of shelter and a bed was almost an overpowering temptation, and yet Gary rode on. What he was looking for, anxiously, was a public livery or some such where he could find another mount to replace the buckskin that could carry him no farther.

He had reached the lower end of the street without success and was about to turn back when a flare of lightning showed him the words "NEVADA STAGES" painted across the front of a darkened building. Riding closer, he saw a battered coach parked in the weeds between the station and its adjoining barn. Beyond was the crisscross of corral poles. More lightning, and he caught a movement of horses in the pen.

A moment only, he hesitated. There was no sign of a night watchmen, no light showing. He sent his limping mount past the parked stage and into the shadows, and stepped tiredly down. He was so near exhaustion that his knees buckled and he had to catch at the saddlehorn to steady himself.

Being relay teams, these horses would undoubtedly be picked ones, sound of wind and limb even if not too familiar to a saddle. To take one in trade for the buckskin would be theft of a kind, he supposed, but Jim Gary was past worrying about that. He moved deliberately, stripping saddle and gear from the spent horse. The shuttering lightning was almost constant now. Brush and trees danced in the glare; thunder growled and bounced off the faces of the dark buildings.

He had his rope, and was stepping to unfasten the swing gate of the corral when the first hard, brief spatter of rain hit him.

Gary paused and stood listening to it pummel the hard earth, smelling the bitter dust it raised. The wind came stronger and as he grabbed at his hatbrim, cold blades seemed to probe deep at that spot of ache in his right breast where the puckered bullet scar was still fresh, not entirely healed. A sizzling fork of electricity fried the sky suddenly, and thunder rocked the ground as a horse in the corral bugled its terror.

Jim Gary said, "The hell with it!"

He coiled his rope and dropped it onto the saddle at his feet. Only the buckskin made him hesitate. He was about to set it loose with a slap on the rump, but it deserved better than that. The horse with the Swallowfork brand had carried him a lot of miles in this past week. Seeing its spent condition he had the stinging guilt of one who has used a faithful friend too severely. Meanwhile, he'd noticed a hay rick and the shine of a water trough in the corral. He slipped the fastenings of the gate long enough to turn the horse inside, and was a little moved at the eager way the lamed animal went limping over to feed and water.

The electric display had eased off abruptly, but the wind still pushed him, like a heavy hand, as he leaned to get his saddle. There was thick brush close by. He lugged the heavy stock rig into the midst of this and stowed it, making short work of that chore. Afterward, he retrieved his saddle roll and tossed it over a shoulder, and turned back toward the main street walking slantwise against the buffeting of rain-wet wind.

He had to cross the street to reach the hotel, and when he gained the other walk there was dust in his eyes and between his teeth. Beneath the swaying, creaking signboard he cleared his throat and spat, before walking into the sudden calm of the lobby.

The doors stood open, to let the cooling night wind enter. Light, here, was the dim glow of a turned-down oil lamp above the desk, that filled the corners with the clotted shadows of a lineup of cane rockers and heavy, sagging arm chairs. Gary carried his belongings over the worn linoleum to the desk and found the night man snoring behind it with head lolling against the wall. His long jaw had fallen open beneath a straggle of tobacco-stained mustache.

About to put out a hand and shake him awake, Jim Gary hesitated.

Keys hung from rows of nails on a board above the man's head. On an impulse he reached across and took one down at random and then, without disturbing the night clerk, shouldered his roll again and turned toward the stairs. He climbed silently, through a muffled rolling of far-off thunder.

Another lamp laid streaky shadows along the upper hall. Gary searched briefly along the double row of closed doors and found the one his key fit. It turned out to be a forward room, above the street. He locked the door and crossed to the window beside the bed and ran it open to look out upon the night.

The sign creaked, a few yards distant. As he leaned there, with the wind blowing past him and cleaning out the stuffy airlessness of the room at his back, the rain began in earnest. His nostrils stung to the pungent smell of it soaking into dust-dry board.

There was a lamp on the washstand, with a few matches. Jim Gary lit up, revealing a room identical with a hundred such he'd slept in. He poured water into the basin and, stripping his shirt, rinsed the sweat and dirt from his upper body. He unhooked his shell belt and slung it over the bed's iron knob, drew and checked the gun and slid it under a pillow. Then, having blown the light, he dragged off his boots and stretched himself out. And in a matter of moments, with the wet wind blowing upon him through the window, Jim Gary slept.

He didn't know how long it was before he awoke. The night didn't feel much older. But some alert part of his brain had stood sentinel and, sorting out the noises of the darkness, now brought him warning. The wind had settled, stilling the constant squeal of the blowing signboard. Rain was a hushed and steady sound, and through it he heard others—the stomp of a hoof, a muttered exchange of talk. Instantly awake, Gary brought his gun from under the pillow and rolled over with it to the window.

Without moving from the bed, he could look straight down the hotel's clapboard front and see the motionless horsemen in the street below. They were two dim and shapeless figures, sheathed in wet rubber conchos that shone like metal through the sliding rain. He knew they were Boyd and Asa

Plank, caught up with him at last. He held his breath as he watched.

Where were the limits of human hatred and endurance? They must be fully as weary and discouraged as he was, and yet here they were, still in their saddles, still pressing after him. The trail was fresh and they knew it, even if this rain had come to wash out tracks. Now the two brothers were arguing, the cranky murmur of their voices rising louder still to Gary's window.

Boyd Plank, with the stolid stamina of two ordinary men, would want to keep going, no doubt; while Asa would be begging for a chance to rest, or perhaps even arguing that they ought to give this town a search before looking further. He could imagine Boyd's scornful answer: *Hell! The cowardly bastard is runnin' for his life. He knows we're close. He's out there somewhere ahead of us. And we got to get him before this storm washes out the last trace of his signs.*

Knowing the brothers, Jim Gary knew which would win the argument; Asa's keener intelligence giving way, as always, to the older man's assertive bigness. So he was not too greatly surprised when he saw them kick their horses forward and so drift away along the silent, shining wet street.

He stayed as he was, leaning in the open window to peer into the farther shadows for any movement while the handle of the sixgun ground into the stiffened fingers that clenched it. It wasn't the first time in this week that he'd found himself thinking sourly, The hell with it! Let them find him, if they wanted to so badly! Let the pair of them try their sorry, unskilled guns against his own.

But he pushed the thought away.

Only after an appreciable lapse of time could he let himself relax, and then by degrees. His pursuers had not shown themselves again, so he could only assume that they had passed him up. He stretched out again, therefore, with his hand on the hard surface of the gun. And finally, weary as he was, he let sleep come once more and claim him.

He awoke with sunlight full across him; he struggled to an

elbow and saw the town spread below his window and a
morning sky swept almost clear of clouds. The mud of the
street steamed under the sun. A horse and wagon creaked
by; voices drifted in clean, washed air. Yonder, a man in a
butcher's apron was sweeping down the walk before his
place of business. He stopped in his work to nod greeting to
a bonneted housewife.

Gary lay back again, still aware of a deep core of exhaustion even after a night's unbroken sleep. A fanwork of cracks
ran across the ceiling plaster and he studied it a long time,
and watched the trembling cloud of reflected light thrown on
the wall by a puddle in the street below. He raised a hand,
presently, passing it across the lean and muscled contours of
his naked chest.

It was tender enough; he could feel the pull of new-healed
tissues when he flexed his right arm and shoulder. But there
was no sign of recurring fever. That was a distinct relief.

Jim Gary levered himself to his feet.

He had a razor in his belongings. As he shaved, taking his
time, the life of this hotel came to him through flimsy walls—
a door slamming, boots moving along the corridor and past
his room, an occasional rumble of voices from somewhere.
Once, downstairs he thought, a woman laughed and the
sound had a musical quality that made his razor hold in mid-
stroke while he looked at his own grave, gray eyes in the mirror, remembering something and wondering how many years
it had been since he had heard a woman, a young woman,
laugh in just that careless, charming way.

Perhaps because of the laugh, he was feeling old and used
as he toweled and slipped into his shirt. The face that
studied him in the glass, watching his lean hands do up the
buttons of the shirt, was too finely drawn, all planes and
angles and with nothing to soften the set of the mouth. It
still showed the traces of his sickness. There was even a glint
of gray at the temples of his straight, brown hair, but that was
premature. He was, after all, only a year or so into his

thirties. And his father had been a grizzled man, from the very earliest recollection of him.

With gun buckled on and hat in hand, he started to pick up his roll but then decided to leave it for the time being. He tossed it on the bed, walked from the room and locked the door behind him, afterward moving along the corridor toward the steps which led below.

The lobby was empty, and the night clerk's post deserted. But when Gary was still a half-dozen steps from the bottom of the stairs a door opened and a girl came out carrying an armload of clean and folded linens.

She went through the drop gate, around behind the desk, and had just set down her burden there when she happened to notice a stranger descending from the second story. Jim Gary saw the surprise that sprang into her glance and was a little amused. While she stood and stared at him, he moved casually down the remaining steps and traveled the worn linoleum to the desk. From his pocket he took his room key and two silver dollars, and laid them in front of her. He said, pleasantly, "That be enough for the room?"

Blue eyes widened, then frowned as she looked down at the money and the key. She was not a tall girl. What he mainly saw was the top of her head—the part, like a ruled white line, and dark hair falling away in soft curls behind small and well-shaped ears. There was a clean smell about her, like that of the linens on the counter at her elbow.

Gary saw her glance stray to the book lying open on the desk. He said, "You won't find me in the register."

She looked up quickly. She was groping for words, plainly puzzled and maybe even a little afraid of him. But when she found her voice, she was completely businesslike. "The charge is three dollars."

He fished up another, and she took it in silence. He liked the way she moved; he liked her voice, and it occurred to him that hers must have been the laughter he'd heard, the sound that reminded him of things so long ago as to be almost forgotten. Now she asked, in the same tone of bafflement, "Do you mean to stay long?"

"No. I'll be leaving. There are some things in the room," he went on. "I'll pick them up later, if it's all right." She only nodded.

Beyond the desk, through a curtained archway, Gary had glimpsed the checkered tablecloths and cane-seated chairs of a small dining room. "Serving breakfast?"

"For the next hour," she told him.

"Thanks." Jim Gary nodded, and walked out of the hotel.

As he drew his hat on and settled it, he reflected with a narrow smile that you really couldn't expect to make a sudden appearance in a place like this, dropping out of nowhere—out of the sky, practically—and not cause some kind of reaction. But he shrugged the thought aside, because there were more urgent things to occupy him.

This town and its people were no concern of his. What he had to do first of all was find out for sure whether Boyd and Asa Plank were here, or had actually ridden through.

## II

THE town was Antler, Nevada. He learned that much from signs on business houses up and down the crooked street. As a town there was hardly anything to distinguish it. He walked along a street that was drying out after the night's storm, and he found himself watching doorways and the openings between buildings and wondering if the Planks would go so far as to lay an ambush. It didn't sound like them, but you couldn't be sure, given their motivation and their fear of his gun.

So he cruised the town warily, and a tired impatience began to take hold of him. But he reached the lower end without incident and so turned back, ready now to believe his precautions weren't necessary, that his pursuers had gone on last night.

A coach and six had just come in over the south road and was standing at the station, with the horses blowing and stomping in the harness. Jim Gary stopped a moment, just across the way, to watch driver and passengers alighting while a hostler hurried out to see to the teams. He was minded of the buckskin he'd left in the corral, and of the saddle hidden in the bushes at the back of the lot. And then, as a sudden thought suggested itself to him, he turned on impulse and moved across the puddled road to where a balding man, wearing steel-rimmed spectacles and sleeve supporters, was at work unbuckling the leather shield of the rear boot. He asked this person, "When does the next stage leave?"

The man peered at him. "Stage for where?"

It hardly mattered. Gary said as much, and saw the faintly suspicious look that he got through the flashing spectacles. But the station agent only shrugged. "This here is the one that goes south twice a week, to connect with the railroad. Won't be rolling again till day after tomorrow. Only other coach we schedule is a weekly feeder stage to Cooper Hill.

291

That old mudwagon yonder," he added, and jerked his head toward the battered vehicle that stood starkly in the barren yard between station and barn. "It pulls out at six tonight."

"Copper Hill?" Jim Gary repeated. "Where's that?"

"Mining camp, in the hills thirty miles east. Ain't surprising you mightn't have heard of it, especially if you're a stranger. It's been pretty dead. But they're reopening one of the old mines and things are startin' to boom again. Were you lookin' for work?" the man asked suddenly.

"Maybe," Gary lied. Let him think so.

"Well, everything's cattle, here around Antler. Now, if it's Copper Hill you're interested in—" The station agent interrupted himself, looking past Gary at someone who was just stepping down from the coach. "Here's the man you should talk to! Webb Toland. He's the one is gonna have that camp back on the map by time he's finished." And before Jim Gary could stop him, the other was calling out, "Mr. Toland! Feller here is looking for a job over at your camp."

Gary turned, a little impatiently. He was a lean, well-dressed man who ran a glance over the stranger's trailworn clothing. Webb Toland said dubiously, "You don't have the look of a singlejack man."

"I suppose not," he agreed indifferently.

But the other's glance had stopped, suddenly, on the gun strapped to Gary's waist. It lingered there a long moment, and then slowly the eyes lifted to his face. And despite himself Jim Gary experienced a slight but distinct thrill of shock.

It was the eyes that did it. In a darkly handsome, almost swarthy face, they were pale and seemingly suffused by a kind of tawny glow. Gary was minded of the eyes of a mountain cat that had come close one night to investigate his campfire.

Toland came just about to an even height with him, but Gary felt he probably edged the man by a good ten pounds. There was indeed something feline in this slim, dark man—poised litheness; some quality that suggested Webb Toland was a man you would not forget.

"I didn't catch the name," Toland said suggestively.

A moment only Gary hesitated. Then he told it, curious to see if the name would strike any spark of recognition in those watching yellow eyes. He couldn't say for sure whether it did or not; the eyes revealed no more than they wanted to. But whether it was the name or the gun, something in Gary had struck an interest in this man from Copper Hill.

"I just don't know," Toland was saying slowly. "I couldn't guarantee anything. But you might look me up at the Copper Queen. I'll be keeping you in mind." Gary had a definite feeling that the other was really considering him, that there was some purpose behind his words for which he could perhaps want a man like the stranger, and a gun like his with its look of frequent use.

"All right," said Gary. "Thanks."

And that ended it. Toland turned away to hail the station man who had just returned to the coach for an armload of stuff from the trunk. "I checked a bag through, Johnson. See that it gets on the other coach and send it up tonight. I'll be leaving right away."

"Sure thing," the man promised. A last stab of the tawny eyes thrust at Gary, as though to place him firmly in mind. Then Webb Toland heeled around and strode away, into the town. Johnson turned to the stranger. "Any luck with him?" he asked.

"Could be."

Johnson nodded sagely. "Toland's a damn big man. He's doin' big things at the Queen. He's ready to put her back in production, now, usin' some newfangled method or other that nobody'd heard of back in the days of the first boom. You get in good with him, mister, and you're fixed."

Jim Gary nodded absently, for he had no real interest in what this Webb Toland was doing at the mining camp. He had learned all he wanted, and already knew his next step, the stage to Copper Hill had supplied the answer.

He was starting to walk away when a passerby happened

to remark to the station agent: "Did the sheriff have any ideas to offer about them three Swallowfork broncs?"

"Hell, no!" Johnson answered as Gary halted, instantly alert. "George Ruby's as much in the dark as I am. No tracks left, after the rain last night. No way of knowin' how they got into the open, or what happened to the horses that were taken in exchange."

"Well, what's he aimin' to do about it?"

"Somebody better do something!" Johnson promised in a dark tone. "The stage company won't cotton to first-grade stock bein' sneaked out of its corral! I figure it'll take a vet and a month of feeding to bring them run-down nags they traded me back into any kind of shape!"

Gary had heard enough. He moved on up the sidewalk, his expressionless face showing nothing. *Three* Swallowforks! Now, what—All at once he understood: Boyd and Asa Plank, their fagged horses stumbling under them as they followed him into town last night, must have figured exactly the same as the man they were pursuing. They'd gone looking for a trade of horses, and found the stageline corral. And if so, they'd undoubtedly seen the buckskin and guessed that Jim Gary had a fresh mount under him. And so they'd been tolled ahead, and by this morning would probably be miles down the south trail.

His spirits rose perceptibly. Sooner or later, of course, his pursuers would know that they'd been tricked, and they'd backtrack then. But he was assured now of a margin of time, to accomplish what he had planned to throw them off the trail for good.

With the pressures suddenly lifted, he realized that he was ravenously hungry. He turned back into the town, ready now to discover what kind of breakfast they served at that hotel.

He saw the girl again, the moment he stepped into the lobby. She was behind the desk, talking to a fat man and another he recognized as the clerk who'd been asleep at his post last night. They all three halted their conversation and looked at Jim Gary as he entered, and they did it in a way that told him he was under discussion. He put his glance directly on the girl, held it until he saw her color slightly and break gaze, biting at her lower lip. He ignored the two men with her, and went on through the lobby and ducked the low arch into the dining room.

He seemed to be the last for breakfast. He chose a table that gave him a view of the lobby door, with an open window at his elbow, and gave his order of eggs and bacon and fried potatoes to the woman who came from the kitchen to take it. As he waited, he sat and frowned at the drab scene framed in the window and realized again how bone-tired he still was.

The bullet wound, the lung fever that had resulted from it, and now these days of trailing—it would be a long time, he supposed, before he had completely overcome the effects of them.

His food arrived from the kitchen, and he had barely started on it when the fat man he'd seen in the lobby came through the archway, looked around, and then walked directly to Gary's table and pulled back a chair for himself. It groaned as he settled his weight in it. The front of his coat fell back and gave Jim Gary a look at the piece of metal pinned to the man's shirt pocket.

The sheriff said, in a rough voice, "You're the man Tracy was tellin' me about. Tracy Bannister," he explained impatiently, when the name drew no sign of recognition. He jerked his big head toward the lobby door behind him. "She owns this hotel. I'm George Ruby," he went on, shifting back onto the hind legs of the chair. "I got some questions to ask you. First off, I think you might tell me your name."

Gary had decided already that he didn't like this man. He didn't like the faintly sweating face, the faintly bulging black eyes. And he didn't like the man's blunt approach. Remembering Webb Toland's apparent failure to identify him, he shrugged and forked another piece of bacon before he answered briefly, "I doubt that the name matters. You've probably never heard it.".

Color was stung into the fat man's cheeks. His head jerked and he brought his chair forward, and laid one wide hand on the table top. "Don't get smart with me!" But he settled again as he met the look the other gave him. He frowned, and ran a fleshy fist across his mouth. "Let's start all over again," he said roughly. "If I was you, I'd answer the questions!"

"Any reason I should? You've got nothing on me."

"No? How about this?" Ruby continued. "It was pretty damned peculiar, you walkin' in here last night without a word to anybody, and helping yourself to a key and a room."

"This morning," Jim Gary reminded him, "Miss Bannister was offered payment for the room and she accepted it. So you can't make anything of that!" Calmly he drank from his coffee cup, set it down. "Want to try again, Sheriff?"

George Ruby scowled into the stranger's eyes. "All right! A couple of horses was took out of the stage company's corral last night, and three worn-out broncs left in their place. I'm thinkin' you must have rode one of them Swallowforks into this town."

"If that's a crime, then you'll have to prove it on me."

"Damn it, you didn't just drop out of nowhere!" The sheriff checked his flare-up of temper. For a moment he said nothing, as though waiting for Gary to speak, but the latter was methodically finishing his plate, and after a moment Ruby took the thing up again. His voice had lowered again to its former rumble.

"I've been tryin' to think where I'd heard of that Swallowfork brand, and it seems to me now I remember. It's a northern outfit. If I ain't mistaken, it's located somewhere up around Mogul Valley, where they been havin' 'em a range war. I know the kind of riffraff always collects for a thing like that! Hired toughs, and gunhands! Now that the fightin' around Mogul has come to a windup, wouldn't surprise me if some of them hired guns should start drifting down this way. And looks to me that's exactly what's happening!" He added pointedly, "Who rode them two other broncs?"

Gary said, with a shrug, "You're telling this yarn." He drained the last of his coffee, pushed the wreckage of his meal aside.

"I see you pack a gun," the sheriff said coldly. "You pack it like it was for more than show. I'm telling you now, we don't need your kind! We got our troubles—the makings of a little range war of our own, right here at Antler. Now, maybe you knew that; maybe somebody even sent up to Mogul Valley, to fetch you. If they did—I'm tellin' you to forget it! And it's the law giving your orders!"

Very deliberately, Jim Gary pushed back his chair. He told himself it was foolish to let this man anger him, but such was his mood and he was too tired to fight it. He got to his feet and, looking down at the sheriff, he said, "You're taking a lot for granted. I admit nothing, and that goes for Mogul Valley and for those horses you say you found. Far as you're concerned, I'm still the man that dropped in from nowhere. Take my advice and don't try to make anything more out of it. As for me, I intend to leave when I'm good and ready!"

He left George Ruby sitting there, and walked back into the lobby. The girl was behind the desk, sorting mail that had come in on the morning stage. She lifted a startled look that she tried to disguise, as she saw the stranger come toward her.

"My key, please," he said.

Tracy Bannister considered the request, her blue eyes searching his. Then very deliberately, and with no move toward the rack of keys, she turned the registration book around and shoved the pen in its holder toward him, and waited.

Jim Gary had to smile a little, amused at the curiosity he had unintentionally roused in these people. The girl, at least, was direct about it, so to satisfy her he took the pen and calmly signed his name. Not answering his cool smile, she very soberly took his key off the rack and he accepted it with a nod of thanks.

When he started for the stairs, he knew she stood and watched him out of sight.

Later, in his room, he stretched out on the bed again and felt weariness pour through him. It was stored up in some deeper well of his being, apparently, than he had realized. Completely relaxed, he let it have its way with him while he thought with a new confidence of the road ahead.

The stage for Copper Hill left at six o'clock. That would serve. Sooner or later, Boyd and Asa Plank would be retracing their course. When they reached Antler they would quickly pick up the trail again, but not soon enough to do them any good. At the mining camp he would get himself a horse and push on east through the hills, able now to take his time and bury his tracks so thoroughly that there could be no hope of finding them. Eventually even those two would have to give up the hunt, and thus he'd be freed at last of everything connected with that grim business at Mogul Valley.

Everything, but the constant reminder of a new-healed wound in his chest. . . .

Six o'clock, he thought, and the whole day till then his own. With the long tensions lifted, the need for rest which had been only partly satisfied last night rose again, stronger now and not to be denied. He set his mental clock to rouse him, and was content to let conscious thought slip away.

# III

It was something in the corridor that woke him this time. He lay a moment, bringing dulled senses into focus, coming out of a sleep so deep that he wasn't even sure for a moment where he was; the past week might never have happened. Then he remembered, in a rush, and at the same moment, recognized the sounds that had roused him: Uncertain footsteps, a noise as of something sliding along the wall beyond his door, an anxious whispering. Then he heard a man's deep groan, and it was this that brought him off the bed.

His gun was in his hand as he padded in stockinged feet to the door and threw it open. For a moment, he could only stare.

Two people were in the hallway—the girl, Tracy, and a big, black-bearded man who looked to be nearly twice her size. She had an arm about his waist and was trying to support his weight but it was plainly too much for her. He sagged heavily against her and against the wall. Gary saw the blood, then, that had nearly drenched the whole left side of the man's hickory shirt.

For a moment they held that tableau, with the girl returning his stare. She looked wide-eyed and frightened, and almost crushed by the blind weight she was trying to support with her own slight frame. But as Jim Gary started to her aid she shook her head and frantically whispered, "No! Don't come near him!"

Then the bearded man went slack and, knees buckling, began to slide down the wall, bearing her with him. Gary didn't hesitate. He stepped forward, shoving his gun behind his waistband, and took hold of the hurt man. He was something of a burden, even for Jim Gary. He thrust a shoulder beneath the other's armpit and got the limp weight settled, afterward saying to the girl, "What do you want done with him?"

Tracy Bannister had a key in her hand, but she seemed to

have forgotten it. She only looked at Gary, and shook her head again with pale lips open on an unspoken protest. And he, waiting, turned impatient. "You want him to bleed to death?" he suggested harshly.

"No. No, of course not!" That had jarred her loose. She turned and hastened to a door across from his own and fumbled the key into the lock. As the door swung open, Gary brushed past her with his burden. "On the bed," she whispered, and moved hastily to draw back the spread. Gary eased him down, lifted the booted legs one after the other, and got him straightened out. The man lay with eyes half closed and the breath sawing in his chest, obviously not more than half conscious. His blood was already staining the sheets.

The girl seemed unaware or indifferent to the ruin of her high-necked shirtwaist. She turned to Gary, hands twisting and knotting and a deep anxiety in her eyes. "You must forget that you saw him!" she whispered. "You must forget what's happened here. Promise me!"

He frowned. "Of course. But can't I help you with him?"

"No!" she answered quickly. "No, I can do everything. Just go away! Please!"

Gary considered her for a moment, and then shrugged. "All right," he said a little stiffly. "If that's how you want it!"

She was a capable person but hardly, he thought, the one for a job like this. Still, she'd refused his help and there was nothing more he could do. He was through the door and had it almost closed behind him when a sudden anguished outburst from Tracy Bannister halted him.

"Wait. . . ."

Turning back, he saw from her look that she was torn between conflicting emotions—her uncertainty about him, and her need for help. "If you will . . .?"

"Name it."

"Down in back of the hotel—his horse. It mustn't be found here. Get rid of it; it doesn't matter how."

He nodded. "All right."

"And I forgot to thank you, Mr. Gary."

Jim Gary considered her for a moment, his total puzzlement over all this tempered by a concern he couldn't help feeling for the girl. She was frightened, pathetically alone in this unnamed emergency. Her eyes were a dark stain against the pallor of her face, and he saw her hand tremble on the bedpost.

He said again, "All right," and left her, carefully closing the door.

He returned briefly to his own room for his boots and gunbelt, and then went quickly down through the silent building. The lobby was empty. He found the door to the rear hall and went past the kitchen and out through a screen door into the weedy lot in back of the hotel. Barrels and empty boxes were stacked against the building's blank rear wall. In the skimpy shade of a poplar tree, a saddled horse stood on trailing reins and cropped at the rank weeds.

It was a spotted gray, a gelding, and a big one, such as anyone the size of the hurt man would need to carry his weight. The heavy stock saddle identified the animal, for it was smeared and slippery with blood. Hard to say how far it had brought its wounded rider, but Gary would judge it had been for some considerable distance. The gray was upset and jumpy. It edged away as he moved toward it and he saw the Spur branded on its shoulder. He spoke to settle the animal, and got the reins.

Tracy Bannister had said merely to get rid of it, prevent it from being found where it was. He had no better idea, so he simply knotted the split leathers and hooked them over the blood-smeared horn, and then gave the gelding's rump a slap. It leaped under his hand like a frightened cat, snorting and shaking its head. Gary scooped up a couple of stones but they weren't needed. The gray had already settled into a trot. He watched it move off into the sage that stretched behind the town, its empty stirrups flopping. When it dropped from sight across a dip of the ground he threw his pebbles aside and turned back to the hotel.

His hand was on the screen when something made him pause and look behind him.

It was not a sound, merely the feeling one sometimes gets of being watched. He stood there in the sun and made a careful survey, his hand drawn near his gun, but he saw no one. Still, there were the windows and the doors and the corners of neighboring buildings where an observer could have seen him driving the horse away and then ducked out of sight to keep from being noticed. Gary scowled, bothered by this thought, but though he waited for a moment there was no sound or movement to confirm that momentary suspicion. He shook his head, and walked back inside.

At the door of the room where he had left Tracy Bannister he started to knock and then held it, remembering his dismissal a moment ago; perhaps she would rather he left her alone. But as he hesitated, there was a sudden burst of incoherent speech, in a man's deep voice, and the girl's quick cry of alarm. He dropped his hand on the knob, then, and pushed the door open.

The hurt man was trying to get up from the bed, and meaningless sounds spilled from his bearded lips as Tracy struggled with him to hold him down. Gary saw the situation and, quickly shutting the door, strode forward to help. Out of his head with pain, eyes wild and unseeing, the man on the bed had a frenzied strength that was enough even for Gary to cope with.

But he held him down, avoiding the thrashing of the booted legs, and suddenly the fight ran out of the other and let him drop back limp. Gary straightened to look at the girl. What he saw in her face settled his mind. He said, "I'll do this," and there was not strength in her to object.

She had managed to tear away the blood-soaked shirt sleeve, to reveal the wound—a clean one, a rifle shot he judged, that had drilled the man's left shoulder and gone on through without crippling damage. The flow of blood had been heavy but the worst of that seemed ended. Gary started to say, "You got any—" but the girl was already offering him the materials that she must have had in a pocket of her skirt. There was a bottle of liniment, a quantity of clean cloth. He took the bottle, saying, "Tear me some strips." It would do her good to have something to turn her hand to.

The liniment was powerful stuff that he could scarcely have brought himself to pour into a raw wound if the man had been conscious. Even as it was the big head twisted on the pillow and a groan broke from the bearded lips as the fiery stuff bit deep into damaged tissues.

The girl had the bandages ready now and Gary placed compresses over both ends of the bullet hole and then wrapped the shoulder tightly. "That's as good as we can do," he said gruffly, and straightened. Turning to the girl, he surprised a look on her white face that alarmed him into moving to put a hand on her arm.

She was trembling; she ran a hand shakily across her forehead and murmured, "I'm . . . all right!"

"You'd better sit down!"

She tried to protest, but he led her to a cane rocker and she seemed willing enough to drop into it. Gary went to the washstand and poured a glass of water from the big china pitcher, and brought it to her.

She drank, and shook her head in disgust at her own behavior. Her color was better now, and he decided she wasn't going to faint. She said, "I'm sorry! It's silly to let the sight of a little blood—"

"Had you ever tried to work on a gunshot wound before?" he demanded.

"No."

"Then there's nothing silly about it!" He took the glass and returned it to the commode. He leaned there, folding his arms and frowning at the girl in the chair. On the bed, the hurt man lay sleeping, his deep chest rising and falling steadily. Gary indicated him.

"Wasn't there anyone else? A doctor he could have gone to?"

"And have the word get out?" she countered. "Have his enemies learn that he's lying wounded and helpless? There's no telling what they would do if they had this chance!"

Gary frowned. "Who is he?"

"You saw the brand on his horse," she reminded him dryly.

"The Spur? That wouldn't mean anything to me." And then, seeing the complete disbelief that came into her face, he said impatiently and in a sharper voice, "Look! You and the sheriff appear to have the same notion, and you're wrong! I know nothing at all about this country. Nobody sent for me, neither him"— he nodded toward the bed—"nor his enemies, whoever they are! You can believe that, Miss Bannister."

"Can I?"

She came out of the chair, and walked over to stand before him where she could look directly into his eyes. Her own were skeptical and troubled, as they tried to read the riddle of this man. "How do I know what to believe about you, Jim Gary? When you just suddenly appear out of nowhere with no way for anyone to tell who you are, where you came from?"

He answered her look with a level regard. "As far as you're concerned, it doesn't need to matter who I am! I assure you I didn't mean anything by the way I walked into your place last night and helped myself to a room. But I had a reason for doing it."

He saw her eyes widen as enlightenment came to her. Her voice sounded a little breathless, shaken at what she had all at once guessed. "There's someone after you! That's it, isn't it?" She added, almost in a whisper, "The law?"

"You're pretty close. But it isn't the law." Gary straightened from his leaning position, letting his arms drop to his sides. His fingers brushed the handle of the holstered gun and the reminder turned his manner brusque.

"I'll be in town only a few hours, and then I'm leaving. Meanwhile I've got no concern with anything that might be going on here. Certainly, I have no reason to do him any harm." He indicated the wounded man.

"Then you *will* forget you saw him? You won't let a word

slip to anybody. Anyone at all? You'll give me your promise?"

"You've already got it."

"Thank you," she said, and he knew then that she had lost her doubt of him. He was as much a mystery to her as ever, but Tracy Bannister must have decided with some obscure woman's knowledge that this was a man she would believe and trust.

Jim Gary, for his part, looked at this girl and he felt a stirring of impulses and regrets that were strange to him. In the world in which he moved, women were the unattractive creatures of cowtown bars and dancehalls; or they were ranchers' wives, drawn out and brutalized by their hard and inescapable existence. He didn't know when he had encountered youth and real physical attraction. Tracy Bannister he judged to be in her early twenties; even the drudgery of trying to manage a hotel in a backward prairie village hadn't yet killed the freshness of girlhood in her, or dulled the color of her cheeks.

He supposed it would happen to her, too, even though there was something about her that suggested here was one who would, at least, manage to escape from that fate by one means or another. But in any event it was nothing that could concern him. There was no place for any woman in his life. Nor would she have a second glance for him if she knew the truth about him and the uses to which his gun was put.

So he put these reflections from his mind and asked "If there's anything more I can do, you'll let me know?"

"I will," she promised, and a smile took the last traces of shock from her face. "You've been more than kind."

Jim Gary walked out of the room, leaving her there. And found a man standing in the gloomy hallway with a drawn gun in his hand.

The meeting was a total surprise to both of them. The man had been looking with close and intent interest at a dark spot on the wallpaper. At the sound of the door opening his head jerked and the gun tipped up, the inch or two it took to bring it full on the other man. Gary, for his part, had begun a move toward his own holster that was almost a reflex action. He quickly checked it.

So the two stood and looked at each other, that gun leveled squarely. Silhouetted against the dim glow of a window at the far end of the hall, the man was an oddly misshapen figure, with one shoulder hitched higher than the other and his head held stiffly as though on the end of a rod stuck into his body. Gary could make out little of his face except the eyes, the whites of them dusky, and a heavy brush of dark mustache. But he remembered suddenly the uneasy impression he'd felt, during those moments in back of the hotel, that curious and unseen eyes were watching everything he did.

He saw now what it was this stranger had been studying with such interest. On the wall, where the wounded man had leaned his weight while Tracy Bannister supported him, there was a dark smear of blood.

The man with the gun looked past Gary at the closed door and he demanded, in a hoarse voice, "Is that where you've got him?"

"Got who?" retorted Gary, letting his hand hang free of the holster. He had a feeling that if he touched it, that other gun would go off.

"Matt Winship!" the man answered loudly. "Don't try to stall me! I seen you chase that gray of his away from here. It ain't all I seen, either—blood, on the saddle! I even rode after and caught the damn bronc, just to make sure. The old devil's been shot, ain't he? Shot bad, I'd judge," he added, indicating the bloodstain on the wall beside him. "Now, where is he?"

Tracy's frightened warning about Winship's enemies came back to him, and now he began to understand it. He said coldly, "Why do you want to know? So you can finish the job while he's laid up and defenseless?"

The man didn't even trouble to deny it. His interest had focused on the stranger who faced him now, and he said, "I guess you must be this gent the whole town is wonderin' about. Gary, somebody read it on the book downstairs. Just what's your game, mister? Where do you figure in this?"

"Put your gun away and walk out of here, or you may find out!"

The head jerked on its mismated shoulders. A sound like a snarl broke from the other. "A bad *hombre*, huh? Don't try anything with me, Mr. Gary! Stand aside and let me see what's in that room."

"I'll say it again," Jim Gary warned without raising his voice. "Be careful what you try!"

For a moment, the tableau held as the man measured the warning and Gary waited to see what he would do. Even with a gun leveled against him, there was something in the stranger's apparent lack of fear that seemed to hold this other one back. Gary sensed the hesitation, and something of his respect for the potential danger in the man began to fall away. Yet even a coward can be dangerous with a drawn gun in his hand.

And then the door behind Gary opened and he heard Tracy Bannister's gasp of alarm. It brought the man's stare whipping to her. For an instant no one moved, or spoke. The heavy mustache lifted, above a crooked and humorless grin that showed the gleam of white teeth. The man said, heavily, "Well, Tracy! Just what kind of room service do you give your guests?"

Gary hit him.

He did it almost without thinking, despite the gun. He made a sharp step forward and the edge of his left hand struck the other's arm while he drove a short and jolting right against his jaw. Taken wholly by surprise, the man was slammed back against the wall and the gun jumped out of his fingers. It hit the toe of his boot and slid away, and he stood there as though dazed with the unexpectedness of the blow.

"What's his name?" Jim Gary asked the girl.

"Vince Alcord."

"All right, Alcord. Let's hear you apologize!"

At this command, the other rallied a little. "To her?" he cried, in a tone of harsh bluster. "Like hell I will! She ain't

foolin' anybody. The whole country's known for a long time
how it was between her and that old goat of a Winship!"

The back of Gary's hand cut him sharply across the
mouth; blood spurted and Alcord's head was jarred sharply
against the wall. Speech broken off, he stared, blinded with
pain, and the blood began a slow trickle down his chin.

"Let him go!" cried Tracy Bannister. She caught at Gary's
sleeve, to prevent him hitting the man again. Her voice
sounded muffled with anxiety and shame. "Please! I don't
care. . . ."

But Jim Gary jerked free, and now his own gun slid into his
hand and it leveled on the other man's lean middle. His
voice trembled with real anger. "Walk down the stairs and
out of here!"

Vince Alcord looked back at him from eyes hot with fury.
His tongue snaked out and touched the lip Gary's blow had
split. At the taste of his own blood he shuddered and his
chest heaved to a sobbing breath. But with the advantage of a
drawn gun shifted now, he could see that the choice wasn't
his. His mouth worked on unspoken words. And then he
jerked about and started toward the stair well.

Following, Jim Gary saw the gun Alcord had dropped and
paused long enough to scoop it up, exchanging it for his own
weapon which he returned to its holster. Stair treads creaked
under the solid tramp of boots, as the two men dropped
down to the deserted lobby. They crossed the room, Jim
Gary herding Alcord at the point of his own gun, to the
propped-open doors. But there, at last, the man balked. He
half turned, and his voice held a tight trembling.

"This ain't the last you'll hear from me," he began. "You nor
that trollop upstairs."

Gary trusted himself to spend no more words on him. He
was in a sour mood, and newly-healed muscles ached with
the savage blows he'd thrown at Alcord. He merely placed
the flat of a hand against the man's shoulder, spun him
around again with a shove that propelled him sharply through
the doorway. Vince Alcord lost balance and in trying to re-

gain it caught the tilted heel of one boot over the edge of the sidewalk planking. He let out a squawk as he went down, to land belly-flat in the street's drying mud.

Standing in the door, Gary watched him scramble. Alcord had lost his hat. He got one knee and a propping hand under him and hunched there panting, black hair streaming into his face as he stared wildly at this stranger. He said, in a voice that was a choked yell, "Mister, if I had my gun—"

Gary looked at the weapon he held. With an indifferent shrug, he tossed it out to the man, and it made a couple of flat spins before it struck the dirt a few inches from Alcord's hand. He watched the man eye it, then lift his stare again to where Gary waited with his gun arm hanging idly alongside his own holstered sixgun. It was up to him, now, and suddenly Alcord wasn't so sure. He hesitated, making no move.

"Pick it up," Gary ordered in tired disgust. "Pick it up and put it in your holster or use it! Whichever one you want!"

"Another time, maybe." The man was making an effort to maintain a certain bluster, but he couldn't hide the clear fact that he was defeated, backing water. He spat blood from his mashed lip, and grabbed up his hat and dragged it on after shaking the hair back from his sweating face. On his feet, he looked for a long moment at the gun. He leaned and picked it up then, carefully, so that the watching Gary should not mistake his intentions. He shoved it deep into its holster.

"Another time," he repeated harshly, with a thrust of his glance at the unmoving figure in the hotel entrance. And then he swung his mismatched shoulders and turned away, striding toward a rawboned black that stood tied to a nearby rack. He jerked the reins free and lifted himself into the saddle. He pulled the bronc's head around and jabbed the spurs so savagely that the bay reared and came down in a lunging run.

Vince Alcord didn't look back. He put the black along the street and went off at a hard lope, one shod hoof striking up a fountain of muddy water from a gathered puddle. He looked like a man with an intent and serious purpose.

But Jim Gary didn't watch him out of sight. He was searching the street quickly to discover how many witnesses there had been to the scene. The sidewalks were deserted but he had already noted a couple of riders who, in passing, had drawn a hasty rein as Alcord came plummeting out of the doorway and into the street mud, almost under the noses of their horses. They were still sitting there, and now Gary looked at them more closely.

As a range-bred man will do, he glanced at the horses first and saw that they were good ones; he caught the Spur brands on them. And then he lifted his cool stare toward the riders of these Winship mounts. The man was young, a handsome and clean-shaven type with yellow sideburns and a spoiled and quarrelsome look in the blue eyes that scowled at Gary; a man who dressed in whipcord breeches and a silk shirt and boots that carried a high and unscuffed polish. But you wouldn't be apt to notice the man, after a first cursory examination, if your eyes happened then to touch upon his companion.

She was a beauty, a redhead with the milky complexion that sometimes goes with hair of that particular deep, rich color. She rode sidesaddle, in a green skirt that hung long over the rounded fullness of hip and thigh, and she carried that handsome head of hers with an erect proudness: her shoulders straight, her bosom swelling in her open-throated blouse, a riding crop across her knees. She looked down from the back of her horse, with a direct and interested stare, meeting Gary's look directly. And he saw her companion turn in the saddle and say something to the woman, his scowl petulant and showing anger.

Gary had no way of knowing their names, but from the Spur brand on their horses he judged they must own some connection with the hurt man on the bed in that room upstairs. Certainly, if they were kin of Matt Winships they would be concerned to know of what had happened to him.

But an obscure impulse kept him silent. Tracy Bannister had said not to let a word slip to anybody. And so, understanding exactly nothing of what he had found himself involved in here, he decided to take her literally.

He turned his back on that handsome pair of riders, walked back inside the building and slowly up the lobby stairs, favoring the slow ache in his hurt right side.

# IV

PAUL KEATING pulled his attention away from that door where the man had vanished, and turned to his wife. She was still staring after the stranger, with an expression that put a cold and clotted tightness inside him and, for the moment, completely knocked from his mind whatever he had been about to say.

He was by nature a jealous man and he knew it, a man completely insecure in his relation with his handsome wife. Even now, even under the pressure of an anxiety that was like a steam gauge on the point of blowing, he could feel this other, crawling emotion of a sick resentment that was always there ready to rise in him at any provocation.

Fern spoke, and her words were enough to make his hand tighten on the reins and bulge the tight muscle along the line of his jaw. "I wonder who he is?"

Keating said, without being able to hold the curt tension from his voice, "Does it matter?"

"It would be interesting to know. You saw how he handled Vince Alcord like a child. Spur could use a few men like that!"

She looked at her husband as she spoke, a tilted glance of her long-lashed and beautiful eyes. He had, as he so often did, the feeling that she was amused and deliberately taunting him, and at this time and place the idea was beyond bearing. His scowl deepened. He said, "Come along!" and jabbed his horse forward with the spur.

A few yards farther on, his wife caught up with him. Reading his mood, Fern crowded her mare against his horse and brought it to a stand, beneath the arching shadow of a cottonwood that had littered the sidewalk and street with branches thrown down in last night's storm. She reached and laid a firm hand upon his coatsleeve, and her voice was stern and vibrant.

"Paul! Remember! Whatever happens, whatever we find,

you've got to act like yourself. Do you understand me? You must manage to be calm and face this through!"

"How can I?" he groaned, and swung his head. "I tell you, the old man was looking right at me when I pulled the trigger. I know he saw me!"

"Surely the distance would have been too great! Be a man, Paul, for God's sake!"

He lifted a flaring look at her. "You can say that! If it weren't for you, and that crook Toland—"

"Are you blaming *me*, now?" She met him with a look as hot as his own. "Did I tell you to do it?"

She felt the muscles of his forearm pull taut and, seeing the shifting of his glance, swung around as George Ruby came toward them through the dappled shade that the big tree cast along the sidewalk plankings. The sheriff gave them a preoccupied look; then he reacted to the woman's beauty. "Afternoon, Miz Keating," he said, smiling toothily as he touched hatbrim. He nodded in passing to her husband. If he noticed anything odd in their unanswering silence he gave no sign, but strode on with his ponderous tread. Fern's hand tightened on her husband's arm and she leaned closer, whispering fiercely.

"You see? The sheriff knows nothing. He doesn't even know that Matt's been hurt!"

Paul Keating shook his head, bewildered. "But where could the old man have got to, if he didn't reach town? I tell you, the last I saw his horse was pointed directly this way!"

"Then it's obvious he didn't make it. He got off the trail somewhere and is probably lying dead."

"I hope he is!" the man said hoarsely, and his clenched fist struck the pommel of his saddle. "Oh, God, how I hope so! I didn't want to kill him, but I had no choice. I couldn't let him see those books; I couldn't have him finding out."

"Be quiet, can't you?" Her fierce whisper silenced him, as his voice began to rise out of control. There was no one in earshot but she looked with apprehension at a wagon and team jouncing toward them over the ruts. "Do you want the whole town hearing? Now, listen to me," she went on as the man subsided under the warning. "There's still one possibility. If Matt did get as far as town, he might have gone directly to the doctor's place and the sheriff wouldn't necessarily have heard yet. We've got to ride around there and find out."

"To the doctor's house?" Looking at her, Paul Keating's face was gray with sickness. Cold sweat made a sheen across the planes of his cheeks. "And supposing he's there? How do you think I can bear to look him in the face, wondering what he knows?"

"Bluff it through."

"I can't!"

She must have seen, then, that he spoke the sober truth. She gave the thing up with a sigh and a grimace dropping her hand away from his arm. "All right," she said coldly. "I'll go alone, then. Wait for me at Laurie Pitkin's. I'll come as soon as I know anything."

Not delaying for an answer, she used her riding crop and the fine bay mare spurted ahead. Keating watched her turn into the street where the doctor's house stood, and vanish. He shook himself, as though to bring himself out of a trance of terror that had locked his muscles. He brought a handkerchief from his pocket and wiped his face with it and his hand was trembling as he stuffed the cloth away again.

He knew what he needed; he could feel the burning thirst for it at the back of his throat, suddenly swelling and choking him. And because there was no telling what ordeal he might still have to face, in the next hour, he formed his resolution and pulled his horse around. He rode back up the street until, at the first saloon, he pulled into the rack, and stepped down. The horse would stand. Keating simply dropped the reins across the weathered pole, not trusting his trembling hands to tie, and walked into the building on unsteady legs.

He was the only customer. When he ordered his drink, he thought the bartender looked at him strangely. He knew he must give something like the appearance of a very unwell man. He threw his money on the bar and managed to pour the rye and tossed it into his throat, and shuddered a little as its potency hit him. But it lent a strength that he needed. He took in a deep breath, and braced his shoulders within the boxed tweed coat.

The bartender, busy with his chores behind the polished counter, suddenly broke in on his musings with a question. "Say, Keating. Did you ever get ahold of Webb Toland, when you was in here earlier this morning, lookin' for him? Somebody said he took off for Copper Hill almost as soon as he got off the stage."

He scowled at his empty glass. "That's right," he said shortly. "That's what I found out."

"Way you talked, I thought maybe you was supposed to be havin' a meeting with him, or something."

"Oh, no. Just something I wanted to see him about. Toland's a busy man. I'll catch him another time."

He thought the bartender accepted this explanation, for the man nodded and turned away, busy with his wet rag on the polished hardwood surface. But to himself Keating thought bitterly, in remembered alarm: *You talk too much!*

This morning, coming into Antler expecting to meet Webb Toland and learn what success the promoter had had outside with his last-ditch attempt to raise needed funds, he'd known the answer when he learned that Toland had left town without even waiting to see him. He should have accepted the fact, not lost his head and gone looking futilely through the place, asking questions that had only served to draw attention to him. When the truth finally came out, and people learned how all Toland's grandiose schemes for the Copper Queen mine had collapsed, they might remember this morning. They'd remember Paul Keating's anxiety, and they might suddenly see a link that he'd been wanting desperately to keep concealed.

*Damn the rotten luck!*

A shaking hand spilled more whisky into his glass. Staring at it, he thought again of the golden pictures Toland had painted. He thought of the constant pressures Fern had brought upon him for those things she couldn't have on the bookkeeper's wage her stepfather paid him. With a weak man's predilection for blaming others, he cursed the pair of them. And then, unbidden, the image of Matt Winship rose before his mind.

Winship, as he'd looked with the rifle's sights notched on his unsuspecting body. And then the resistance of the trigger, the kick of the weapon, the sudden film of muzzle smoke that swept stingingly into his face. The memory set his hand to trembling again and he grabbed up the drink and threw it off, trying to drown the searing horror of it.

Panicked!—so Fern had called him, when he came galloping into the yard at Spur and babbled a confession of the terrible thing he had done. Panicked by the knowledge of what his unlucky association with Toland had done to him, what it would mean if old Matt were to learn his guilty secret. Panicked because, only the night before, the old man had said, "I ain't takin' no syndicate's offer for Spur, but just the same it'd be worth knowin' some figures to throw in their face if they come at me again. I'd like to go over them books with you tomorrow, son, and get me an idea just how we're standin' with the bank."

Winship was no fool. He'd know, if he looked at the figures, that they were all wrong. He'd have probed until he uncovered just what had happened to his money. And so, riding home to Spur, full of the thought of Toland's deceit and the depths to which it had hurled him, sight of Winship on the trail ahead had been enough to strike panic and terror into Keating, and put a desperate solution into his head.

He shuddered, the need of another drink rising strongly. But he had control enough not to succumb to it; he knew his limit. In despair he pushed bottle and glass aside and walked back out to his horse, trying hard to discipline his features and not to show to any casual passer-by a hint of the turmoil within him.

He turned into a side street where a small clapboard house stood well back among rustling poplars. A sign, fastened to

the pickets of the fence, said: MRS. LAURA PITKIN, DRESS-
MAKING. He saw at once that his wife had beaten him here,
and the sight of her mount waiting at the iron hitching
post beside the gate filled him with mingled emotions. He
didn't know if this was a good sign or a bad one. He pulled in
and dismounted, but then stood beside his horse with the
reins in his hands as he saw the door of the cottage open and
Fern and the Pitkin woman came out upon the porch, chatting.

They had been standing just inside the door, no doubt
watching for him. He lifted his hat to the dressmaker, and
got her birdlike, flashing-eyed nod in return. There was something about the woman that always repelled him: something
greedy and knowing in her black eyes, something secretive
in the tight mouth and the narrow, pointed face.

"Wednesday, then, for the fitting," Fern Keating was saying as she came down the steps to the path.

The pale head nodded, the old woman's glance darting to
the man waiting by the gate. "Yes ma'am. I'm real sorry I
have to make you wait again. I thought I'd have the dress
ready by today, but I couldn't get the thread I need."

"It's perfectly all right," Fern said, and flashed her such a
warm smile that for an instant Keating wondered. She was not
one to accept delays gracefully, or a needless trip to town.
Why then should she make the concession to a mere seam-
stress?

But his own needs and worries crowded the thought from
his mind. He waited impatiently as Fern came toward him.
When she walked through the gate and closed it behind her
he saw the smile quit her face to be replaced by another
expression. "You took your time getting here!" she whispered
coldly, as he moved to help her to the saddle. Then, with
him bending close to place his hands for her boot, she re-
coiled a little and he knew she had caught the whisky on
his breath. "I might have known!"

He shrugged the remark aside irritably. "What did you
find out?" he demanded.

She waited until he had lifted her up and she was settled

on the saddle, her full skirt smoothed across her thigh. Riding crop in hand, she looked down at his anxiously waiting face. "Matt isn't at the doctor's," she told him. "If his horse hasn't carried him in to the ranch by this time, I suppose he's lying out somewhere. Dead, perhaps."

Keating closed his eyes a moment. "If only we could know for sure!" He opened them again. His weak mouth twisted with the pain he felt. "He was good to me! To think that I had to repay him like this! I'll answer for it, and so will you!"

"Blaming me again?" she said sharply. "Because you got wild and lost your head?"

"Because it was you that got me mixed up with that grafter, that Toland!" he answered doggedly. "You made me dig into the books so deep there was no way to straighten them."

She swung her head, the coppery curls brushing the white column of her throat. "You wanted what Toland might have given us as much as I did!"

"Very well. We were both fools! But he isn't going to get away with this, either! He didn't have the nerve to meet me as he'd promised, and tell me the bad news. Well, I'm going right up there to Copper Hill and have it out with him!"

"Paul!" He was turning back to his own horse. He didn't see the look she gave him—the consternation, the sudden fear of what despair and whisky might lead him to. But then Fern subsided, biting her lip, and her fingers crept into the pocket of her skirt and touched the fold of paper they found there.

It was not the first such note Laurie Pitkin had slipped to her. The dressmaker had been serving a useful function as go-between, now, for many weeks. This note was unsigned, as of course they all had been. Still, she knew well every loop and downstroke of the strong, bold writing: "Tonight, at the usual place and the usual time. I must see you."

Yes, she thought suddenly. Let Paul take his useless ride up to the camp. It would be convenient, at that. Best to get him well out of the way, in this crazy mood of his in which almost anything could happen. "Suit yourself," she said. "But you can't leave me alone until we've learned something for certain about Matt."

He shrugged, not answering, as he pulled his horse around. There was a felt distance between these two, riding their horses down the slight hill from the dressmaker's house. They turned again into the wide, limb-littered main street. And there, all unexpectedly, saw the confused mill of horses in front of the hotel, and heard the excited shouting and a sudden muffled shot.

Keating pulled in so quickly that his nervous mount pivoted and Fern nearly lost the saddle, trying to avoid colliding with him. She heard his gusty exclamation: "What the devil?"

Someone on the sidewalk cupped hands to mouth and yelled the answer, in a voice cracked with excitement. "Hey! It's your paw, Miz Keating! Old Matt Winship! I heard somebody say he's been shot. They got him trapped in the hotel—Burl Hoffman, and Alcord, and their boys! Looks like they're set to smoke him out of there."

Jim Gary stood before the mirror in his room, smoothing back his long hair with the hard palms of his hands, eyes only half paying attention to the image in the watery glass. He was thinking of the expression on Tracy Bannister's face when he'd come back up the stairs after getting rid of Vince Alcord, and found her waiting, her cheeks drained, her eyes dark with apprehension.

"It's all right," he'd assured her. "Our friend decided to leave."

"You're certain?"

He nodded, and then as they stood there a sound had come from Matt Winship's room: a faint murmur of pain. It broke into the moment. It pulled the girl back to her concern for the injured man. She looked into Gary's face an instant longer, as though there were things she wanted to say. Then she turned and slipped back into the room and he stood and stared at the closed door before returning to his own drab quarters across the hallway.

Now he considered his unsmiling face in the glass and noticed how long it had been since a barber had touched scissors to that full and slightly grizzled thatch. He realized suddenly that he was seeing himself through Tracy Bannister's eyes and he shook his head, dissatisfied with this discovery, and walked over to the window.

It was midafternoon, he decided; three or four hours to wait, perhaps, until the stage left. An impatience filled him, for the time to pass quickly now and be over. He didn't like the things that had been happening to him. He feared he was becoming involved in something. He could sense the tendrils that were reaching to him from the affairs of this place, trying to weave and trap him in a web of circumstance. He couldn't afford to have that happen. He certainly would be a greater fool than he credited himself, if he let himself be swayed out of his purpose by the words or the smile of anyone he knew no more about than he did about Tracy Bannister.

Scowling over his thoughts, he stood looking down into the street and rolling a cigarette from the materials in his shirt pocket. He had placed the twist of paper and tobacco in a corner of his lips, and was reaching for a stick match on the washstand beside the lamp, when the knock came on his door.

His head jerked at the sound. For a moment he waited, his thumbnail against the match head, almost reluctant to answer. But when the sound didn't come again, he said finally, "Yes?" and the sulphur popped to life. He was putting the flame to his smoke as the door opened slowly.

It was the girl. She entered rather diffidently, with a fleeting and somehow apologetic smile. Hand on the knob of the opened door, she said, "He's resting," and indicated that other room across the corridor. "When he stirred I was afraid there might have been some internal bleeding."

"Not where he was shot," Jim Gary said gruffly as he shook

out the match and flipped it through the open window. "It's a good, clean hole. I told you that."

"I know," she admitted, and pushed a hand tiredly through her dark wealth of hair. "I—I'm afraid I'm still a little upset, with it all."

"Of course."

He regarded her through the film of smoke from the cigarette, which the draft of the open door sucked against his face. He knew there was something more on her mind, and he waited.

"I didn't get to thank you," she said, "for . . . what you did afterward."

"Your friend Alcord?" Gary shrugged. "He talked trouble but he didn't make much. He's mostly wind, I figure."

"Some of the others aren't."

"The others?"

"Burl Hoffman, for one," Tracy answered, with a hint of impatience in her voice, almost as though she had forgotten he was a stranger who knew nothing of the background of the trouble he had stumbled into here. "He's the leader, and I don't think he'll stop at bluster!"

"But who are these men?" Gary insisted. "What's their grievance against Winship?"

"It's simple enough. He's too big to suit them, and they're too little. That's what it comes down to. Myself," she added, "I've always thought that a man was small by nature, that you couldn't make yourself any taller by trying to cut down someone else to your own size."

He liked that; he liked the flash of scorn in her eyes as she said it. But he asked, studying her gravely while he dragged at the cigarette, "Would they hate him badly enough to risk murder?"

"You're thinking about the sheriff." The girl shook her head. "They're not afraid of George Ruby. And anyway, who else could it have been?"

He frowned. "It wasn't Alcord, I'm sure of that much. That was no act he put on for me. He saw the horse, and the blood on the saddle, and he was trying to find out just what it meant. It tickled him to think Winship might have been hurt, but he certainly had no previous idea it had happened."

Tracy didn't seem convinced. She said only, "Any one of the others could have done it."

"Did Winship say anything to indicate he might have seen who it was?"

"No. He was too far out of his head."

"But not far enough gone to stop him riding to you for help. You said he knew he'd be safer here than going to the doctor's."

"Or anywhere else. Yes, he'd always know that." The words died on her lips, suddenly. At something that came into Gary's thoughtful look, her own eyes widened. Color crept up from her throat, touched her cheeks. She tried twice before she managed to get out: "You're thinking of something that Vince Alcord said, about Matt Winship and me!"

Somehow, he couldn't meet her hurt stare. He looked at the burning end of his cigarette instead, put it back between his lips. "There's no need to explain anything to me!" he said gruffly.

"Meaning, you thought it was true!" He heard the break in her voice, and glancing up at her saw the shame in her eyes as she shook her head. "I suppose," she told him heavily, "there are lots of others who think so, then. I didn't know there'd been talk! But they'll have to think and talk as they like!" she added defiantly. "I owe too much to Matt Winship to turn against him. There's no one else who understands him, how alone he is. . . ."

He saw a shine of tears in her eyes. Embarrassed himself, he remembered something and said, to change the subject, "I saw a couple a little while ago, riding Spur horses. A young man and woman. Are they his kin?"

"That would have been the Keatings," she answered, her emotions settling. "She's Matt's stepdaughter. Her husband keeps the books out at the ranch, handles business details and paperwork. They're all the people Matt has since his wife died, three years ago."

Her look told him more than her words—told him that she had small use for that handsome and glittering pair. He considered this, as he turned and snapped the butt of his smoked-down cigarette through the window toward the street far below. He turned back, and his mind was settled and his manner changed. Firm and yet a shade apologetically, he said. "Miss Bannister, I've asked too many questions. I had no business taking up so much of your time with them, because they were none of my concern and in the nature of things they can't be."

He knew she read his meaning. She said quietly, "I understand. And I don't mind. You did help me. It gave you a certain right." But having said that much she paused, and Gary knew she was searching out the words for something else she wanted earnestly to say.

She took a step toward him.

"You're in trouble yourself," she blurted. "It isn't fair that there's no way someone could return the favor!"

"By helping me?" He shook his head, and a faint smile edged his lips. "Bad business! The men I mentioned—"

"The ones you're running from?"

Gary nodded. "They made that mistake. They saved my life. Now they're wishing they'd let me die! You've heard of the doings up in Mogul Valley?" he went on, prompted to talk about himself, against his better judgment, by something he saw in her face. "I was mixed up in that, as your sheriff guessed. You see, I'm just what Ruby thinks I am—a hired gunfighter. It's nothing to be proud of, nor was my part in in the Mogul Valley affair."

"You don't have to tell me anything," Tracy Bannister said.

"Somehow I want to. Maybe it's so you'll understand why I've got to be going on, this evening. The Planks," he continued, and a frown took shape between his eyes, "were on the other side of that fight. There was quite a gun battle, and

I took a bad one." He touched a finger to his chest, above the puckered scar.

"By all the rules I ought to have died of it. But when I woke up, I found that Boyd and Asa had taken me in. Six weeks they spent, waiting on me hand and foot, just because they couldn't watch a man die—not even one who'd been fighting for their enemies. They did a good job. Got me on my feet again."

Tracy was staring at him, frowning her puzzlement. "But I don't understand! Why would they be trying to kill you, now?"

"That's the rest of the story! You see, there was a third brother in that family. I'd made myself an enemy or two, on the other side, the one I was supposed to be fighting for. They wanted me, bad. And this other boy—Lane Plank, his name was—fixed up a deal to deliver me. For pay. But when he tried it—"

"You killed him?"

Gary nodded. "I didn't want to. He wasn't much of a man, not worthy to sit at the same table with a pair like Boyd and Asa. But he was their brother, and all they knew was I'd killed him after what they'd done for me! So now they want to find me. If we should meet over gunsights, they'll be playing for keeps."

"While you won't be able to," she finished. "Because you owe them your life. And that's why you're running! Isn't there anything to be done? Any way to make them understand?"

He shook his head and shrugged. "Don't worry about it. I've thrown them off my trail now, for a few hours anyway. I plan with any luck to lose them permanent."

"Then I wish you the luck you need!" she said earnestly. "Thanks."

But her eyes were still studying him, still troubled. "And after you've lost them?" she persisted, with a directness that made him somehow uncomfortable. "You don't really enjoy this kind of life? A professional gunman—I just don't believe it! You're not the kind who'd take to it of your own choice."

"You're well acquainted with the type?" Cary suggested, his thin smile widening while his eyes chilled a little. He saw the look bring the color again into her face.

"I'm sorry. I didn't mean to pry!"

And then, before he could apologize or answer to the stiffness in her voice, the noise breaking in the street below drew him around quickly to the window.

There seemed almost a dozen in the mill of riders that had pulled up before the hotel. Some were already dismounting, while others held to their saddles in seeming indecision. Almost at once Jim Gary's raking glance singled out Vince Alcord's high-shouldered shape, and from this he knew what was happening even before Tracy's startled voice spoke, at his elbow.

"That's Burl Hoffman!" she exclaimed, and he knew she was pointing out the big sandy-haired figure who towered above the other horsemen, already giving orders. "And Priday Jones, and—Alcord's fetched the whole lot of them!" She swung away from the window, starting for the door. But Gary moved quickly and his hand closed upon her arm, stopping her.

"No," he said quietly, as her look raked his face. "Stay here. It begins to look to me that I'm not finished with this business after all."

Her quick protest followed him, unheeded, as he moved at a quick stride through the doorway and toward the stairs. He was already loosening his sixgun in the holster.

# V

He moved into the door and put his shoulder against the edge of it, and for a moment none of the men in that mill beyond the hitch racks seemed to notice him. It was Vince Alcord who finally glanced his way. He stiffened, and with dark anger flooding his face reached to drop a hand on Burl Hoffman's shoulder, as the latter was about to swing from saddle. Jim Gary saw Alcord's mouth form the words, "There he is now! That's Gary!"

Hoffman slowly settled back into the leather. What Alcord said must have carried, because the rest were turning to look in Gary's direction now, and suddenly the noise and confusion stilled. Gary stood and let his glance run over them all, sorting them out, deciding which were owners and which were hands. And then their leader's voice rang a challenge.

"Don't stand in our way, mister! We're coming in!"

This Hoffman was a good-sized figure of a man, all right, and he looked like a man governed by temper. He had a ruddy face and scalp, that showed through thinning strands of sandy hair that he combed in a saddle straight across his head. His jaw thrust forward as though he expected someone to take a poke at it. He had a restive intensity that he transmitted to the big chestnut under him; it kept the horse moving edgily about. Like the man, the horse seemed ready to explode.

Gary said calmly, "Come ahead if you really think you want in bad enough."

Nobody moved. They were waiting on their leader, and as he sensed this the redhead's scowl deepened. His eye touched on the gun thrusting up from the stranger's hip holster, lifted again to his face. His big shoulders stirred and he said, "All right, Gary. I'll lay the cards out. You already know who we are, I guess. Hoffman's my handle. This old-timer is Priday Jones." He indicated a slight, small-boned man with a thick shock of snow-white hair edging beneath the brim of his hat.

Gary only touched Priday Jones with a glance. "I don't need to hear names," he said coldly. "Just tell me what you want with the gent who's lying upstairs with a bullet in him." His mouth hardened. "Didn't take the bunch of you long to gather! What's the matter? Isn't one try at murder enough?"

Hoffman's angry jaw settled. "It was none of us who shot Matt Winship!"

"No?"

"No. But we ain't above using a situation somebody else has set up for us!"

"And who would you say *did* shoot him?"

"How would I know that? We ain't the only enemies he's got. Especially not since people have learned about the syndicate!"

"Syndicate?" This was a new one to Gary and he didn't hide his puzzlement. "*Now* what are you talking about?"

"Not that this is any of your business," Hoffman told him. "But it's some Eastern outfit. Back in Cleveland."

"Chicago, is what I heard," Vince Alcord corrected him.

The big man shrugged. "All right, Chicago. Word has it they're out to buy Winship's ranch off him. We understand he's ready to close a deal."

"You understand a lot, don't you?" Gary gibed dryly. "Do you know any of this for certain?"

"We intend to find out. And right now! We mean to have a plain answer from Winship as to whether he really intends throwing this range into the hands of some corporation."

"It's his ranch," Gary pointed out, "to do with what he pleases. But supposing the rumors are true?"

"We've told you all we figure to," Hoffman said. "Now you just get out of our way!"

Still the man in the doorway failed to move. He stood at ease, seemingly; but anyone looking closely at Jim Gary might have noticed the faint narrowing of his eyes, the slight stirring of the muscles along his cheeks. He said, "The odds

327

seem a little heavy. A crowd like this against one wounded man."

"It's your neck," Vince Alcord warned him, "if you try to buck this crowd!"

Then, from the head of the stairs behind Gary, Tracy Bannister's cry of warning rang sharply through the lobby: "Jim! Behind you!" It brought him pivoting against the point of his shoulder, as he whirled back into the room.

His gun lifted from holster in a single, unthought motion as he saw his danger.

A couple of men had entered by the hotel's rear door, while he was occupied with the rest out front. They had come silently into the lobby and only a few feet separated them from him. They were ordinary cowhands by their looks, but one already had a gun leveled and the other, at his heels, was even now pulling his revolver up from the leather.

Seeing Gary's sixshooter, they stopped like men frozen. The second man failed to complete his draw. Jim Gary let his gun settle on the other and told him sharply, "Drop that!" And when the man was slow about complying, he coldly and deliberately worked the trigger.

Sound exploded in the room. The man with the gun shouted in pain and fell back against his companion, grabbing at his upper arm while the Colt tumbled to the floor. "Move when I speak!" Gary snapped, real anger boiling in him. "Now, come here!"

This brought the pair to him, the hurt man stumbling and cursing the pain of his skewered arm, while blood began to redden the fingers that clamped it. His companion, white-faced and scared, was holding onto him and helping to guide his steps. Gary motioned them both out the door, drawing aside to make room for them to pass. "All right," he said then, turning back to the group at the hitch post, "whose men were these?"

The answer was slow in coming. They exchanged uneasy and frightened looks, and finally Burl Hoffman settled his shoulders and answered defiantly, "Mine."

"Then take them! And the next time anybody tries coming at me, front *or* back, he'd damn well better be ready to shoot first. Next time I won't be aiming for his gun arm!"

He had never been so furious, and there must have been something in his voice and in his eyes that carried fear to these men. Not one of them tried to meet his gaze. A couple hurried forward to help the man Gary had shot. Somebody said, in a shaky voice, "He's got to see the doctor quick! That arm is in a bad way!" For just an instant Gary felt a qualm of regret. He could have stopped the man, probably, without using a bullet. But his anger at the attempted trickery rose and utterly swamped this other feeling, and he shrugged it aside. He lifted his voice across the confusion in the street.

"Alcord!" he said, and the head on the mismated shoulders swiveled quickly. "What did you do with the bronc?"

"What bronc?"

"Winship's. The gray that I turned loose. I don't imagine you'd let it run, to show up at the ranch and get the Spur crew headed this way too soon!"

Alcord said gruffly, "I don't know nothin' about it!" But his eyes showed he was lying. And with the muzzle of his gun, Gary pointed to a hitch pole.

"He'd better be tied to that post inside of twenty minutes!"

There wasn't any answer. All at once the only interest seemed to be in getting away from there. The hurt man was being hustled off down the street, supported by his friends. There was a scramble for saddles, as the group broke apart and lost its unity. The whole town had come awake by this time, roused by the shot. A block distant, Gary glimpsed the fat sheriff heading that way at a puffing dogtrot, which was probably the closest George Ruby could get to a run.

Only Burl Hoffman seemed to have defiance still left in him. Face livid, he shouted Gary's name; he stood in the stirrups, the reins cramped tight in a grasp that made the restive horse under him fight the bit and toss its mane. "Whoever you are," Hoffman said as Gary turned his attention on the man, "wherever you came from, don't buy into this. We ain't always going to be so easy to stop!"

Gary measured him, unspeaking. Then, deliberately, he turned his back.

Tracy's heels tapped a light rhythm on the stairs as he came into the lobby. Her face was white; the hand she laid on his arm trembled with the strain of these last minutes. "Is it over?"

"For now, anyway," he assured her. "They lost their nerve. They talked when they should have been acting. It's a common mistake."

She closed her eyes and her breathing tremulously swelled her bosom. "For a minute I thought you'd be killed."

"I might have," he admitted, "if you hadn't warned me. Now they've sobered down, and with the town roused and the sheriff on his way I doubt if anything more will happen. So you can stop worrying. About him," he added, jerking his head toward the stairs that led above.

Tracy was looking at him again, and her blue eyes held concern. "But what of you, Mr. Gary?" she demanded. Only then did he realize that a moment ago, in the stress of excitement, she had called him by his first name. "You won't take any chances? You won't have more trouble with them?"

He shook his head. "I won't be here long enough. It's only a few hours till stage time." And, touched by her obvious concern, he gave her one of his rare smiles before he walked out of the hotel.

A few townspeople gave him curious stares. As he started along the street he heard his name shouted and knew that would be George Ruby. He walked on, ignoring them all.

He had spotted a faded barber pole fastened to the front of a small building down the street. He walked down there without hurry and found the barber standing in the open door. The man blinked and backed hastily as he saw the stranger turning in.

"I need a haircut," Jim Gary said.

"Yes sir, Mr. Gary!" The barber nearly stumbled over his

own feet, ushering him in. Gary stepped to hang his hat on one of the row of nails on the wall. He was working at the buckle of his gun harness when, through watery plate glass, he saw on the farther walk a couple of the men who had been with Hoffman in front of the hotel.

His hands stilled as he regarded them narrowly. Then, leaving the belt in place, he swung back to the chair where the barber waited, with comb and scissors and towel. He shoved his filled holster around to the forward part of his leg, and stepped into the chair. And when the big towel whisked into place covering his body, his hand rested on the butt of the holstered gun.

The muzzle pointed at the door.

When, a half-hour later, Jim Gary left the shop and walked back upstreet to the hotel, he saw that Matt Winship's gray horse now stood, saddled, at the tooth-marked and sagging hitch pole. A look of bleak satisfaction settled about his eyes and his mouth, seeing the effect of his threat: Vince Alcord, at least, had learned something from the events of the afternoon.

There were two other broncs at the pole, both fine animals, wearing the Spur brand. Gary studied them a moment before he recognized them, and then remembered he had seen the Keatings riding them into town earlier. The Keatings: the sullen, glittering young man, and the woman with her coppery hair and flawless skin and her direct, bold stare.

Gary shrugged, and walked into the lobby and up the stairs to his room.

There was no real hurry. He had no packing to do except to reassemble his roll. His saddle was probably where he'd left it, in the bushes behind the stageline corral. He still had time to kill, through what was left of the long summer afternoon, before the stage would be pulling out for Copper Hill.

The door of Matt Winship's room stood partly open and, hearing a rumble of voices within, he hesitated a moment. But now the door swung wider and a seedy little man came backing out, one hand on the knob and a worn doctor's bag in the other. "I'll look in again in an hour or so," Gary heard him say, "and find out how you're doing. Main thing you need is rest." Past his shoulder, Gary saw Paul Keating standing at the foot of the bed. Somehow that changed any thought he had about going in and he swung away instead toward his own room, hearing the doctor's footsteps retreating along the corridor.

But then Tracy Bannister was saying, "Will you come in a minute, Mr. Gary?" He turned to find her looking at him from that door opposite.

. He frowned, reluctant. "Is it necessary?" However, he shrugged and she stepped aside for him, and now he saw Keating's copper-haired wife standing beside her stepfather's bed, a hand on the hurt man's shoulder.

Matt Winship had regained consciousness. He sat propped up with a couple of pillows against his back. His face, for all its weathered ruggedness, showed a pallor that was hardly darker than the neat, professional bandage with which the doctor had replaced Gary's own makeshift effort.

All their eyes rested on Gary as he walked in—Keating's, scowling and perturbed; his wife's, coolly curious. It was big Matt Winship who spoke, in a deep rumble of a voice that suited his massive frame.

"I understand I'm in your debt."

His eyes were blue, their contrast softening a little the rugged contours of the bearded face. They regarded Jim Gary with a level directness that he instantly liked.

Gary shook his head. "You're wrong. You don't owe me a thing."

"Tracy tells me," the hurt man persisted, "that you patched me up so I wouldn't bleed to death, and then kept the cur dogs off my hide, I'm grateful."

"There are things any man would do for another."

"Not just any man," Winship corrected him dryly. He nodded then toward the Keatings, who were watching all this in silence. "You've met my children? Fern and her husband Paul?"

Gary acknowledged the introduction with a brief nod that was not returned. He looked again to the man on the bed. "How you feeling?"

"Tired," said Winship. "Tired, like I never been in all my life! Funny what a little piece of lead can do to a man. Over fifty years I been a fighter." He shook his massive head. "Now suddenly it's like there ain't no fight left in me!"

Looking at Tracy, Gary saw the concern that grew deeper in her eyes as she heard what Winship said and the tone of his voice. Gary was watching her as the hurt man turned to his son-in-law. "Paul."

"Yes, Matt?"

"That syndicate," Winship said slowly. "I've changed my mind."

"What do you mean?"

"I'm takin' their offer!"

The reactions were varied and immediate. Gary saw Paul Keating's head jerk, with an undefined emotion. But it was Tracy Bannister who spoke, as though the words had been jarred out of her. "Oh, no!" she cried, and Gary noticed how the red-headed woman's glance lifted sharply to the other girl.

"It's a fair enough offer," Matt Winship said, his manner dogged and with a listless quality that seemed so odd in the type of man Gary had taken him to be. "Probably as good as anyone will ever make me for the ranch. And . . . I dunno. I been lyin' here thinkin' maybe I better play it safe and take this while I can.

"Ain't as though I had any real reason for holdin' out; ain't as though I wanted to pass Spur on to my family. It's been plain to me for a long time that they got no interest in takin' the place over when I'm gone—and why should they? Because it means something to me doesn't mean I should expect them to want to be saddled with it."

He nodded to himself, as though admitting the force of his

own arguments. The blue eyes, under their black brow thickets, turned on his son-in-law. "And so, Paul, I want you to have the books all in shape. And tell Ed Saxon he's to be ready for the syndicate inspectors so they can make range count of the stock."

Jim Gary happened to be looking at Keating as Winship said this, and so it was that he surprised a look on him that he could only interpret as startled shock. The young fellow covered up quickly enough, but Gary knew what he had seen and it left him frowning, wondering over a question he didn't quite put into words.

Paul Keating asked, after the slightest lapse of time, "When will this be, Matt?"

"Right away. Soon as we can get a wire off to Chicago."

"I see. Very well." Saying it, Keating glanced at his wife. Whatever he was looking for from her, he didn't get it. A tiny muscle worked for an instant at the corner of his mouth; a small, pulsing pit of shadow against the smoothness of his too-handsome face. Then abruptly he turned on his heel and went out of the room, without even a glance for the other people in it.

Fern watched him go. Afterwards, a coppery highlight played across her hair as she placed her long-lashed stare on Jim Gary, considering him in a way that made him think she might be wondering if he had noticed anything in her husband's manner. Gary met her look but it lasted for an instant only, before she again faced the man in the bed.

She said, "I think you're absolutely right, dad. You've worked hard enough and long enough. It's time you thought about something else for a change. Time you enjoyed what you've worked for!" She gave her stepfather a smile and laid a hand on his knee. "Now don't give the ranch a thought. You just lie there and get well. Paul will take care of everything. I'll see that he keeps his mind on his duties."

She was gone, then, her footsteps light as she followed her husband from the room. Looking after her, Gary heard Tracy's indignant exclamation: "Enjoy what you've worked for!

How can *she* know! How can she pretend to think she knows what Spur has been to you?"

The hurt man smiled a little. "You don't want to be unfair. Fern never took much to this life out here. But then, her mother didn't either."

"You just can't sell the ranch!" Tracy cried. "You can't *do* it!"

"What else is there?" Matt Winship demanded, with a shrug. "With the hounds snappin' at my heels—"

"You can fight! You've always been a fighter. It isn't like you to lie down!"

He shook his grizzled head against the pillow. "I dunno. I feel like they've killed something in me. Maybe the next time they'll finish the job. I don't think I could stand a next time!" The heavy-lidded eyes closed. "I'm an old man, suddenly. And I want to be let alone!"

"Oh, Matt! Matt!" Suddenly Tracy was beside him, going down on her knees by the bed. She flung an arm across his chest, pressed her head against him. "It breaks my heart to see you like this!"

Jim Gary watched the man raise his arm about her, the big hand closing upon her shoulder in an affectionate embrace. It was no more than a fatherly one, surely. But Gary frowned a little as he looked away, remembering what Vince Alcord had had to say about this man and this girl. And why, he wondered suddenly, should it make any difference to him, one way or the other? What if she actually was the old man's mistress? It could be no concern of his.

"Your name's Gary?"

Matt Winship's words, directed at him, brought his eyes back to the man. Gary nodded briefly. "That's right."

"I like your looks," Winship said bluntly. "Tracy says you're quite a scrapper. I was one, myself—reckon I know the signs." He paused, a question printed in his eyes. "Wish I was free to ask you another favor."

"Such as what?"

He asked only because he was curious, expecting almost

any answer. He was totally unprepared for the one he got.

"I need someone at Spur, to take charge while I'm laid up. Get things ready for those syndicate buyers. Keating can handle the paperwork. And there's Ed Saxon, who's a good enough range boss. He'll be able to get the stock shaped up for a range inspection. But I need somebody with more to him than either of those."

"You aren't offering *me* a job?" exclaimed Gary, the words jarred out of him. "You never even laid eyes on me before?"

"I size a man pretty quick," Matt Winship said with quiet confidence. "Saxon would like to be foreman but he's a lightweight, and that ain't good enough! You've seen the men who hate me; you seen what they already tried. Maybe you know by now that they'll do anything at all to keep this sale from going through. The man I need is one who can hold 'em off until it does. From what I've seen, he could be you, Gary! Say the word and I'll write a note that will give you authority to ride out there right now and take over."

Tracy had pulled back and was staring at him, still within the circle of his arm. "No, Matt!" she said hastily, a little too loudly. "He can't!"

"I'd pay well. I'm pretty desperate."

"You don't understand!" she insisted. "You're asking something it's impossible for him to give!"

A frown etched itself into Winship's craggy brow. He twisted his head to look at the girl, and then back again to Gary. He said gruffly, "Reckon there must be something here I don't know about. If I spoke out of turn, Gary, just forget I said anything!"

Sunlight lay full upon the hurt man and on the girl who knelt beside him with his arm about her shoulders. Jim Gary looked at the two of them, wondering suddenly what he was doing in this room, in this town.

And he was astonished to hear his own voice saying quietly, "That's all right. If you think I'm the man for the job, Winship, I'm ready to take it!"

## VI

HE HAD finished packing and was just pulling tight the lashings of the saddle roll when Tracy Bannister knocked and entered. She placed her shoulders against the door and stared at Gary a moment, watching the neat, deft movements of his hands. "Why did you do it?" she asked finally.

Jim Gary shrugged. "I figured he needed help pretty bad, to ask a total stranger. Being needed is kind of a new experience for me! Besides, I like the man.

"But it seems like a hell of a service," he added with a frown. "I can't think he really wants to sell. Still, those are my orders."

"And those other men? The Planks? You're in danger every minute you stay here, without taking on Matt Winship's enemies!"

"I've always pushed my luck pretty hard. Maybe it will stand a little more pushing."

He picked up the blanket roll, slung it across his shoulder, and took his hat from the bed. "Do me a favor?" And when she nodded: "Since I haven't got a horse of my own, I'm going to take Winship's gray for the ride out to Spur. My saddle's stashed away in the bushes down near the stageline corral. Could you have somebody dig it out and fetch it up here to the hotel, to keep for me?"

"Of course."

"Which is the road?"

"You take the north trail from town. Bear right when it forks at the crossing of Antler Creek. It's a ten mile ride from there."

He nodded his thanks. "I'll find it." But in the doorway he halted, as she stood aside for him. "Oh, one other thing. Did Winship give you any idea where this ambushing took place?"

"Why, yes. He said it was just as you pass the turnoff of the Ute Flats Road. You'll see a signpost. He told me the shot

337

seemed to come off the ridge." She frowned, puzzled. "Why did you want to know that?"

"Just to be asking." He left her with that, and went down the lobby stairs and outside.

The two Spur-branded horses the Keatings had ridden were now missing from the hitchpole. Winship's gray gelding stood alone, hipshot and idly pawing the drying mud. Gary slung his roll behind the cantle and strapped it down. He was testing the cinch when he heard his name spoken and, turning, recognized the small, white-haired man who came striding toward him.

It was one of the Alcord and Hoffman crowd, the rancher he'd heard called Priday Jones. There was something ill-at-ease in his manner as he came to a halt, his hands shoved into hip pockets of his denims, and scowled up at Gary through white thickets of bushy brows.

Gary met his look coldly. "You want something with me?"

"Look, Gary!" the old man blurted. "I'm sorry about what happened awhile ago. I'm not a quarrelsome man. But I got to look after my own interests, and I figure my interests are the same as the others'. I have to go along."

"What were you planning for Matt Winship if you'd got your hands on him—to finish what that bushwhacker tried?"

The old man colored but shook his head emphatically. "Oh, hell no! Nothing like that! Actually, we were thinking we could take him out of the hotel and hold him awhile, until we got satisfaction."

"Kidnap him, you mean?"

"Well, something like that. A crazy idea, I suppose, when you think it over. But we're desperate enough to try anything."

"Wouldn't your sheriff have had something to say about it?"

Priday Jones's waxen cheeks bunched in a look of distaste. "George Ruby," he said, "ain't too much of a man."

"I don't suppose it even occurred to you that, in his condition, you might have been committing murder by trying to move someone as badly shot as Matt Winship!" From the way

338

the old man slid his eyes away, uncomfortably, Gary knew he'd hit solidly. He added, "Just what did you think you were going to get out of him?"

"Well . . ." The old fellow hesitated, and then plunged ahead. "You heard of Ute Flats?"

Gary shook his head. "Nothing more than the name."

"It's a good stretch of graze, well-watered. The way it sets it makes sort of a buffer between Spur and the rest of us. It's a bone of contention between us and Matt Winship. Not only do we all need the grass, but we're thinkin' ahead, to that syndicate moving in. You know how it is with them big outfits! We'll trust 'em a lot better, if we can only get control of Ute Flats before they take over Spur.

"The Flats is open range," he went on. "Never did belong to Winship, except as a matter of prior usage. And if Winship won't hand it over peaceably, we'll use other means."

"Then you'll have a fight on your hands!"

"Maybe not. With Matt laid up, it leaves Ed Saxon and that weak sister of a son-in-law to hold down Spur. We'll never have a better chance." He hesitated, and his faded eyes set a speculative regard on the tall stranger. "But meanwhile, I got me an idea."

"Yeah?"

"It's pretty much dog eat dog around here just now, and my teeth is kind of blunted with age. I admire the way you handled yourself, facing the bunch of us there a while ago, and the way you used that gun you wear, when the situation demanded. George Ruby or somebody was telling me you wore that gun during the trouble up in Mogul Valley. If you ain't got other commitments and if your price ain't too steep, I'd like to see you wearin' it for me!"

Jim Gary looked at him coolly, through a long and silent moment. "You're offering to hire my gun?"

"Plain as I can put it. Never paid gun wages before, in a long and pretty busy lifetime; always fought my own wars. But a man don't always know if he can even trust his own friends! What's in your holster could make a lot of difference, come a real showdown."

Gary looked behind the words, read the real note of anxiety in them. Another time, he might have been a little sorry for this old fellow who was trying to run with wolves like Burl Hoffman and Vince Alcord. But his loyalties were already engaged, and Priday Jones was aligned on the wrong side with those who would take advantage of a man laid flat on his back by an ambush bullet.

He shook his head. "Sorry," he said bluntly. "You spoke a little late. I've already been hired."

The news took the old man hard. It straightened him like a blow, and the hands jerked out of his hip pockets to dangle aimlessly at his side. "Who by?" he demanded hoarsely. "Not—"

"Exactly!" Jim Gary had whipped the gelding's reins free of the gnawed pole and now he stepped into the saddle, favoring the pull of muscle in his half-healed chest. From the gelding's back he looked down at the other man, gave it to him straight. "I've signed with Winship. I'm rodding Spur."

The old man's mouth dropped open. His seamed face sagged and looked suddenly very sick. And Jim Gary left him like that, touching his bronc with the steel and swinging away from the rack.

He rode up the street, falling into a canter and splashing through the sky-reflecting pools of rainwater. He knew that within the hour all Matt Winship's enemies would have heard the news. That suited him. Let them take whatever warning they would from it.

The rain had done wonders for this land. It had brought out a flush of green on the bare, autumnal sweeps of thin-soiled range; in the hollows, water had collected and thirsty cattle gathered there to stand hock-deep. Nearly every dry arroyo had its miniature torrent of chocolate-brown runoff.

It would be gone in a few hours, of course, most of it sinking into the thirsty soil or finding its way to the few drainage streams. Still, the range was better for it, however brief.

Gary followed a plain trail, and when he reached Antler Creek, half-drowned willows along its turbulent course told how much it had risen above its regular level. The gray was edgy about taking the crossing but he encouraged him with a word, and they made it without trouble. Beyond, remembering Tracy's instructions, he swung his bridles toward the better-marked right-hand fork. This wasn't really necessary, because the horse knew it was heading home and it took the trail of its own accord.

There was considerable travel over this trail, and the sign failed to tell him much. He kept riding steadily and only pulled up when he came to a second forking, which was the one he had been alerted for.

As Tracy had promised, there was a faded signpost, indicating that the secondary trail he saw snaking off through the juniper led to Ute Flats. He sat saddle a moment, staring slit-eyed through brilliant sunlight in the direction of the Flats which, according to Priday Jones, was a prime bone of contention between Spur and its neighbors. Afterward he turned his attention to the low ridge that flanked the main trail here. He studied it, in silence broken only by the wind that sang in the junipers, and the whistle of a meadowlark somewhere.

The ridge was nearly bare: pink, shaley rock studded with low clumps of brush. No end of places, there, for an ambusher to lie and draw his bead on an unsuspecting victim.

Gary shook his head. He could waste hours on that bare-ribbed hill and find no clue. Nor would it matter very much, which one of Matt Winship's enemies happened to have been the one that tried to kill him. The real, vital damage was done.

He rode on.

At the end of the ten miles Tracy had estimated, the wagon road topped up out of a shallow barranca and there, suddenly, lay the ranch, its buildings tucked into the shelter where two bare ridges formed an angle. The main house was a big one, built of logs and fieldstone, and seemingly over a period of time, as though Winship had kept adding to it as he prospered from small beginnings. There were barns, and sheds, and a large bunkhouse with a kitchen. There was also a good-sized system of corrals. Everything looked business-like and trim, and as he rode in Jim Gary saw every evidence that Spur belonged to a man who thought a lot of his property.

In brief, it had everywhere the plain stamp of big Matt Winship. It had been built of his sweat and his years of loving effort, and the idea that it should be sold now to an impersonal corporation didn't sit too easily with Jim Gary.

Except for a dribble of smoke from the kitchen stovepipe and the cook's voice raised in some mournful cowboy dirge as he clattered around in there, Gary at first saw no sign of anyone. But then the clear note of a hammer striking on anvil began to sound, and he followed this around to a small three-sided frame shed that was the ranch smithy.

Here, fire glowed redly in a portable forge and three men stood about a saddled horse that was getting a hasty shoeing. They looked up as Gary rode toward them and at once all activity ceased. The puncher who was doubling as blacksmith, with a leather apron tied on over his jeans, let the hammer rest as he stared at the rider, and particularly at the gelding with the Spur brand on its flank.

It was a young fellow with a wild thatch of yellow hair who spoke. "Why, that's the old man's horse he's riding! Where'd you get him?" A rifle was booted on the saddle of the animal that was being shod. Quickly the puncher slid it out and swung the muzzle toward Gary, as the latter reined in. "Mister, you better start talking!"

The third man knocked the rifle barrel aside, shaking his head at the young fellow's rash anger. "Take it easy, Cliff." This was an old-timer, nearly as old as Priday Jones himself. He was a little stooped with the years, his head as round and dark as a nut. But the eyes that looked at Gary were sharp and shrewd. "He must have some kind of a story that makes sense, or he wouldn't dare ride in like this. Let's hear what it is."

"Thanks," Gary said dryly, and dismounted. The youngster, Cliff, held his rifle slanted toward the ground but his eyes were smoldering. Gary directed his words to the oldtimer, who seemed to have a monopoly here on cool common sense. "The name is Jim Gary. I'm here because Matt Winship sent me."

"On his own horse?" The old fellow's eyes narrowed. "What's happened?"

"Somebody tried to kill him."

There was a shocked reaction—first, disbelief, and then a rush of stammered questions. Gary proceeded to give them the facts as briefly as he could. When he was done all three stared at him in silence. Finally, the old puncher said, "We still don't know what *you've* got to do with this."

"There's something here that will explain. That is, if you know Winship's handwriting."

He handed over the note Winship had scrawled for him, and watched while they gathered close to read it. As one man they finished and raised incredulous stares. "It's his hand, right enough," the grizzled puncher said heavily. "Otherwise I'd never believe this! Selling out to the syndicate—and hiring a stranger to do the job!"

"I'm not sure I do believe any of it!" the towhead muttered.

"Easy enough to check. Go in and ask him. You'll find him in bed, at the hotel."

The oldster shook his head as he handed back the piece of paper. "It's the truth, I reckon. Though it ain't easy to accept. Pete Dunn's my name, Gary. These here are Cliff Frazer and Hack Bales."

"Glad to know you." Gary offered his hand and shook with old Pete Dunn and with Bales, the blacksmith. But Cliff Frazer only looked at the hand, his cheeks drawn tight with suspicion, the rifle still clutched tightly. Gary's mouth hardened but he didn't make an issue of it; he couldn't blame the kid for the way he felt. He withdrew the hand and said, "Will one of you take care of the horse?"

"I will," Hack Bales said, picking up the hammer again. "Soon as I finish here."

"All right. Now, where's the nearest telegraph office?"

Pete Dunn answered. "Reckon that'd be Elko."

"Winship wants a wire of acceptance got off to the syndicate. I'd better be getting it written, and tomorrow morning somebody can ride with it." He looked around at the silent ranch buildings. "What does Winship use for an office?"

"Yonder." Pete Dunn indicated a tacked-on wing of the main house. "Everything's there—all the books and records, anything the syndicate'll need to know." His mouth was a grim white line, his voice heavy with bitterness. Gary thanked him with a nod.

He started to turn, then held up. "As soon as Ed Saxon gets here, I'm going to want to see him."

"That's one thing you can count on!" Cliff Frazer said and showed his teeth in a mirthless grin. "It's gonna take more than a piece of paper to convince Ed that some stranger's moving in over him!"

Gary looked at the youngster sharply, and then saw Pete Dunn's confirming nod. He shrugged. "That's how it'll have to be, then."

From what Matt Winship had said about the current top rider, he had been led to suspect he might have to face some argument from this Ed Saxon when he learned the new state of affairs. But the look these men gave him made it appear more as though what he'd have on his hands would be a fight. . . .

The study was a big room, big enough to have its own stone fireplace, with the stuffed head of a lobo wolf mounted over it. Matt Winship's throne was a swivel chair that stood in front of a scarred, broad-topped desk holding a blotter and pens and pencils and a rack that contained a half-dozen much-smoked pipes. As he sat in the chair, a man could make a quarter turn and look out through a window onto the ranch yard, and the wide dun sweep of rangeland stretching out toward the hills clouding the horizon.

Jim Gary sat for a long time staring at that view, thinking of the hours big Matt must have spent here, judging how much it undoubtedly meant to him, how much he must hate to give it up. The more he learned about this man, the more Gary disliked the job he had undertaken to do for him.

On a smaller desk, that stood beyond the fieldstone fireplace, Gary found a stack of account books and briefly thumbed through them. They were kept in a spidery hand and were replete with ink blots and careless erasures. Paul Keating's work, he judged. The figures meant nothing to Gary, for he had no knowledge of accounting. Keating would have to fill him in on the details of Spur's finances.

He shoved the ledgers aside and returned to the big desk, took pencil and paper and laboriously worded the telegram that would have to be sent to Chicago in the morning.

It was late as he finished and stood the paper up against the pipestand, and now the first sounds of arriving horsemen brought his attention to the window. He sat and watched the Spur crew ride in on the tail of the day's work, through the golden glow of sunset.

There were a dozen of them. They came off the range singly and by twos and threes, converging on the home ranch over as many different trails. They formed a clot around the corrals as they took care of their horses and ran them into the trap. Then the men came tramping toward the buildings, and there was something in their collective manner and in the looks they turned upon the main house that told Gary the news had spread: they'd all heard of the stranger who had arrived with word of Matt Winship's ambushing, and of his own authorization to take charge.

Here was one phase of the job he wasn't particularly looking forward to, but it had to be got through, one time or another, and better to have it done than to leave the men stewing in rumors and growing resentments. He stubbed out the cigarette he had been smoking. Leaving his hat on the desk, he stood and left the house.

Emerging, he saw a man approaching along a graveled path that led from the bunkhouse area. As Gary appeared, the man halted. Beyond, the Spur riders hovered about the doorway of their quarters, gone motionless and attentive. There was almost no sound as Gary closed the office door carefully behind him, and then paced forward through the deepening gold of the fading day.

The man in the path stood and let him come.

He was a stocky, tightly-knit shape—a man in his thirties, blunt-featured and with a stubborn, honest look about his brown eyes and wide mouth. Just now he was scowling, in a dogged and forthright show of dislike. His eyes met Gary's challengingly; he made no move to step out of the way.

Coming to a halt in front of him, Gary said, with a nod toward the men before the bunkhouse, "This the whole crew?"

The other only looked at him for a moment, without answering. Then he turned his head deliberately, glanced at the silent group and back again. "I reckon. All that'll be coming in tonight."

"Good. I'm Jim Gary. While we're together, I've got some things to tell them."

He started forward, to step around the other man. But the latter set his boots and brought up a hand, the blunt fingers against Gary's chest and blocking him. "You'll do your talking to me!" he said. "I speak for the crew. Saxon's my name. I'm top rider with this outfit.

"So I understood," Gary answered levelly, not letting any trace of anger into his voice or his answering look. "Matt Winship said I'd find you the most valuable man on the payroll. And I suppose, actually, it's for you this note is intended."

As he spoke he was taking the scrawled paper from his shirt pocket and offering it to Ed Saxon. The puncher barely flicked it with a glance. Next moment he batted it out of Gary's fingers, so that it skimmed and fluttered to the path.

And he said, in a tone that carried sharply in the sunset quiet, "I don't give a damn what the boss may have wrote on that paper! He must have been out of his head. He's got all the crew he needs, and I reckon I can rod it as well as some nobody he never laid eyes on before!"

An angry tightening bunched the small muscles of Gary's jaw, but he ironed it out again. He dropped his hand to his side, and said calmly, "Winship told me you'd feel this way. I can understand you might resent being passed over, but that's how he called the play. After all, I'm only taking orders, myself. Sorry if you don't figure you can cooperate."

Saying which, he turned away from Ed Saxon and moved to walk around him and on to the bunkhouse. But with a quick sideward step the puncher again confronted him, and this time Saxon's furious stare was inches from his own. "Maybe you don't hear so good, mister! I said you give no orders to this crew!"

I'll give my first one right now," Jim Gary said quietly. "Stand out of my way!"

Ed Saxon's fist swung directly at his jaw.

The blow was telegraphed in the leaping, angry shine of the man's brown eyes and the quick lift of his chest. Gary's forearm lifted and fended it aside, and the puncher was left wide open for the answering blow that took him on the side of the head. Ed Saxon was knocked spinning off the path, and hit the dirt in a loose sprawl.

He was surprised but this failed to stop him for more than an instant. He loosed a bellow of rage and at once the drive of his boots sent him springing up and charging straight for the man who had flattened him.

Gary squared away to meet the attack. They were well matched. Gary was an inch or so the taller, but Saxon was solidly built and bound with hard, firm sinew and muscle while Jim Gary himself was honed down by his recent bout with illness. So he knew he had trouble on his hands, and that his best hope lay in staying out of the puncher's reach and making his own efforts count as quickly as possible. He moved

faster than Saxon. But the man's reaching hook missed him
and threw Saxon off balance with the force of his lunge, and
Gary threw a fist at him and felt the ache as his knuckles
struck the bone of the man's forehead. Saxon fell back, blinking his eyes.

But he was only surprised, not actually hurt. He swore,
dashed a hand across his eyes, and lunged at Gary with both
clubbed fists swinging. Giving ground before him, Gary felt
one of his bootheels turn on gravel. He stumbled, steadied
himself, and in that helpless moment a blow like the drive of
a piston sledged him full in the chest.

Agony went through him, a burning that told him the half-
healed bullet wound had been wrenched open. He gasped
and took a second wallop across the side of his face, that
rocked his head on his shoulders.

They stood toe to toe, then, slugging. At the first exchange
of blows the men from the bunkhouse had come running.
They crowded around the fighters, and Gary had no doubt
all of them were cheering Ed Saxon on. He heard shouts of:
"Cut him down to size, Ed!" "Show the bastard up!" Grimly,
Jim Gary stood and paried blow for blow, trying to break
again through the other's guard and find a vulnerable spot.

But now the pain in his upper body was swelling with
every savage blow. He could feel the steam leak out of his
muscles. He lost his hat. Sweat plastered his hair against his
forehead. His arms felt leaden and his knuckles seemed to
bounce off the other man's toughly muscled shape.

A second piston-stroke found that spot of torture high on
his right chest. This time it seemed to drive right through him.
And this time, the watchers must all have seen he was hurt.
Someone—it sounded like the young towhead, Cliff Frazer—
shouted triumphantly, "You got to him that time, Ed! Finish
him!"

The red tide of pain, receding, left a numbing blackness.
Desperately Jim Gary willed strength into his arms; they were
too heavy. His head rocked. Blows rained on him. And then

he was falling, and the hard earth came up and struck him with solid force.

As from a great distance, voices spoke:

"He made out to be real tough, but Ed licked him easy!"

"Sure caved, all right. Reckon this will change the Old Man's notions of him, when he hears."

Gary tried to speak, tried to stir. He could do neither. Then another voice—the old-timer, Pete Dunn—breaking in on a sudden tone of alarm. "Ain't that blood, there on his shirt?"

"Hey! Pete's right, the guy's bleeding!"

Hands worked at his shirt buttons, ripping it open. Somebody swore. "Why, that's a bullet wound!"

"And only about half closed," Pete Dunn said. "The fighting tore it open. No wonder you licked him, Ed! Standing up to you with a thing like that in him—Well, he's a game one, that's all I can say!"

Ed Saxon cried, in a tone of horror, "But how was I to know? He never said—"

"You never asked!" Pete Dunn retorted sharply. "Well, are you gonna just leave him lay there? To bleed to death?"

Hands were under him then, lifting him. And as they raised Jim Gary off the ground, the last gray of twilight seemed to fade. Consciousness ebbed and then darkness swept cleanly over him.

## VII

AT LEAST a dozen times, in her lonely waiting, Fern Keating heard a sound which brought her hurriedly to the door of the shack, certain at last the man she looked for was coming. Each time ended in disappointment that drew her nerves tighter with frustration and suspense. Then, as sunset painted the range and the sky, iron shoes struck an echo from a stretch of shale rock and she sprang up from the chair by the table, where she sat with empty hands. She was in the doorway as Webb Toland rode into view.

Now that the waiting was over, she stood with a hand at her throat and impatience roweled her cruelly. It seemed to take forever for the red roan horse to thread its way up the slope, through the thin stand of pine whose trunks were dyed to a rich red by the glow of the setting sun.

"I've been waiting for hours!" she exclaimed, and there was frantic urgency in her voice and in the hands that clutched at him as he dismounted. "I thought you'd never come."

The darkly handsome face drew into a frown. "But I said in my note it would be tonight."

"I know, I know. I couldn't help it. I was so anxious to see you—to learn what happened."

"Happened? What do you mean?"

"Why, in Denver, of course!" She almost shook him. "Did you get the money?"

He shook his head. The failure of his mission was already ancient history as far as Toland was concerned, so that he had almost forgotten she didn't know. His own busy mind was already ranging far ahead; he never looked back. "No," he admitted curtly. "I couldn't raise it."

"Oh, Webb!" She backed away, staring at him, aghast. "Then what about the mine?"

"It wouldn't have mattered anyway. I've had some expert opinion now, on the amount of flooding in the lower drifts.

350

My first estimates were wrong. It would be too costly an operation trying to reclaim it."

"But the money I talked Paul into giving you?"

"I can't return it just now. I'm sorry."

Her eyes brimmed with tears of anguish. "Later will be too late!" she insisted. "Can't I make you understand? Paul's out of his head with worry! He—" She corrected herself just in time. "Somebody shot the old man this morning, on the road to town. Now he's made up his mind to sell to the syndicate. It means the books will have to be examined. The whole story will come out."

"Are you worried about Paul?" he cut in, his eyes hardening. "If you are, then I suppose I've been wasting my time!"

"Don't say that!" She seized his arm convulsively. "You know I love you. Only you! Paul means nothing any more. But think of the scandal! He's so weak! When it's found out the money's gone, he'll blurt everything. He'll say that I told him to take it and put it into developing the mine. Before the thing's finished, the whole range will know about us!"

"There'll be no scandal," Toland assured her sternly. He had no intention of confessing that only a matter of an hour or so ago he himself had been ready to panic. Right now the saddlebags on the roan held the few possessions he'd cleaned out of his safe and desk in the office at Copper Hill, everything he owned. With the mining venture proven to be a fiasco, he had returned from Denver able to think only of meeting Fern here at the shack, talking her into running away with him, tonight, and leaving the rubble of his scheming behind.

But in the past half-hour, something had happened to change the whole course of his thinking.

"I ran across Burl Hoffman on the way up here," he said. "Hoffman told me all about Winship being ambushed. He told me more. He said the old man had hired himself a foreman, some gunslinger that suddenly showed up today."

The woman's eyes widened. "Not Jim Gary? I didn't know! It must have been after I left town."

Toland regarded her with sharpened interest. "You've met this fellow? What did you think of him?"

"He's a wild man! He fought with Vince Alcord and threw him into the street. And he shot one of Hoffman's riders. . . ."

Webb Toland nodded to himself, and his mouth took on a tilted smile of satisfaction. "Good! Good! He certainly seems to have stirred up the animals! Alcord and Hoffman and the rest of them are ready to fight, before they'll see a syndicate take over Spur. And with a roughneck like this Gary throwing his weight around, they'll be in a mood to fight even harder. Can't you see the opportunity for us in that?"

Fern stared in complete bewilderment. "For us? I'm afraid I don't follow you."

"With a stronger man than your stepfather at the head," he explained patiently, "Spur could be twice as big as it is. Even now it's worth many times over what he'd likely get from that Chicago outfit. Certainly you don't want him selling, not when there's a chance of building Spur bigger than it's ever been!"

"What chance?" She shook her head. "I still don't understand!"

"It's very simple." He took her by the shoulders. His voice was eager and intense, but he spoke slowly, almost as though he were explaining a problem in addition to a child.

"Hoffman and the others can't really buck an outfit the size of Spur, especially not with some tough gunman running it. They'll be broken, and leave Spur to pick up the pieces. Matt Winship will end up with an empire on his hands, whether he particularly wants one or not."

"But how does that help *us*? What about the books? How can Paul explain the money that should be there and isn't?"

"He won't have to. The sale will fall through. Eastern money isn't going to knowingly buy into a range war. As for Jim Gary, he probably doesn't know a debit from a credit; and besides he's going to have his hands too full to worry about figures written in a ledger. So you see, it give us the time to find some way to cover up the shortage.

"I said there'd be no scandal. I meant it! I'll let nothing hurt you, sweetheart."

She was in his arms again and their lips met, long and lingering, as he stilled her questions with his kiss. They were questions he wasn't ready yet to find answers for, though in in his own mind he already saw many possibilities.

Today Matt Winship had nearly died. In an all-out war with his neighbors, who would question too seriously if another ambush bullet proved more successful? Fern would be left as his only heir to the enlarged Spur that Toland saw rising out of the embers of the coming range dispute.

And, should there be any doubt of its outcome, Toland had a good half-dozen gunfighters in Copper Hill who could be used effectively wherever needed. With Fern Keating in love with him, he didn't see how he could fail to come out on top in the confused shape of events ahead. He'd come out with something far more valuable than some played-out copper mine.

There was Paul Keating—no problem! He could be gotten rid of at any time. And . . . oh, yes. This foreman at Spur, this gunman—Gary, was that the name? He was a cipher, at the moment. He might need more careful handling. But Webb Toland had no intention of letting some fiddle-footed gun-slinger stand in his way when the time showed itself ripe for taking over Winship's ranch, and Winship's daughter.

For minutes after he woke, Jim Gary tried to imagine where he was and then, as memory of the fight with Ed Saxon came to him, decided he must be in the bunkroom at Spur. Morning light lay on the empty room, with its wood-framed bunks built in double tiers against the walls, and the gear and clothing hanging from nails. There was a deal table and chairs, a space heater sitting in a box of cinders. Beyond a partition, male voices and a clatter of dishes sounded in the kitchen that occupied one end of the building. The crew was at breakfast.

He tried to sit up and made it on the second attempt. His face and body felt like one huge bruise, testifying to the beating he'd taken. The ache of the bullet wound in his chest was a piercing throb. He examined it, found someone had bandaged it tightly. The cloth was unspotted, so he didn't seem to be bleeding any longer.

Whoever put him on the bunk had removed his shirt and his boots, but not his trousers. Gary looked around, saw his boots nearby and hooked and dragged them over. He worked them on and then got carefully to his feet. He was in good enough shape, he thought, considering.

As he stood holding to the timber of the bunk, the connecting door opened letting in a burst of noise from the kitchen. He turned, and saw Ed Saxon standing in the doorway looking at him.

For a moment neither moved or spoke. Then Saxon closed the door, shutting away the racket. His face was sober and he was ill at ease. He said, "How do you feel?"

"I've felt worse."

"It took nerve walking into a fight when you knew you had that bullet hole in you!"

Gary shrugged. "I couldn't see myself using it as an excuse to duck out."

"I still wish I'd known," Saxon said heavily. "I don't like beating hell out of a man and then finding he was already hurt."

"Forget it! The important thing is, I may have got licked but I'm not backing down. I'm still foreman here and I still intend to give the orders. So where does that leave us?"

He saw a flush creep upward through the man's blunt features. Ed Saxon was the one to break gaze. He said, doggedly, "It's no pleasure half-killing a gent as nervy as you, Gary. But, by God—"

He never finished. A shout from the yard outside broke in on him: "Ed! Where's Ed Saxon?" A hard-ridden horse plowed to a stand. In the adjoining kitchen, there was a hurried trampling of boots.

Ed Saxon gave Jim Gary a startled look. "Sounds like Johnson, the rider we had with the herd on Ute Flats."

Gary was directly behind him as he rushed out. The rest of the crew were gathered around the newcomer and his lathered horse. He was wild-eyed, bareheaded. His holster was empty and one shirtsleeve was blood-soaked.

"It's Alcord and Hoffman, and that crowd!" Hack Bales relayed the word as Saxon and Gary hurried up. "They've hit the Flats. Driven off our herd and tooken possession!"

"When was this?" Ed Saxon looked white beneath his tan.

"Gray light," Johnson answered. "They planned it good. Priday Jones and a couple of his men jumped me while I was still in my blankets; they held me and the rest started movin' our stock into the junipers. Claim they're gonna hold onto the Flats come hell or high water or a syndicate army!"

Jim Gary frowned. "Wouldn't the law have something to say about this? What's the sheriff's office for?"

"That fat-headed George Ruby?" young Cliff Frazer snorted. The veteran puncher, Pete Dunn, nodded sober concurrence.

"Spur don't actually own the Flats," the old man pointed out. "It's a matter of customary usage. By every right except legal title, the Flats belong to Matt Winship for as long as he continues to run cattle on them. But Sheriff Ruby isn't going to stick his neck out as long as he can find a technical excuse!"

Ed Saxon was looking at the blood on Johnson's shirt. "Who shot you?"

"It's no more'n a nick. One of 'em tried to stop me when I seen my chance and made a break."

"What are they doing now?" somebody wanted to know.

"Time I left, they was digging in and putting up breastworks. You ask me, they're getting ready for a battle!"

"Well?" Hack Bales demanded. "And what about it? They gonna get one?"

All eyes turned toward Saxon, then. He felt the weight of their looks. He seemed suddenly tormented by doubt: he ran a hand across his cheeks, down over his mouth, and the hand was trembling. And looking at him, Jim Gary understood the man.

Saxon was a good cattleman—an honest plodder, excellent for seeing that the routine of a working ranch was accomplished. But here, faced with an emergency, he was floored. And this was precisely what Matt Winship had foreseen, when he decided to look elsewhere for a foreman.

Gary settled his shoulders. Without preliminary he took over the reins. With the first word he spoke, leadership passed to him like an invisible mantle.

"Whatever they think they're going to do," he said, "we have to catch them while they're off guard, before they expect it. Everybody get horses and guns. But remember," he added sharply, "those guns stay in the holsters until you get orders!" And to Hack Bales he said, "Rope out a bronc for me, will you, Hack?"

"Yes, sir!" Hack said eagerly. "You bet!" And he joined the general rush for the corral. Gary turned to the man named Johnson.

"Have the cook take a look at that arm," he ordered. "See if it needs a doctor. Otherwise, you're to stay here at the ranch."

Johnson didn't argue. But as he started away, he paused to give the stranger a closer look. "Never seen you before," he said. "You must be this Jim Gary, that I heard Priday Jones mention. The new foreman Winship signed on?"

Gary only nodded. As Johnson walked off toward the kitchen, Ed Saxon asked him, "What's your plan?"

There was no trace of hostility in the question or in Saxon's blunt, honest face. As abruptly as that, he seemed to have accepted Gary's right to authority, his position of leadership. Perhaps the truth had been borne home to him that, in the showdown, he himself was no leader.

"No plan," Gary had to admit. "We'll just see what the

thing looks like when we get there. You have to be ready to improvise, and then move fast, to carry out whatever you've thought up!" He added, "I better finish dressing."

"You sure you can ride? You in shape for it?"

Gary answered the anxious question with a nod. In the bunkhouse he found his roll and dug a clean shirt out of it. He didn't bother with shaving. Remembering he'd had no breakfast, he went next door to the kitchen and let the gimp-legged puncher who served as the ranch cook pour him a china mug full of coffee. He drank it standing in the doorway, munching at a bacon sandwich as he watched the activity in the yard. The crew members worked fast and efficiently to catch up their mounts and cinch saddles into place. Rifles slid into saddle scabbards. Sixguns were checked for loads and replaced in holsters.

Suddenly, in an upstairs window of the main house, Gary saw a woman looking silently down on the scene.

It was Fern Keating. A dressing gown was belted at her waist and, as she leaned with hands on the sill, her long, copper-colored hair lay unbound upon her shoulders. The morning sun shone on it as on a new-minted penny. She was a beautiful sight, Gary admitted, the coffee cup forgotten for a moment in his hands.

Then he saw Hack Bales hurrying up, leading a skewbald gelding. Prompted to his immediate duties, Gary put the woman from his thoughts. He finished off his coffee, handed the cup to the waiting cook, and hurried out.

"Mount up!" he shouted, and rose into the saddle as leather creaked and horses stomped restlessly in the yard. "Let's ride!"

The Spur crew left the ranch yard in a rush and a quick thunder of hoofs. They rode into the morning. The last thing Gary saw, glancing back, was the coppery glint of the woman's streaming hair, framed by the window.

They were a sober group and they rode quietly, without much talking, thinking of the thing that lay ahead. Once, as they halted to breathe their mounts, Gary found himself next to Pete Dunn and something prompted him to ask the old puncher, "You known Matt Winship long?"

"Longest of any man here," he answered promptly. "Rode with him in Texas and the Indian Nations. And I was at his stirrup the day he come into this Nevada country and sized it up as likely cattle range."

"Then you must have been with him all through the building of this ranch."

"Every step of the way! And I can tell you, it's been the nearest thing to his heart, 'specially since his marriage went sour for him. He's sunk a lifetime and a fortune trying to improve the land and the stock. Wait till you see the special herd of Black Angus he's got spotted over by Buck Ridge! That cost him real money." The old man shook his head, his face clouding. "And now to give it all up. . ."

"Sounds to me you think pretty highly of him."

Dunn stabbed him with a clear, undimmed gaze. "No finer man ever forked leather! You take what he done for the Bannisters—"

"Tracy Bannister, you mean? The girl at the hotel?"

"Her and her pa, Luke Bannister. He was another old hand of Matt's. He got throwed and rolled on in the Spur corral, by a bad cayuse Matt had ordered him not to ride. Now, any other boss would of said it wasn't none of his blame, and washed his hands of it. Not Matt! He paid all the hospital bills, and when we seen that Luke wasn't gonna be able to get out of a wheel chair, let alone ride, Matt still took care of him.

"Made a down-payment on that hotel in Antler, footed all the bills till Luke and the girl could make a go of it. And since Luke Bannister died he's been with Tracy like she was his own daughter!" At a thought, the old puncher's mouth pulled down. "Wish to hell she *was*, in place of that stepdaughter his wife left him! Josie Winship was a real good woman, but that red-headed first husband of hers must really

have been a pip! Handsome as hell, most like, and no damn
good at all!"

They rode on, after that, and Gary mulled over what the
old man had told him.

He knew a strange sense of relief. Pete Dunn's opinion of
Fern Keating didn't concern him. But what he'd had to say
about Tracy Bannister eased his mind more than he would
have cared to admit. He told himself he had never really
believed the nasty hints Vince Alcord had passed about the
girl. Even so, it was good now to hear the facts concerning
her relationship with Matt Winship—the real link between
them, the true basis of her gratitude.

Ute Flats was actually a grassy depression in the sparse
juniper forest, hemmed by low hills to the west, and on north
and south by slanting rims. It would be a couple of miles
from end to end of it, and perhaps half as wide. In a land of
fairly dry range, its acres of graze that were well watered by
a natural collection tank could be valuable indeed.

"Johnson said they were digging in," Ed Saxon remarked.
"I guess I see what he meant."

He stood with Gary on a rise that gave them a view toward the Flats, where water glinted under a high, cloud-
dotted morning sky. Silently Jim Gary studied the near end
of the depression, and the wagon trail that snaked toward it
through the sage and juniper. Where this trail dipped onto
the Flats, the low rims drew together, like a funnel, making a
gap of little more than a quarter of a mile. And there he
could see tiny figures frenziedly at work.

They were throwing up breastworks of dirt and stone and
timbers hauled down from the rims. They had a pair already
built, flanking the road, and were starting on a couple more
which would tie in with the protecting rims and make a barricade that could be held against an attack from the direction
of Spur.

"Looks to me like Burl Hoffman's thinking," Saxon said
dryly. "He was a corporal in the Army Engineers, once.
This is probably his idea of a real military maneuver!"

359

"Could be a pretty good one," Gary answered. "That is, if we gave them time to finish. But I don't think we're going to!"

The puncher looked at him sharply. "You already got a notion?"

He nodded. "Could be. This juniper gives pretty good cover, and the ground's still too soaked to raise a dust. How long would it take you and half the crew to circle wide and come in on that south rim, without letting yourselves be spotted?"

Saxon computed, eyeing the lay of the land that was cut by arroyos and overgrown with the twisted, bushy trees. "Fifteen minutes, maybe."

"I'll give you twenty. This has to be timed or it won't work. Who's your most reliable man with a rifle?"

"Cliff has a good eye, and he's cool."

"The kid? Will he follow orders?"

"Sure."

"Then let's go." And he led the way back down the rise to where the rest of the crew were bunched, waiting for the word.

The shaggy, blue-berried junipers were washed to a brilliant green by the recent storm. As Jim Gary picked a careful way through them, with Pete Dunn at his stirrup and five members of the Spur crew trailing, the red hide of an occasional steer showed among the twisted trunks—part of the herd Matt Winship's enemies had thrown off its customary graze on the Flats. The porous earth soaked up hoof-sound. Gary rode with a confidence that they would be giving the enemy no warning of their approach.

The trees grew almost to the dropoff of the rim. He dismounted, turned his reins over to one of the men, and moved forward on foot for a look, dropping to all fours as he neared the edge.

The wide depression of the Flats lay directly below him here. Long waves of shadow flowed across it as clouds intermittently shuttled over the face of the sun. The only stock in sight was a small bunch of saddle horses belonging to th men who were sweating and toiling in evident haste to get the logs and stones piled up and tamped with dirt to complete the barricade.

Two of the men—the only ones with guns in their hands—stood guard at the breastworks that were already completed; they were keeping an anxious watch on the approach through the junipers, waiting for the attack they knew they had invited by their move in ousting Spur cattle from the Flats.

Only one thing was wrong with their calculations: The enemy was already at their backs.

Directly opposite him, now, on that other low rim some four hundred yards to the south, Gary saw movement as Ed Saxon and his half of the riders came into position. Cautiously he lifted an arm, wig-wagged and received an answering signal. Afterward he drew back, got to his feet, and returned to the riders he'd left waiting. Rising to the saddle, he shouted, "Let's go!"

They came down onto the Flats with a rush, dust and gravel spurting under braced hoofs. As they finished the drop Ed Saxon and the rest of the crew were breaking over the opposite rim. Both groups hit the level, then, and were spurring directly toward the work party at the barricade. They fanned out as they rode.

The surprise was complete. Their busy picks and shovels making a covering racket, the workers failed even to hear the horses until they were nearly on top of them. Whirling, they stared helplessly at an enemy sweeping in on their rear, and were too surprised at first even to drop their tools.

Gary's attention was on the two guards. His sixgun was in his hand and he flung a shot that dropped one of them with a smashed leg. The other, suddenly realizing he was on the wrong side of this barricade they'd put up with so much effort, turned and made a desperate effort to fling himself to cover across the top of it.

But now Cliff Frazer carried out the precaution Gary had taken against this. Out in the junipers, a rifle cracked. A steel-jacketed slug raised a film of dirt from the top of the breastworks and whined skyward. The guard, losing his nerve, dropped his carbine and slid back down the mound of wood and stone. By the time he scrambled to his feet, the Spur riders were menacing the entire group. Shovels and crowbars were flung aside and hands were quickly raised.

Altogether, two shots had been fired. The only one to be hurt was the man whose leg Gary's own bullet had skewered.

Young Cliff Frazer came whooping in along the wagontrail, out of the junipers, spurring his pony and brandishing his smoking rifle. Pete Dunn was crowing as the Spur crew disarmed their prisoners. To a scowling, black-haired man named Marshall who, as Burl Hoffman's foreman, seemed to be the leader of the detail, he said, "What's the use building a fort, if you let your enemy sneak in and grab you from behind?"

Marshall, glowering beneath his brows, said nothing. But another man retorted, "You just didn't give us time to finish. Half an hour more and we'd been ready for you."

Ed Saxon gave Gary an openly admiring look. "You're dealing with a gent who ain't going to give you any extra half-hours!"

But Gary, for his part, took no share in this. He wasn't wholly satisfied. Looking at Marshall, he saw the way the foreman's scowling glance seemed to keep returning to a spot on the far western edge of the Flats, where the ridge of rocky hills edged it. Never a man to take any victory for granted, he suddenly took warning and said sharply, "Ed! You and Cliff watch these birds. Have one of them do something to keep this one from bleeding dry." The rest he signaled to follow him.

A notch in the ridge yonder commanded his attention. He knew that was where the trouble would come from and he spurred directly toward it. While the Spur riders were still some fifty yards short, the first rumble of plodding hoofs and clacking of horns and mutter of bawling cattle began to sound Then a steer broke into view, up among the rocks and brush, then two more hard on its tail. Legs braced against the downward pitch, the lead steer saw the horsemen suddenly blocking the way ahead and he hauled up, swinging his horns. He tried to turn back as the other steers crowded down on him.

Jim Gary's sixgun snapped flatly and the lead animal buckled at the knees and rolled over on his side, and Gary saw Burl Hoffman's Box H brand on the steer's flank. The cattle immediately behind bawled in fear and stopped short. Farther up in the notch, a man's voice shouted faintly in alarm.

More cattle appeared, pressing hard on those in the fore. No orders needed to be given. The Spur riders opened fire, and several more steers dropped. By then, a racket of bellowed fear rose above the echoes of the guns. In the narrow gap, cattle were turning, trampling, goring in their frantic anxiety to escape from what waited for them at the foot of the pass.

Suddenly horsemen were visible, shadowy figures trying to buck the snarl of frightened beef. One of them was Burl Hoffman. He saw the defenders at the foot of the slant and at once a gun in his hand was blazing. Jim Gary fired back, saw the hat jump from the man's sandy hair. Other guns opened up on both sides.

For a matter of minutes there was real madness in the rocky throat of the gap. Steers bellowed and tried to climb over one another. Men shouted, fighting to hold their horses steady. Burnt powder spread its stench.

Actually the fight was quickly over. One of the attackers took a bullet and, dropping his gun, clutched for the saddlehorn. His horse, turned by the pressure of steers trying to escape in the direction from which they'd come, swung broadside against one of the other riders. In an instant, the confusion was too great for any attack to continue.

Burl Hoffman, the last to admit defeat, took a last angry shot at Gary and missed, then savagely he swung his horse's head and he too was gone, in the wake of his men. Echoes died among rocks and brush. Now all that remained behind were a half-dozen dead steers, stiffening where the bullets had dumped them—a plug of slaughtered beef that should block further attempts by Spur's enemies to drive their cattle onto the Flats, through this route at least.

The fighting had been so brief there had been no time for the Spur crewmen to dismount. Empty gun smoking in one hand, Jim Gary settled the frightened skewbald and said, "That's that! Now we'll move our own stock back where it belongs and turn loose the prisoners, without their guns. And we'll keep a three-man guard here, until we're sure they aren't going to try anything like this a second time."

"Gary!" somebody cried in a tone of horror. He looked, and only now realized they hadn't got through this encounter unscathed.

For the old-timer, Pete Dunn, lay in the dirt where he had fallen from his saddle. When Jim Gary got to him, he found the man still alive but unconscious. Blood pumped from a bullet wound in his chest at an alarming rate.

At this price, victory had come high indeed.

# VIII

WITH shadows thickening among the town's buildings—though the last light of day made the sky overhead the color of steel—the figure of the man swinging out of saddle before the saloon had a familiarity about it that hauled Jim Gary up sharply. He said, aloud, "Boyd Plank!" Next moment, as he got a better look, he saw there was really nothing more than a similarity of shape. But the experience had been a disturbing one.

As he rode on to the hotel hitchrack and there dismounted to tie, he was thinking that events had so far taken over his mind as to make him lose all sight of his own personal affairs, until reminded by an accidental look at a casual stranger.

Alarmed by this, he stood a moment with his hands upon the tooth-gnawed smoothness of the tie-pole, thinking now about the Planks and wondering what might have happened to them—wondering if they wouldn't have guessed by now that they'd missed the trail somewhere. Then he shrugged; he was committed here, and he couldn't do justice to two worries at one time.

He'd known what he was doing, and risking, when he took on the chore for Matt Winship. So be it.

Lamps were burning in the lobby. The night clerk was already at his post behind the desk. Gary, looking for Tracy Bannister, shook his head at the man and went to look into the dining room, where a handful of townspeople were scattered among the tables. Not seeing the person he wanted, he was about to turn away when a voice spoke his name sharply and halted him, drawing his eye to a table where two men were seated.

It was the fat sheriff, George Ruby, who had spoken. He was pushing back his chair, which creaked under his gross weight. He made a move to rise but then stayed as he was, for Jim Gary had altered his course and was crossing the room toward him. Gary touched the second man at the table with a brief glance, still so preoccupied with his own thoughts that he didn't immediately recognize the dark features. But when he saw the tawny eyes he remembered Webb Toland, from that single meeting at the stage station. Their eyes met briefly, and then Gary returned his gaze to the sheriff's scowling face.

"Well?" he prompted.

"What's this I heard about some gunplay out at the Flats this morning?"

"I wouldn't know what you heard," Gary replied shortly. "There's probably no telling, since I suppose you heard it from the other side!"

The sheriff didn't like his tone. His flabby cheeks colored and he said quickly, "Far as that matters, I've known Burl Hoffman and Vince Alcord for a long time, and I've known *you* about two days. I warned you I didn't much cotton to some strange gunslinger riding in here from nowhere, and turning a bad situation into open warfare!"

This view of the matter was so blatantly unfair that Jim Gary shrugged, seeing no point in arguing it, or bothering to point out that Spur's enemies had made the initial move by their attempt to grab Ute Flats. "All right," he said curtly. "So you warned me." He turned to leave.

"How's Pete Dunn?" the sheriff asked gruffly. His tone held real concern, and Gary paused long enough to give him an answer.

"Doctor was with him a couple of hours. Did everything he could. But the old fellow's still unconscious."

Ruby wagged his head. "Bad. Damned bad! Can you tell me who it was put the bullet in him?"

"No," Gary admitted truthfully. "There was a lot of lead being flung around. How'd the other side make out?"

"Nothing to fuss about. A skewered leg and a rib smashed. Doc had better luck there."

"I'm not apt to waste tears over them." Concerned as he was about Pete Dunn, he had little mercy for those who had followed Burl Hoffman in his unprovoked attack on what, by custom and usage, was recognized to be legitimate Spur graze.

Webb Toland's eyes regarded him across the rim of a coffee cup. "You sound pretty cold-blooded, my friend," he observed, and got a hard stare from Jim Gary.

"And what's *your* stake in this business?" Gary demanded bluntly.

The other lifted a shoulder. "None at all," he said, "being a mining man myself." He set the cup down, appearing to take no particular offense at Gary's manner. Laying money beside his plate, he rose and took an expensive flat-topped hat from the seat of an empty chair.

"Well, my stake," Gary said in the same cold tone, "is the promise I made to a man lying, hurt, upstairs in this hotel. When I sign on a job, I try to do it. And if I think the man I hire with is in the right, then any man who works against him has to count me for an enemy!"

"And I take it," Webb Toland murmured, with what Gary read as an edge of mockery, "that you figure yourself as a fairly bad enemy?"

"As bad as I can manage!" He added, with a curt nod at George Ruby, "Good evening, Sheriff." Not waiting to discover if the lawman had anything more to say, he turned on his heel and walked back through the lobby archway. He left the dining room in complete silence, with everyone's eyes following his straight, solid back.

In the lobby he confronted Tracy Bannister. She must have heard the exchange, for her face was stern, her eyes troubled. "Were you trying to pick a fight in there?"

He shook his head tiredly. "I dunno. I dunno what I was trying to do. Your sheriff rubs me the wrong direction. And there's something about that other gent that doesn't set with me, either."

"Webb Toland?" She made a small gesture. "I can't really say I blame you. But he's on the sideline, as far as Spur's troubles are concerned. He at least is one man you shouldn't need to worry about. So why let him upset you?"

"A good question, I suppose." He didn't know what nagging thing it was that worked at him—something he had seen in the pale eyes that made him feel this Webb Toland wasn't really as disinterested as he pretended.

The girl was watching him with an anxious look. She said, "Come in the office."

It was the room that lay behind the lobby desk, a small room taken up by a rolltop desk and a couple of chairs. In the doorway, Jim Gary glanced back into the lobby and saw Webb Toland walking into the night, pulling on his hat. Gary frowned thoughtfully as he closed the door.

From this room, Tracy managed the running of the hotel. It was neat, like everything else about her, but it had been furnished by a man. Probably Luke Bannister had consciously copied Winship's study at Spur, aping the tastes of the man he had admired, and Tracy had left things untouched when her father died.

She took the swivel chair behind the desk and watched Jim Gary slack into the deep leather chair opposite and drop his hat upon his knees. "You're really tired, aren't you?" she said.

"It's been a long day." He didn't bother to add that ever since the fight with Ed Saxon the half-healed wound in his chest had been aggravating and troublesome.

"Tell me what really happened at the Flats. I've had nothing but rumors."

His account was brief, succinct. He ended, with a glance toward the ceiling, "Has *he* heard anything of this?"

"Matt?" she shook her head. "Not from me, and I haven't let anyone near him except Dr. Walsh. The doctor said he shouldn't be told anything to alarm him, or put him in a worse mood."

"How is he?"

"Physically good enough. I think he could go back to the ranch if he wanted to bad enough. But he doesn't seem to want much of anything. That bullet did more to hurt his spirit than his body. It frightens me to see a man like him suddenly beaten."

Gary rubbed a palm across his jaw, feeling the shaggy stiffness of unshaven beard. "Damn!" he exclaimed, an explosion of breath. He went on: "I know what you mean! I've seen that special herd of Black Angus that means so much to him. And the crew.

"Not a man of them that doesn't want to fight this thing, instead of sell. Especially after the business at the Flats. This evening they're out on guard, working overtime voluntarily to make sure there aren't any more such surprises." He hesitated. "The real reason I came in," he said then, "was that I thought—if he really knew what's been going on—"

"He might change his mind?" she finished. "Get mad enough to fight?"

"Something like that."

She shook her head, a crease of worry forming between her brows. "You can try it if you like, I suppose. But I hope you won't take the risk."

"Why's it a risk?"

"The strange mood he's in—I just don't know. He'd have to be told what happened to poor Pete Dunn. And I'm afraid that that, on top of everything else . . ."

She let it go unfinished. Jim Gary looked at her for a long moment in silence. Then he dropped his eyes to his boots. "Well," he said finally, "you know him better than I do."

"I'm sure I'm right!" Something made her lean in her chair and place a hand on his wrist. It was hard with muscle and bone, weather-roughened. "I'm sorry," she told him earnestly. "But I *do* know Matt Winship. He's a stubborn man. He hired you to do a certain thing. He's going to expect you to do exactly that, and nothing else."

"To take part in dismembering a fine ranch," he interpreted, and he swung irritably to his feet and prowled to the window, slapping his hat aginst his knee. He stood a moment with his boots spread and his head shot forward a little, peering sightlessly through the glass into the growing dark outside. Tracy watched him, and when he suddenly swung toward her again she saw the hardness that had come into his jaw, and into the set of his mouth.

"I better tell you this," Jim Gary said curtly. "I wrote the telegram he ordered me to, telling them in Chicago that they had a deal." He spoke as though the words tasted bad to him. "I wrote it, but then I tore it up!"

She stared. "You had no right!"

"Maybe. But I'm a stubborn man, myself! I can't send that kind of a wire, whether Winship likes it or not! He'll have to send it himself. I'll hold the line against his enemies, until he's on his feet. If he still wants to sell then, that's his busines."

Tracy said, "Don't you see you're taking a terrible risk? You'll be facing his enemies, and you'll be going against direct orders!"

"I have to take the chance," he retorted. "If Winship doesn't like it when he finds out, that's too damned bad. But still better than if he'd think it over and be sorry—too late!— for a decision he made when he was flat on his back with a bullet in him!"

Her breast rose on a long, slow breath. She shook her head, the hair glinting softly in the lamplight. But she said, "Very well, Jim. I'll say nothing more. I give you credit for doing what you think you must. And I'll be praying that you're right!"

"Thanks," he said gruffly. "For now, I guess I'll be riding. I have to check the guard at the Flats, before heading back. And there doesn't seem much point in discussing anything with Matt tonight."

A moment afterward, he left. And for a much longer time, Tracy Bannister remained seated at her desk, staring with brooding, sightless eyes at the place where she had watched him standing, before the darkened window.

Paul Keating, in the lamplit study at Spur, with the hopelessly botched account books spread before him, was lost in a bad state of funk. Knowing there wasn't any whisky in the house, he wished for a drink with an intensity that made his hands tremble. His nervous system had taken too many shocks in these last few days, too many ups and downs that fluctuated too violently between tremulous hope and total, engulfing despair.

The worst moment had come yesterday when, alarmed by Matt Winship's announcement of his plan to sell the ranch, he'd raced the miles to Copper Hill to locate Webb Toland and pin him down to some definite statement about the money. But at the mining camp he'd found Toland come and gone, his office empty, the desk and safe hurriedly ransacked. People he'd questioned had told him alarming news. It was rumored now that Toland had been advised the Copper Queen was a hopeless proposition, that all his reports had shown the tunnels were flooded past any hope of reclaiming.

Certain of the worst—that he'd been swindled, left to face the wrath of his father-in-law—he'd returned to Spur this morning nursing desperate thoughts of suicide. And had learned from his wife about this man Jim Gary, being appointed foreman, with the job of pushing through the sale of Spur to the syndicate. Fern had tried, with ill-concealed scorn, to shame him out of the despair the news threw him into.

"Will you listen to reason, Paul? What is this Gary, but an illiterate gunslinger? If you can't pull the wool over his eyes, you're even more a fool than I think you are!"

"But I'll never fool a syndicate lawyer! One look at those books—"

"It may never happen," Fern had cut in mysteriously. "Worry about the syndicate lawyers when you see them walking into the office."

Whatever might have been in her mind, he could get nothing more out of her. She'd been less than reassuring. As for Gary, he hadn't even seen the man yet.

Ranch headquarters was silent at this late hour. Practically the whole crew, or so he understood, was out riding range against further attempts like the one at Ute Flats. The

windows were closed and a small blaze crackled in the fireplace. A chill that came with the setting of the sun had
warned that summer was ending and fall was nearly on
them. When a mutter of running horses began to swell out of
the night, it was some moments before Keating's distracted
mind registered the sound.

His head jerked up suddenly. The sound was unmistakable.
Even as he got to his feet a swarm of riders swept into the
yard. He heard the thunder of the hoofs; the hoarse bawling
of voices. When the first guns began to roar, he understood.
This was an attack!

A first knotting of terror gave way to fear for his wife. He
found himself running from the study, across a hallway and
into the main portion of the big house, calling her name.
Empty stillness echoed him. The outer noise swelled to a
crescendo, muffled by these thick walls that seemed to tremble with the pound of hoofs on hard-packed earth, the slam
of gun echoes.

A window went out, close beside him. He dropped to all
fours and crouched, shaking, as broken glass sprayed him
and a shard of it ripped his cheek. No sound at all from the
room upstairs, where Fern had retired an hour ago claiming
a headache. Pushing to his feet, Keating shouted her name
from a tight throat and then groped through darkness to the
stairway, went stumbling up them two at a time.

Her door was locked. He pounded on it and rattled the
knob, calling. Thought of her lying wounded, perhaps even
dead from a flying bullet, sent his shoulder ramming hard
against the wood. It was a sturdy slab but with the third
lunge the lock pulled loose and the panel sprang inward.
Keating grasped the edge of the doorjamb to steady himself,
as he stared toward the bed.

Enough moonlight came through the window to show
him it was empty. Wherever Fern was, she wasn't in this
room.

His mind limped and stumbled, trying to understand and,
in his confusion, failing. Then a flurry of gunshots in the yard

carried him to the window. He stared below, incredulous.

It was madness! Mounted men spurred at will through the yard, raising dust and banging guns. Over at the bunkshack a couple of Spur hands were firing back, from cover—the crippled cook for one, he supposed. Perhaps even Pete Dunn had dragged himself off his bunk to put up a fight, so far as he could. But it wasn't enough.

Above all the other racket, he thought he recognized the voice of Burl Hoffman shouting hoarsely, "Burn 'em out! *Burn 'em out!*"

Already, one of the sheds was in flames, spreading a wind-whipped, ghastly light over the scene. Smoke and dust rose cherry-red. Torches made circles of fire as the attackers brandished them. Even as Keating watched, one let fly and a firebrand lobbed end-for-end, in a crazy pattern. Next moment came the smash of a downstairs window as it hit.

That sound broke him from his dazed inaction. "Oh, my God!" cried Paul Keating, in a throat that felt scraped and dry. He whirled and ran wildly from the room.

A hellish glow already showed at the bottom of the steps as he stumbled down them. Fire had seized on heavy drapes at the broken window, was licking toward the ceiling. The torch, rolling, had spread oily flames clear across the room. Heat and smoke caught at him.

There was nothing he could do here. He edged past the fire, and then shaking legs carried him again through the hall and back into the study, to stare wildly around. On pegs above the mantelpiece was Matt Winship's rifle. Paul Keating hurried and snatched it down, and with untrained motions checked its load.

But he was no gunman. He had no business in a fight! Helpless, he stood in the middle of that hated room, that held so many evidences of the father-in-law whom he so strongly feared. He listened to the hullabaloo in the night outside, and even with a gun loaded and ready, he knew he could take no part in the defense of the ranch.

And then his eye lit on the open ledger, on the other

account books that held the proof of his downfall. He coughed on acrid smoke that swirled through the hallway door. He looked at the small box safe in the room's corner, and suddenly it was perfectly clear to him what he was going to do.

It was no worse than what Webb Toland had done, he thought, picturing the empty safe in the office of the Copper Queen. Even bluff, confident Webb Toland—who Fern had often told him, scornfully, was twice the man Paul Keating could ever hope to be—had cut his losses and run when the hole he dug for himself proved too deep!

Keating could act when his course was set, and there was a certain cunning in him that his wife might have found astonishing. First he pulled open all the drawers of Matt Winship's big desk, as a hurriedly rummaging intruder might do. The box safe presented no problem. He'd often thought a petty thief could pry it open at will, using the fireplace poker.

He spun the dial hastily, and squatting before the box he scooped greenbacks and a sack of coins into the pockets of his coat. He got the poker then and took a moment to batter the door and the lock, completing the illusion of a forced entry. The sounds he made were lost in the continuing racket outside.

Smoke swirled thickly now, stinging his throat to rawness. He was held for an anguished moment in a paroxysm of coughing, as he clung to a corner of his own scarred desk. Afterward, driven by a desperate need for haste, he proceeded with the rest of his program.

He heaved the desk over. Account books and ledgers spun to the floor in a fluttering of leaves. Taking the burning kerosene lamp, he stood looking around to make certain of his arrangements. Then he lifted the lamp and slammed it down, hard, into the mess of fallen books and papers.

Burning oil spattered and pooled. Blue flame licked at the ink-blotted pages that had cost him so many hours of anxiety and toil. But not fast enough. He needed a cross draft. Quickly he hurried to a window and ran it open. Chill night air spilled into the room, bringing the racket of the yard outside. And now the fire leaped, beginning to eat greedily at whatever it could reach.

Hastily, Paul Keating grabbed the rifle and rushed through the hallway door, Sparks floated redly about him; past the living room archway he looked into the heart of a roaring furnace. He gave it no more than a single awed glance, before he turned in the other direction, hurrying toward the rear of the house.

He found a window, on the blind side of the building. It was locked and had been seldom opened. He struggled with the catch, then impatiently smashed it out with the butt of the rifle. He knocked out all the jagged splinters of glass and slipped through, dropping the short distance to the ground.

There was no action here; no one saw him. Keyed-up excitement pulled the lips back from his teeth as he started running.

More than once, climbing the barren hill behind the ranch, he slipped and fell in the dark. Rocks and brush tore at him; he was panting when he reached level ground. And here he turned, for a look at the scene he had left below.

The raid was over; the attackers had done their work and gone. He could see the Winship men—two or three shadowy figures who moved about the yard—looking like men dazed and stunned by catastrophe. The second fire, started by Keating himself, had helped seal the doom of the Spur house. It was a flaming pyre, sending red billows of smoke toward a high cloud ceiling that covered the stars. With the night wind whipping at it, there was only the question of how long it would take to be consumed.

He felt no touch of remorse, no sympathy for Matt Winship, who had spent so many years of his life building this ranch. Paul Keating had always hated the building, which had been a kind of prison for him since his marriage to Winship's stepdaughter. Now, its ashes would serve to bury all traces of his own guilt, and of the foolish trust that had led him to embezzlement. The books with their damning figures were gone; no one would ever know how much of

Winship's money had gone into the hands of a smooth-talking swindler, how much of it might have been taken from the safe by one of the perpetrators of tonight's raid.

New riders were pounding into the ranch yard—Spur crewmen, summoned by the torchflare of the burning house that must be visible for many miles. Keating scarcely noticed them. He was thinking of the money that weighted down his pockets. He must dispose of it somehow. Best to hide it, for the time being, somewhere right on this hill. Then, later recovered—and the thought filled him with sudden elation —it should be enough to buy him independence of this harsh country that he hated. A new start for himself and Fern, somewhere far from the shadow of Matt Winship.

Large slabs of rock crested the bare hill. At the foot of one of them he should find a temporary burial for the loot. He was busily searching when a sound made him freeze, to crouch motionless in shadow as two riders came walking their horses along the ridgetop. His hand tightened convulsively on the balance of the rifle.

The pair reined in, not a dozen yards from him, making a confused silhouette in the thin light. They must have been drawn by the reflection of fire that boiled at the sky. One spoke, and in astonishment he recognized the voice of his wife: "My God, Webb! What's happening down there?"

And Webb Toland's cool, cynical answer: "It should be obvious. Somebody's getting even for the loss of Ute Flats to that roughneck, Gary. I'd say it was Burl Hoffman's doings."

Paul Keating stared. Webb Toland! Here with Fern, when Keating would have supposed he was hours gone by now! His thoughts boggled as he began dimly to sense what this could mean.

He wasn't to be left long in doubt.

"Do you suppose," he heard his wife say, "anybody was hurt? What—what if Paul—"

Toland's sneering laugh jarred in Keating's ear. "Only wish we could count on it! If he could just get himself conveniently killed, it would make things all that much simpler for us!"

"Why, what a dreadful way to talk!" she exclaimed, but she didn't sound too shocked. And Toland laughed again.

"Come off it! You don't really care what happens to him. You've told me so yourself. It's me you're in love with!"

"Just the same—" But then the talk broke off and they both turned in their saddles, as Paul Keating strode toward them with the rifle braced against his hip.

"Damn you!" Keating's voice was a shaking, bleating scream. "At last I see you for what you are! You've made a fool of me at every step, Toland. You tricked me into embezzlement, and now you take my wife!"

Trembling hands lifted the rifle. But before he could work the trigger, the other man was already in motion. A gun leaped into Webb Toland's hand, glinted light as it slanted down across the saddle. It roared, with a flare of muzzle flash.

The rifle in Keating's hands went off in a wild and unaimed shot, and then the thrust of the explosion flung the weapon from his hands. He stumbled, going down with a great, exploding pressure tearing his chest apart. In his ears, his wife's startled scream mingled with the echoes of the guns.

# IX

Jim Gary lifted a hand sharply, to cut off the tumble of excited words spilling from Ed Saxon's lips. "Hold it! he snapped. "Thought I heard more gunshots!"

The puncher's face twisted in concentration. "You're right! Sounded like up there on the hill!"

Promptly they kicked the spurs and sent their already lathered horses pounding across the yard, that was lighted eerily by the wind-whipped torch that had been Matt Winship's ranch house. Seasoned timbers had caught the flames readily, and though some of the Spur hands were rushing about in futile efforts to curb the fire or at least salvage something, Jim Gary had known with the first look that nothing could be done, other than keep the drifting brands from starting more fires.

Such pointless, wanton destruction had left Jim Gary stunned. He had thought Winship's enemies might have some further ideas of grabbing off strategic sections of graze, but he'd never imagined a guard was needed for the home ranch itself. Still, it had been his responsiblity and he blamed himself for this disaster. He was in a bad mood as he raced toward the rise of the hill, with Ed Saxon at his stirrup.

Their horses were blowing before they topped it. Gary pulled in, and his gun was in his hand as he hunted the shadows. After those two shots there had been nothing more, nor could he see anything moving here. But suddenly Ed Saxon grunted, "Yonder!" Someone was standing beside a horse. As they rode over, the figure raised its head and it was Fern Keating.

At the same moment Gary saw the man lying at her feet. She said, in an odd voice, "I—I just rode up and found him like this. I think he's dead."

Gary was already piling out of the saddle. Kneeling, he

saw at once that the man on the ground was Paul Keating. "Ed!" he ordered sharply. "Give me a light here."

The match that Saxon snapped alight on a thumbnail showed Keating's condition plainly. He was still breathing, but dark blood welling from the hole in his chest could mean only one thing. Knowing he had only moments, Gary seized the dying man by a shoulder and spoke his name.

The head rolled limply. The eyes wavered open and glinted oddly in the matchlight. Blood flecked his lips as Keating strained for breath.

"Keating!" Jim Gary demanded. "Who did this?"

A name struggled to frame itself on the slack lips, but there was no breath behind it. Blood ran thickly from a corner of the dying man's mouth.

"Can't you speak? Can you show me where he went?"

A hand was able to raise itself, feebly, and gesture into the surrounding darkness. Then it fell limp. The eyes wavered past Gary, to touch the face of the woman who bent close over the latter's shoulder. They came to a focus and Jim Gary saw in them a look of such utter revulsion as he had never seen. Keating appeared to be trying to draw away from her. The lips stirred again, wordlessly.

As he stared at the man, the match flickered and died. By the time Saxon had dug up another and got it burning, the moment was over. Paul Keating's eyes stared sightlessly. The labored breathing was still.

Ed Saxon swore as the second match burned his fingers. He shook it out, but the image of that last, hating look was imprinted on Jim Gary's mind as he got to his feet and turned to face the woman. "How did you happen to find your husband?"

"I was riding," she said. "Alone. I saw the reflection of the fire, and it made me head back across the hill."

"Then you didn't see the shooting?"

"No. I already told you—"

"Did you see anyone riding away? Or hear them?"

She shook her head—a little too quickly, he thought. "I didn't see or hear a thing."

Somehow he knew she was lying.

"I suppose he must have run up here to get away from the fighting," Fern went on. "It's just about what he'd have done."

An exclamation broke from Ed Saxon. "Jim! Would you look at this? What the hell you suppose he was doing with this much money in his pockets?" The puncher rose with what he had found: a double handful of greenbacks, held together by wide rubber bands, and a canvas sack that gave out the clink of coins. As Jim Gary looked at it, he had a sudden picture of the box safe in Winship's study—and, with it, a half-formed thought that he didn't like.

He asked the woman, "You know anything about it?"

"Why, no. Of course not! How would I?"

"Well, it'll have to wait. Get him down below," he told Saxon, "and take charge. Nothing much left to do down there, except try to keep that damned fire from spreading."

"We could take the fight to the skunks that started it!"

"Maybe later. Right now, my feeling is that it's more important I get on the trail of the one who got Keating."

"Not alone! You need someone with you."

"I can manage."

"But you'd be riding blind!" Ed Saxon pointed out. "And at night! You could run into an ambush. Jim, let me—"

It had been a long day, and his beaten body was too near exhaustion to give him patience. "You've got your orders! You're needed here."

There was no more argument. In strained silence they lifted Keating's body across the saddle of Saxon's horse, and Gary stood and watched the puncher lead it away down the slope. Afterward, alone with Fern Keating, he turned and faced her in the faint reflection from the burning house. Night wind blew its chill breath along the ridgetop, rattling dry grass and scrub growth as it rushed in toward the fire.

# THE LURKING GUN

Gary said, "I'm wondering how much you really care. About losing him."

Her head jerked at his bluntness. But she showed no outrage. "I can't see," she retorted calmly, "what business it is of yours."

"None, I suppose," he admitted. "I never even really knew the man. But I saw the expression on his face as he was dying—his look when he saw you. If I were a woman, doesn't seem to me I'd want to remember hatred like that on my husband's face—"

She slapped him, a stinging blow. "You're contemptible!" she flared between set teeth. "Because my father hired you, I suppose you think it gives you a right to talk that way to me!"

"Nobody gave me the right," Jim Gary said. "I helped myself."

"While you're at it, why don't you just go ahead and say that I killed him?"

"I thought of that," he admitted. "But I don't really believe it. I don't think you're this good an actress! What I do know is that there's something going on here that I don't understand yet. And if it's of concern to Matt Winship, then I'm making it part of my job to dig it out."

Her face was a pale blur that he couldn't read, but he could see the rapid fall of her breath, hear the rasp of her breathing. "Don't be too sure!" Fern Keating told him harshly. "You were hired and you can be fired again. You may find out you're not as important to anyone here as you seem to think you are!"

In a flash she whirled, caught up the reins of her horse. She fumbled at the stirrup and lifted into saddle, as Jim Gary stood watching, with no move to help her mount. She gave him a last flickering glance, then swung her bridles with an angry wrench that made the horse toss its head.

She was gone then, flinging the horse at a reckless pace down the slope. Jim Gary let her go. He turned tiredly to his own horse and swung astride, with more than this woman to occupy his attention.

He had nothing to go on but a vague gesture he thought he'd seen Keating's dying hand make. He pointed his horse in that direction, over the top of the ridge and away from what was left of the raided ranch. It stood to reason, anyway, that this was the course the killer would have had to take.

Riding blind, he let the animal carry him into the head of a shallow gully that deepened as it funneled down off the ridge. Loose rubble skittered past him. Wind rattled the heads of dry brush that cloaked this face of the ridge. But where the earth leveled off, he swung down and fished up a match which he scraped alight upon a spur rowel.

Almost at once, he saw what he hoped for. It was the distinct, freshly printed mark of a shod hoof. Casting ahead, he found another before the match died and left him momentarily blinded. Another rider had used this route, only minutes before him, and the horse had been traveling with a widespaced, reaching stride.

Quickly Gary remounted and took up the chase, knowing all the odds were against him. The killer had too good a lead for night hunting. Besides, he would know the country and Gary did not. But the circumstances of Paul Keating's death were so tangled with the other problems of this range that he wasn't going to give up the chase without at least a token effort.

A dry ravine seemed to open into a notch in the next low ridge, and he took it, using the spur and trusting the horse to find good footing. The ground was sandy and muffled the thud of hoofs. Once he reined in to use another match. The bottom of the ravine was often used by cattle and was pocked with their sign, but he thought he saw fresh hoofprints.

He kept going, coming up out of the ravine and across the flinty comb of the succeeding ridge. Beyond lay sagebrush and a dark line that looked like willows following a dry watercourse. Gary reined in briefly, and as he did the wind blowing against his face brought him the brief and sudden rattle of hoofs crossing rock, somewhere distantly ahead. That spurred him, and turned him reckless. He came down off the low ridge at a full gallop. Tall sage whipped against his legs as he drove the horse through it, and its pungent odor surrounded him.

And then, as the willows swept blackly nearer, muzzle flame lashed out of their shadow. He heard the snap of the rifle, even as he felt the horse start to stumble under him. By instinct he kicked free of the stirrups. The skewbald, having taken the bullet in midstride, tripped and went down in a complete somersault, and Gary sailed across its rump and narrowly missed the flying steel of its rear hoofs.

He was able to loosen his body and hit the ground limply, but he felt for a moment as though all the life had been slammed out of him.

The rifle in the willows flatted off a second time, but this shot flew wild. It alerted Gary, however. With the night still spinning around him, he groped for his holster and his fingers closed on empty leather. The gun had dropped out in his fall. Alarmed, he started up to his knees. Pain shot through him. He found himself dropping weakly forward, and when he put out a hand to catch himself his palm touched metal. It was the barrel of his own gun!

Fumbling, he grabbed it up and then he was moving crabwise, in a scramble for the protection of his dead mount. Even as he did so, a third bullet chewed up the dirt, just inches from him.

Jim Gary flattened himself and triggered twice across the warm barrel of the horse, paused, and fired again. He had to duck as a bullet came screaming low above his head, but instantly he raised himself and shot twice, directly at the smearing after-image of the muzzle flash. An unlearned instinct that kept count of the shots told him, then, his gun was empty. Without triggering on a spent shell, he dropped back and proceeded to reload.

He was feeling sickly dizzy from the pain in his chest; the

earth seemed to rock beneath him, and he felt the cold sweat on his face. The hand that thumbed fresh shells from his belt loops dropped them into the dirt. Panting, he paused to slide a hand in under his shirt and test the bandage, but he could find no warmth of blood. The wound in his chest hadn't reopened, at least.

Then he had the gun refilled and he rocked the cylinder into place, turning back to his hidden enemy. It occurred to him that minutes had passed since there had been any sound from the willow thicket. Perhaps one of his blind shots had been lucky. On the other hand, the ambusher could be waiting for him to be fooled into exposing himself for a better target.

Impatience had its way. After a long count of twenty he brought his feet under him and came cautiously to a stand, the reloaded gun leveled and ready. Still nothing, there in the shadows.

Then he heard a rider coming—but from behind! He whirled, to seek this new danger. Moonlight filtered by the high overcast showed him the horseman picking his way through the thick sagebrush, and he placed his gun on the figure and his finger took up triggerslack.

The rider halted. Hack Bales's voice sounded across the stillness: "Gary! You there?"

He eased the tension out of him, lowering the gun as he called answer. The puncher rode quickly up, reining in as he saw the other man standing beside a dead horse. "Saxon told me to come after you," he said. "What's happening here, anyway?"

Gary gave him a quick explanation. "Whoever he is, I'm sure he's the one that murdered Keating. I've either plugged him, or he's pulled out."

"We'll soon see which!"

Ignoring Gary's warning to caution, Hack Bales circled the dead horse and spurred straight toward the trees. Gary stood with the night wind blowing against him, straining for a sound and hearing only the noise the Spur rider made as he crashed through the dry branches. For a long moment there was dead silence.

At last he saw Hack Bales returning. The man rode up and reported briefly, "Got away. Did you get a look at him?"

"No. Maybe, in the morning—"

Hack Bales shook his head. "You'll never pick up a trail. Not in those flint hills! If there'd ever been rustlers in this country, they could have stripped the range clean and not much anyone could of done about it. Only luck for us they never tried!" He added anxiously, "Hey! Are you hurt, Gary?"

He must have seen something in the other's manner that alarmed him but though he was still shaky from the fall he'd taken, Gary shook his head. As he turned to strip the saddle off the dead horse, he said, "What about the ranch?"

"The house is still burning. We couldn't save it. Johnson says it was Burl Hoffman and his crowd, all right. He got a good look at some of them during the raid."

"They're a bunch of mad dogs!" Gary said grimly. "No more casualties, I hope? Aside from Keating?"

Bales didn't answer during the moment it took him to accept the heavy stock saddle and swing it up in front of him. Reluctantly he answered, "One more I'm afraid."

About to step into the stirrup Bales had cleared for him, Gary paused and looked at him sharply. "Who?"

The answer was heavy with anger. "We found Pete Dunn afterward. We figure he must have tried to get off his bunk and take a hand in the fighting. Bad hurt as he was, it was just too much. . . ."

There was nothing to say. Face grim, Jim Gary pulled himself with a painful effort to a place behind Hack Bales. Silently, the horse with its double burden started back for the raided ranch.

All that remained of the house, by now, was a pile of charred timbers and stone, and glowing coals that leaped to blue flame when the ground wind breathed upon them.

False dawn stained the eastern sky as the Spur crew, gray with fatigue and soot-grimed, gathered in the kitchen for coffee and a grim discussion. Sound of an approaching wagon sent someone to the door, and then the shout went up: "Hey! It's Matt! It's the Old Man!"

Quickly, Jim Gary strode outside and, with the rest of the crew, watched the rig and team pull into the yard. On the seat, Matt Winship stared around him with a bleak expression. Tracy Bannister, in a heavy coat and with a shawl knotted about her head, handled the team. It was only when he saw Fern Keating, following the wagon on her horse, that Gary realized how Winship must have learned the news of disaster.

"He made me bring him," Tracy said quickly, as she kicked on the brake. "She came and told him what had happened, and he insisted." Gary saw tears on her cheeks as she looked at the ruin of the house. "Oh, how terrible! And—and is it true, about poor Pete Dunn?"

"I'm afraid so."

Matt Winship stirred, but he made no move to step down yet. His bearded face, in the sickly dawn light, was ashen, lined with bitterness and shock. He sought Jim Gary and his eyes settled sternly on the man. He said, in his deep rumble of a voice, "Gary, I hold you responsible for this!"

The words were like a blow. Gary heard the small stir they made, among the crewmen grouped about the wagon.

Tracy cried indignantly, "Matt! You know that isn't fair! They pulled this raid in retaliation."

"Yes!" he retorted. "Retaliation for the fight he took it on himself to stage at Ute Flats. I gave him no such authority!"

"Would you rather he'd stood by and let them grab whatever they wanted, without lifting a finger?"

"Then at least," the old man answered, "Pete Dunn would still be alive! Rather that, a thousand times, than try to hold onto a few acres of open range that never really belonged to me, and that I'm not going to need much longer, in any event!

"It's a good thing," he went on doggedly, "that my daughter forced her way into my room and made me see what kind of thing's been going on. Plain to see nobody else would have told me." His gaze settled on Jim Gary. "Any more than you would have told me you disobeyed my plain instructions about sending that wire of acceptance to Chicago!"

"When it comes to that," Gary said flatly, "you knew the kind of man I was when you hired me. You must have guessed that if Hoffman and that crowd threw me a challenge, I wasn't the one to walk away from it!

"I'm sorry as hell about Pete Dunn. But he was another man who preferred to fight." He lifted his shoulders, let them fall. "Still, you're the boss. If you say so, then I did wrong. I can still send that telegram."

"No need to bother," Matt Winship said. "You're fired!"

Gary couldn't believe it. "Are you serious?"

"Since you won't do the job I hired you for, I'll pay you your time, and then manage the job myself!"

There was a silence. Jim Gary drew a long breath. He ran a glance over the faces around him, saw the same stunned look on all of them.

On all but one. Fern Keating returned his stare with a look of triumph, and he knew suddenly that this was exactly what she had hoped to accomplish by running to her stepfather with this news of disaster—without bothering to care how the shock of it might affect him.

Tracy Bannister's voice shook with hurt and anger. "Matt, I'm ashamed of you! Really ashamed! You knew he never wanted this job. He only took it as a favor. No other man would have troubled to do what he's tried to—"

"Let it go, Tracy." Jim Gary shook his head tiredly. "Thanks, but let it go. I'll be leaving." He started to turn, then paused. "Forget about the pay," he told Winship. "I'll take it out in the loan of a horse to get me into town. I'll leave him at the stable."

He walked toward the corral, a tall, weary shape of a man

whose face showed the aches in his tired body, the harsher hurts that roiled his spirit. As they watched him go, the raw, burnt stink of the gutted house tanged the chill mists of dawn.

# X

BURL HOFFMAN's home ranch was a bachelor layout, the main house being a mere tar-paper shack where he lived with his crew; he was apparently a man with no need for either solitude or privacy. The morning after the raid and fire at Spur, the yard filled early with saddle horses. By prior arrangement, the ranchers who had pooled their interests in opposing Matt Winship and the syndicate sale were gathering for a council of war.

A glum mood lay on all of them, though there was some good news, at least, as a result of last night's grim doings. Jim Gary had been fired, for one thing. No one seemed to know for sure whether he had already left the country, or perhaps was in town somewhere. But George Ruby, someone said, had unpinned his sheriff's badge and laid it on the desk in the dusty jail building and got on his horse and ridden out of Antler for good, rather than face the risks of trying to deal with a worsening situation. It meant that for the time being they had a free hand.

But if there was reason for satisfaction, it was strangely muted. News of the death of old Pete Dunn rested heavily on all these men, like the pall of smoke that hung in the motionless upper air over Spur headquarters. They had all known and respected the old cowpuncher. There wasn't a one who didn't regret what had happened, or wouldn't have avoided it if he could.

Filing into the house, they saw with some surprise the man who sat at ease in a chair by the oilcloth-covered table smoking a slim cigar and evidently waiting for the meeting to begin. Old Priday Jones stopped dead and, scowling, demanded of their host, "What's *he* doing here?"

Burl Hoffman felt himself on the defensive, after last night. "Webb Toland's our friend," he said. "He sees our side of this fight, and he's been telling me some ideas he has for helping us win it."

"That don't make sense," Jones retorted. Someone else said, with suspicion, "Yah! Why should he stick his neck out when it's none of it any of his business?"

If Toland sensed hostility, he didn't show it. He coolly tapped ash from his cigar and answered the questions himself, before the sandy-haired leader had time to frame a reply.

"Don't make any mistakes," the mining man said, his whole manner unruffled. "I've got no more love for a syndicate than the rest of you. And with good reason. I've seen how they operate! They get in here with cattle, and sooner or later they're going to hear what I've been doing at the Copper Queen. Next thing, they'll be wanting to cut in for themselves. With their money, they can beat me out of some valuable properties I've got my eye on. I have no intention of letting that happen!"

"There you are!" said Burl Hoffman, eyeing the silent group. "You all ready to admit you yelped a little soon? You willing now to listen to what Mr. Toland is offering?"

Except perhaps for old Priday Jones, to whom this outsider had always appeared too well-dressed, too well-spoken, they had all tended to be impressed by Toland's facade as a successful and resourceful man. Their hostility melted and now Vince Alcord said, "I'm never too proud to accept help from any source, when I'm in the middle of a fight!"

"Good enough!" Hoffman was pleased as he saw the change of attitude. "As I say, I've been listening to Mr. Toland's ideas and I think they answer our problem. But you've got to decide. I'll go along with whatever the rest of you say."

And so Webb Toland took the floor, and he chose his words carefully.

"I think you're set on the right track," he told them. "What you've got to do is create a situation to convince the syndicate bigwigs that buying in Spur will cost more in the way of trouble than it's worth. Burning out the ranch last night—that was a good move, because it shows you're in dead earnest. And if Matt Winship gets hurt, or loses a man or two . . . well, he started this; *you* didn't ask for the fight. But you've got too much at stake to pull your punches!"

Heads were lifting among the listeners. Shoulders straightened and jaws set, as Toland cleverly helped them justify the very things some had begun to regret. He sensed this and smiled inwardly, knowing that now he could count on their complete support.

"This morning, I happen to know, Winship sent off a rider to the telegraph office at Elko, with a wire accepting the syndicate's offer. They'll undoubtedly have their men here within a week. Before then, you'll have to strike, and strike hard. The sooner the better."

"Where?" Vince Alcord demanded. "If you think you know the answer, spell it out for us."

"I'm thinking there's one move that would cinch matters—create a situation no Eastern outfit would even consider touching." He paused for effect. "Just suppose," he said slowly, "that Spur was all at once to begin losing stock."

This caused a stir of shocked reaction. Priday Jones cried hoarsely, "You—you ain't trying to suggest we turn cattle thieves?"

"I'm suggesting it's no time for half-measures," Toland replied firmly. "The setup for rustling is perfect, here. In the hills east of Spur, a trail can be lost beyond any chance of finding it." He might have added that he had just finished proving this himself. He wondered if that arrogant roughneck, Jim Gary, had wasted any more time trying to pick up sign on the man who ambushed him from the willows last night.

He went on: "I can think of no better beginning than the special herd of Black Angus stock Winship's holding on that graze under Buck Ridge. It's a valuable bunch of stock, and being that close to the hills, it makes a natural target. The syndicate will really be impressed!"

"Maybe." But Vince Alcord, frowning, was troubled. "I ain't saying you're wrong; I'm near ready to tackle anything that might settle this matter. But Winship sets a lot of store by that damned herd of his. It won't be taken without a fight. And what happens if some of us are recognized?"

"You won't be," Toland assured him. "Naturally, I thought of that. And it's the place where I come in.

"Up at the Queen, I've got some men on my payroll that I'll be glad to make available for this job. They're good men—I hire them to guard my property and my interests, and I pay them enough that they follow orders. What's more, they're not the kind to lose their heads if some Spur rider should empty a cartridge or two at them. It's true, of course, they know nothing much about handling cattle, but that's your department. The beauty of it is that even if they're seen none of their faces are known here on Antler range."

"So?" Alcord still didn't catch the drift of his thought.

"So we work together. My boys will go in first and take care of any guard. And when that's done, some of you will be standing by to move in and help yourselves to the beef. It's as simple as that."

Alcord's eyes narrowed. "And how about you? You going to be taking any personal part in all this? Any of the risk?"

"Naturally," Toland answered curtly. "I'll be there." His part was a feature he meant to keep to himself. If these fools could guess even a little of what was working in his crafty mind, they would have been in for a shock. Triumph tugged slightly at a corner of his mouth, as he saw them rising to the bait he had carefully spread for them.

"It's entirely up to you," he finished, prodding for a decision. "If it's too risky for you, say so. There's other ways I can protect my interests. But let me say this: Once a syndicate *does* move in on you, you'll find them a lot harder neighbor to deal with than Matt Winship ever was!"

Burl Hoffman said loudly, "I'm convinced! I vote to go along with Webb Toland, and waste no time about it! What do the rest of you say?"

They said it, in a general chorus of agreement. Webb Toland's keen eye discovered only one holdout. Old Priday

Jones, scowling to himself in a corner of the room, didn't like any part of what was happening here.

If he had the rest, then the hell with Priday Jones! The old bastard could be silenced if he tried to make trouble. Toland listened to the noisy outbreak of voices eagerly discussing the plan that had been adopted. It was always an immense pleasure, to see how he could lead fools to his wishes, to see the parts of a well-laid plan dropping smoothly into place.

Tracy Bannister, sorting mail behind the desk, looked up at a step and a shadow in the doorway. When she saw who had entered, her eyes darkened and she quietly put down the letters she was holding. Not speaking, she waited.

Despite her emotion, she had to admit that Fern Keating had never looked more beautiful or self-assured than she did this afternoon, in divided skirt and whipcord packet. Her blouse had a bunch of frilly material at the throat, and a pert riding hat sat perfectly upon her gleaming hair. In one hand she carried a leather riding crop which she slapped against the other palm, as she looked with superior aloofness about the cramped and ill-furnished hotel lobby, and then let her glance settle on the girl behind the desk.

Without a word of greeting she walked forward, and from her pocket she drew out a couple of bills and tossed them down in front of Tracy.

"What's this?" Tracy demanded coldly.

"Payment for the room my father used. Does that cover it?"

"Are you trying to make a joke? You know I'd never charge Matt Winship room rent, no matter how long he stayed!"

"I'm paying for the room," Fern repeated crisply. "So there'll be no obligations left unsettled. And after that I want you to stay away from him, and from Spur. I think you have entirely too much influence over my father!"

For a moment Tracy could not believe what she'd heard. But what she read in those eyes turned her cold with understanding. She said, icily calm, "I owe more to Matt Winship than to any man I ever knew, outside of my own father. If I

393

can ever help him, in return, I'll always do it. And there's no way you can stop me."

"I think there are ways," Fern answered. "I've heard talk around town—nasty, childish talk, about you and Matt Winship. If you were to cross me, I could make plenty of people believe those rumors aren't so entirely childish!"

Tracy Bannister stared, incredulous at such a threat. Suddenly she couldn't refrain herself. She heard herself calling Fern Keating a name—an unladylike word she had never thought would cross her lips. The other woman's breast lifted on a quickly drawn breath. Next moment, the leather whip in her hand was raised and came slashing squarely at Tracy's cheek.

Moving too quickly for her, Tracy caught the blow against her forearm. Then she seized Fern's wrist, wrested the riding crop from her, and flung it angrily across the lobby. She said tensely, "I'd just like to know what your really after! You deliberately maneuvered to have Jim Gary fired. Now you want me to stay away from Matt because you know I have his interests at heart, and that he listens to me. *Why?* He's almost your own father. Do you really *want* him to lose the ranch that means so much to him?"

Fern Keating jerked her arm free. She stood rubbing the wrist that was red from the grip of Tracy's fingers, her eyes flaming with fury and hatred for the girl across the desk. But what she might have said went unspoken, for a sudden anguished voice pulled them both quickly around, toward the sun-filled doorway.

"Miz Keating!"

It looked like an apparition that came lurching through the door, his shoulder striking the edge of the frame and throwing him off stride. But it was only old Priday Jones, clothing awry and white hair streaming into his face. "Miz Keating!" he said again, hollowly, and set a weaving course across the linoleum flooring. He put a hand on the desk and leaned heavily, peering at Matt Winship's daughter.

"You're drunk!" she said in disgust.

"Yes, ma'am. If I wasn't, I wouldn't be here! It's tooken me all day to find the nerve to do what I know I have to. Then, when I seen your bronc tied at the pole outside—"

Alarmed, the quarrel of a moment ago forgotten now, Tracy seized the old rancher by a trembling arm. "What is it, Priday? What is it you're trying to tell us?"

"That I don't hold with rustling, even if it means turning against my own kind! Oh, I told 'em I wouldn't go along, but that ain't enough! I got to stop it! I got to tell—"

"Tell what?" she insisted. "Stop them from what, Priday?"

Then it came out, the whole sordid story of the scene at Hoffman's, and the program Webb Toland had sold the men who met there. "Reckon maybe I'm a traitor," he finished despondently. "But, by God, there's some things a man just can't hold still for!"

Jim Gary spoke from the lobby stairs. "You did right," he said. "Don't blame yourself, if your conscience said it had to be done."

They hadn't seen him there, listening to the old man's troubled story. Now he came down to the lobby, carrying his bedroll and the saddle Tracy Bannister had recovered from the bushes at the stageline corral. He set them down near the doorway, and turned to Jones. "When's this business supposed to take place?"

"This very afternoon," the old man answered miserably. "They ain't lettin' any grass grow under their boots. May be too late already to do anything."

"And it may not!" Gary turned to Fern. "You'd better get started for Spur as fast as you can ride! Let them know what we've learned. Tell them Webb Toland's gone and got himself mixed up in it now, for some reason we don't yet know. And get the crew burning leather for Buck Ridge! Meanwhile I'll head directly out there to see if there's anything I can do."

Fern Keating only looked at him, as though she hadn't understood. Impatiently, he took her by an arm and pushed her toward the door. "Didn't you hear? There's no time to lose! Get on that horse of yours and try to act as though you had some stake in what happens to your father's ranch!"

She didn't argue. She gave him one hate-filled stare, and then she pulled away from his hands and hurried out of the hotel and down the steps to her waiting horse. She mounted and quickly left town, heading north.

But with the town behind her she pulled rein and sat a moment, debating. Directly ahead lay the road to Spur, where there were the riders Jim Gary would be counting on to help save Matt Winship's precious Black Angus holding.

She gave that road no more than a glance. Instead, she pulled out of the trail and then was cutting north and east toward a higher fording of Antler Creek, and a short route to Buck Ridge.

If Priday Jones had told the truth, Webb Toland would be there. Her lover must be warned that his plans had been betrayed, and that he was in danger.

Jim Gary and the girl watched old Priday Jones peg away into the glare of the sunlight. Tracy shook her head. "I'm so sorry for him!" she exclaimed. "It must have been a terrible decision!"

"I don't think he'd ever have forgiven himself if he hadn't made it." A need for action turned Gary back into the lobby then. He had slept and was feeling fresh. The wound in his chest was no more than a dull ache as he leaned to take up his saddle and blanket roll. When he straightened, the girl was standing before him.

"You're going out there? Alone?" She shook her head. "Even after all that's happened, you still mean to fight Matt Winship's battles. After he threw your help back in your face? No one would expect it, Jim. Not when you could just ride on out of this country and forget its problems. They're not yours."

He shrugged. "A man doesn't always have a reason for what he does. When he's once picked up a problem, even for a day or two, it sometimes isn't easy to lay it down again. How do you know? Maybe I resent having a horse shot out from under me. Or maybe it's just that I'm curious to know what that smooth-talking Webb Toland has in his head. Maybe it's no more than that."

Tracy shook her head. "All the talking in the world won't make me believe you're anything but what I've known you were: a very fine and very unselfish man!" And then, without warning, she came up onto her toes and her warm mouth pressed against his.

Gary was taken utterly by surprise. He stood with arms loaded down by his possessions, and before he could move to drop them the kiss was over and she was stepping back, fast, a mingled sweetness and confusion in her face. He stood and stared at her like a fool. And then, because there was nothing to say, he turned and walked out of the building.

The softness of her kiss was still on his lips and his mind was a maze of bewildered thoughts as, moments later, he stood in the gloom of the public livery stable, fastening his saddle on the back of the horse he'd ridden in from Spur this morning, after being fired. Whatever had possessed her? he asked himself, and got no answer. Yet he knew that nothing in his experience had ever changed the shape of his world so completely. You couldn't just ride away from a thing like *that*. Once this business at Buck Ridge was settled, one way or another. . . .

Still, who and what was he—with his dubious past and uncertain future—to make too much of what could have been a mere impetuous gesture, that the girl perhaps already regretted?

So filled was he with these thoughts that, as he finished saddling and took the reins to lead his horse from its stall, he scarcely noticed the two men who stood waiting in the gloom near the double doors. Not until the bigger one spoke to him in the unforgotten voice of Boyd Plank: "All right, Gary. It's been a long chase you led us, but we finally run you down. Now, stand and take it!"

## XI

Their guns were in the holsters, he saw. But their hands were tight upon the grips. Caught flat-footed, Gary could make no move toward his own weapon. He said heavily, "So you found me."

"We come near never doin' it," big Boyd Plank told him. "We was halfway to Arizona before we knew for sure we'd tooken a wrong trail."

"It was the bronc you left in the corral that fooled us," his slighter, younger brother Asa explained. "We thought sure, when we seen it there that night, you must have roped you a fresh mount and pushed on." He frowned, a man darkly puzzled. "But I just don't get it! You've had three days, now, when you could have been losing us for good. Why are you still here?"

Jim Gary, thinking of all that had happened, said a little bitterly, "I wonder the same damned thing!"

A horse stomped in one of the stalls. High in a corner of the rafters, a couple of hornets hummed about their mud-daub nest.

Asa said, "It's your move, Gary!"

Gary's chest felt cramped. The pressures on him were roweling him hard, and even though his life hung on the trigger fingers of this vengeful pair, they could be no more than a distraction. He took a deep breath. "Now, listen—" he began.

"Listen, hell!" Boyd Plank snapped. "We ain't letting ourselves be slick-talked! We got a score to settle. There's a gun in your holster. Pull it!"

"Against the two of you? You call that fair odds?"

"It's as fair odds as a trained gunfighter goading a youngster like Lane into the draw!"

Gary's mouth pulled down hard. "I never goaded your brother!" he started to answer, but then the hopelessness of it

398

all quieted him. "All right, skip that! I know you'd never in a million years believe my side of the story!

"You've caught me, and I suppose you'll do what you want. Just the same, there's something I've got to ask you to let me do first, a job that's waiting. If I can have just two hours—"

"Two hours for what?" snapped Asa. "A head start?"

"You ain't going nowhere!" Boyd Plank told him. "You're not getting away from us a second time!"

They were implacable, beyond reasoning. A kind of despair touched Jim Gary as he felt the moments tick by. His hand moved nearer the jutting handle of his gun, tempted to drag it out and make a showdown. "I won't try to escape," he promised hoarsely. "My word of honor on that."

Asa Plank sneered and his scorn was like a blow across the face. "The honor of a hired gunman?"

"Mister," Boyd Plank said, "we wouldn't take your word for nothing!"

"I'm afraid you're going to have to!" Tracy Bannister said, behind him.

She was a little breathless, and white of face, but she was determined, and the shotgun she held braced against a hip was steady enough. The Planks stiffened, and very slowly they turned. When they saw the weapon's shining tube, and the girl's hand white-knuckled on the trigger guard, they reacted visibly. Slowly, without bidding, they raised their hands.

Asa said, "Now, lady—"

"Get their guns, Jim!" she said. "And please hurry! This thing makes me nervous!"

Quickly he stepped forward and took the sixshooters from the brothers' holsters, dropping them into the straw of a manger. "I think they'll be good now," he said. "Thanks, Tracy."

She eased her grip on the shotgun, but she kept it ready. "They came in the hotel," she answered his unvoiced question, "checking the desk register. I knew who they must be, the minute I saw them."

"Can you hold them here a little longer?"

"I'll hold them!"

Jim Gary turned and swung into the saddle. He looked down at the scowling brothers. "I made you a promise," he said earnestly. "And I'll keep it. I'm not running again. I can see you'd find me eventually. I want this settled, but you've got to wait till my other business is finished."

Their faces were hate-filled, uncompromising, unbelieving. Seeing he would get no answer, Jim Gary kicked his horse and rode from the stable, ducking to clear the low doorway. Straightening, he let the bronc out, and used the spurs.

Webb Toland, standing beside his horse, watched Vince Alcord ride away through the scrub growth of Buck Ridge— a formation so-called because someone had once said its silhouette resembled that of a sleeping Paiute warrior. Toland's mouth quirked and he said, contemptuously, "Sucker!"

St. Cloud laughed shortly. He was a lath-lean shape of a man, who affected black clothing that made his face appear sallow and accented the shadows of his gaunt cheeks. His eyes, also black, glinted as coldly as chips of obsidian. With black-gloved hands, he settled the heavy shellbelt about his hips, checked the lashing of the tong that strapped the cutaway holster carefully in place.

He had done many jobs for Webb Toland, in the past, and between these two there was a complete meeting of minds. He said now, with cruel amusement, "The stupid bastard will never know what hit him."

This ridge, and the lower one beyond, formed a sheltered draw that was ideal grazing for Matt Winship's prized herd; once the pair of riders who guarded it had been disposed of, that trough down there would serve equally well as a funnel to pour the herd straight into the flinty hills eastward. Just now Vince Alcord had ridden up to inform Toland that he and Burl Hoffman and their men were in position, ready to pick up the beef as soon as it could be started moving in their direction.

St. Cloud slanted a look at the sun, and then at the three

other men who waited, a little distance off, for instructions. He said, "About time to start this ball?"

"I told Alcord five minutes," Webb Toland answered. "There's no great hurry." And then both men turned, instantly alert, as they caught sound of a horse and rider approaching along the comb of the ridge, breaking through the scrub growth.

St. Cloud swore and the gun was in his hand in a sudden, effortless swipe of motion. But his boss told him sharply, "Put it away!" and was hurrying to meet Fern Keating when she rode up and dropped quickly from the saddle.

"What are you doing here?" he demanded.

She showed the effects of her breathless ride from town. She'd lost her pert riding hat and her beautiful auburn hair had come down in a wind-blown tangle. Her eyes blazed with shock and anger. "I came to find out if it was true—and I guess it is!"

"Don't talk in riddles! If what was true?"

"That you've joined Spur's enemies!" And she poured out what she had learned from Priday Jones in the hotel lobby. As she talked, Webb Toland's handsome face seemed to settle into hardness, his tawny eyes took on danger.

"So Jones talked!" he said quietly. "I didn't think he'd have the nerve!"

"Then you admit it's so?"

"Of course not!" He took her by the shoulders. She tried to shrug his hands away but he wouldn't free her. He spoke levelly, earnestly.

"Have you forgotten what I said about letting Hoffman and Alcord and the rest of those fools break themselves, and then picking up the pieces? That's exactly what I'm working on. Only I saw an opportunity to give things a little push!"

"How? By helping them steal our stock?"

"Will you be quiet a minute and let me explain?" He drew a long breath, summoning the patience he needed. "We only get the cattle started for them. Then they take over. I've already convinced them my boys aren't experienced in handling beef, which isn't exactly the truth."

"And then?"

"Well, naturally—being law-abiding citizens, who believe in justice and order—if we should see someone in the act of driving Spur cattle into the hills, we'd be expected to stop them. Any way we can."

She said, aghast, "I think you mean to wait for them somewhere and ambush them!"

"Why not? They're the ringleaders. With those two out of the way, the opposition to Spur collapses like a punctured balloon!"

"But the rest, who were at the meeting this morning, will know exactly what you've done! So will Jim Gary, and that Bannister girl!"

He shrugged. "Let them go to court and prove it! I can produce witnesses of my own to give iron-clad testimony that I couldn't possibly have been at their damned meeting." A smile tilted his mouth. "In a thing like this, a little cool bluff will beat an implausible truth, any time!"

"You may need more than bluff against Jim Gary! When I left he was all ready to take the saddle to stop you."

"Alone?" The name of Gary had caused Toland's face to darken slightly. "He must be crazy!"

"He has his share of cool nerve, too," she reminded him. "He thought I was riding to Spur to alert the crew. Instead, I came straight here."

"Then that means he's expecting help that won't be coming!" Toland nodded, satisfied, and made his quick decision. "It changes nothing. We'll proceed as planned, except that we'll leave a man posted, to watch for friend Gary and take care of him when he shows!"

He turned away, quickly giving his orders. One of St. Cloud's men pulled a saddle gun and checked the loads, and went looking for a spot to keep his watch for Gary. Toland was gathering the reins of his horse when St. Cloud came to him, carrying a rifle. With it, the gunman indicated the draw at the foot of the ridge.

"I might be able to pick off those guards from here," he said. "It's not an impossible shot."

Toland's eyes narrowed as he considered. The two Spur riders had a fire going, near a shallow bay of rocks near the farther ridge. They were over there now, heating up a pot of coffee. Toland gauged the distance, then reluctantly shook his head.

"You could miss, too," he said. "And then they'd be into those rocks and we'd have to dig them out. No, we'll ride down. They know me; they'll not think anything suspicious, before we're close enough to make damned sure of our shots."

Fern Keating couldn't hold back the exclamation: "You're not going to ambush those men, too? My father's own punchers?"

"What's the lives of a couple of illiterate cowhands, against saving Spur?"

She was looking at him as though she had never quite seen him clearly before this moment. "Is it your method to murder every man who happens to get in your way? The way you did Paul?"

"That wasn't murder!" Webb Toland said sharply, his eyes cold. "The fool came at me with a gun. I had to protect myself."

"You killed him because he was in your way," she repeated. "And how can I be sure that next time it might not be my father? Or—" She shuddered, as the idea touched her like a cold wind. "Or—even *me?*"

For a long moment his eyes rested on her, and they were the eyes of a stranger. She faced him, a woman waiting for an answer, for some assurance, something she could hold to and believe. But Webb Toland was canny enough to see that there was nothing worth saying. He wasted neither time nor breath.

He turned abruptly, toed the stirrup and swung astride. St.

Cloud fell in beside him. With the two others trailing, they dropped slowly down the slope.

The two Spur crewmen were Hack Bales and the towhead, Cliff Frazer. As Webb Toland predicted, they recognized him at once and, seeing in him a successful businessman who was well respected by the people of this section, took no alarm at having him ride up on them. They straightened, leaving the coffee pot sitting in its bed of coals. As the newcomers reined up Hack Bales nodded greeting.

"Howdy," he said. "You're in time for a bait of java, if you don't mind that we only got two cups."

Webb Toland shook his head and piled both hands on the saddlehorn. Beyond the little fire, the black cattle herd grazed peacefully. A three-stand fence of barbed wire, snaking across the draw, cut it in two and held the beef in a grassy pocket that headed up where Buck Ridge joined its lower neighbor. A single-panel gate, now closed, would free the herd and let it be driven into the waiting hands of Alcord and Hoffman and their crews.

"No, thanks," said Toland. "We're not here to drink up your coffee. I heard somewhere you had a fire and a killing at Spur last night. Wondered if it was a fact."

"Your hearing's good, Mr. Toland!" young Cliff Frazer answered grimly. "They burnt the house and they same as murdered Pete Dunn."

"Mr. Keating, too," Hack Bales added.

Toland showed them a look of shock. "Keating? I hadn't heard that!"

"Shot him dead. No knowing what they'll try next. That's why we're doubling the guard, here and any other place they might take a mind to hit." The coffee on the fire suddenly came to a boil. Brown liquid fountained sluggishly from the spout as Hack Bales swore and leaped to snatch the pot from the coals. "Reckon this is hot as we need it," he said. "Sure you won't have a shot with us?"

Toland hesitated. Then he said quietly, "Why, sure. Why not?"

As Hack Bales turned to take the tin cup Cliff Frazer handed him, Toland's fingers closed around the butt of his gun. His eyes on the puncher's back, choosing a target, he heard the slight whisper of gunmetal against leather and knew St. Cloud was clearing a weapon.

"Hack! Cliff!" It was Jim Gary's sudden shout, breaking across the stillness. "It's a trick! *Look out!*"

Surprise stayed Toland's hand. Whipping around, he saw Gary on a lathered horse, spurring down the ravine where the two ridges headed up. Fury locked his jaw muscles tight, brought the gun out of its holster.

Where the hell was that guard he'd posted?

"They're after the herd!" Gary was shouting. His drawn gun winked reflected sunlight. But now, above and to his right, Toland's gunman came belatedly into view, rifle snapping to his shoulder. As flame and white smoke sprang from the muzzle, the bronc under Jim Gary squealed and then man and mount piled up in a wild, rolling tangle.

The horse pawed and struggled quickly to its feet, and with reins flying came sliding on down the trough, raising a huge boil of dust. And as this thinned and settled it became clear that Gary, too, had survived the spill. Was he indestructible?

Webb Toland swore, brought up his sixshooter and fired. At the same instant, St. Cloud or one of the others triggered also. It seemed to explode almost in Toland's ear, and it startled him and spoiled his own aim. With his whole head ringing he saw Gary take cover, safe, behind a half-buried boulder.

Furious, he turned back to the two Spur crewmen. Hack Bales stood like a man dumbstruck, the coffee pot still in his hand. Deliberately Toland fired and saw him spun and knocked off his feet as a bullet drilled his thigh.

That jarred Cliff Frazer into action. As Toland was leveling for a second, finishing shot, the young towhead gave a cry and grabbed wildly for the gun in his own holster. He jerked it out and emptied it blindly into the group of mounted men.

A bullet stung Toland's horse and brought the animal up rearing, to slam sidewards into St. Cloud's mount. For that moment all the horses were out of control and the riders had their hands full trying to settle them. And this was time enough for Cliff Frazer to get to his hurt companion, slip an arm under his shoulders, and start frantically dragging him toward the jumble of rocks just behind them.

Cursing his roan to a stand, Webb Toland looked for them, just in time to see them disappear into cover. He gripped his weapon in a fist that shook with impotent rage, as he saw how this Jim Gary had blown apart what should have been a very simple operation, and made it all suddenly very complicated.

In his relief at seeing Cliff and the injured man reach safety, Jim Gary almost forgot his own peril. The whine of a rifle bullet, and the stinging impact as it slapped within inches of him and showered him with rock pellets, warned him that he was still exposed to that marksman on the ridge. He whipped up his sixgun, threw a shot that came close enough to drive the man into cover. Then he changed position, hugging what protection the half-buried boulder could give him from that direction.

Down below it looked as though Webb Toland, in his determination, was about to rush the two Spur crewmen. Deliberately Gary fired. It was a long range for a revolver but in that clot of mounted men it wasn't hard to reach some target. He saw one of the riders lifted from his saddle and slammed to the ground. At the same moment, one of the Spur men—Cliff Frazer, most likely—started shooting.

That was enough for Toland's men. They turned and pulled back quickly for the protection of Buck Ridge, leaving their dead companion sprawled in the grass beside the fence. Silence returned then, broken by an uneasy stirring of the cattle; terrified by the gunfire, they might have tried to bolt from it except that it apparently was coming from every side.

Gary, bellying the dirt, checked the position of the rifleman but failed to find him. As he jacked empties from his six-shooter and reloaded from the loops in his belt, he called down to the pair trapped in the rocks below: "Hack? Cliff?"

Cliff Frazer answered. "You all right?"

"I'm doing fine. How's Hack making it?"

The hurt man answered for himself, his voice tight with pain but wholly defiant. "Got the bleeding stopped. Reckon a little old hole in my leg won't kill me. Damned if I'll let it, without I take a couple of them bastards along! Since when are they mixed in this fight, anyway?"

"It's a long story," Gary called back. "Just sit easy. Don't do anything foolish."

He wished he could tell them of the trump card they were holding. He couldn't, because Toland would be listening to every word. It didn't matter. Webb Toland's work was cut out for him, now. He was going to have to try and dispose of all three. And meanwhile, figuring from the time Fern Keating left town, it would certainly seem she'd have managed by now to reach Spur home ranch and warn her stepfather, and so get the crew started for here. Help should be only minutes away, if they could stick it out.

Only Jim Gary was not the man to sit and wait for help, when at any time young Frazer—or even Hack Bales, hurt as he was—might take it into his head to make some rash move, not realizing how things stood.

Then the rifleman on the ridge dropped another shot so close to him he knew the man must have changed into a better position. Gary waited no longer.

Tensed muscles drove him to his feet, during the instant the rifleman would need to lever a new shell into the breech. He caught a glimpse of his target and drove off a pair of shots as fast as he could work trigger. Though he fired instinctively, without time to aim, the second shot was lucky. The sharpshooter appeared to dive face forward into the brush, as a man might dive into deep water. He crashed from sight, and the rifle leaped from his hands to go skittering, end for end, down the slope, disappearing.

Gary saw this from a corner of his eye; he himself was already running, boots fighting the pitch and loose dirt of the hillside. With each step he cast ahead for some glimpse of his remaining enemies. Then, as he crested a slight hump and the whole flank of the ridge suddenly lay before him shagged with buckbrush and thick sage clumps, he saw the thing that brought him up short, in disbelief.

There was Webb Toland and Fern Keating, standing close, her face lifted to him and her hand laid against his chest in a way that suggested an astounding intimacy. Gary shook his head, for that first moment too stunned to think. Then the fact of her presence here descended full on him, like the crash of a wave breaking over his head.

Suddenly, half-guessed truths, things that had halfway suggested themselves to him last night as he knelt beside Paul Keating and saw the hating look he gave his wife as he died—all these hints began to drop into place. And one thing came through, with an appalling clarity: *If she's here with Toland, then she never took the message to Spur! You've been looking for help that isn't going to come!*

It was while he absorbed this, and adjusted his thinking to it, that he suddenly caught the drum of hoofs in the draw below. Looking, he saw a half-dozen riders filing up the trough between the ridges. Among them he recognized Burl Hoffman, and Vince Alcord's unmistakable, nearly deformed shape. They were heading for the rocks where Bales and Frazer were holed up. And they came from a direction that would take the pair on an unprotected flank.

Those two were doomed unless Gary could somehow manage to help them.

He drew a bead on Burl Hoffman but then lowered the gun, chagrined at knowing he had no target for a sixshooter. And as he debated what he could possibly do, a gunsear clicked behind him. A voice he didn't know said, "Don't try to use the gun, mister!"

# XII

SLOWLY he turned. The man in black was a stranger, but he had been one of the group with Toland down there by the fence. Though Jim Gary didn't know him, the type was familiar enough. Like Gary himself, he was obviously the kind who made a living from the hire of his gun. Judging by the way he held it trained on Gary, he was undoubtedly good with it.

Jim Gary didn't drop his own gun. His chances were gone if he let himself be disarmed, and so he took the greater chance and tried for a shot, hurling himself to one side as he brought the weapon up. The black-clad gunman fired, with the first motion. Gary felt the bullet strike and was knocked bodily to the ground. But he kept his hold on the sixshooter and even as he landed, prone, his sights were on his opponent and he fired a second time, from there.

He saw the other jerk and whirl clear around, a convulsive pressure of his trigger-finger sending a last bullet winging wildly along the slope. But Jim Gary didn't see him fall. Blackness and pain swept over him. As he lay fighting it, he thought he heard a woman's scream mingle with the roar of the guns. He was too dazed, at that moment, to think clearly.

The pain was gathering itself now. He could feel it centering in the general region of his left arm and shoulder. Pushing to his knees, he looked down and saw the blood beginning to work through the fabric of his coat. But then he forgot his injury, as he became aware of gunfire beginning in the draw below him. Remembering the plight of the two men trapped there, he struggled to his feet.

What he saw astounded him.

More riders—a second, and larger bunch of them—had appeared from somewhere and were pouring in on Alcord and Hoffman and their crews. All at once the attackers found themselves outnumbered and under fire. Dust arose, mingling

409

with the fumes of burnt powder. Saddles emptied. Even as Gary watched, he saw guns flung down and arms raised in surrender.

It could mean only one thing: Spur! Yet he failed to understand for he knew that Fern Keating couldn't have warned them.

But that reminded him of Webb Toland, almost forgotten, in these past few minutes. He whipped around, hunting the man and finding no sign of any living person on that ridge except himself. Yet Toland could not have gone far. Not if he had a woman with him.

Quickly, ignoring the throb of his thawing shoulder wound, Jim Gary went looking, wading and crashing through waist-high clumps of brush that cloaked the hillside and held him back.

Under some scrub trees near the top of the ridge, he saw a clot of saddle horses and at once turned toward them. When he came upon Webb Toland, it was so unexpectedly that he almost overran him.

For Toland was on his knees, with Fern Keating cradled motionless against his breast. Gary, halting, stared at the two of them for a long moment before Toland seemed aware of his presence. Then the dark head lifted, the tawny eyes met Gary's, and they were clouded with grief. Webb Toland said, as though it were something he could not really believe, "My God! She's *dead!*"

Jim Gary saw the blood now, and remembered the scream that sounded on the heels of the black-clad gunman's second shot. A wild bullet, it must have streaked aimlessly along the hillside and found its target, quite by accident. He shook his head at the irony of it.

"Too bad," he said, without emotion. Then, gesturing with the point of the gun: "On your feet, Toland. I'm taking you with me."

Toland looked at the gun and at Gary's hard face. He said, "You're a cold devil, aren't you?" And when the other made no reply: "We can't just walk away and leave her lying here!"

"I'll see she's taken care of."

"No!" Toland clutched her tighter, one arm sliding under her body as in readiness to pick her up. "I'll carry her myself! Damn it, I can't think of her lying in the dirt—"

"She's not your responsibility," Jim Gary snapped coldly. "And she never was, whatever you two may have had between you while she was Paul Keating's wife! Now, get up from there."

Quietly Webb Toland answered, "I hope I see you in hell!" And his right hand slipped into sight, holding the gun he had managed to palm under cover of Fern's body. Toland slanted the weapon up at Gary and his face was a mask of hatred. But before he could fire, Gary triggered deliberately. He shot Toland in the chest and knocked him over backward. Gun smoking in his hand, he walked over and looked at the man.

Toland's arms were spread wide, empty hands plucking convulsively at the grass and weeds. He peered at Gary with dimming eyes. "Damn you!" he whispered. "I should have made sure and got you, last night, instead of your horse."

"Then it was you, there in the willows? And it was you that shot Keating?"

There was no answer. The tawny eyes glazed over. The man was dead.

By now, the last of Spur's enemies had surrendered. Matt Winship stared down from his saddle at Burl Hoffman and Vince Alcord, with a fine, flashing scorn. He seemed a different person from the beaten, dispirited man who had first hired, and then fired, Jim Gary. One would have said this attack had been the thing he needed to drag him out of an uncharacteristic lethargy. "I'd be in my rights," he said furiously, "to throw the book at you. Maybe I will, I ain't decided. But you damn well better walk easy!"

Vince Alcord cringed before his fury, and Hoffman said, flushing, "We was only trying to look after our interests. We don't want no syndicate on this range!"

"Syndicate?" Winship gave a snort. "Don't jump to con-

clusions. I ain't so damn sure there's gonna be any syndicate!
I'm beginning to think Jim Gary had it straight, that it's time
I got up off my hind end and fought for my rights!"

If he sensed the pleased surprise that went through his
crewmen, the rancher failed to show it. He had caught sight
of Jim Gary walking up, leading the horse someone had
caught up for him. His bearded face held a scowl of alarm
as he saw the blood on Gary's coat. "You took a bullet!"

Gary shook his head. "It's nothing much. Did Spur lose any
men?"

"Nobody hurt to speak of, outside the hole in Hack Bales's
leg, that is." Winship paused. "Gary, I'm thinking now I owe
you an apology. You seen I was making a damn fool of myself,
with that talk about quitting and selling out. I dunno what
could have got into me! But I sure knew it was time to fight
when that rider Tracy sent from town brought us the word
of what was going on here!"

"Tracy sent the word?" Suddenly he could guess what had
happened. With a woman's intuitive suspicion, she'd never
really trusted Fern Keating. She must have decided to play
safe, make doubly sure Spur got warning. Bless her for that!

"I got plenty to thank you for," Matt Winship went on, his
deep voice heavy with embarrassment. "I'd like you to forget
that firin' business. Spur still needs a good foreman, permanent. I'm asking you to come back."

"Thanks, Matt," Gary said and meant it. "I'd like to." But
then he remembered, and he frowned. "I don't know, though.
I'm afraid there's something else I've got to take care of—
some unfinished business."

The other's black brows drew together. "You mean you're
turning me down?"

"I'll have to see. I've made a promise. One I can't back out
on. And it means that, right now, I have to be riding."

In a dead silence, they watched him turn and lift himself
into the saddle. He winced, stretching his hurt shoulder. Matt
Winship saw, and said, "You better let us do something about
that, before you ride anywhere!"

He shook his head. Reining away, he caught Ed Saxon's eye. He rode over to the man, leaned to speak softly enough that no one else would hear. "Up on the ridge: Webb Toland, and Fern—both dead."

Astonishment and horror warped the other's face. "*Fern?*"

"I'm only beginning to guess at what it all adds up to. Damned if I know how you're going to break it to Matt!"

"That's all right. I'll think of something."

Gary thanked him with a nod. And thus, he rode from there—rode for town, and the rendezvous he had promised Boyd and Asa Plank.

His left shoulder throbbed dully, but the wadded handkerchief he'd stuffed inside his coat seemed to have absorbed the bleeding. He shoved the hand into his waist belt and let that support the weight of the arm and keep it motionless.

A kind of depression rode him, a letdown after the tensions of gunplay. His entire battered body seemed to be one tired ache. But there was more to it than that. These last days, since immersing himself in the affairs of this range, had worked their change in him. He'd begun unknowingly to put down roots. As he'd told Tracy Bannister, it was a new experience for him to feel needed.

Now Spur's worst troubles appeared settled. There was the offer of a permanent job. And finally, there was Tracy—that moment in the hotel lobby, when her kiss had made it certain that, whatever else happened, he was never going to forget her.

Yet in the face of all this he was riding to meet the Planks! He drew his gun, thinking to replace the spent shells, but knowing that in a showdown he would never use it against that pair to whom he owed his life. He shrugged and shoved it back again. Perhaps this was crazy, perhaps it was a kind of suicide. Or on the other hand, maybe it was only justice; a man with his past didn't deserve such rewards.

He took the fording where the road crossed Antler Creek. Topping out on the south bank, he climbed a slight rise in the trail, and saw the two horsemen approaching, a mile down the road. Even at that distance, he recognized the Planks. They were coming to meet him!

Something rose in Gary, nearly choking him. He settled it and then rode on. His hand was steady enough on the rein, his jaw set firm with the determination to have this out, to whatever hard ending.

Slowly the distance narrowed. They were close enough now that he could see their faces—grim, implacable, expressionless. Their guns rode their holsters, their gunhands hanging awkwardly near the jutting grips. Presently, when only yards remained to separate them, Jim Gary hauled up. His horse tossed its head, then settled. Wind across the sun-scorched grass fingered its mane, fanned the brim of Gary's hat, touched his cheek. Motionless, he waited.

Still Boyd and Asa Plank came on. They edged their horses slightly apart, now. So they meant to take him from both sides, put him between them. . . .

They drew nearer, still at that same unbroken, plodding pace. Now they were abreast of his horse, one on either side.

They rode straight past. Their eyes did not even touch his face or appear to see him!

Astounded, Jim Gary whirled his horse. Feeling that he was the victim of some kind of trick, he stared at their backs as the distance continued to widen. Unable at last to hold it in, he called harshly, "What the hell is this? Where do you think you're going?"

They pulled rein, then. They looked back, without turning their horses. For a moment, neither spoke. It was big Boyd Plank who answered him, in a strange, flat tone.

"Ask the girl. That Tracy Bannister—she's quite a woman. And quite a talker! She told us things we hadn't heard. About Lane, and how you come to kill him." He hesitated, scowling. "Could all be a lie, of course. But *she* believes it. And, by damn, she near convinced us!"

"We wouldn't want to make any mistakes," Asa said. "She told us you been cutting quite a swath in this part of the country. Looks like we could have been wrong in the kind of man you are, and I reckon we both knew Lane wasn't no angel!

"Anyway, killing you wouldn't bring him back. And that girl seems to think a lot of you, Gary. You just better the hell be worthy of her!"

Without another word, they were gone—toward Mogul Valley, turning their backs on the revenge they could have taken. Jim Gary let the cramped breath from his lungs slowly. For a long moment he watched that pair grow small against the immensity of rangeland.

He spoke to his horse, then, and rode on—toward Antler, and the girl who had given him a new life, and a new beginning.

**D(wight) B(ennett) Newton** is the author of a number of notable Western novels. Born in Kansas City, Missouri, Newton went on to complete work for a Master's Degree in history at the University of Missouri. From the time he first discovered Max Brand in Street and Smith's *Western Story Magazine*, he knew he wanted to be an author of Western fiction. He began contributing Western stories and novelettes to the Red Circle group of Western pulp magazines published by Newsstand in the late 1930s. During the Second World War, Newton served in the U.S. Army Engineers and fell in love with the central Oregon region when stationed there. He would later become a permanent resident of that state and Oregon frequently serves as the locale for many of his finest novels. As a client of the August Lenniger Literary Agency, Newton found that every time he switched publishers he was given a different byline by his agent. This complicated his visibility. Yet in notable novels from *Range Boss* (1949)—the first original novel ever published in a modern paperback edition—through his impressive list of titles for the Double D series from Doubleday—*The Oregon Rifles*, *Crooked River Canyon*, and *Disaster Creek* among them—he produced a very special kind of Western story. What makes it so special is the combination of characters who seem real and about whom a reader comes to care a great deal and Newton's fundamental humanity, his realization early on (perhaps because of his study of history) that little that happened in the West was ever simple but rather made desperately complicated through the conjunction of numerous opposed forces working at cross purposes. Yet, through all of the turmoil on the frontier, a basic human decency did emerge. It was this which made the American frontier experience so profoundly unique and which produced many of the remarkable human beings to be found in the world of Newton's Western fiction.